Praise for Christine Feehan's

"[A] dark and seductive paranormal romance series."
—HeroesandHeartbreakers.com

"Hot-blooded . . . intense and thrilling . . . You don't want
to miss it!"
—Joyfully Reviewed

"With a Feehan novel you know you will get well-developed
characters and an engaging plot, so when you add a dose of
sizzling sexuality, you have an unbeatable mix."
—*RT Book Reviews*

"Heady, passionate, seductive . . . Ms. Feehan does a fan-
tastic job of building up to the climax for a smashing finale
that leaves you breathless and satisfied."   —Smexy Books

"Readers . . . will be seduced by this erotic adventure."
—*Publishers Weekly*

"Another wild ride . . . enter the lair of the shapeshifters."
—Romance Reviews Today

"A passionate, jam-packed adventure."
—Fallen Angel Reviews

"The passion runs high and the sex is hot!"
—The Romance Readers Connection

"Sizzling and exciting . . . surprises erupt at every turn."
—Fresh Fiction

"A phenomenal story . . . Christine Feehan knows how to
weave a tale of action, suspense and paranormal passion that
has earned her so many fans and keeps bringing new ones."
—Romance Junkies

Anthologies

EDGE OF DARKNESS
(with Maggie Shayne and Lori Herter)

DARKEST AT DAWN
(includes DARK HUNGER *and* DARK SECRET*)*

SEA STORM
(includes MAGIC IN THE WIND *and* OCEANS OF FIRE*)*

FEVER
(includes THE AWAKENING *and* WILD RAIN*)*

HOT BLOODED
(with Maggie Shayne, Emma Holly, and Angela Knight)

LOVER BEWARE
(with Fiona Brand, Katherine Sutcliffe, and Eileen Wilks)

FANTASY
(with Emma Holly, Sabrina Jeffries, and Elda Minger)

Specials

DARK HUNGER
MAGIC IN THE WIND
THE AWAKENING

CHRISTINE FEEHAN

JOVE BOOKS, NEW YORK

JOVE

An imprint of Penguin Random House LLC
375 Hudson Street, New York, New York 10014

WILD CAT

A Jove Book / published by arrangement with the author

JOVE® is a registered trademark of Penguin Random House LLC.
The "J" design is a trademark of Penguin Random House LLC.
For more information, visit penguin.com.

ISBN: 978-0-515-15609-6

PUBLISHING HISTORY
Jove mass-market edition / December 2015

PRINTED IN THE UNITED STATES OF AMERICA

10 9 8 7 6 5 4 3 2 1

Cover images by Shutterstock.
Cover design by George Long.

Penguin
Random
House

For Tarah, who loves Leopards!

For My Readers

Be sure to go to christinefeehan.com/members/ to sign up for my PRIVATE book announcement list and download the FREE ebook of *Dark Desserts*. Join my community and get firsthand news, enter the book discussions, ask your questions and chat with me. Please feel free to email me at Christine@christinefeehan.com. I would love to hear from you. Each year, the last weekend of February, I would love for you to join me at my annual FAN event, an exclusive weekend with an intimate number of readers for lots of fun, fabulous gifts and a wonderful time. Look for more information at fanconvention.net.

Acknowledgments

With any book there are many people to thank. In this case, the usual suspects: Domini, for her research and help; my power hours group, who always make certain I'm up at the crack of dawn working; and of course Brian Feehan, who I can call anytime and brainstorm with so I don't lose a single hour. A special thanks to Irma Camargo for my Spanish endearments. If I got anything wrong, that's totally on me. For the salsa and dip recipes, thanks to Irma Camargo (the above Irma's mother) for her help, and again, I certainly hope I made them correctly.

A Special Note

When I was a child growing up, my mother would tell me stories of when she was young and first married to my father. She married him never having cooked or held a baby. One day while he was gone working, she wanted to surprise him with one of his favorite meals. She burned her hands on the chilies and he came home and was *very* upset with her, but of course he took great care of her. I always wanted to retell that story because I loved it so much. Irma Camargo (the mother) allowed me to do so by providing me with the recipes so Elijah would have to take very good care of Siena.

1

"Siena, *bella*, come see your old *nonno* for a minute."

Siena obediently dropped her car keys on the table and hurried into the sitting room her grandfather preferred. The room was cozy and always just a little too warm. As a rule that didn't bother her, but for some reason lately, her body seemed overheated. She was restless and edgy and *hot*. Very hot. Her skin ached, felt too tight, stretched over her frame. Even her jaw hurt. Her breasts felt swollen and achy, and for the first time in her life, she burned between her legs. Like crazy. It was awful.

The condition seemed to come and go at will for no apparent reason. It had started a couple of weeks earlier and was getting significantly worse. She was grateful she had just earned her master's of science in oenology and had come home, although being in the same room with her beloved grandfather when her body was on fire was decidedly uncomfortable.

She needed to get out of the house—immediately. Lately,

the condition had gotten so bad she was seriously thinking
about visiting an adult store and getting herself a toy. A really
good one. Sheesh. She'd never looked at a man like that. Well,
that wasn't strictly the truth. She'd once seen Elijah Lospostos
when she was fifteen. They sat across from each other at a
dinner when she'd been home from boarding school. He was
at least eight years older than her. Maybe ten. It hadn't mattered. The moment she'd laid eyes on him, something wild
unfurled deep inside of her. She'd barely been able to keep
her eyes off of him. He was the most gorgeous man she'd ever
seen. *Ever.* And her grandfather employed a lot of men.

She tried as hard as she could not to stare at him, but
sometimes she'd felt his gaze on her, and every time she'd
looked up, his eyes were looking at her. There was no mistake.
He smiled. She didn't. She blushed. A horrible reaction. He'd
tried to engage her in conversation and she'd stammered.
Blushed more. It had been horrible. She was smart. Brilliant.
She was already doing college courses. And she couldn't say
a single intelligent word to him. Even the memory embarrassed her.

"What is it, Nonno?" she asked, bending to brush a kiss
along his jaw. She ruffled his hair. He still had a wild mane
of hair. All silver, but thick as a cat's pelt. His eyes, a dark
chocolate, were faded, but still sharp. "I'm off to the gym."
Because she really, really needed to work out hard. Tire
herself to the point of exhaustion so she could actually get
some sleep. She was desperate for sleep.

"I need a favor, *bella*, a small one for an old man, eh?" he
coaxed.

As if she had ever in her life turned him down when he
asked her for something. She was rarely at the house. She
had been in boarding school most of her life and then college, but she treasured her times at home with him. He was
her only living relative. It was just Antonio Arnotto and his
granddaughter. The two of them.

"What would that be, Nonno?" she asked, trying to sound

stern. She knew she failed when the laugh lines around his eyes crinkled. She sank down onto the arm of his chair and ruffled all that silver hair again.

"I want you to take a case of my best reserve to a friend. His birthday was last week and I forgot to send a gift around. My beautiful granddaughter delivering it personally will make up for this mistake, no?"

She laughed. "It seems you have a lot of friends with birthdays and anniversaries you forget until your granddaughter comes home."

He shrugged his shoulders. "I'm not getting any younger, Siena, and you might start thinking about marriage and babies. Come to think of it, Elijah isn't married, and *he's* not getting any younger. He's quite good-looking." He winked at her.

She bit down on her lower lip to try to keep from blushing. Just the mere mention of Elijah's name set her heart pounding and her stomach whooshing a slow somersault. He *was* good-looking. Hot. Gorgeous. And way out of her league. She wasn't going to tell her grandfather that.

"Stop being a matchmaker. You'll get your babies in due time, I promise." Maybe sooner than he wanted if her body didn't stop with the meltdown-frantic-for-sex-*now* routine.

She'd taken to looking at her grandfather's bodyguards. And his number one man, Paolo, the man her grandfather dreamed of having her marry. Paolo watched her all the time. He always had. His gaze burned through her. He was good-looking and always very polite to her, but she knew he was a hound dog. He went through women, and word was, he wasn't very nice about it. She'd heard rumors from some of the maids and the cook that he ruled his women with an iron fist. She wasn't hooking up with him, even though she knew he was more than willing.

"I'm not getting any younger," he repeated, patting her hand. "Be a good girl and deliver the wine for me. Give Elijah my best. Tell him not to be such a stranger and to drop by once in a while to see an old man."

"I will, Nonnino," she murmured and kissed the top of his head.

The hair on the back of her neck stood up and her stomach tightened. She knew without turning her head that Paolo Riso had stepped into the room. He was all roped muscle and fluid grace, and for such a big man he moved in complete silence. She knew he was very intelligent, and her grandfather relied heavily on him. She had always gotten along with him, even liked him when she was younger, but the last few years she'd visited home, he made her very uncomfortable.

She turned her head and forced a smile. His eyes were on her. Gleaming. Watching. Hooded. Holding secrets. Secrets she was certain involved her—none of them good. He was very close to her grandfather, and her grandfather treated him as he might a son. She wanted to love him for that alone, but instead, each time she came back home, she found herself becoming more and more uneasy around him.

Not like her grandfather's second-in-command. Alonzo Massi made her entire body tense, shiver even, with revulsion. The man's body was massive with ropes of muscle, and he was just plain scary. His eyes were always following her around, and he appeared as cold as a snake. She wasn't certain what kind of job he actually did for her grandfather, but she was fairly certain it had nothing to do with the winery.

"Hey, Paolo." She gave him a smile. She was very good at smiling and making it seem genuine. "How's it going?"

"Good, *bella*." Paolo moved right to her.

She forced air through her lungs, knowing what was coming. He was getting bolder and bolder, and always in front of her beaming grandfather, who clearly approved. He took both hands and pulled her to her feet. Pulled her into him. He leaned down, and she turned her face slightly so his lips brushed her cheek rather than her lips.

Deep inside something that was out of control and wild leapt toward the surface. She was shocked and pulled back, although Paolo didn't release her hands. He stared down at her face and there was speculation there. His eyes changed color, yellow flecks spreading through the dark brown until they almost looked like a cat's. Wholly focused on her. Unblinking.

Heat moved through her body. This wasn't good. She tugged on her hands to get him to release her.

"I have to go. Nonno asked me to run an errand for him, and I want to get to the gym tonight as well."

Paolo frowned. He didn't release her hands, but looked over his shoulder at her grandfather. "Perhaps someone else should run the errand, Antonio."

There was something very subtle in his voice. A warning. An order? Whatever it was, she didn't like it. Siena very firmly pulled her hands away, not bothering with being polite. She always thought the infamous Arnotto temper had skipped her, but right then she knew it hadn't. Edgy and restless turned to fierce and formidable. She drew herself up—and wished she was wearing her heels—but she could look haughty without them and she gave Paolo her best princess to peasant look.

"I told Nonno I would take the gift to Signor Lospostos and I will." She tossed her head, the long mane of very thick hair flying around her face and down to her waist. Bending down, she skimmed another kiss on her grandfather's head and then left the room with a small wave. "*Addio* Nonnino. *Addio*, Paolo, please take care of Nonno for me."

She ran back upstairs to her room without a backward glance. If she was delivering wine to Elijah Lospostos, arguably the hottest man in the universe, then she was going to take a little care with her appearance. She quickly stuffed her gym clothes in a bag and changed. She didn't want to look like she went all out. He probably wouldn't even notice her, but still, she was going to look good.

Siena knew she was pretty. She looked in the mirror, and she knew. She had great skin. Perfect skin. Italian skin. Her eyes were unusual. Very large, shaped like a cat's, so she looked exotic to people. They were green. Not just any green;

a deep, pure brilliant green, and she had lush, thick, very black eyelashes. She was blessed with those eyes.

She had the most annoying hair in the world, although even she had to admit it was beautiful. There just was too much of it. It grew and grew and never seemed to stop. She'd tried cutting it, but that seemed to make it grow faster and even thicker than ever, so she gave up and just went with the old-fashioned look. Thick, rich, luxurious, her hair fell well past her waist in waves. It was impossible to tame, so she mostly wore it up when she was home, pulled back in a pony-tail or braid. At school, of course, she had to appear a little more sophisticated, so she used updos of intricate braids spun in all kinds of lovely knots.

Her nose was straight, her cheekbones high and her mouth a little too generous, but she did have straight teeth without having to go to the orthodontist. She was short. There was no getting around that. She had tried to gain a few inches by hanging upside down on the bars when she was a child, but that hadn't helped at all. She had a small waist and a narrow rib cage, but along with that generous mouth, her hips and breasts were a little bit on the generous side too. No matter how much she worked out or watched what she ate, she had curves. Lush curves.

She sighed. She'd seen Elijah with a tall, thin model once, coming out of a coffee shop. The woman had blond hair and blue eyes. His arm was around her and they were laughing together. She saw him in the distance at another party her grandfather had thrown when she was sixteen, and another one at nineteen, and he'd had a different model on his arm. Tall. Thin. Beautiful. Blond. And yet again, a few years later in a magazine. Tall. Thin. Beautiful. Blond. *Again*. He had a type and that type was *so* not her. She was short and dark and totally curvy. She looked even younger than she was, not at all sophisticated. She knew when she delivered the wine, Eli-jah would look at her like she was a little kid, like he always did. Antonio Arnotto's little granddaughter. Still, she was determined to go looking her best.

She chose soft, vintage faded jeans and a camisole that was pale green with satiny straps. The camisole emphasized her small rib cage and tucked-in waist. The color was great against her skin and really brought out her eyes. The only real problem was shoes. She wore heels all the time. She hesitated, looking at a pair of strappy green designer heels, her favorite paired with the camisole. She didn't want to look as if she were trying to be his type. Still, she needed confidence and heels gave her that. She shrugged and strapped them on.

Biting her lip, she stared at her wild hair. How in the world was she going to tame all that hair? There was nothing else for it on such short notice. She swept it all back away from her face into a long ponytail. She left all jewelry off.

Looking into the mirror, she practiced. "I'm on my way to the gym and just stopped by to deliver your birthday gift from Nonno. I'm sorry it's late, but my school didn't let out until this week and Nonno likes me to personally deliver . . ." Siena groaned. That made her sound like a silly schoolgirl when she was twenty-four. "Damn it," she whispered, and turned away from her image. She *looked* like a silly schoolgirl. She needed a lot more inches and a lot less curves to be the type Elijah Lospostos went for, so really, why was she bothering?

She caught up her gym bag and hurried down the stairs before she did something crazy like change her clothes again. She rushed back toward the sitting room her grandfather seemed to occupy more than ever these days, but stopped abruptly when she heard the whispered but furious conversation between her grandfather and his first-in-command. They kept their voices low, but lately she'd noticed her hearing seemed to be very acute. At the same time, her vision messed up, so that she saw in weird bands of color. Whenever that happened, she felt restless. Edgy. Need burned hot and wild between her legs.

She held the back of a chair just outside the sitting room, her grip so hard her knuckles turned white. She took in long, deep breaths, trying to regain some semblance of control. Her bones ached. Her fingers curled, and she felt that strange feral entity unfolding deep inside of her. Her skin itched, a terrible wave that refused to stop, and she swore something was pressing on her from the inside out, needing to escape. She was afraid of that something. It was wanton, hungry and in terrible need.

She put her head down and breathed more, desperate for the feeling to pass. She was very happy Paolo was nowhere near, because the sound of his voice seemed to trigger a deeper reaction in her.

"I'm telling you, Tonio, this is not a good idea. Something could go wrong."

"You worry too much, Paolo. Always you worry. She's young. Beautiful. His mind will be on her. Not my reserve. Not what day of the month it is. On her."

"I don't know why you have such an obsession with making certain you exact your revenge. You are putting not only Siena in jeopardy, but you as well. If evidence is left behind . . ."

"Marco knows what he is doing. Always you worry," her grandfather repeated.

"She is close to the Han Vol Dan. I feel it. My other feels it. She's *very* close."

"You saw evidence of this?"

"No evidence, just a feeling. She can't do this, Tonio. Stop her. I'm telling you, something could go wrong. If the timing is off, if she lingers . . ."

"She's a good girl. She will do as she's told and then go to her gym where many witnesses will see her there."

Witnesses? She is close? What did that mean. *Evidence?* What were they talking about?

"Tonio." Paolo bit out the name between his teeth.

"Paolo." Her grandfather did the same. "The subject is

closed. Go find her. Tell her the wine is in her car and she must go now."

Paolo swore in Italian, but she knew he would obey. Everyone obeyed her grandfather. He'd built an empire with his wineries and his amazing grapes. He had more money than he knew what to do with, and he'd made good friends and many enemies along the way.

The breathing helped and the wildness in her subsided. She turned away from the sitting room to make her way to the landing at the top of the stairs, acting as though she hadn't come down already. She had no idea why she did that, but it was instinctive. She knew her grandfather and Paolo would both be upset if they knew she heard their strange conversation. The knowledge came from the tone of their voices in their whispered exchange—almost as if they were involved in a conspiracy.

"Siena." Paolo's voice came up the stairs. "I'd like a word with you before you go. Your grandfather wants you to get moving. He says he doesn't want you to miss Elijah."

She winced at that hard authority in his voice. He was becoming more and more bossy with her. When she'd been a teenager, he'd been less so. Now, he watched her all the time. She wasn't certain why. She looked young, so he might think she was still a teenager. She'd just turned twenty-four while she was away at school, and no one, not even her grandfather, had remembered her birthday, so how could she expect Paolo to know? Still, she had studied oenology and viticulture for years and had so many degrees you would think Paolo would consider her intelligent, but he always spoke as if she were a child. Of course no one had come to her graduations—not any of them—so maybe he didn't know that either. Maybe they all still thought she was in boarding school.

"Coming, Paolo," she called, as she once more gripped her gym bag and began her descent. "Did Nonno have someone put the wine in my car?"

She hurried down the stairs again and immediately felt the impact of his gaze like a hard punch. He reached out and caught her arm, jerking her close to him, his fingers a vise.

The instant he touched her, the wild unfurled in the pit of her stomach. Something dangerous and scary. She heard her heart thundering in her ears. She felt the need to rake and claw at him. She stayed very still, breathing hard.

"You changed?" He growled it. "To see Lospostos, you changed your clothes?"

"I could hardly wear my workout clothes on an important call for my grandfather, Paolo," she pointed out, keeping her voice even and calm when she uncharacteristically wanted to rake her fingernails down his face. "You're hurting me. Let. Go." She stared straight into his eyes. His eyes were weird. Scary. He looked as if he might kill her any moment.

"Not until you listen to the rules of this visit." He pulled her from the staircase, away from the sitting room where her grandfather watched television and into the foyer.

"Paolo." His bruising grip really hurt and she was fairly certain he knew it. She decided on another tactic. "Why do you dislike me so much? I thought we were friends. What did I do to make you so angry with me all the time?" She forced herself to ask the questions, mainly because she knew he would relax his hold on her, but partly because she really wanted to know.

It was the right way to approach him. Instantly his grip loosened and his face changed. Grew softer. "I don't dislike you, Siena. Don't be silly. You're grown up now, and you know your grandfather has all but promised you to me. I don't like you running around looking like you do where other men might take advantage of you."

Siena wasn't certain how to respond. She knew her grandfather was always matchmaking, and she couldn't deny he always said when he was gone, Paolo would look after her. He sometimes went so far as to tell her he would plan the wedding of the century for them.

"Paolo." She took a deep breath and let it out. "Nonno is always pairing me with someone. Just a few minutes ago he told me it was time for Elijah Lospostos to settle down." Something dangerous moved in his eyes and she was suddenly afraid. "I'm not old enough to settle down. I still have to learn the business end of the winery right here at home. I'm not looking at anyone right now. Yes, I go to clubs to dance, but I'm careful about drinking and I don't take men home. You know I don't. One of Nonno's men is always looking after me. I know they report back to you."

"You go to his house and give him the message from your grandfather and give him the wine. You do *not* go inside with him. He's a dangerous man. Your grandfather thinks everyone is his friend. Lospostos is not. Deliver the wine, talk a few minutes and get out of there. Do you understand me?"

"I hardly think I'll be . . ."

"Do you understand me?" He roared it. His fingers sank deep again, and he gave her a little shake.

Siena nodded submissively when all she wanted to do was kick him very hard in the shins and claw his eyes out. She kept her head down so he wouldn't see the rebellion in her eyes. "Yes, Paolo."

He stared down at her another minute and then let her go. Siena forced herself not to rub at the finger marks on her arm. She knew she would have bruises and she was tempted to march in to her grandfather and show him what Paolo had done to her. The only thing was—she was beginning to think he wouldn't do anything other than ask her why she would upset such a good man. In his eyes, Paolo could do no wrong. As she'd gotten older, her beloved grandfather had gone from doting to watchful as well. She didn't know what they were all waiting for, but the longer they waited, the more upset everyone got.

"The wine's in your car," Paolo said. He caught her chin in a firm grip. "You be careful, Siena."

She blinked rapidly, trying not to show fear. Or anger. Or

any other emotion. She felt as if her life was turning upside down and she didn't even know why. His eyes searched hers.

"Did I hurt you?" His voice was gentle. "I'm worried for you, and sometimes my temper gets the better of me. Your *nonno* and I disagree about some of the things he asks you to do. I don't ever like the idea that you could be in danger."

"Paolo, I'm just delivering his wine. He's asked me to do it each time I've come home on a break, and I have. It's the least I can do after all the things he does for me. It's no big deal, honestly. I don't mind. And I'll be careful. It's possible Lospostos isn't home and I'll leave the wine and a note."

Siena knew she was placating him, but she did it anyway. She didn't understand the dynamics of her household anymore. Maybe she'd just been gone away so much she never really knew what they were.

Her parents had died in a car bombing. Siena understood why her grandfather was so protective of her. He'd never really gotten over his son's death. When she was little, she had her grandmother, who doted on her. When her grandmother passed away, she was immediately sent to a very private and exclusive boarding school. She'd been six and terrified, but no amount of tears would convince her grandfather to keep her at home.

Of course she was home every holiday, and he spoiled her rotten. She sat with him, laughed with him, played games until all hours, and he seemed to delight in her company. His men were always close, always watchful, and when she asked, he told her that there were bad people out there who didn't like that he'd been so successful with his wine making and vineyards. He needed to make certain she was protected, so he had bodyguards watching her.

When she was ten years old, she found out the hard way he was right. Men broke into her room at the school and dragged her, kicking and screaming, into the night. She had spent two nights in an old abandoned warehouse, terrified, in the dark, a blindfold over her eyes, tied to a bed. One of

her kidnappers had been kind and given her water and reassurance, but the others were terrifying. Her grandfather's
men had come, and there was a terrible gunfight. Two of the
men who had been holding her were shot and killed. The other
two had been outside the building and got away. She knew
her grandfather had hunted for them for two years.

When she was fifteen, someone had tried kidnapping her
again. Alonzo had stopped them. She didn't remember much
about it, but she had terrible nightmares. One day, after she
told her grandfather her nightmare, he simply said she didn't
have to worry anymore and to stop. The nightmares didn't
stop, but she never told him about them again.

"Stay out of his house, Siena," Paolo warned her again.

She nearly startled, so lost in her thoughts she had almost
forgotten he was standing in front of her. Paolo had always
helped her grandfather. She guessed he was fifteen to twenty
years older than she was. He had been one of the men to rescue
her from the first kidnappers, assigned as her bodyguard back
then before he moved into the number one position.

He was handsome, she supposed, now that she was really
up close to him. She had never thought of him that way, but
she wasn't attracted to him. Not really. So why did that edgy
feeling begin to creep back over her?

"I will," she agreed, turned and left without a backward
glance. What was wrong with her? Paolo had manhandled
her. She shouldn't have noticed that he was good-looking.
She shouldn't have felt tingles anywhere on her body. Not a
single place.

She drove fast with the top down and the wind in her hair.
She didn't care if the long strands got tangled and she looked
terrible when she arrived at Elijah's house. She needed the
cool air on her hot skin. She needed to breathe, far away from
the house that had once been her home but was now a prison.
Everyone watched her. Waiting. She detested that her every
move was scrutinized. It was the reason she didn't use the
state-of-the-art gym her grandfather had put in for her, instead

choosing to have a little respite from all the eyes on her ever since she'd returned home.

Elijah owned a large estate not far from where her grandfather lived in the hill country west of San Antonio and Austin. His property was close to Jake Bannaconni's huge, sprawling ranch. It was where all the millionaires lived, although Bannaconni was a certified billionaire according to *Forbes*. Most of the bigger estates and ranches were out away from the city. She knew Bannaconni took a helicopter to work. She didn't know what Elijah did, but she wondered.

There were rumors, of course. Her grandfather was Italian. He'd actually emigrated from Italy with his wife to raise his family in the United States. He'd worked hard for his winery and, although he made his money legitimately, the rumors persisted. They did about Elijah's family as well. His family was Spanish and had come from somewhere in South America. Because she knew her grandfather was a good man who had worked hard all of his life for his family, she didn't judge Elijah or the whispers surrounding him.

The high wrought-iron gates to his ranch were closed, and she leaned over to look into the camera and state her business. There was a moment of silence while her heart pounded. She twirled a thick strand of hair from her ponytail around her finger, which she often did when she was nervous, but couldn't help it. The gates swung inward. Heart pounding, she drove through and up the long, winding driveway to his house.

She knew this wasn't the family home, the huge one Elijah's father had owned before he'd been murdered. Rumor had it that his own uncle had ordered the hit on his father and then his uncle had been killed, leaving Elijah the head of his family business. No, this was the house Elijah bought to entertain his women in. His tall, thin, blond, *beautiful* women. She sighed, knowing she spent far too much time at school where she had developed low self-esteem for a variety of reasons. It hadn't helped living in her grandfather's house with all the men coming and going.

She'd always felt like an outsider. Not always, she corrected herself. Not when her grandmother was alive, but she could barely remember those days anymore. She'd spent her school years fairly isolated. There was no having friends at school, her grandfather's men saw to that. Having two hulks go with her everywhere made her seem pretentious. Even some of her professors balked at them entering the classrooms. It had left her without many social skills. She didn't exactly relate well to others and kept to herself most of the time, even at home, although she did go dancing because she loved to dance.

The drive up to Elijah's house was very long and winding. It was paved, but on either side, the land rolled away, wild and filled with trees and brush as far as the eye could see. This wasn't at all like her grandfather's manicured estate. The only flowers growing were wildflowers. She glimpsed a couple of oil wells as she drove along the fence line of his property, and she wasn't surprised. Bannaconni, his closest neighbor, was noted for finding oil, even in the most obscure places.

She slowed her car and pulled to a stop to stare out over the wild land. A part of her longed to leap out of her seat and just start running, lose herself there, in the middle of all that rough terrain. She sat there a long time, feeling tears on her face. She was lonely. Lonely at school. Lonely at home. Just plain lonely. She didn't have girlfriends to go out clubbing with. She didn't have boyfriends to take her to dinner or sit and watch movies with.

She had her grandfather, who these days seemed far away, cut off from her, more under the thumb of Paolo and Alonzo. She rarely saw her grandfather without one or the other of them close. In fact, her last three visits, she'd never really been alone with him. They were continually at his side. Alonzo was ice-cold. Paolo stared at her hungrily, like an animal scenting something weak and ready to pounce.

She didn't consider herself weak. Just lost. She had no real direction. She had just finished school and had no more excuses to stay away. She'd spent most of her summers and vacations gaining hands-on experience in the vineyards, learning to care for the grapes. She stood to inherit everything. The vineyards and the winery. All of her grandfather's businesses. She had no other living relative. None.

She stared out into the wild, beckoning land. She needed to take some control in her life. She'd escaped to school, she realized. Ran away. She didn't want to be home anymore. It wasn't a sanctuary or a haven; it was an alien place filled with men who walked all over her. She needed to talk to her grandfather, without either Paolo or Alonzo around, and explain she was due a lot more freedom.

She had her own money. Her grandmother had left her a trust fund. Her parents had left her a second trust fund. She didn't need to stay under her grandfather's thumb if he disagreed with her. She needed to get some guts and actually confront him. It was time to get rid of the bodyguards. She was tired of living her life under the scrutiny of his army of men. She actually thought of them like that. Soldiers.

With a small sigh she took a deep breath and started up the drive again, toward the house. Her heart beat hard in anticipation of seeing Elijah. She hadn't really been close to him since that last dinner, when she was nineteen. Just as when she was fifteen, his gaze had rested on her more than once, making her heart pound just the way it was doing now. Given that her body seemed to be raging with runaway hormones, this wasn't the best time to be alone with him.

She decided to put the wine on his front porch and obey Paolo's rule of staying out of the house. It was the only safe thing to do to keep from making an absolute fool of herself. She wasn't even certain she could talk to him. Say a word. Maybe she'd gotten lucky and it had been his security people who had allowed her inside the high gates.

She pulled into the circular drive and stared up at the house. It wasn't a mansion like her family home, but it was beautiful. Perfect. Homey. Not in the least ostentatious. She loved the wraparound verandah with the huge columns holding up a sloping roof that shaded the wide, inviting porch.

Elijah stood waiting at his front door, wearing a tight-fitting pair of jeans that rode low on his hips and fit very lovingly around his extremely nice butt. The breath left her lungs in a long rush. His jeans were carelessly buttoned, the top two left undone. He wore no shirt, displaying a heavily muscled chest. His black, black hair was unruly and damp as if he'd just stepped out of the shower. She swallowed hard, trying not to stare. Her already soaring temperature went up a couple more notches. She had forgotten how good he looked. He was definitely a man—no soft edges to him at all. Right now, intimately barefoot, his anger seemed to simmer right below the surface.

She couldn't understand his anger, unless she had interrupted him with another woman. She blushed. Of course there would be a woman there. She hadn't called. Her grandfather never had her call, saying he wanted it to be a surprise when she delivered his best reserve for whatever the occasion. She could see how intruding on a date with a willing woman would make Elijah mad.

Still, he looked so gorgeous. Handsome. Masculine. *Dangerous.* Immediately, that wild thing inside her stretched and unfurled. She felt hot. Very hot. She couldn't tear her gaze away from him. She told herself he probably had a woman in the house with him, but it didn't matter. Already, her blood rushed through her veins, so heated she knew she was flushed. Her breasts ached. Her sex spasmed. There was a burning between her legs that was worse than anything she'd ever experienced. She had the mad desire to fling herself at him, tear his clothes off and beg him to pound into her, filling her.

She gripped the steering wheel until her knuckles grew white. His eyes drifted over her, an intense scrutiny that saw way too much. She had never seen a man more sensual in her life.

"Siena." He said her name softly and took a step toward her.

Her heart hammered madly. God. He was beautiful. Masculine. All roped muscle, wide shoulders and thick chest. With every movement, his very defined muscles rippled. Her mouth watered. Her pulse throbbed deep in her core. His wide shoulders tapered to a narrow waist, and her eyes dropped lower. Her breath caught in her lungs.

"Siena," he said again, this time firmly. A command.

She swallowed hard and let out her breath slowly. "Elijah." She could barely get his name out. Her voice didn't sound the same at all. It sounded husky. Sexy. Not at all her.

They stared at each other. Her breath refused to leave her lungs. He'd sucked all the air from the atmosphere until her lungs burned and felt raw. He looked predatory. Dangerous. Scary. He looked delicious. She licked her lips, holding on for dear life to the steering wheel, otherwise something terrible was going to happen. Her blood thundered in her ears, drowning out common sense.

"My grandfather sent you a belated birthday present, Elijah. A case of his reserve." She nearly stammered the words. Her voice wasn't her own. Husky. Sensual. Needy. Hungry.

His gaze drifted over her face and dropped to her chest. She couldn't control her breathing. "So this is how he does it. He uses you. You're a part of this? He uses you for his dirty work?" He nearly snarled the words at her. "And you let him?"

She had no idea what he was talking about. She barely heard the words through the roaring of her blood in her ears. She could barely think. Her mind was melting along with her body. So hot. Her breasts were on fire. She needed to drive away. Her finger instinctively went to the starter.

"Don't." His voice was low. She froze, her gaze skittering to his. "Get out of that fucking car right now."

She didn't dare obey him. His voice was every bit as husky as hers. Predatory. Hungry. She tried to shake her head, to tell him it wasn't a good idea, but he was down the walkway and leaning into her car to unhook her seat belt. He simply lifted her into his arms, pulling her right out of the car and striding back to his house. *Into the house.*

She felt his hands burning like brands where he touched her. She clung to him, staring into his eyes, shocked at his behavior. All the while that burn got hotter until she was afraid she'd burst into flames. He slammed the door behind them and put her down, leaving her breathless. Her breasts heaving. Her stomach rolling. Damp heat spreading like wildfire between her legs.

"Take off your shoes." It was a clear order, delivered in a harsh, rough voice that seemed to stroke her skin and leave behind flames.

She licked her lips, looking up at him. She was in way over her head, but he was so compelling she couldn't move.

Impatient, a snarl on his face, he bent to the pale green strappy sandals and undid them, lifting her leg to force her to step out of them. She backed away from him on bare feet, unsure what to do.

"I'm not supposed to be in here. In your house," she blurted stupidly.

2

ELIJAH stalked toward her. Siena backed up at the fury gathering in his eyes. It was so intense, the room smoldered with his temper. She had no idea why he was angry, but when her back hit the wall, she gave a small cry and turned to flee the house. Elijah smacked the wall hard, his hands on either side of her body, caging her in.

"I'll just bet you're not supposed to come in the house," he hissed, his body utterly still. His eyes were so focused on her, she felt pinned beneath his stare. Mesmerized. His prey. Unable to move.

One hand came up to her hair, his fingers going to the elastic holding her ponytail in place. He dragged it out and sifted his fingers through it. "Soft as it looks. Is your skin as fuckin' soft as it looks?"

She couldn't look away from his eyes. His pupils were nearly gone. His breath was an invitation. And then his fist was in her hair, dragging her head back. Her heart stuttered.

Pounded. A dark whisper of a thrill crept down her spine. Her breasts swelled. Ached. Her sex clenched. Burned. She couldn't look away from his eyes, mesmerized by the hunger there and a dark lust so intense, her own hunger escalated.

Elijah's mouth slammed down on hers, and she was lost. There was no telling him she didn't know what she was doing. She didn't have time to think. She couldn't think. There was thunder in her ears, her blood roaring, her mind melting completely.

There was only his mouth brutally taking hers. Hard. Demanding. Almost savage. She caught at him, arms sliding around his neck, fingers searching for the thick, wavy hair at the back of his neck, standing on her toes, giving herself completely to him, lost in the beauty of his mouth. Of his dark, wet, terrible kiss. Her mouth was as out of control as his, following wherever he led, seeking the fire, needing it. She wanted him to devour her. She wanted to devour him. She was ravenous for him. She couldn't get close enough to him.

His skin was hot and she had to feel it, the hard surface, the heat—he was nearly as hot as she was. Her fingers curled in his hair as their mouths consumed each other. His hands went to her camisole, ripping at it, jerking the material down, so her generous breasts spilled out over the top, the material holding the soft mounds up to him like an offering.

She cried out when his mouth left hers to travel down her throat to her left nipple. His hand went to her right breast, kneading, massaging, tugging and rolling while she sobbed with need against his chest. He wasn't in the least gentle. He was rough, demanding, possessive. He wrenched her body's responses out of her, driving that hunger until she was so needy she was nearly sobbing for him.

His hands and mouth were relentless, refusing to allow her to catch her breath or her mind. The hunger in her was so sharp and terrible and savage she wanted to strip him of his clothes and climb over him like a cat in heat.

She licked at his chest, tasting his skin. Tasting the fine

sheen that coated him. He tasted all male. Feral and as wild as she felt. It wasn't enough, and she was desperate to get at him. Her hands fell to the buttons of his jeans, fumbling, her breath ragged and needy. His hands dropped to the waistband of her jeans. He shoved the offending material off her hips, taking her panties along as well. The relief against her burning skin was tremendous.

"Step out of them."

The sound of his voice stunned her. She almost couldn't hear him with the strange roaring in her ears, with the pounding of her blood rushing through her veins or the hammering of her own heart.

He practically ripped the jeans off of her and was down on his knees, pushing her thighs apart, and then his mouth was there. His tongue plunged deep. Then his finger followed. She came apart. Legs shaking, thighs dancing, her breasts on fire while an earthquake took possession of her body. He didn't stop. His mouth was as relentless as his hands.

"More," he growled in a kind of fury. "Again."

Her body was already consumed with fire, burning hot, burning out of control. She didn't have time to think. To catch her breath. There was only feeling. Pure feeling. She caught at his hair, one hand on his shoulder, trying to stay upright when she was coming apart. Flying too high. She had no choice. He gave her no choice, driving her up fast and wild a second time so that a tsunami hit this time, taking her completely.

Then his mouth was gone, and he yanked his jeans to his ankles, dragging her down to the floor beside him, his hands on her head, guiding her mouth to him. He was big. Bigger than she thought a man could be. He looked intimidating, as if he wouldn't fit anywhere. Not her mouth. Certainly not inside of her. She knew she should slow down. Tell him she'd never done this. She had no idea what to do, but the fire was inside of her and his hands were insistent.

"Your mouth, baby, right now. I need it."

His voice was harsh. Thrilling. In as desperate need as she felt. She licked up the shaft, closed her eyes and sucked the large head into her mouth. She felt him jerk. Swell impossibly larger. His hands were firmer. Tugging on her hair. The bite of pain in her scalp only added to the crazy hunger building until she wanted to weep with need.

Deep inside, tension coiled tighter and spread, building again, and she needed release. She needed satisfaction. She needed that terrible hunger assuaged, and only Elijah seemed to know what to do. She didn't. So she used her mouth and tongue, following his harsh, whispered commands. Or tried to. He was nearly as brutal with her mouth as he had been when kissing her.

Then he was pulling away from her, pushing her to the floor, yanking her legs apart to kneel between her thighs. His eyes were on her face. His dark features were a mask, sensual lines carved deep. Eyes alive with lust. With hunger. With possession.

"Hurry," she whispered.

He took her fast, driving through her tight folds ruthlessly, slamming deep, his hips a jackhammer, pushing through her protesting muscles and her thin barrier to lodge deep inside her. Pain ripped through her. Bright. Hot. She opened her mouth to scream, but nothing came out. Her eyes were on his. He bent his mouth and took her breast, his teeth rolling her nipple and then sucking the soft weight into his mouth.

"*Fuck.* You're so tight. Like a scorching-hot fist." He bit the words out around her breast.

She couldn't answer, couldn't say a word, because almost immediately the heat began to build. Hotter than before. A firestorm this time, and with every stroke jolting her body, slamming deeper and deeper, the pleasure spread, overtaking the pain, pushing her high. So high. Terrifyingly high. Still, she went willingly, her nails scoring down his back to find his hips. Trying to pull him deeper. Lifting her hips to meet the pounding of his.

Then he reached between their bodies, his thumb finding her clit, and she exploded a third time. She opened her mouth to scream again, but no sound emerged. Siena was too stunned by the fierce flames and the consuming hunger that had engulfed her. By the pleasure that was unlike anything she'd ever experienced.

He thrust three more times while her body gripped and strangled his, forcing him with her over the edge, milking every last drop of his seed from him. Taking him deep inside of her. They lay locked together on the floor in his foyer, breathing ragged, sweat on both bodies. Her jeans were completely off, her camisole torn. His jeans were around his ankles. Her top remained pulled down, exposing her breasts, and when he lifted his head, his mouth nuzzled her there. At the touch, another wave of fire rushed through her and bathed his cock in hot liquid.

Without warning his face changed completely. He'd been looking at her with soft eyes and suddenly, his eyes changed. Went hard. Alert. He rolled fast, taking her with him, even as he slid out of her, his hand coming to rest beside a table. He reached up, ripped a gun from beneath the table and half lifted up on his other hand, his body between her and whatever he'd seen or sensed. She started to lift her head and he slammed her back to the floor.

He fired his weapon three times in rapid succession. She heard his shots as two other shots came at them simultaneously. One bullet hit the wall behind them, just over her head, the other the floor in back of her. She heard something very heavy hit the floor with a thud.

Elijah rolled completely off of her, gliding smoothly to his feet, jerking his jeans up, the gun steady as a rock when he did it. She lay in shock, hardly comprehending what had happened until he moved. Stepping away from her, he kicked a gun away from the outstretched hand of a man in a dark coat. The intruder lay in a pool of blood, not five feet from her.

She gasped and scrambled backward on all fours. Elijah

searched for a pulse. Evidently he found none because he turned toward her. The look on his face terrified her. He crossed to her in three long strides, reached down and yanked her up by her arm, fitting the muzzle of his gun to her temple.

"Give me a reason not to blow your fuckin' head off. Setting me up. Fucking whore. Did you think I was so stupid I wouldn't figure out what you were doing? Distracting me to let that bastard get to me?" He shoved her away from him and transferred his hold to her hair, his fist buried deep, all the while swearing in Spanish. Over and over. Harsh, dirty, ugly words.

"Elijah." She whispered his name. A protest. She had no idea what he was talking about. Worse, her brain wouldn't work. She was in shock. A dead man was only a couple of feet from her. She'd just had sex for the first time in her life— violent sex—mind-blowing sex, and now he was accusing her of aiding the intruder in some way.

"What?" he snarled, dragging her back through the foyer by her hair.

She cried out and tried to grab at his hand. His fist was buried deep, right next to scalp, and the pain brought tears to her eyes. His grip was brutal and there was no escaping it as he dragged her by her hair to the front door.

"You thought your amateur performance was going to distract me while your fucking hit man killed me? Is that how you got those other poor bastards? You're the worst cocksucker I've ever experienced, so they should have known better, but I guess being old men they didn't care as long as they had a mouth around their dicks. Get the fuck out of my house before I change my mind and kill you." He snagged her jeans as he pushed her past the dead man on the floor.

She knew she was in shock. His voice barely registered. She knew the things he said to her would be branded on her brain for all time, but right then, her horrified gaze was on the dead man—the dead man she knew—the dead man who worked for her grandfather.

"If you're going to be in the business of whoring yourself out for your grandfather, Siena, you seriously need to get someone to give you a few lessons in fucking. How could a woman possibly get to be your age and not even learn to suck cock?" The contempt in his voice lashed at her already raw emotions. "You're laughable. I had far better back in high school. Hell. Grammar school. I would never have bothered fucking you if I hadn't wanted to see how far you'd take it. Get the hell out of my sight and hope to hell I never see you again."

He propelled her out the door, threw her jeans at her, then slammed and locked the door. She knew he locked it because she heard the bolt. Siena stood on shaking legs, blood and seed trickling down her thighs, her body in shock. Her brain in shock. Leaning against the door, she tried to put her jeans on, an automatic gesture, but she was trembling so hard she couldn't lift her leg up without falling down. She took several deep breaths, her movements slow, but she managed to make her way to her car and climb in, the jeans still crumpled in her hand.

The terrible things he'd said reverberated through her head. *The worst he'd ever had.* She'd been so caught up in their sexual encounter she had built entire fantasies about him. She'd *loved* him. Was making love to him. Worshiping him. She was so stupid. So naïve. *The worst he'd ever had.*

Elijah had been her dream man, literally. She dreamt of him almost every night. She fantasized about him. She searched for pictures of him in magazines and articles about him in the newspaper. She knew when he left the country for South America. She knew when he returned. *Better in high school. Hell. Grammar school.* He'd called her a whore.

Whoring herself out? Distracting him for her grandfather? She knew that man, the one who lay dead in a pool of blood in Elijah's foyer. She knew Marco Capello. She'd known him her entire life. Elijah thought she'd gone to others, went down on them, old men. Old friends, because the only men she'd ever taken her grandfather's reserve to were men she had known all of her life. Elijah thought she would get on her knees and suck their cocks to allow a hit man to kill them. *Elijah* thought that of her.

She clapped her hand over her mouth to keep from screaming. Tears ran down her face until she couldn't see. She wiped at them, knowing she had to do something. Wanting to run. Knowing she had nowhere to go because what happened, the things Elijah said to her, would go with her. This evening would be forever with her.

She became aware of her breasts heaving, pulled right out of her camisole. With a trembling hand she started her car and drove a little recklessly away from the house, down the long winding drive, her jeans still in one hand, her breasts exposed, her blood and his seed staining the driver's seat under her.

She didn't care. She had to get out of his sight and she did, driving almost to the gates where she stopped the car, got out and was sick. She had to crouch down to empty her stomach. Her shaky legs barely held her up. The first time she'd come home from grad school was on her break several months earlier. That had been normal; she always returned home on her breaks.

Her grandfather had asked her to take a case of his reserve to one of his oldest friends, Don Miguel, a man his age who often graced their table, played dominoes with her and spent a great deal of time laughing. She was very fond of him. She'd stayed at his home for an hour, played their favorite game before kissing his cheek and leaving. She left for school the next day. Her first day back to school, her grandfather called her and told her that Don Miguel was dead. She hadn't asked how because the man was in his eighties. Everyone knew he had a bad heart. She should have asked.

She bit back a sob and pressed her hand to her mouth again. The second visit she'd been called home because her grandfather was ill. The flu, it turned out. He'd asked her just before she left to deliver a case of his best reserve to another friend, Carlo Bianchi, a man who had actually worked for him for a long time. He'd started his own businesses and become very successful, but the two men remained good friends. She'd stayed an hour, laughing and joking with him. She liked him too. He was her grandfather's age and always treated her like a granddaughter. Three days later she learned he had died—that someone had broken into his home and shot him.

Siena had come back home for his funeral. Her grandfather had spoken at the funeral, in fact, he'd gotten so choked up that Siena had gotten up and taken over his talk for him. He had quietly wept through the entire service. She had stayed close to her grandfather, worried that he might become ill at the death of such a close friend on the heels of the first that had come only a few weeks before.

She found a bottle of water in her gym bag, rinsed her mouth and spit, wishing she hadn't removed her gym clothes when she had gone upstairs to change before she had left the house. Then she pulled her camisole up over her breasts, trying to smooth out the material with shaking hands. The fabric was torn, shredded around the cups, but she managed to cover up. She rinsed her mouth a second time, trying to keep her brain blank, but she couldn't.

The third time she'd delivered her case of reserve was to Luigi Baldini, a man in his sixties, one she didn't know as well as her grandfather's other two friends, but he came often to the house to consult with her grandfather on several business dealings. He was always very polite. She'd stayed a few minutes, given him the congratulations from her grandfather on his latest business coup and left. She didn't know he was dead until two months later when she came back for another short weekend.

She pressed the water bottle to her throbbing head. She was in no state to drive. Her body felt used up. Shaky. Achy. She hurt in places she didn't know she had and worse, she could feel him inside of her, stretching her, leaving skid marks. She knew she would carry Elijah's mark on her. She also knew she never wanted to see him again. She never wanted to repeat what happened between them with anyone else. *Ever.* She couldn't get his voice out of her. *The worst I ever had. Don't even know how to suck cock.*

The fourth time she'd delivered wine had been to Angelo Fabbri. Angelo was the son of her grandfather's best friend. Angelo had taken over his father's restaurant when his father had a massive stroke a few years earlier. She'd known Angelo since she could remember. He had bad luck in his relationships and she could never figure out why. He seemed like a good man. She had met him at his restaurant after hours to give him the wine, had coffee, talked for a while and then hugged him good-bye.

Angelo had been on his way home, the day's take in his car, when someone who had been hiding in his backseat shot him in the back of the head. The police had questioned her. She had been the last person to spend time with him. They wanted to know if she'd seen anyone out in the parking lot, or near his car. The wine was in the trunk. She didn't understand how Angelo could have put the wine in the trunk of his car and not see the robber.

She'd cried for days over Angelo's death, her grandfather trying to console her. Never once had it occurred to her that any of those deaths were related. Not one time did she put it together that she had been the last person to see all four men. The deaths were weeks and months apart. Could her grandfather really have had those men killed? Murdered? His friends? Men who sat at their table with them frequently. Could he really be such a monster and she not know?

Marco worked for him. He'd been around as long as she could remember. She knew Marco would never act on his own. He was quiet, unassuming, but his eyes were watchful and often very cold. Not necessarily when he looked at her or her grandfather. Marco had headed the team of men rescuing her when she was kidnapped that first time when she was ten. He'd held her in his arms and rocked her back and forth once they found her, shielding her from the sight of the bodies of the dead men. He always watched over her grandfather, and cared nothing for the business, only for the protection of Antonio Arnotto.

Elijah clearly had been waiting for him ever since she'd driven up. He knew a hit man would be coming, and he probably knew who that man was. Her face turned scarlet. Her heart shifted in her chest and her stomach lurched alarmingly again. Elijah had deliberately had sex with her. He hadn't been overcome with passion as she had been. Another sob escaped. She'd been a complete and utter fool. *The worst I ever had.* She knew she would never get his assessment of her abilities out of her mind until the day she died. He'd branded her in more ways than one. *Don't even know how to suck cock.*

"Oh. My. God. What did I do?" she whispered. There was no taking it back. No way to change what happened. How did she live with it? With being the distraction that allowed her grandfather to have his friends murdered? With wild, dirty sex that she wasn't any good at. With Elijah knowing what she was, a whore her grandfather sent out to distract his friends while he sent someone to murder them.

With shaky hands, she pulled on her jeans. She was sore and achy. Worse. That horrible, disgusting hunger was beginning to build again. She hated herself. She hated her grandfather. She hated her life, and most of all she hated Elijah. She wasn't the person he made her out to be. He had to have known it was her first time. She couldn't have been whoring herself out for her grandfather. And if her grandfather was guilty of being the man it had been rumored he was—what did that say about Elijah? He ran in the same circles.

She got back in the car barefoot. He could keep her beautiful strappy green sandals that gave her four inches when she wore them. She never wanted to see them again. Or the camisole or her bloodstained jeans. She was going home to inform her grandfather Marco was dead. Then she was packing her bags and leaving.

She cried all the way back to the estate. Parking in the cavernous, heated garage, she ran up the back stairs and let herself in that way, going through the kitchen, hoping to avoid everyone. She needed a shower, although she didn't think she could ever scrub hard or long enough to erase what had happened. Erase the feel of Elijah's hands and mouth. She couldn't brush her teeth long enough to ever get the taste of him out of her mouth, or the scent of him out of her lungs.

Siena hurried through the house to the stairs leading to the upper story. The more she thought about it, the less she wanted to confront her grandfather and the more she wanted to just leave. She dashed at the tears still falling and skidded to a halt as she entered her bedroom. Paolo sat on the edge of her bed. His gaze jumped to her face and he looked—terrifying.

His face was dark, almost red with anger. The anger radiated throughout her room, filling the air until she nearly choked on it.

"What are you doing in here?" she asked.

Even as she spoke, she found herself looking beyond him to the bed where he sat. Her comforter, the one her grandmother had given her, was shredded, great long tears right down the center of it. She looked around her. The room was in shambles. The walls had rake marks, as if a giant cat had scraped its claws from ceiling to floor, peeling paint and wood off in strips.

"Shut the door."

Her heart seemed to stop for a minute and then began to pound. She tasted fear in her mouth. Paolo looked—evil. When she didn't move, he stood up, stalked to the door and slammed it closed behind her. He came close to her, inhaling her scent as he walked around her.

He was close. Too close. She felt his body heat. His rage. She wanted to move, but her feet refused to cooperate. She could actually hear herself screaming inside.

"I can smell his stench on you," he spat out.

She remained silent, the tremors seizing her body worsening. Something terrible was happening and she didn't know how to stop it.

"Did he fuck you?"

She took a breath and remained silent.

"Did you let him fuck you?" Paolo roared the question, his voice like thunder, his features contorted with anger.

"That's not your business," she replied in a whisper. She couldn't look at him. She could never look at another man again.

"You *fucking* whore."

He slapped her hard, the blow sending her flying. She landed on her side, beside the dresser, facing away from him. She didn't see the immaculate Italian leather shoe coming at her. She felt it though, kicking her twice, and then he rained blows on her with his fists. She curled into a ball, hands over her face as he beat her. She sobbed. Pleaded. He didn't stop for what seemed an eternity but could only have been a couple of minutes.

Finally. *Finally*, there was no more, just the sound of his heavy breathing and her broken sobs. The worst of it was she didn't know if she was crying because she hurt everywhere, or because of the terrible things Elijah had said to her, or seeing Marco, a man she actually liked, dead on the floor in a pool of blood. She was utterly and totally humiliated. Utterly and totally beaten down. She'd never felt so small or so scared in her life.

Paolo crouched close to her, gripping her hair in his hand and pulling her head up so he could look down into her face. "You. Belong. To. *Me*. If you insist on acting like a slut, I'll treat you that way. This is what sluts get, so make up your mind what you're going to be, Siena. My adored wife, or my slut I use any way I see fit."

There was disgust in his voice. So much. He made her feel filthy. She didn't understand her behavior with Elijah.

She'd never done anything like that in her life. Never. She'd never even dreamt of having sex like that. Wild. Abandoned. Out of control. But just the thought of Elijah had her body burning, wanting more. Paolo was right. She was a slut and a whore. She was everything he said, and she wasn't any good at it either. She would never—ever—make that mistake again. She felt vulnerable, fragile, and Paolo had just taken anything she had left of herself away from her.

Paolo released his grip on her hair, spit in her face and then was gone, leaving her lying there, hurting so bad she didn't think she would ever be able to move, with spittle running down her cheek. Her stomach lurched. The waves of itching grew stronger as if something raced beneath her skin, pushing and shoving to escape. She hurt so bad everywhere, but now, she was aware of every joint, her knuckles, her knees, her ankles and even her jaw. She rolled, trying to get to her knees. The moment she did, she began to vomit. She couldn't even get to the bathroom.

Once she was able to stop the terrible retching, she crawled toward the bathroom and the cool tiles. Her clothes hurt her skin. She couldn't stand the weight of the fabric, and her body temperature seemed to be soaring. The burning between her legs was back. Horrible. Needy. Her body wanted him—Elijah. She despised herself—and him.

Siena pulled herself into a sitting position and then shakily, using the sink, pulled herself to her feet. Her face was already swelling. There was blood streaking down her face from several cuts where Paolo's knuckles had split her skin open. Her camisole was torn from Elijah, the material in tatters, exposing the tops of her breasts. There were bruises forming there as well. Every breath she drew was painful.

She yanked down her jeans and kicked them away from her. Wetting a washcloth she cleaned the evidence of her innocence and Elijah's possession from between her legs and thighs, but she couldn't take away the feeling of him there inside, filling her. She pulled off the ruined camisole and let it drop to the floor while she stared at herself in the mirror, hardly recognizing herself.

She had to tell her grandfather. No, she had to *show* her grandfather what his beloved, first-in-command had done to her. Then she had to confront him about Marco. She wiped the spit from her face, her stomach lurching again dangerously.

Her movements clumsy, she dragged on a T-shirt and a clean pair of jeans and went slowly down the stairs, using the bannister to keep herself upright. Each step jarred her bruised ribs so she wrapped her arms around her middle as she walked into her grandfather's sitting room, her face still bloody, her breath hitching in her lungs with every step.

Paolo stood just inside her grandfather's sitting room. She felt the instant tension in the room as she moved inside, bloody, swaying, holding her arms around her bruised ribs. Her grandfather looked up slowly, his old, faded eyes moving over her face and then going back to Paolo. She didn't see censure there, only resignation.

Paolo licked at the blood on his knuckles, but said nothing, his eyes on her. She waited, her gaze fixed on her grandfather. He should be yelling. Ordering Paolo out. Instead, his gaze came back to her and he shook his head.

"Tell me you did not do this thing, Siena. You allowed the *bastardo* Lospostos to put his hands on you?"

She flinched at the disgust in his voice, but she didn't move. Didn't respond. They couldn't make her feel any lower than she already felt. She wasn't going to defend herself. There was no defense. Still, there was no defense for what Paolo had done and certainly none for what her grandfather had done. They were all guilty of something.

"I did not raise my granddaughter to *puttaneggiare*."

Her breath left her lungs in a long rush. "To play the whore? To be a slut? You didn't? You just send me to your friends, men who have been at our dinner table, to distract them so Marco can slip into their home and *murder* them.

You raised me to assist a murderer. All those rumors, Nonno, all those rumors about you are true, aren't they?"

There was a long silence. Her grandfather exchanged a long look with Paolo.

"Siena." He whispered her name, for the first time looking his age.

Her stomach lurched. She'd been holding out hope that there was some other explanation, but she read the truth there. She saw it in his eyes. In the way he looked at her. In the exchange with Paolo.

"He missed, Nonno. Marco is dead, and Elijah knows you tried to have him killed. In fact, he was waiting for it. He knows about the others." She kept her gaze on her grandfather, but she was fully aware of Paolo watching her closely. She forced her lungs to keep breathing, although every breath she took hurt.

The others. Their friends. She still held out hope, even though she knew better. She didn't want to be a part of killing their friends. Friends who had laughed with her, believed she was simply visiting. They were glad. Grateful. She actually felt dirt coating her skin, grinding into her pores, making her ugly and filthy. Her own grandfather had used her to kill his friends.

"I have enemies, Siena," her grandfather said softly. He pushed himself out of his chair and walked over to her, leaning down to tip her face up to his.

She tried to jerk away, not wanting to feel his touch. Not wanting to be any part of him. Of his world. She didn't want to hear what he had to say. He caught her chin firmly, murmuring soothingly in Italian to her. His thumb touched one of the cuts on her face and he turned to look at Paolo. This time, the censure was there. Paolo glanced at the floor, managing to look ashamed.

"I didn't know what I was doing, Tonio," Paolo said. "For a moment, I lost control."

Paolo hadn't apologized. He hadn't lost control, not in

the way he meant. She wouldn't forget what he'd said to her. His threat. She could be an adored wife or his slut, and he would treat her according to her choice.

"Rafe Cordeau has disappeared, is presumed dead, and that has left a vacuum in the business world—a world you don't yet understand, Siena." With a sigh, her grandfather smoothed back her hair and returned to his seat. "Our world is made up of great danger. You know that. My son and your mother. Lost to me. To us. You nearly taken *twice*. I had to move to protect us. Elijah Lospostos is a man who would take what is not his."

A low growl rumbled in Paolo's chest. Her gaze jumped to him. She was fearful, in spite of the fact that she still wanted to rip his face off. In spite of her defiance and the famous Arnotto temper he had aroused in her. She didn't want him to hit her again. Or kick her. She already hurt enough, and truthfully, she was afraid of him and what he might do to her.

"You used me. Not only to target Elijah, but four other of our friends, men I knew from the time I was a small child. You're right, Nonno, I don't understand this world, nor do I want to." She lifted her head and stared him straight in the eye. "This man"—her hand swept toward Paolo—"this man punched me with his fists. He kicked me in the ribs with his shoes. He hurt me, and you do not punish him, you do not even reprimand him, and in failing to do that, you condone what he did. You speak of a marriage between us . . ." There was total contempt in her voice. "You show me I don't have your protection or his."

"You do not understand. After your marriage . . ."

She glanced at Paolo, her arm once more sweeping out, her hand shaking. "This is the man you want me to marry? Seriously? A man who would do this to me? You approve of him and his behavior?"

Her grandfather's gaze softened and he shook his head. "Paolo is headstrong. Passionate. He didn't want you to go to the house of Lospostos, but I insisted. He knew better. He knew you were close . . ."

"Close? Close to what? What I'm close to doing, Nonno, is leaving and never coming back."

Paolo moved then, shifting his weight to the balls of his feet as if he would stop her. Her grandfather held up his hand, and Paolo froze in place.

"This is not your fault, Siena," Antonio said softly, his voice weary. He pushed his hand through his hair. "Forgive an old fool for his egotistical leanings. I wanted to send a message to my enemies and I used you to do it. This isn't Paolo's fault either. He warned me but I didn't listen to him."

Her legs weren't going to hold her up anymore. Blood trickled down her face and onto her T-shirt. Her ribs hurt with every breath she drew. In her life, no one had ever raised a hand to her and to have a man she knew, one she thought cared about her, beat her so severely was terrifying.

Siena wrapped her arms around her middle to try to ease the burning pain, breathing shallowly in an effort to control it. She was swaying, trying to hold herself upright.

Paolo took her arm and she winced, trying to pull away from him. She hadn't heard him move, but she knew, she didn't want him touching her. She jerked again, a slow hiss escaping. "Get away from me."

"Let me help you, *cara*," he insisted softly, his fingers tightening, although his hand was gentle as he tugged her to the chair beside her grandfather. "Listen to him, Siena, but if you don't sit, you will fall down."

"Please don't touch me. Not ever again," she whispered. "I mean it, Paolo. You raise your hand to me again, and you'd better kill me." She didn't look at him. She didn't care if he believed her or not, but he wasn't ever going to touch her again and live through it unless he killed her.

3

"YOU must forgive Paolo, Siena. We are not what we seem," Antonio informed her. "We are much more. We are shifters. Leopards. The leopard lives inside of him, and we have those passionate traits. Good and bad. Paolo knew you had been with Lospostos because he smelled him on you, and the scent was offensive to his leopard. His leopard reacted, driving him with his hot temper."

Siena closed her eyes and shook her head. Her grand-father's voice was matter-of-fact, as if he were telling her a truth and not something totally crazy. Now she was sup-posed to believe in fairy tales. Shifters. Leopard people like in a Tarzan novel. Did he think she was a silly schoolgirl, ready to believe anything he chose to tell her to justify Paolo's reasons for beating her? He had justified his own actions of murdering his friends, so she supposed he would believe anything and expect her to as well.

"The next thing you're going to tell me is that you had

to kill those men, using me as a distraction because some leopard made you do it."

"You do not believe me."

"I lived in this house for years, Nonno. At no time did I ever see a leopard."

"You lived in boarding school. You came home on holidays. We have control of our leopards and we made certain they stayed locked up tight."

"Control?" She spat the word at him. "Is that what Paolo had tonight? Control? Because if that is what he had, I'd hate to see him lose control."

Her grandfather sighed. "That was unfortunate, Siena. The circumstances . . ." He broke off. "You need to understand. A male has his leopard almost from birth, but a female, that is much more complicated. She does not come out until she wants to do so. She is capricious. Her male must wait for her. Sometimes that waiting is long. Your leopard is close, Siena, and she wants out. When that happens, the passion is hot and the hunger doesn't let up. It burns through you and there is no denying it."

That was the first thing he said that made her pause. She had never looked at a man and wanted him with every breath in her body. Her body had never burned relentlessly, insistently. Not like this. Not like now. Not the way it had for Elijah.

"Show me."

"When we shift," Paolo warned, "we do so without clothes." Already, his hand was at the buttons of his shirt, clearly eager to show her.

She didn't look at him. She couldn't. If he thought having some leopard inside of him would make her forgive him, he was insane. Her grandfather was insane. She had no intentions of forgiving either of them. She was leaving the moment she could, but she realized by the way Paolo was acting, so proprietary, that he wouldn't let her go so easily. Even if she convinced her grandfather—and she knew he loved her in spite of what and who he was.

She licked her lips and tasted blood. She closed her eyes, and when she opened them, a huge golden leopard crouched in front of her, its malevolent, greedy eyes staring straight at her. Wholly focused. She should have screamed. She should have fainted. She should have done anything but what she did. Later, she recognized that she was in shock, that one too many things had happened and her brain couldn't assimilate them. She leaned toward the leopard, one arm still wrapped around her ribs. "You should have killed me, Paolo. I will never forgive you, leopard or no leopard."

The animal snarled, showing large teeth. A blast of hot air hit her face, and she realized what she was doing. She sat back, her heart accelerating. Maybe if she were really lucky, the large cat would kill her right there.

"Paolo," her grandfather said sharply. "Enough. You showed her. She knows we are telling the truth."

The leopard stared at her for a long time before suddenly leaning toward her, the tongue coming out. He licked up the side of her face, tasting her blood. The tongue felt rough. Hot. Obscene. She shuddered. Her heart pounded so hard she had to press her fist over her chest in an effort to try to still it.

Something like satisfaction gleamed in the leopard's eyes before he turned and moved off, back to the pile of clothes Paolo had placed on the chair to her left. Just out of her vision. She didn't turn her head to watch him. She knew now what she was up against. Paolo had made it as plain as he could make it. He intended to have her, and he would treat her the way he saw fit in spite of her grandfather. What he didn't seem to understand was Siena would rather be dead than give herself to him.

"You see now," Antonio said. "We are leopards. Passion runs deep. Tempers as well. We love well and often with our mate, but the fighting, that is something we cannot always help. Your leopard is close, Siena. She will come to you soon and you will need a man. Paolo wants to be that man, and I want that for you."

When she simply stared at him, her grandfather shook his head. "It will be Paolo or Alonzo. I need someone strong, Siena. You will need protection. Our business must survive my passing, and without a strong hand at the helm, it will be consumed by our enemies."

She stood up on unsteady legs, avoiding Paolo's hot gaze. She could feel it. The demand. The fury building in him that she continued to deny him what he wanted, and in front of her grandfather. Just movement alone took her breath and sent waves of pain crashing through her, hardening her resolve.

"Nonno, you have two choices here. You can hand over everything you own to Paolo or Alonzo and disinherit me. I'm fine with that. I have my money from my parents and Nonna."

"You are my beloved granddaughter, my only flesh and blood," Antonio protested. "I leave everything to family. To my blood. You will marry and have children. That is what you will do, Siena. Our bloodline is strong."

"Then choose another for me to marry, Nonno. Or let me choose. I will never, under any circumstances, accept Paolo or Alonzo." She looked at Paolo for the first time, her eyes meeting his. She saw the fury there and didn't care. She shivered, knowing she was riling him all over again. She also knew without a shadow of a doubt that at some time he would do his best to retaliate—hurt her again for this night.

"*Never*," she hissed. "You knew," she added, looking at Paolo with contempt. "You knew what was driving me and still you beat me. And you called me a whore and a slut. As did you, Nonno. You knew there would be no controlling what happened this night and still you said those awful things."

"My leopard reacted—" Paolo started.

She shook her head. "Don't. If you can't control it better than that, I would be terrified for our children. You were thinking of yourself. Only you. It didn't occur to you I would be scared and humiliated and needing reassurance and someone to hold and comfort me. You knew what was happening to me and I didn't. Still, you felt the need to use me for a punching bag."

"You don't know what you're saying, Siena," her grandfather said softly. "Sleep on it. Think about it before you make a decision."

She shook her head. "*You* need to think about it, Nonno. You had better reconsider if you truly believe that this man would be good to me. Protect me. Put me first. He's going to have affairs, beat me and force me to do whatever he wishes. Is that what you want for me? A man who wants my money and estates, not one who loves and cherishes me?"

"That is not true," Paolo hissed. "Tonio, you know it has always been Siena."

She shook her head. "I will never accept you, a coward who beats on women. *Never*, Paolo. *Never.*"

She looked into his eyes and what she saw made her heart nearly stop beating. Rage was gathered there. A kind of killing wrath she'd never seen before. She turned and stalked out of the room as best she could when her ribs hurt with every step she took. As best she could when every single cell in her body urged her to run for her life. She walked, keeping her shoulders as straight as possible. She didn't look back. Not at her grandfather and not at Paolo.

Once in her room, she closed and locked the door and then put the back of a chair beneath the doorknob. She collapsed on her bed, running her hand lovingly over the ruined quilt, wishing her grandmother were there to comfort her. To talk to. She had no one at all. Leopard? She had a leopard inside of her, and when she came out, she would desperately need a man? Who could she possibly tell anyway? Who would believe her? Because she was getting so hot again, her temperature soaring and her joints hurting, she got up and moved the dresser in front of the door before she sat on the edge of the bed and tried to determine what to do.

She had blood on her hands. If she went to the police, they'd probably arrest her. In any case, her grandfather entertained the district attorney, a councilman and even the senator. She knew he was very connected to the governor. She had no idea if any of those officials were dirty, but she couldn't take a chance. Still, she had money and that would allow her escape. She could leave. Go to Europe. Disappear.

She wasn't naïve. She knew her grandfather would send an army after her. He'd always kept a close watch on her. She'd believed it was to keep her safe. Now, she wasn't so certain.

Siena shivered in spite of the fact that her temperature seemed to be soaring. Beneath her skin, that itch came back in waves. She glanced down at her arm and saw the skin was actually raised as if something moved, pushing hard from the inside out. She bit back a scream and flung herself backward.

Her joints popped. Her jaw hurt. Her fingers curved downward as if she were convulsing. Her ribs, so sore from Paolo's fists and shoes, flashed with pain so that she found herself on the floor. Tears streaked down her face because it hurt so much. She was terrified. Absolutely terrified. A part of her had denied what was happening to her even after she saw the proof of Paolo's leopard. Now, there was no denying anything.

Resolutely, in complete silence, Siena removed her clothes. She wished she'd asked more questions, but she'd been in shock ever since she'd been with Elijah. She closed her eyes, feeling the burn along her ribs again, something pushing, expanding. The pain made her want to black out. She was certain her ribs had gone from bruised to cracked. Her breath came in spasms. Hard. Raw. Desperate.

She slid off the bed to the floor on her hands and knees. *Just come. Take me over. I don't do so well as a woman. Maybe you'll do better than me.*

She wanted to disappear, and becoming a leopard was as good a way as any. She just had to be very quiet so those downstairs wouldn't hear. Every now and then she heard raised voices, men shouting to each other in Italian, and she knew Paolo and her grandfather were having an argument.

They didn't do so often, but when they did, it usually got very heated.

Her body contorted. Her teeth ached. Her jaw was painful. Most of all, the pain along her ribs had become agony. She dropped her head down, breathing through it, welcoming the leopard. Wanting to become anything but what she was—a woman so covered in vile filth—a party to the murder of four men and almost a fifth. Her grandfather—the man who was supposed to love and protect her—had done that.

She had thrown herself at Elijah. She dreamt of him nearly every night, and had since she was fifteen years old. Sometimes the dreams felt so real, she couldn't imagine that they weren't already together. Often, the dreams were just silly, the two of them laughing together and walking along a road holding hands. Other times, they were highly erotic, two lovers unable to keep their hands off of each other.

She groaned but the sound came out more of a low growl. The itch increased until she wanted to scream. She tried to bite down on her lip, but her mouth felt strange and then she found herself inside a cocoon, surrounded by another, and she knew her instantly. Her leopard prowled the room, every step painful as her ribs protested the action. She lifted her head and scented the male who had come there. The one who had done the damage to both woman and leopard. Her lip lifted in a silent snarl.

Deep inside the animal, Siena found a kind of solace. She wasn't gone, she was right there and fully aware of her leopard padding softly through the bedroom to the wall where the male leopard had raked deep rivets in the wood. Every step hurt. It hurt to drag in a decent breath, and Siena felt that right along with her leopard. She soothed the leopard, talked to her, told her everything. Part of her was hysterical, thinking she was having a complete breakdown, but it didn't matter to her.

The leopard moved to the bathroom and looked in the full-length mirror there. Golden, with black rosettes, there

was a tinge of fire to her fur. She was beautiful. She had
Siena's exotic eyes, and that deep green stared back at her.

You're beautiful, she whispered to the animal. Her savior.
She wished she could put her arms around the little female
and hug her tight. If she was crazy, she would be happily so.
Much better to live as this beautiful creature, even if she was
put in a zoo, than to live as a woman who clearly was no good
at being a woman. Being a leopard had to be better than being
a woman who was an accessory to four murders.

The leopard returned from the bathroom to leap onto the
bed. The movement, as fluid and graceful as it was, sent
waves of excruciating pain through the animal—through
Siena. The cat forced its head out the window, looking at
the tree branch that curved invitingly close. One leap and
she would be gone. It was close to midnight and few people
would be out. She could get to her car and escape.

The sound of a gunshot was loud, reverberating through
the house—coming from downstairs. Deep inside the leopard, Siena froze. Opened her mouth in a silent scream. She
knew. She knew the gunshot had come from downstairs,
and her grandfather was down there. Four more shots were
fired. She winced with every one.

The leopard whirled around as Siena, without any real
thought, seized it, forcing herself to the forefront, shifting
back in a sea of pain as her ribs protested. She found herself
on the bed, naked, the itch settling down as the leopard
withdrew. It had wanted to run free, but it had immediately
obeyed when she called it back.

Siena pulled on her clothes as fast as she could with her
ribs screaming at her. They hurt far more now than earlier
and she knew shifting had somehow aggravated whatever
damage Paolo had done. Quickly she moved the dresser and
chair and hurried out of her room to the landing to lean
down over the railing.

Men moved in the house, guns drawn, as if searching.
She recognized Alonzo as he raced up the stairs. His eyes

were moving around, searching every alcove before coming back to rest on her face. For the first time ever that she could remember, there was compassion in his gaze.

Her knees sagged. She gripped the bannister for strength. "Nonno?" She hadn't kissed him when she left the room. She hadn't told him she loved him. She did love him. He was her only relative. The only person in her life that cared about her. He'd done terrible things, but she loved him.

"Siena." Alonzo said her name. And that told her everything.

She started down the stairs. He caught her arm, bringing her to a halt. "He was executed, sweetheart, and it isn't pretty."

She nodded, swallowed hard and inhaled the scent of gunpowder. It was on his clothes. All over him. She didn't react, but moved away from him, down the stairs. She had to see for herself.

Paolo met her at the doorway to the sitting room, reaching for her. She evaded his hand, but she caught the scent of gunpowder again. It was much stronger and she knew. Siena raised her eyes to the man who had murdered her grandfather. Maybe both had. Alonzo and Paolo.

Paolo ignored her attempt to elude his grip. He caught her bicep in a strong grip and tugged her to him. "He's dead, Siena," he told her.

She knew that already without looking. Death smelled. Her leopard recognized the unique scent. She smelled the blood as well. She nodded and looked away from Paolo to the chair where her grandfather always sat. He was slumped back, blood pouring down the back of his head into the fine material of his chair.

"You can't touch him, we've called the police."

"I want to go to him."

"It's a crime scene, Siena," he explained, as if she were a child. "You can't touch him or anything around him."

"What happened?" She already knew what happened. "I heard you arguing."

He didn't deny it. He nodded. "Yes. We argued." His grip on her tightened. "Over you. What I did to you. It got heated. I was angry and I went to the kitchen to cool off. He wanted his nightcap, and Alonzo had come in to take over for me and he went to the bar to get it for Tonio. We heard the shot. Both of us ran, each from a different direction, to the sitting room."

He was lying. She heard the lie in his voice, but it was not only plausible, he was so good at telling the story that she would have believed him had she not been able to smell the lie. Smell the gunpowder. Smell the rage lingering in the room. Already sirens could be heard in the distance.

"I heard more gunshots."

"We saw a man disappearing through the connecting door, over there." He indicated the door behind her grandfather. One had to have intimate knowledge of the house to know the door existed. It looked as if it was part of the wall.

"A man?" she echoed.

"We were fairly certain Elijah Lospostos would retaliate, but this soon?" Paolo shook his head.

She shook her head. Now he wanted to make her believe that she had sex with the man who murdered her grandfather. She couldn't tolerate his touch one more moment. "I need to sit down, Paolo. I think I'm going to pass out."

He immediately led her to a chair just outside the door to the sitting room. Alonzo had already let in the police. Paolo and Alonzo immediately turned over their guns and gave their stories. She knew the bullet that had killed her grandfather wouldn't match either gun. Still, she knew Paolo and possibly Alonzo had killed him.

The first questions the police asked after inquiring if she had seen anything or anyone were about what had happened to her to get the cuts and bruises on her face. She made up a story about working out with Paolo in the gym, boxing earlier, and she'd taken a couple of hard punches. They discovered the state-of-the-art gym complete with boxing ring and martial arts equipment and they seemed to believe her.

Paolo raised his eyebrow at her and nodded as if he was pleased with her story when the detective went to him to confirm what she'd told them.

Hours later, after answering question after question, her ribs burning and her head throbbing, after crying her eyes out until she was certain she had no tears left, her grandfather's body was gone and the detective was still talking to Paolo and Alonzo. She knew it was now or never. Paolo was watching her like a hawk. Her grandfather's murder had been about her. About her declaration that Antonio find her another man to marry because she wouldn't accept Paolo or Alonzo. She knew her grandfather had known she meant what she said and he argued with Paolo about it.

Maybe the two men had conspired to kill her grandfather in order to take over his business. And they needed her to do it. She was directly responsible for her grandfather's death. There was no other way to look at it. She knew Paolo had mentioned that her grandfather was in a feud with Elijah Lospostos. She knew because she had been questioned closely. She denied knowing anything about it, because she didn't know they were in a feud. Only that her grandfather had sent a hit man to kill him, and no one mentioned that.

"I'm exhausted and I need to lie down." She looked up at Paolo as if for permission. As if she were looking to him now that her grandfather was gone.

Instantly satisfaction crept into his eyes. Solicitously he went to her, taking her arm to help her out of her chair. "The house is a crime scene, *cara*. You will have to sleep in the guesthouse. The detective said the gatehouse and the guesthouse can be used. You take the guesthouse. Alonzo or I will be watching over you."

She bit her lip and looked up at the officer who had come over to stand beside her. "I'll need clothes," she said, her eyes filling with tears again. She had to allow Paolo's hands to steady her when her ribs screamed at her and her legs shook. "I don't know what I'm going to do." And she didn't. She felt more lost than ever.

"I'll go up with you," the officer said gently. He looked compassionate.

"Alonzo, keep an eye on her," Paolo said. The officer raised an eyebrow, and Paolo shrugged. "We're not losing her too. They shot him right under our noses."

Alonzo trailed after them. She packed as many clothes as she could without looking suspicious. Most importantly, she packed one of her best suits, and went out to the guesthouse with the policeman and Alonzo. An idea for escape had formed. Two years earlier, on a visit home, she had overheard Paolo and her grandfather talking.

Her grandfather had mentioned a man named Drake Donovan. The reason the conversation and name impacted her so much that she remembered was because Antonio sounded admiring. He had told Paolo that Donovan headed a security company and the man was incorruptible. He said if any of Donovan's team or Donovan himself was involved in any way in security or any of the problems the man took on, everyone else should stand down and walk away, no matter the cost of losing to him. She'd also heard that Donovan was a friend of the local billionaire, Jake Bannaconni. She had no idea where to find Donovan, but Bannaconni had offices in downtown San Antonio.

The moment she was safely in the guesthouse, she took a long hot shower, wincing as she lifted her arms to try to cope with the mass of wild hair falling past her waist. So much of it. She thought about grabbing scissors and whacking it off, but it would only grow thicker and longer and drive her crazy, so she left it down to dry after squeezing all the water out of it with a towel. Very, very carefully, she applied makeup over her bruised, swelling eye and the lacerations at her temple. Thankfully, most of the damage Paolo had done couldn't be seen when she wore clothes.

He would come to check on her, or Alonzo would, so she left her bag packed, slipped into the bed and waited, praying they would come while it was still dark enough for her to slip away. She couldn't drive her own car because the garage she'd parked in was attached to the house and part of the declared crime scene, but there was another garage down by the winery where the cars her grandfather collected were installed. All keys were hung in that garage and she had the password to the lock.

She sat for a long time, her hair falling all around her, afraid to actually go to sleep. She hadn't been lying when she'd said she was exhausted, and she couldn't miss her opportunity. By tomorrow, Paolo would have her grandfather's army of men looking for him to give the commands, and he would assume that role. He would also act as if she belonged to him, and the men would take it for granted that she did.

She tried to take a deep, calming breath, but her ribs protested and she forced herself to just sit, mapping out every move of her escape. They didn't know about her leopard. That would be her first line of escape, but she had to find a way to take clothes with her. When she heard the soft footfalls—and it was more a feeling than an actual sound—she slid between the sheets, swung her head to allow her hair to fall over her face, closed her eyes and feigned sleep.

Paolo stood over her for a long time and then his fingers brushed at her hair with surprising gentleness. "Siena?"

She lifted her lashes instantly, but didn't move her head. "Is something else wrong, Paolo?" Her voice trembled. She knew she gave the appearance of being broken. Fragile. Lost. Because she was. Letting him see that vulnerability aided her this time.

"No. I'm just checking on you. The doctor said he could give you a sedative."

"Please tell him thank you, but I'm so tired I think I'll sleep for a month. I don't want to face this. What will I do without him?" Her voice broke, and it wasn't even feigned.

"I'll look after you, Siena. Go back to sleep."

"Paolo? If he was a leopard, a shifter like you, won't they find out when they do an autopsy?"

He brushed back her hair with his fingers. "Don't worry, *cara*, your grandfather's body will never be autopsied. There will be a fire tonight. Now, go to sleep."

She closed her eyes obediently and was a little surprised when his thumb slid over the bruises on her face and the two cuts, as if he could erase them. She waited until she sensed he was gone and then she waited a half hour more, her heart pounding. If she did this, if she tried to escape and he caught her, he would be furious, worse than when she'd come home with Elijah's scent on her.

She could stay. Stay with a man who beat women. Who murdered her grandfather. Who wanted her for the money and power she could bring to him. Siena threw back the covers and sat up gingerly, one arm around her middle. It wasn't happening. She'd rather die trying to get out than be forced into a situation that would be that intolerable.

She packed her clothes, rolling them into a tight pile and slipping them inside a backpack she'd found in her closet when she was packing. That had given her the idea. She included her driver's license and credit cards and all the cash she had in her wallet. Makeup, hairpins and a brush followed, and there was really no room for anything else.

Stringing the backpack loosely around her neck, she stripped and moved to the window, raising it up quietly. She stood there listening. Scenting the air. She knew Alonzo was out there, on the other side of the house, by the front door. Outside the bedroom window, the manicured lawn stretched out for several feet to the strips of plants and then behind that, the wilder, bushier plants before the roses and grapes of the vineyards extending behind that.

She called up her leopard, uncertain what she was doing. Coaxing. Needing. At once the animal responded, pushing to the forefront. Siena had forgotten the agony as the cat

pushed against her sore ribs. It hurt so bad this time she saw
spots on a field of black and had to blink rapidly to clear her
vision.

Then the leopard stood where the human had been, the
backpack hanging around her neck, heavy, but doable. She
wanted to roar with elation. Instead, she directed her female
out the window and across the lawn. The cat used a slow,
freeze-frame stalk, crouching low, to cross the lawn. In the
distance, she caught sight of Alonzo, but the wind was blowing in the opposite direction and if he was a cat—and she
suspected he must be or he wouldn't have been named by
her grandfather as a possible spouse—then he could catch
the female's scent if the wind shifted.

Siena wanted to scream at the cat to hurry, but she left the
leopard alone, allowing it to make its way safely across open
ground. They made up time in the heavier foliage and then
used the vineyard. The leopard made a wide circle, backtrack-
ing to the large building on the other side of the massive
winery. She sent her leopard a million thanks, lots of warmth
and shifted back to her own body. She found herself on her
hands and knees, her body aching, her joints painful, but she
was free—or almost. The door to the garage was right in front
of her and she punched in the code without even dressing
first. Once inside, she hurried to the bathroom there, dressed
hurriedly in her suit, left her heels off, put her hair up, and
flung the backpack on the front seat of the Mercedes.

She grabbed the car keys, didn't bother with lights, hit
the door opener and backed out, using the road that led to
the back side of the property. Once she was off the estate,
she drove fast, putting the hill country behind her so that
she could hit the city early. She wanted to be there first thing
in the morning when Jake Bannaconni got to his office. If
he did. Her heart tripped double time. He *had* to go into
work. She knew he had a helicopter pad on top of his building and used that to get to and from work. If he wasn't there,
she planned to have his secretary call him. She couldn't

imagine that he wouldn't know her name. Her grandfather's winery was very famous.

She parked her car in the underground garage of Jake's building, hoping that Paolo didn't find the car right away if he was tracking her. She hoped he wouldn't realize she was gone for another few hours. Surely he would wait to let her sleep in after such a terrible trauma. She waited through dawn, to working hours, watching out for anyone coming after her. Finally, she was able to go into the building. Using the ladies' room on the lower floor to touch up her makeup and hopefully cover up most of the bruising, she stared at herself in the mirror. She barely recognized herself.

She'd been innocent when she'd gone to Elijah's house. A woman with her master's and several other degrees and a good background in her chosen field, but still, she'd been innocent. In one night, everything had been ripped from her. Every single thing, including her self-esteem. "Who are you?" she whispered. "Because I don't know anymore."

She lifted her chin and went to the security desk. "I don't have an appointment with Mr. Bannaconni, but please call up to his office and tell him Siena Arnotto is here and it's an emergency. I really, really need to see him. Immediately."

That was the best she could do. The security guard at the desk looked at his consoles, into each screen as though she might be a terrorist bent on Bannaconni's destruction, then at her, the door, and lifted the phone, speaking into it briefly. When he put it down, she honestly couldn't tell if she'd been granted an audience or not. The one thing she did know was that Jake Bannaconni was in his office.

Her leopard suddenly reacted, going on alert. She turned her head and saw two men in dark suits closing in on her. She waited.

"Come with us." One of the men motioned her toward the elevator.

She went with them, taking shallow breaths. Every single step seemed to jar her injured ribs. Her ribs really, really needed attention. She had bruises and knew they were still visible in spite of her makeup, because both men scrutinized her face carefully and she could see the look they exchanged. These men were not happy, and they would never believe the boxing story.

In spite of the fact that she couldn't hide the beating she'd taken, she had dressed carefully for the occasion, her best dove gray suit, the one that made her look all business in spite of her age. Short jacket with a series of ruffles from waist to the middle of her bottom, flowing over her matching skirt with her soft pink shell. She loved that shell because she could match it to her favorite high heels, the ones that made her legs look long when they really weren't. She had put her hair up in a thick intricate braid that wound in a figure eight at the back of her head. She had armor, and right now she really needed it.

Bannaconni's secretary looked up as the security guards walked her through the enormous outer office with its artwork and comfortable furniture. She waved her hand and reached for the phone, presumably to inform her boss she'd arrived. The man who had spoken opened the door for her, stepped back and indicated she go in alone. Siena didn't hesitate. She lifted her chin and walked in. The door closed with a soft snick and she found herself in a large corner office with glass for two walls, overlooking the city.

The suite was so large she couldn't see into every corner, but her leopard went wild, suddenly edgy, as if she might be in danger.

"Miss Arnotto," Jake said, standing as she entered. He indicated a chair. "Please sit down." His eyes jumped to her face and narrowed, his darkened gaze studying her carefully. "Do you need medical attention?"

He was observant, and she knew, in spite of the fact that she tried to hide that she could only breathe shallowly, he noticed.

She shook her head. "I don't want to waste your time, Mr. Bannaconni. Thank you for seeing me on such short notice. I'm grateful."

He walked around his desk and leaned one hip against the granite top, his eyes on her face. Seeing the bruises in spite of her makeup.

She ignored his frown. "I know that you are friends with a man named Drake Donovan, a man who runs a security company. I once heard my grandfather say he was incorruptible and if he or his men were involved in something, that everyone else should walk away. My grandfather was very admiring, and he didn't admire many people. I need to find Donovan." She didn't feel she had conveyed the urgency of the matter fully. He didn't look in the least as if he was going to help her. His expression hadn't changed. She leaned forward, her fingers twisting together until her knuckles turned white. "Immediately."

Bannaconni studied her face. He didn't blink. The edgy restlessness began to hurt, to burn. Her temperature soared. She tried breathing the feeling away, but her ribs prevented that from working very well.

"You'll have to do better than that, Miss Arnotto."

"My grandfather was killed last night. Murdered. I'm not safe . . ." She broke off as her leopard leapt, surging forward. She turned her head toward the shadows.

Elijah Lospostos walked out. He looked as gorgeous as ever. Not at all like she looked. Not as if one single thing had been ripped from his life. He walked like a jungle cat, and he stared at her bruised face with the same unblinking focus as Jake Bannaconni had.

She was up, out of the chair and across the room instantly, shaking hand on the door. "I'm sorry. I made a terrible mistake in coming here."

Jake Bannaconni was associates with Elijah Lospostos. That meant he was part of the underworld her grandfather had alluded to. She could barely breathe. Worse, with her cat raging at her, and the way their eyes had changed, she feared they were also part of the shifter world.

"Siena." Elijah said her name and her stomach lurched.

She couldn't face him. She wouldn't. Not after what she'd done with him. Not after the things he'd said to her. Not after knowing that he was right and she'd been whoring herself out for her grandfather as a distraction for his hit man.

She yanked the door open and hurried out, rushing past the secretary to the elevator. Fortunately the doors to the elevator were open, allowing her to step in and go down fast. She was terrified one of them would issue an order to stop her so she all but ran out of the building, tears swimming in her eyes, blinding her. She had nowhere to go. No one to run to. She had no idea what she was going to do.

She wasn't looking where she was going and she ran straight into a solid body, a man standing right outside the double glass doors. He caught her arms in a viselike grip and dragged her to him. To her horror, she knew instantly who had her, without even looking. She knew his scent. She knew that fury.

Struggling, she tried to escape as he manhandled her into a waiting vehicle. When she tried to throw herself out, he shoved hard on her belly, and then slapped her, knocking her into the vehicle and climbing in after her. The door slammed closed and the car sped away with her in it.

4

ELIJAH took two steps after Siena to follow her. The sight of her bruised face both infuriated and sickened him.

"She's leopard, Elijah," Jake said. "And she's terrified. There is no way that woman was whoring herself out for her grandfather."

"You think I didn't figure that out?" Elijah snapped. "Hell. I was so fucking pissed and my leopard was so insane I couldn't think straight. I was all over her, took her on the damn floor like an animal. When I shot Marco, I was so angry, thinking she was involved. Too angry. I should have known what was happening; I'd figured out, after Don Miguel was murdered, that Arnotto was making a move on territories, but I didn't know how he was getting away with it, making everyone drop their guard. When she showed up with the wine, I knew then."

"But she didn't know," Jake persisted.

"I got that after I threw her out and called her every

disgusting name I could think of. After she was gone, I could see blood on the floor where we'd been and on me. She was a fucking virgin, and the things I said and did . . ." He shook his head and raked his fingers through his disheveled hair. "I don't have a clue what to say to her, how to fix this, but she's mine. There's no going back from this. I know she's mine. If she's really in danger, I have to help her."

"Do you think her grandfather beat her?" Jake asked. "You knew him. Would he do that to his own granddaughter for failing in her mission?"

"No way. Antonio was many things, but he loved that girl."

"I'll get the police report and see what happened last night," Jake offered. The phone buzzed and he picked it up to listen for a moment. At once his face darkened as he slammed down the phone, cursing. "Elijah, front desk just reported a man pulled Siena Arnotto into a car. She fought him and he shoved and slapped her before getting into the car after her."

Elijah swore in his native Spanish. "Did they get the license plate?"

"They said it was one of Arnotto's men. A leopard. That has to be either Paolo Riso or Alonzo Massi, since Marco is dead." Jake was on the move as well. "Where will they take her?"

"My guess, back to the Arnotto estate. It's large. A lot of acreage to cover. He won't take her anywhere near the house. That has to be crawling with cops, possibly even Feds. He's going to take her somewhere private, somewhere no one will hear her."

"I'll get a bird in the air," Jake said, and fished out his cell phone as they raced through the building to the garage where both kept vehicles.

Elijah drove and he drove fast, weaving in and out of traffic, fear pushing at him hard. He wasn't a man who was fearful. He'd faced death on several occasions and he had come out on top, but this wasn't him in the fire. This was Siena.

He had spotted Siena when she was a teen. He'd been drawn to her then. She was beautiful, but it was more than that, something he couldn't put his finger on, but he found himself dreaming about her, which, because of her age, made him very uncomfortable. The few times he saw her over the years, as she'd grown, hadn't changed the way he felt about her. The intrigue. The mystery of her. The fantasy of her.

Elijah had always been a generous lover, wild, rough, but always generous. He hadn't been generous with her. Partly anger at her for showing up with the wine. Partly his leopard going crazy. But he couldn't blame his behavior all on his anger. He'd been lost in passion, consumed by it, and that had never happened to him before.

It had been easy, at first, to say he was furious that her grandfather had sent her to seduce him. More than furious. Disappointed in her. But that wasn't the entire truth, and he just didn't like admitting it to himself. He didn't like that he had lost control with her, because a man like him could never lose control.

Elijah had deliberately kept away from her over the last couple of years, feeling like a pervert for even thinking about her, although the chemistry between them, from the very first time he'd laid eyes on her, had been the strongest he'd ever felt and it just grew stronger each time he did see her—even from a distance.

He had solved the mystery of how Arnotto had lulled his friends into a false sense of security the moment he heard Siena's voice on the intercom. Anyone wouldn't think twice about letting her get close. She'd said she was delivering wine. A birthday present. It wasn't his birthday. It wasn't even close to his birthday, but he'd let her in, intrigued to see how far the charade would go, when the hit man would actually show up and what she'd say.

And then he saw her. Sitting in her car. Eyes hot. Face so beautiful and sensual. Her lush body. He could see the naked hunger in her eyes, and there was no way he could stop himself. He was so caught up in his own hunger and lust he hadn't realized his leopard was raging at him, driving him, savage in its need to claim its mate. He hadn't realized she was close to the Han Vol Dan, the moment when a female leopard was ready to emerge and accept her mate.

Siena Arnotto belonged to him. He felt it when he touched her. Knew it when he kissed her. She was branded in his very bones the moment she ignited for him, a wildfire burning out of control right along with him. He hadn't even noticed she was innocent. He nearly groaned aloud right there in the car thinking about it as he drove like a madman through traffic, heading to the hill country. He'd taken her innocence roughly. Without thought for her. He'd been so far gone that it had barely registered until afterward.

After he had shoved her out the door, furious at her, at himself, after he'd closed the door and locked it, leaning against it, breathing deeply to control the killing fury welling up in him, he became aware of his own body and saw the smears of her blood, evidence of her innocence.

Another surge of anger hit him, this time at himself. He should have known. She was so tight he hadn't been certain he could get inside her when he'd first pushed into her. Had he not been savage and crazy with lust, insane with his own need, like a madman, driving into her, desperate to feel her surround him with her heat and fire, he might have noticed that he was her first.

He realized, far too late, his leopard had been welcoming. Leaping toward the surface, pushing to cement the relationship. Every trait of the leopard was mixed up with his own insane emotions, and he'd treated his own woman in a disgusting, vile way. The things he'd said to her reverberated in his head. The accusations. His temper. Everyone knew his temper was lethal. That made him angry all over again.

She hadn't said anything at all to him. She looked at him with shock in her eyes. Shock at what he said. Shock at what he did. Shock that she recognized Marco. Shock at the realization that her grandfather wasn't the innocent man she thought him.

He swore under his breath. She'd been beaten. Both Alonzo and Paolo were leopard. They would have smelled his scent all over her. They would have known what had happened between them. He stiffened. Her leopard had been so close to emerging. It had to have emerged or would any time now, and if she was with another male, he would claim her. Fight to keep her.

A cold fury settled deep in his bones, poured into every cell of his body. Whoever had beaten her was as good as dead. If they harmed her again, in any way, he would hunt them to the ends of the earth.

"Trey's spotted them. The car is heading into the hills, straight for wine country," Jake reported.

Elijah wound in and out of traffic. Fortunately, one of the advantages to being leopard was amazing eyesight and hand-eye coordination. Still, it took too long, whoever had taken her had too much of a head start. Enough that a leopard could kill or do a tremendous amount of damage in a short time.

Time had never passed so slowly. Fear had never choked him like this. He tasted it in his mouth, became intimately acquainted with it on the long drive. He knew, because the helicopter pilot, Joshua Tregre, reported it, that the car had stopped in heavy brush on the Arnotto estate, and two leopards had tumbled out, rolling, fighting. The car had been driven away, the driver leaving Siena to her fate.

Joshua and Trey reported they lost sight of the two cats in the trees when the smaller, female leopard tried to escape in the denser woods. Jake cursed steadily, but Elijah remained silent, his heart pounding, trying to keep his mind blank. If he thought about what her assailant was doing to her he knew he'd go crazy and never be able to hold back his leopard. More, if her leopard had already come out, the male may have claimed her.

Elijah barely managed to turn off the engine before both men were out and running toward the sounds of screams—human screams, not those of a female leopard. The cries were those of a woman in agony, and the sound chilled him to the bone. He burst through the brush, dodged around trees, leapt over fallen trunks, moving without thought but to get to her. He knew Jake was shedding clothes and that Joshua had found a place to put the helicopter down, which meant Trey was rushing to join them, but Elijah just ran toward those terrible, haunting, *chilling* cries. Without warning the cries stopped abruptly, and his heart stopped right along with the sound. He rounded two more trees and saw them.

A large male leopard tore at Siena's naked body, ripping deep furrows in her back, while his teeth held her in place. She wasn't moving. Her body looked like it might be a doll, a rag doll covered in blood. The cat dropped her on the ground and turned toward Elijah, eyes malevolent, targeting him. Jake slammed into the male from the side, knocking him away from Siena and toward Elijah.

Elijah drew his gun and fired, hitting the leopard in the left shoulder as it spun around. The leopard roared and turned, desperate to escape. Elijah reached Siena and crouched beside her, keeping his body between her and the wounded leopard. Before Jake could hit it again, the male had rushed into the brush. Jake started after it.

"I need the helicopter and your doctor," Elijah shouted, calling Jake back. "Leave him. We'll get him later."

There was blood everywhere. *Everywhere.* Soaking into the ground, coating her body, thick in her hair. He didn't know where to touch her without hurting her. She had four deep rake marks down her back; the claws had cut through muscle and tissue. Two puncture wounds at her shoulder. One terrible rake from the top of her hip all the way to her knee, and it was deep. The leopard had ripped her open.

Elijah was afraid of turning her over, afraid of what he would see. He didn't even realize he was silently praying, his fingers gentle in her hair, pulling it back away from her face. Blood coated his fingers, her hair sticky with it. His heart sank. Fear was metallic. "Baby," he said softly. "I'm right here. He's gone. I'm right here."

He couldn't see her chest moving up and down. She didn't look as if she was breathing, and he had to feel her pulse. He had to know she was alive. He circled her throat with his palm and was still. Listening. Feeling. There it was.

"I've got to pick you up, Siena. It's going to hurt, baby, but I'll be as gentle as I can. We have a helicopter and we'll get you to a hospital." He wasn't certain she could hear him, but he wanted to reassure her. He needed to reassure himself.

Very, very gently he rolled her partially over, careful not to let any of the rake marks touch the rotting vegetation. The breath left his lungs. His stomach dropped. The leopard had ripped her face open from her temple to the top of her cheek and it was a deep gash. She must have rolled immediately into the fetal position because that was the only laceration on her front that he could see.

"We've got to get moving," Jake hissed. He had pulled on his jeans and was tugging his shirt in place. "I've called for Doc to meet us at the pad on the roof. He knows the injuries are severe and that she's one of us. He's the best, Elijah. You know he'll take care of her. Trey can take the car back."

Elijah didn't know if anyone could take care of her. She'd lost blood. A lot of it. He'd never seen anyone so torn up. As gently as possible, he lifted her into his arms, the worst laceration on her hip facing away from him, but that meant her ripped face was against his chest and his arm was a band across the furrows on her back. He could see swelling on her face and on both hands. She'd fought her attacker. She'd fought him hard.

"I want that bastard," Elijah snapped, looking down into her face as he ran with her through the trees toward the clearing where the helicopter had landed. "I want ten minutes with him before he dies."

Jake was silent, keeping pace. They'd left the keys in the car, and he'd barked an order into his radio so Trey had made his way through the trees to get to the vehicle.

"Too much blood," Elijah said.

"Don't think, let's just get her there."

Elijah tried to keep his mind blank. He didn't slow down when he reached the helicopter, he just ducked and ran, leaping at the last moment with Siena in his arms to get inside. Jake was right behind him. Both threw themselves into seats and Joshua took the bird into the air.

Siena moaned softly as the helicopter banked and then moved fast toward the hospital. Jake covered her naked body with a blanket, dragged on headphones and talked into the radio, obviously communicating with the doctor, relaying as much information to him about Siena's injuries as they could see.

Elijah wanted to brush away the bloody strands of hair that hung in chunks over her face, but the thick strands were helping to stop the flow of blood. Instead he ran his finger along her eyebrow. "I'm here, baby. Right here with you. Hang on for me. Can you do that, Siena? Promise me you'll hang on."

Her lashes fluttered. His breath caught in his throat, but she didn't open her eyes. Everything after the landing felt like a terrible blow. The gurney waiting, the team of doctors racing her to the operating room where Doc was waiting for her. He couldn't go with her—he tried—but four huge security guards blocked him from the room.

He would have gone right through them had it not been for Jake and Joshua. The two men moved up on either side of him, and Jake backed him up with one hand. With three words. "You're not helping."

It was the longest wait of his life. Hours. He didn't sit down. He paced. His leopard raked at him savagely, needing to get to his mate, to ensure no harm was coming to her—to ensure she lived. Elijah found he couldn't pace away the rage that rode him so hard, or the need to go find Paolo and

Alonzo and retaliate in a way that would make them suffer for a long time before they died.

He pushed both hands through his hair and stopped moving, going completely still, his breath holding there in his lungs as the doctor came through the doors. Jake and Joshua immediately were there, on either side, caging him in. Not touching him, but close just in case.

"She's alive. She's strong. She fought him off of her. She fought hard. There was no evidence that she was raped, thanks to her determination. Because you told me you had sex with her last night, I gave her the more advanced pregnancy test, but it hasn't been twenty-four hours. Her body is flooded with hormones, so we treated her as if she were pregnant. I'll give her another test tomorrow, because if she's pregnant that will determine the pain medications we can give her."

Elijah shook his head and took a deep breath to let it out. Of course she could be pregnant. With her leopard rising, both the cat and the human were fertile at the same time. He'd been so out of control he hadn't thought about anything but being inside of her.

"She has four cracked ribs and another one fractured," Doc continued. "The laceration on her hip and leg is the worst. It took us hours to close that one. Michelle, a friend of mine, is an amazing plastic surgeon. She spent a long time on Siena's face as well all other surface closings. The four rake marks on her back are deep, and she's going to experience pain for a long while. She was lucky. He wanted to hurt her. He wanted to punish her, but he didn't want to kill her."

"Her leopard didn't accept his," Elijah guessed.

"I would say that's what happened," Doc agreed. "The puncture wounds indicate he tried to cement a relationship. The fact that the male leopard raked her like that, it wasn't a marking, it was a punishment, a leopard out of control when he's denied what he wants." Doc's dark eyes pierced Elijah directly. "Her leopard was already bonded to yours, yet there was no mark on her from you."

That wasn't exactly true and Elijah knew it. He had marked her with his teeth, with his hands. His marks were all over her and probably deep inside as well.

"What are you not telling us?" Elijah prompted.

"Infection is bound to set in," Doc said. "We have to anticipate that. We flooded the wounds with antibiotics, but this is a cat and those lacerations are deep. *Very* deep. We're not out of the woods yet."

"You're not happy," Jake observed.

Doc sighed. "She lost a lot of blood. We gave her transfusions and we'll blast her with a cocktail of intravenous antibiotics, but you need to be prepared." He stood for a moment, head down, and then he looked up, his eyes meeting Elijah's.

For the first time Elijah could see the leopard in him. That fierce nature.

"Whoever did this to her needs to be . . . eradicated. Gone. For all time. It's not right. She's a young girl. I've never been so angry in my life."

"I'll find him," Elijah said, and made it a vow.

SIENA floated in a sea of pain for days, moving in and out of awareness. Once she opened her eyes and Elijah was there, his hands stroking her hair, whispering softly to her, assuring her he was there. That she was safe. At times she thought she was dreaming, but that time she knew he was really in the room with her. She couldn't bear his touch. Couldn't stand the idea of facing him. She would never be safe again. She would never look the same again. She closed her eyes and he was gone.

Another time she heard muted weeping. It was heartbreaking. She wanted to get up and go to the person to comfort them. They sounded so alone and wept as if their world was gone. It was only when she felt a hand on her forehead, brushing back her hair, and heard Elijah's voice soothing her that she realized *she* was the one crying.

She surfaced a few more times and always he seemed to be there, no matter if it was dark or light. She had to have been dreaming, but it was such a strange thing to dream that she wanted to stop. She didn't even want the man in her dreams, let alone in her hospital room—and she knew she was in a hospital. She remembered what had happened to her—every single detail.

In the car, Paolo had tried to rape her. She fought him hard, but when he hit her in the face, nearly knocking her out, her leopard had pushed forward to save her and she'd allowed it. It had angered Paolo that her leopard had already emerged. His male leopard had immediately attacked the little female. Her female had only come out twice before and had no clue how to fight off a huge male, and he wanted to mate with her. The attack on the small female leopard had been brutal and Siena couldn't stand it; she'd shifted again to protect her cat.

Siena didn't want to think about it. She didn't want to remember the pain knifing through her when the cat mauled her. She didn't want to think about her grandfather's death and how her demands of allowing her to have a different choice for a husband had precipitated his death.

Siena tried to force her body back to wherever it had gone, but she could hear the sound of machines and the noise was persistent. A heartbeat. Drumming. And then there was the pain. She wanted to move, to try to get away from it, but found it impossible. She took a breath and forced her eyes open. She found herself staring at a wall. She was hooked up to all kinds of bags with all sorts of liquids in them, and none seemed to be the painkiller that she needed *desperately*.

Her face felt stiff and throbbed with every beat of her heart. Her ribs hurt. Her back and one side all the way down to her knee felt like agony. She was lying on her right side, only a sheet covered her, and it was her left side that felt as if someone had poured gasoline on it and started a fire.

"She's been moaning," a voice said—a male voice, one

of hard authority—and he sounded pissed. "She's in pain. Give her something."

Her breath left her lungs in a long rush. She knew that voice. She prayed it was a dream only that Elijah Lospostos had been holding her, whispering to her to hang on, but there was no mistaking that voice of absolute authority. *The worst I ever had.* She squeezed her eyes tightly closed.

She couldn't face him. Not ever again. Certainly not like this. She hadn't glanced under the sheet, but she knew what she would see if she did. She looked like Frankenstein's monster, sewn back together in patches. She pushed her fist into her mouth to keep from weeping. She wouldn't do that in front of him.

A woman bustled around by the machine and stuck a needle into the line going into her arm. "You're awake," she said brightly. "This should take care of the pain. I'll let the doctor know you're awake."

Siena didn't respond. She bit down harder on her fist, wanting to scream at Elijah to leave. What was he doing there? Had he been there the entire time? The woman left the room, and she felt his hand on her hair—hair that was braided. She nearly groaned aloud, remembering the feel of hands in her hair, a brush. That low male murmuring as he braided her hair to keep it out of her face and make her more comfortable when she'd been so hot.

"Go away, Elijah," she ordered flatly.

"You know I'm not going to do that, baby," he said softly.

She opened her eyes and there he was. Close. Too close. His hand stroked a caress through her hair and tears burned behind her eyes. She didn't want his pity. "I can't face you right now. Please just go."

"We'll get through this. You're on the road to recovery finally. The fever has subsided, and it looks like the antibiotics have finally kicked in."

She was afraid to move. Whatever drug the nurse had given her was actually beginning to work and she didn't feel like screaming in pain for the first time since she'd become aware. She didn't want that agony to come back. That meant staring into Elijah's eyes, eyes that changed color continually, one moment light mercury and the next as dark as night. Her breath caught in her throat. He needed a haircut, but the need suited him, giving him a disheveled, sexy look that went with his handsome face. He was a beautiful man, with his black tee stretched across his heavily muscled chest and his jeans fitting his narrow hips and tight butt perfectly.

He was breathtaking. She didn't want him to look at her, and she certainly didn't want to meet his eyes. She couldn't. *The worst I've ever had.* His words were burned into her brain.

"Don't, Siena," he said softly, as if he could read her thoughts. "I was full of shit, saying those things to you. I fucked up. I know that. You know that. We have to move past that because we both know I'm not going anywhere."

She stared at the wall just over his head.

"Siena. I told you I fucked up. I'm saying we need to move past it."

Something inside her broke. She wanted to leap at him, anger moving through her humiliation. "Move past it? Exactly what should I move past, Elijah? Move past the things you said to me? Sorry, the things you said can't be unsaid. Move past the fact that you shoved me out a door naked when I was in shock? I don't think there is moving past those things. Please leave before I call security."

"I *am* your security," he snapped. "No one is going to throw me out, baby, least of all you. You're going to have to come to terms with that fact. You know everything I said to you was bullshit, so move on."

"Oh. My. God." She forgot about the pain—probably because it had subsided—and she lifted her head, glaring at him. "You are so arrogant. And idiotic. Seriously idiotic if you think I'm just going to forget what you said to me. I can repeat it word for word if you like."

"I wouldn't like," he said, his eyes nearly glowing at her

as if he had every right to be angry. "And lie down before you hurt yourself."

"You can stop giving me orders and get out of my room."

He put a hand on her shoulder and applied pressure until she had no choice but to subside against the pillow. For a moment satisfaction gleamed in his eyes. She saw the leopard there, and she knew he was one of them. She *knew* it. His temper. His arrogance. The sheer power he exuded just walking into a room.

Siena narrowed her eyes at him. "I can't believe you. You have no right . . ."

He leaned so close her breath caught in her lungs and her angry retort caught in her throat. His mouth skimmed her ear. "I have every right. *Every* right, Siena. You're mine. Your leopard accepted me. You gave yourself to me. You have my child growing inside of you. Believe me, baby, you belong to me. I don't give up what's mine. So move past the bullshit and let's deal with what we've got going on now."

She stared at him, feeling another body blow. A hard one. *You have my child growing inside of you.* Did he just say that? Did she hear him right? She opened her mouth but the only sound that emerged was a soft cry of anguish. She closed her eyes, jammed her fist back in her mouth and bit down hard. It didn't help. Tears started. Once they did, she couldn't stop them.

She cried silently, a storm that couldn't possibly be held back. She wept for the men who had died after she'd distracted them, allowing a hit man to get into place. She wept for her grandfather who she loved more than anyone on earth. She wept for the fact that her beloved grandfather had used her to do something that vile. She wept because she'd given herself to Elijah Lospostos and he'd thrown her out his front door naked.

"Baby, enough," Elijah soothed, his hand back in her hair. "We'll work this all out. No one can get to you. We've got the team in place . . ."

She couldn't stop the tears. There was that awful first time. The only time. The *worst* he'd ever had, and now there were consequences because she had been so out of control and burning up for him that she hadn't thought about what could happen. A child. Elijah's child. If Paolo or Alonzo found out they'd move heaven and earth to get to her. They'd do something terrible.

She lost sight of Elijah and then felt his weight on the bed. He actually stretched out beside her, careful of her back, but his arm went around her waist and his breath was on the nape of her neck.

"Baby. Go ahead and cry, then. Let it go. All of it."

"Go away, Elijah." It came out muffled and teary because of her fist. She also sounded a little desperate.

"You need to cry, then cry, but you're going to do it in my arms."

She didn't fight him. What was the use? Right then she felt too raw and exposed, and truthfully, there was comfort in his closeness. She didn't want to feel that way, not when he was the cause of her total humiliation, but still, he made her feel as if she really were safe, and she hadn't felt that in a long while, not even as a child. Not since the kidnapping attempts.

There had always been rumors about her grandfather, but even the Feds hadn't found anything. His businesses all had appeared legitimate. Sometimes she'd been suspicious because the army of men who worked for him clearly carried guns and did little more, it seemed, than watch both her grandfather and her closely. She had come to believe they were bodyguards, there to protect them, and even if they completely ruined any chance of dating, or having friends, they gave her grandfather peace of mind. Now she knew none of that was the truth.

Nothing she had believed had been the truth. Elijah was a part of that world. In fact, the Feds had investigated his family business *numerous* times. He'd always managed to come out without them finding the evidence they were certain was there, but everyone knew his family's reputation. She had made herself believe he was just like her grandfather, wealthy, an astute businessman who had made enemies on the way. Her grandfather was guilty, so there was no doubt in her mind that Elijah was guilty.

"I'm not pregnant." She announced it firmly through her tears, into her clenched fist and the knuckles she'd bitten. Her hands were sore when she curled her fingers but she needed something to focus on.

"Okay, baby." He pressed a kiss to her nape.

She closed her eyes. If he'd argued, there might have been a possibility he just threw that out there. She didn't know how many days had passed while the fever raged and she'd been in and out, but she knew some of the bruises had really faded and that meant some time had passed. Still, surely they couldn't know for certain, but he wasn't arguing with her. That was just plain scary.

"Elijah." She said his name softly. A protest. "Please." Fresh tears burned her eyes. He had to say he was lying. He just had to.

He held her closer, shifting so that her buttocks were pressed tightly against his front. She could feel him, the very male part of him. She should have felt threatened, but instead, something inside of her settled. It was all too much. She couldn't fight on every front, nor could she process everything that had happened to her. She just couldn't. If he'd just take it back, tell her it wasn't true, that she wasn't pregnant, she could cope—at least for the next few minutes.

"Siena, sweetheart, just stop thinking. Let it go. Drake Donovan is here and our team has you completely surrounded. No one can get to you. Your job is just to heal."

She moistened her lips. She remembered something else he'd done. She'd surfaced a couple of times to the feel of his finger rubbing something soothing on her dry lips. He'd leaned into her and brushed a kiss across her forehead. Gently. She couldn't quite reconcile the two men. Elijah was rough and demanding. Bossy. Arrogant. The man who braided her hair and applied a lip balm was gentle and sweet. She *had* to have been dreaming, but if so, why was he lying on the bed with her holding her so gently, so careful of her injuries? Why was he pressing a soft kiss onto her nape?

The door opened. She stiffened, her heart accelerating. She was turned away from the door out of necessity and it was truly frightening not to know who had entered, but Elijah didn't move.

"Relax, baby. It's just Drake."

The man came around the bed to lean down toward her. He didn't make a sound. He had the hard, powerful look of the leopard she was coming to recognize, but his eyes were kind. Tender even. He smiled at her.

"I'm Drake Donovan."

The moment she saw him, fresh tears started. She hadn't cried so much since the time she'd been kidnapped. She covered her face with her hand. "Thank you for coming." But what was he doing there? Who had called him? "I want . . ." She sniffed. "To hire . . ." She couldn't stop the tears coursing down her cheeks so she gave up trying, accepting that she needed to cry. "You," she managed to get out.

Elijah nuzzled her neck, his hands stroking her. His palm at her waist, his fingers splayed wide, feathering caresses and heat at her back, tracing along the path of each of the rake marks with the pads of his fingers as if that would erase the lacerations forever.

"You have to make him go away and stay away from me."

"Who has to go away?" Drake asked.

"Elijah." There. She'd done it. She'd sent him away, and she wouldn't be touched or soothed or humiliated by him ever again. She wouldn't be pregnant. She wouldn't remember *the worst I ever had* every time she saw him or heard his voice. She wouldn't remember being a part of murder.

Elijah didn't so much as shift position. His hands didn't pause, not even for a moment.

"He's one of them. Like my grandfather." Now, she'd even betrayed him. There would be no going back from there.

Elijah pressed his lips into the nape of her neck. His teeth scraped along her skin, and instead of scaring her, it felt erotic. *That* scared her.

"He has to go," she blurted. She sounded desperate.

"Elijah is a big part of my team, Siena. He is not like your grandfather." Drake's voice was impossibly gentle. "He walks a very fine line, half in our world and half in the underbelly, but I can assure you, he is on your side. If you trusted me enough to come looking for me and to hire me, you have to trust my judgment."

Elijah couldn't stay. She shook her head, her gaze jumping to Drake's face, eyes pleading.

"Baby," Elijah whispered softly against her bare neck, his lips leaving a trail of kisses. "I'm not going anywhere. Not now when you need me to protect you. Not ever. Get that through your head. *I'm* your security. I'm part of Drake's team, and that means all of his men. All the men who work for me. Paolo and Alonzo will never come near you again."

A shudder went through her body at the thought of Paolo getting close to her. She couldn't think about him, so she pushed him out of her mind. She couldn't think about her grandfather or Elijah or anything else. She closed her eyes, pulled the sheet up to her face and hid from the two men. Hid from the world. Hid from herself.

5

SIENA stood shakily by the side of the car, her legs feeling like rubber. Any minute she was going to collapse in a little heap onto the ground. No one listened to her. Not at all. No matter what she said. How much she protested. She was *not* going back into that house. Not ever. She didn't care what any of them said.

Elijah had announced he wasn't leaving her *ever* and he'd said it in his low, firm voice, with his *bossy*, commanding tone, but she hadn't considered even for a minute that he might mean that literally. He barely had left her hospital room during her stay—and that stay had been lengthy, Doc insisting she stay for over two weeks. The doctor and nurses addressed him instead of her when discussing her progress or care. Drake deliberated security details with him. It was her life, but everyone had the very false impression that she belonged to Elijah—even Elijah.

She realized her mistake now. She'd let him take control

in the hospital because she was in too much pain, both men-
tally and physically, to cope or process. It was easier to let
Elijah take her over. She didn't have to think about anything.
Her mind felt numb most of the time and she just seemed
to drift. She thought a lot about her grandfather, and to her
shame, she found herself angry at him. *Really* angry. He'd
deceived her her entire life. He'd kept her shifter heritage
from her. He'd used her. Antonio had been her only family
and he'd betrayed her. He'd promised her to a man like
Paolo, and when Paolo beat her, he had condoned it, calling
her a whore.

Siena stood, staring in horror up at the huge house, tucked
into Elijah's side, swaying and weak, shaking her head. Her
life had been taken out of her hands and now she was surrounded by another army of men, most of whom she didn't
know. She had gone along with everything, staying silent,
withdrawn, but not this time. Not over this. No way was she
setting one foot in that house.

"I'm not staying here," she declared.

"Siena."

Her name. A soft reprimand. So gentle her heart turned
over. She tried to pull away. Elijah seemed to control her
with his voice, but not this time.

"I mean it. I will not go in there." Humiliation stained
her tone. She knew it. She couldn't help reliving that moment
when he'd looked at her with such contempt, said horrible,
brain-searing things to tear down her self-esteem as a
woman and then shoved her out of his home as if she were
a piece of garbage.

A small sound escaped—a whimper of pain—and that
embarrassed her further. Her face flushed red, the color
creeping up her neck. She knew he was reliving the same
moment right along with her and that made it so much worse.
More than she could bear.

Siena tried to pull away from him, but his arm tightened
around her waist and he bent his head toward hers.

"Look at me."

She shook her head and continued to strain against his arm, which had somehow turned into a steel band.

"Siena, look at me. Right. Fucking. Now." He bit out the last three words between his teeth.

She stilled, her heart fluttering. There was a distinct warning in his voice. Almost of its own volition, her gaze jumped to meet his.

"Stop. I mean it. You're weak and about to fall down. If you don't stop, I'll be carrying you into the house."

"I'm not staying here." She forced herself to meet his steely gaze even though panic welled up as his eyes darkened and he scowled at her. She'd wondered when the real Elijah would come out. The mean, jerky Elijah who bossed her around and threw her naked out of his house. This house. The one he wanted her to go back into.

"I'm done arguing with you." He swung her up into his arms, cradling her against his chest, forcing her to grab on to him.

"That wasn't an argument," she protested, her panic becoming full blown.

Elijah ignored her and stalked up the walkway toward the front door. She buried her face against his neck, not wanting to see the foyer, her fingers clutching at his shoulders so hard her nails bit into him.

Holding her still with one arm, he began to slide his key into the lock. He went still. Unmoving. Inhaling. He left the key in the lock and turned toward the two men trailing behind them. Drake Donovan and a man named Joshua Tregre. He lifted his hand, fist closed, and both men halted abruptly.

Siena's heart began to pound. Something was wrong, but she didn't want to ask what. She didn't dare. Whatever it was, Elijah was backing slowly off the porch. Once he was down a couple of steps, he hurried away from the house with her.

"I smell a male leopard." Elijah set Siena on her feet and

pushed her toward Drake. "Joshua and I will search for him or whatever he left behind. Keep her safe."

"No." She caught at his arm, suddenly terrified. Suddenly comprehending. She didn't want to be with him but she didn't want him dead either. Paolo had to have visited Elijah's home while he was in the hospital with her. "Let's just go away from here. Come away, Elijah, right now."

He cupped her face in his hands, the pad of his thumb sliding over her lower lip. "It's going to be all right, baby. This isn't new to me—to any of us."

"I'll stay with you, Elijah," she offered, her hold on his shirt tightening. "I will. If you come away with me now, I'll stay with you." Trying to save him. Desperate to save him, and she didn't know why.

His eyes darkened even more and he bent his head to brush his mouth gently over hers. "You'll stay with me anyway, Siena, but I appreciate the offer more than you'll ever know. Go with Drake. I'll take care of this and be with you in a few minutes. This is what we do, what you wanted to hire Drake for."

She shook her head. "I wanted to hire him as a bodyguard. *Before*. Not now when I know Paolo wants war with you. With anyone who is helping me. With my grandfather dead there is going to be a fight for the businesses. Alonzo may be working with Paolo now, but believe me, he's looking to take over. That means he's looking at me."

"*Mi corazon*, go with Drake." Elijah gently pushed her toward the other man.

Drake immediately took charge as Elijah turned away, shepherding Siena back into the vehicle with its bulletproof glass and heavy armor on the body. Elijah wouldn't have trusted Siena to too many other men. He believed in Drake and knew the man would guard her with his life.

Joshua joined him. He'd done a quick search around the house, looking for scent and tracks. "Someone was here. The front and back doors are rigged to blow the moment you open them. Whoever did this knows what they're doing. They didn't go into the house. The bomb is below the deck itself and wired to the door so that when it swings open, whoever is in the near vicinity scatters to the winds."

Elijah nodded and went to investigate for himself. He'd met both Paolo and Alonzo on several occasions. He knew Paolo had been the male leopard attacking Siena at the Arnotto estate. He said as much to Joshua. "This doesn't smell like either of them."

Joshua had followed him, slipping beneath the deck so they could both examine the device. "He knows what he's doing," Joshua said. "It's going to take some work to remove this safely. Whoever put this here doesn't care if Siena dies as well."

"Not necessarily. I doubt anyone would suspect she would come home with me. I was questioned in her grandfather's murder. It was all over the news," Elijah pointed out. "It was only by coincidence that I had gone to Eli's that night." To talk to him. To get drunk. To tell him how badly he'd fucked up.

Eli Perez's land bordered both his and Jake's properties. Eli was an ex–DEA agent. The cops investigating Antonio Arnotto's murder had to believe him. Eli's wife, Caterina, vouched for him as well. Paolo's plan of implicating him had gone up in smoke thanks to the fact that he'd felt so guilty over his treatment of Siena—and he'd needed help to dispose of Marco's body. Marco had been leopard as well, one of Antonio's oldest friends. The body had to be incinerated so there was no evidence of a leopard.

They'd put a story out about a leopard escaping from one of the upstate hunting properties. Rich men with too much time on their hands wanted to hunt large game. The animals were bred and raised on the large property and then hunted and killed. It was easy enough to claim a leopard had escaped and then attacked Siena. Her wounds certainly bore that out.

"If not Paolo or Alonzo," Joshua said, "then who?"

Elijah inhaled again. He frowned. The scent was definitely male, elusive, but he'd smelled it before. He searched his memory and called up his own leopard. His male was good at identifying other leopards.

He moved positions beneath the deck, looking up at the very neatly made bomb. He'd seen one similar. But where? Partially shifting, just enough to allow his big male access to the smell, Elijah waited patiently. There it was. He shifted back.

"I met him at Rafe Cordeau's home, a few years back when I went there for a dinner. My uncle and Cordeau were cementing a deal. This man was there, but he didn't eat at the table. He prowled around the grounds. I went outside twice. Both times he circled around me, watching closely until I went back inside."

"You weren't introduced?" Joshua asked, as he pulled out a small tool kit.

"No, not formally, but I met him. I wanted him to know I knew he was watching me, so I walked right up to him and introduced myself, forced him to tell me his name. Gaton. Robert Gaton. Cordeau introduced us to four of his top soldiers, all of whom were leopard. They were killed on Eli's ranch," Elijah pointed out. "This was Cordeau's reserve man—the one he held back. His shifters ran his army. Everyone answered to them. Whoever he is, he must be taking over Cordeau's territory and is making some kind of a statement. This attack has nothing to do with Siena."

Elijah felt relief when he hadn't even known he'd been tense. Siena had been through enough and he didn't want her to have anything more to worry about than she already did. She was very fragile. He knew she hadn't dealt with any of it. Not what had happened between them. Not the beating Paolo had given her. Her grandfather's death. Not the leopard attack and, most of all, not their baby growing inside her. She didn't want to acknowledge anything between them, let alone a child. Elijah could give her all the time she needed, but she was taking the time with him right at her side.

Joshua's forehead beaded with sweat. He wiped at it with his forearm to keep the beads from running into his eyes. "He's a hell of a bomb maker. He's got a couple of false tags on this thing. Why would a man who is taking over a territory deliver a bomb himself? That doesn't make sense, Elijah."

Joshua had a point. A good point. Elijah would never deliver a bomb. He'd send someone he trusted to do it. Antonio hadn't sat in wait for Elijah, he'd sent Marco to do it.

"Someone else, then," Elijah said softly. "Someone with a big enough reputation that Cordeau's shifter will give him allegiance and do his bidding. Or, he was Rafe's bomb man and didn't trust it to anyone else."

"We'd better find out or your lady is in trouble. Her grandfather was murdered. Regardless of who did it, some of the other bosses are going to be looking at his territory with hunger in their eyes. Unlike Paolo, they aren't going to worry about how they acquire it, which means Siena won't be safe." Joshua held his breath for a moment, snipped a wire and allowed his arms to drop to his sides. "One down."

They stayed still for a few minutes, knowing they had to crawl under the back deck and do the same thing.

"She doesn't want any part of me," Elijah said.

Joshua frowned. "I thought you said your male recognized her female."

"Absolutely he did. He's crazy to get at her."

"Then what's the problem?" Joshua asked, wiping at his forehead again with his arm. "Is it hot under here, or is it just me?"

"It's hot," Elijah said. "I totally fucked things up, and now she's pregnant and doesn't want any part of me."

"What did you do?"

Elijah almost didn't say another word. Joshua had sounded a little too amused for his liking, but Elijah had to admit he was out of his depth. He had never had a problem getting a woman he wanted. Not ever. The trouble was, once he had them, he didn't want them again. He didn't have a lot of experience with having to work at keeping one around—in fact, he had zero experience.

"I knew Arnotto was making his move to acquire new territories. He's always been one to take advantage when there was a vacancy. My uncle used to tell me to watch him. He said Arnotto had the brains to keep the Feds from looking too close. He surrounded himself with legit businesses, high-society friends and had valid reasons for keeping an army around at all times. His son's car bombing and his grand-daughter's kidnappings. When bodies started falling I knew he was behind it, especially because each death seemed entirely unrelated. He's that intelligent."

Joshua followed him out from under the deck and around toward the back of the house. Elijah turned to face him, folding his arms. "Before I tell you the rest, just know: you laugh and I'm going to knock you out."

Joshua grinned at him. "You can't do that, man. You need me to disarm that bomb and help you make certain there aren't any others."

Elijah shook his head. "We fucked, and then Marco showed up and I shot him. I accused her of being part of a plot to divert attention so the hit man could get in and then I threw her out." It was a watered-down version, but he guessed Joshua would get that.

Joshua looked shocked and then a slow smirk settled over his face. "You did that? You really are a jackass, aren't you?"

"Shut up. I knew I shouldn't tell you. It was bad enough admitting what I did to Drake. He was pissed, and I mean really pissed. For him it was all about controlling my leopard, and clearly I didn't do that. My temper got the best of me."

"Your temper or your dick?" Joshua sneered, and then burst out laughing. Hastily, he moved around Elijah and dove under the deck.

Elijah stood a moment, staring after his friend. Men had never dared tease him until he became part of Drake's crew. He still felt a little stiff around the others. His upbringing had been serious. Once his parents were dead—murdered by his uncle—he spent his youth protecting his younger sister Rachel from his uncle. That had been *very* serious business. He'd also spent a number of years cementing his relationship with the men working for his uncle. Plotting against his uncle with two of his childhood friends in the organization. Finally, taking him down.

He wasn't good at the softer things in life. He'd cared for one person—his sister—and he'd had to protect that relationship by acting as if she didn't matter that much to him so his uncle wouldn't know he had as much leverage. He was a hard man, and he got the job done however it needed doing. He'd done things out of necessity he wasn't proud of. He'd done other things—illegal and dangerous—and never looked back.

He had been an enforcer. He was good with his fists. Fast. His leopard was savage and strong. He'd always wielded power, and he'd learned from his grandfather, father and uncle how to command a room just by walking into it. Silence worked for him. He didn't explain himself. He didn't apologize. He had a tendency to take what he wanted. More than anything he was always, *always* in control. Until Siena.

He followed Joshua under the deck. The device was the same as it had been on the front door. Robert Gaton had covered his bets by rigging either door to blow. He considered what would have happened had he opened the front door with Siena in his arms. They both would have died.

A cold rage snaked through him. He was familiar with that feeling. He had waited years to avenge his parents. He'd played his part and developed his strength right under his uncle's nose. He had patience for revenge. The man who had struck Siena, leaving bruises and fractured ribs, the leopard that had torn her flesh open, and now this man, they would all go down, just as his uncle had.

He didn't believe in the justice system. He'd seen it bought and paid for too many times. He wasn't going to trust anyone with Siena's safety, not completely, not even Drake. He would oversee everything.

Siena didn't have a chance, and he recognized that. Owned it. He was a man with a passionate nature and a savage but cold-as-ice temper, but he'd learned a few things about himself he hadn't known since he'd been with Siena. He could be possessive and jealous, two traits he had never considered would ever be in his nature. Being dominating and controlling was inherent, bred deep, but it was really solidified with his upbringing.

Siena was his. *His.* He was rough and mean and expected those around him to obey him without question. Siena wasn't going to do that. He could tell her nature would rebel if he came at her wrong. Still, she was his.

He had never been moved by a woman's tears. He considered tears a manipulative weapon. Until Siena. Her tears had undone him. He'd ordered her to stop, not because he thought she was trying to control or sway him in some way, but because her weeping was truly heartbreaking. In the end he'd needed to hold her more than she needed to be held.

Siena brought out things in him he didn't know were there, and truthfully, it was a little frightening. She stripped him bare, exposing raw emotion. He kept his emotions under tight control at all times, but with her, he couldn't do it. He'd lost control when he'd taken her innocence and when she'd cried . . .

"Got it," Joshua said. "What are you going to do about this, Elijah?"

Elijah kept his features carefully blank. "I don't know what you're talking about. The bomb? Hand it over to Drake."

"About Robert Gaton," Joshua said patiently, his cool gaze drilling into Elijah's. "And don't give me crap that you're not going to do anything. You're going to hunt him down, just as you're going to hunt Paolo and Alonzo."

Elijah didn't reply. What was there to say? Hell yeah, he was going to hunt them, but not now, not when they'd be expecting it. He was going to wait them out. Paolo didn't have the patience for chess. He would make a move soon to get Siena back. He wasn't the type of man to let his dream go. He wanted the power of the Arnotto family, and he saw Siena as his way to get it.

Alonzo was different. Hard to read. He had a reputation, a bad one. No one ever messed with Alonzo, and if he showed up on your doorstep, chances were good you weren't going to live through his punishment. No one knew much about him or his family. Unlike Paolo, he wasn't from any of the leopard families in the United States or South America. He didn't say where he came from. He'd met Antonio by chance and for some reason, best known to him, had stayed.

Elijah always sized up his enemies, and one thing he was very good at was reading them, knowing them, learning everything about them, but Alonzo was an enigma. He'd have to get Drake to use his sources to find out about the man because he was definitely a wild card.

Elijah had learned in a hard school not to show anyone who mattered to him. He protected those he loved by acting completely emotionless around others. He wasn't going to make the mistake of showing the rest of the world that Siena Arnotto had suddenly become as necessary to him as the air he breathed.

That strange thing was, he didn't know how it had happened. It wasn't something that had come on suddenly. He'd been acutely aware of her for years. So much so that he'd deliberately dated the complete opposite of her, but that hadn't gotten her off his mind—or his radar. He fantasized about her. He dreamt about her. He had been obsessed with her.

He hadn't let anyone in on that secret until he spoke to Jake about her, there in the office when he'd confessed he'd totally fucked up, because he wasn't a man to put a woman in jeopardy. Any woman who became his would be living a shadow life. He'd be asking her to allow everyone to think she lived just as dirty as the world believed he did. She would be in danger and would have to walk a very fine line.

"Elijah?" Joshua pushed.

Elijah shrugged casually, his only answer to Joshua's question, and sauntered back to the car where Siena waited with Drake. She had offered to go away with him right then, to protect him. No one had ever made such an offer, giving herself to him so he would be safe. He liked that. Something deep inside had shifted at her plea.

Drake was out of the car and around to the passenger side before Elijah was there. His eyes asked a question. Elijah answered with a nod.

"Your woman is fragile, Elijah," Drake warned softly. "She's in some pain, and she's been worried but tried not to show it." He opened the door.

"I'll handle her with care." He didn't know if he knew how, but he did acknowledge that he should.

Before Drake could reach inside and get Siena, Elijah did. He drew her into his arms. "You're safe, sweetheart," he promised. "We'll get you inside and settled."

She stiffened, but this time she didn't protest. She settled her face in his neck and held on as he carried her back up the stairs to the verandah. He'd given Joshua his keys and Joshua was already inside, disarming the alarm system.

He carried her through the house, straight back to the master bedroom. It was very spacious. The bed was large, on a platform with two steps leading up to it. The rest of the room was space. He liked space. He liked to see what was coming at him. The bed was positioned in such a way to hide two escape routes. One route was beneath the platform through a disguised trapdoor leading to a tunnel that wound underground beneath the house to exit just to the west.

In the underground chamber just beneath them was a room filled with weapons, with a go bag, passport and money at the ready. He could leave in an instant and start again with no problem. He had vehicles stashed on the property and a route mapped out for his leopard should he need it.

The second escape route had been cleverly incorporated into the design of the wall at the headboard of the bed itself. One simply stepped from the bed, through the hidden door and into the narrow hallway that led throughout the house. There were other openings in various rooms, and small, tucked-in chambers to hide in should there be need. He had stashed weapons and a second go-bag there as well. Elijah was a man who believed in being prepared.

Very gently, he eased Siena down onto the bed. He stayed bent, his fists on the mattress on either side of her hips, caging her in as he leaned close. "I'm having your things brought here. Jake arranged for a police escort to remove your clothing from your room. My people will get whatever else you want out of the house. Make a list, Siena, before you take a nap."

She shook her head, her gaze downcast, refusing to meet his. "I'm not staying here. I mean it, Elijah. I know you don't want to hear me, but I'm not."

"Babe." He brushed back her hair with gentle fingers, inhaling her scent. He loved how she smelled, that faint scent of honeysuckle that clung to her skin and hair. "Look at me."

He waited, allowing the silence to add to the tension in the room. He was patient. He had all the patience in the world, especially with her. Her fingers twisted together in her lap. He felt the knots in his stomach unravel. Even with the bandage on her face, she was gorgeous. His stomach went from knots to mush. His cock stirred. Yeah. She was his, all right. Her thick black lashes lifted, leaving him staring into her brilliant green eyes.

"You are," he stated firmly, uncaring that he sounded bossy and arrogant. He used the tone that brooked no argument—from anyone. "Staying here. You aren't in any condition to fight me on this. We can protect you here. In a hotel or somewhere else, it would be much more difficult."

"Why? I don't understand any of this."

"You burned hot for me the moment I touched you. I burned just as hot for you. You're the only woman in my life I've ever been out of control with." He gave her that because he'd been brutal in taking her self-esteem. She deserved the truth, even though he was opening himself up further than he'd ever done. "You can't give me that, baby, and then think you're going to walk away from me."

She blinked. Looked vulnerable. "You threw me out."

He leaned down and brushed a kiss across her forehead and then straightened. "I fucked up, Siena. You're going to find I do that a lot. I'm leopard. I've got all those traits that make me leopard . . ."

She shrank away from him, fear stark in her eyes.

"Don't. Don't you ever be afraid of me. Don't look at me like that. I'm not like Paolo. I would never physically hurt you. I'd hurt myself before I'd ever harm you. I'm willing to die for you, Siena. More importantly, I'm willing to kill for you."

"I don't want you to do that," she whispered.

"Paolo shouldn't have laid his fucking hand on you." He slid the pad of his thumb across the bruise fading at her temple and then down over her eye. "No one does that to you. No one."

Elijah turned abruptly and stalked to the door. He couldn't take the look in her eyes. She was afraid of him, and he couldn't really blame her. He had to have scared her to death when he'd turned on her and put a gun to her head. What a damn fool. It was going to take time to repair that damage.

"Make a list," he reiterated. "Be thorough. Pen and paper are on the nightstand. I'll be back in a few minutes. I want to make certain our team is fully in place."

Siena watched him leave the room, her heart pounding. She glanced at the phone on the nightstand. She could call a taxi, but if she did, how would it get through the gates? Elijah would never let a taxi through. So all right. She was going to have to stay for a few days, at least until she felt stronger and her leg and hip didn't hurt so much.

She tried to figure out Elijah's motives. If he was really a good man as Drake had tried to convince her in the car, then none of this made sense. She knew better than to think he was attracted to her, no matter what he said. Her world had been turned upside down. She knew Paolo had tried to come to the hospital on several occasions, ostensibly to talk to her about her grandfather's memorial service. She hadn't been able to go. She had a raging fever, the infection spreading through her body like a wildfire. She knew her grandfather's body had disappeared and why.

Leopard. She moistened her dry lips and pushed off the bed. She was leopard. A shifter. Instead of being upset by the news, she was grateful. Her leopard was company. Part of her, yes, but still company, and she'd felt very, very alone most of the time.

She found an enormous closet through double doors. The closet was so large it appeared to be a room all in itself. Just to the left of that was the master bathroom. An apartment could fit into the bathroom. It was a room one would indulge themselves in. An open shower with beautifully appointed gold hardware and a long marble sink with double faucets, a makeup mirror and a beautiful, deep bathtub-Jacuzzi took up one side of the room. On the other was a deep, inviting pool. The cover appeared to be thick glass. Steam fogged the glass on the inside so she was certain she was looking at very large hot tub.

She couldn't imagine Elijah living here. He was just too—*rough*. She swallowed hard and forced herself to walk over to the bank of full-length mirrors behind the pool of steaming hot water. Her hands shook as she stopped and slowly raised her eyes to her image. In the hospital, she had felt the bandage, but no one had given her a mirror and she hadn't asked for one. She didn't want to see herself with anyone around.

The side of her face, from her temple to the high point of her cheek, was covered in gauze. Very slowly she worked the tape loose in order to see the actual laceration. Her breath caught in her throat as she observed the jagged, puckered scar. Pain exploded through her and her body shuddered, remembering the pain of the claw tearing through her flesh. Her face, once pretty, had been patched together with tiny neat stitches. The actual stitches were gone, but she could see where they had been.

A small sound escaped but she choked it back and slowly undid the buttons on her dress. It was long, almost to the floor, and she let the dress slide off her shoulders to pool around her ankles. The material was soft and flowing to prevent hurting her skin when it touched her leg and back. She turned sideways to look at the laceration running from above her hip all the way to her knee.

Paolo's leopard had held her down with his teeth—she touched the back of her shoulder without taking her eyes from the horrendous, *ugly* line of raised, red, *stitched* skin that looked as if someone had created her by throwing pieces of flesh together and then using a needle to sew them together. The stitches weren't gone from *that* laceration; it had been too deep and they'd had to stitch up the inside as well as outside.

She couldn't tear her gaze from the horrible sight. Bile rose in her throat. Everything she'd ever had was gone. Her grandfather . . . She blinked rapidly to keep tears from falling again. It seemed the only thing she knew how to do these days was cry. She had nothing left, and now she didn't recognize her own body. How could everything in her life be ripped away in twenty-four hours?

She swallowed down the lump in her throat threatening to choke her and turned so she could look at her back. Her heart thudded loudly as she saw the four long furrows Paolo's leopard had ripped down her back. The pain had been excruciating. Even now, after all the time that had passed, her body throbbed with pain.

The marks ran from the top of her shoulders all the way to her spine. Those stitches had also been removed, but she could see where they'd been. The marks had been deliberate. Paolo had shifted his head halfway down, placed his mouth against her ear and taunted her.

"No man will ever want you with my mark on you. You belong to me and, by God, you will marry me. You and all of this is mine. I earned it. A little slut like you is not going to take it away from me."

No man will ever want you with my mark on you. You're the worst I've ever had.

She stared at herself in the mirror for a long time, mesmerized by the sight of her patchwork body. The shine of tears in her eyes. The absolute hopelessness in her mind. She thought she was lost before, but now, she didn't even know who she was.

If she could shift there might be a chance she could escape—and she had to. She couldn't stay here, not with Elijah. That was the worst thing she could possibly think of. Elijah had seen this. He had been there, when pain engulfed her completely, when every breath she took was so difficult she tried desperately not to breathe. He was there.

He'd been so gentle, his voice soothing her, his arms trying not to hurt her more, to jar her pain-wracked body. She remembered that. She remembered the blood everywhere—her blood. Elijah had been covered in it. His face had been grim, set in stone, the lines carved deep and his eyes alive with ice-cold fury. She hadn't moved or spoken, afraid if she did she would shatter. Still, he had come to save her. Paolo had run, and she was left . . . broken. Torn apart. Ripped to pieces. Elijah had seen her like that. He'd seen—*this*.

She felt her cat rise, push close to the surface in an attempt to comfort her. She stroked a hand over her tummy. The doctor had come in to talk to her before she left, giving her a pep talk on how she was so lucky to be alive. But no one had mentioned a baby again. A part of her shied away from the thought. Thinking it might make it real, but on the other hand, if she had a baby and she could get away from everyone, she could take it far away from this mess. She wouldn't be alone.

She'd have a part of Elijah. The dream part. The man she had believed he was. The one who had fallen in love with her and wanted to be with her forever. Not this one. Not the mean, jerky, arrogant, *cruel* man who said those terrible things to her. Things that woke her in the middle of the night. She would have thought her nightmares would mostly be of Paolo attacking her, or the more familiar ones of her kidnapping, but no, they were of Elijah, throwing her naked out of his house, slamming and locking his door, leaving her alone and vulnerable with the terrible things he'd said forever branded into her mind.

Elijah's words in her brain. Paolo's marks on her body. That was who she was now. Except . . . She pressed her hand tighter over her stomach. Maybe she was more. Maybe there was something inside her left to protect. Something worthwhile. Her eyes burned as she stared at her image in the mirror.

She was so ugly now. What would a child think of her? What could she even tell her child? She would be bringing an innocent baby into a world of ugliness. Of vile deceit and murder. Their mother was a product of that and she was disgusting. She'd helped murder four men and then her actions had caused the death of her grandfather. She'd been so selfish she hadn't considered what Paolo would do if she stripped him of all chances to inherit his kingdom.

"Siena." The name was spoken softly. A reprimand.

Startled, her gaze flew up to see Elijah standing right behind her. He looked handsome. No, more than handsome, gorgeous, in a rough masculine way, of course. Sheer beauty. His skin was a deep olive, his eyes alive with passion and focus. She didn't understand how he could even look at her patchwork of a body.

She froze, unable to move. Unable to cover up. He had come in so silently and she'd been so lost in her thoughts that she hadn't heard him. Deep inside where no one could hear her, she screamed and screamed.

6

"SIENA, the lacerations will heal over time," Elijah said gently, his hand settling on the nape of her neck.

Gentle. So gentle. So at odds with his personality. When he touched her like that, she could almost believe he cared. As it was, she stood frozen, shocked that he could see her nearly naked body. Her breasts were bare, she hadn't worn a bra because she couldn't stand anything tight against her back. She had worn panties, although the material hurt against her hip. She was grateful she had done that much—she'd been tempted to go without.

A slow flush began somewhere in her sex and began to move upward toward her face. Instead of covering her breasts with her hands as she should have, she moved her palm over the bandage on her face. It was difficult enough to face him, but to have him see her like this—so exposed—so vulnerable—was the absolute worst.

Elijah reached around her to capture her wrist. "Don't,

baby. Don't hide from me or anyone else. You're beautiful and you'll always be beautiful, even if these scars didn't fade, which they will. You're shivering. The fireplace is going in the bedroom and I'll get one of my shirts for you to wear."

He didn't move. He stood directly behind her. She could see his head and shoulders above her own in the mirror. "Stop looking at the lacerations, Siena; look at *you*. Your beautiful body. You take my breath away, you're so beautiful."

His eyes on hers in the mirror, he bent his head and brushed a kiss over the puncture marks on her shoulder. Her heart stuttered and her breasts tingled. She moistened her lower lip. She wanted to look away, but she couldn't. His unruly, dark hair brushed her back, a sweep of silken strands that caused a flutter deep in her core. His mouth, feather-light, moved down the first rake mark. Small butterfly kisses, so soft and barely there that she held her breath, afraid of missing the sensation.

His hands moved under her arms on either side of her, slowly sliding down the sides of her breasts, so gently over her rib cage to her narrow waist where his fingers bit in possessively. All the while his mouth continued to distribute soft kisses down each terrible rake mark. Wherever his mouth went, the pain seemed to subside just a little.

He was so tender she felt the burn of tears. How could he touch her like that? How could he stand to put his lips on those rigid puckers of red, mottled flesh complete with stitch marks? She stood frozen, unable to move, mesmerized by the sight of his darker skin against hers. By the way his fingers at her waist made the statement that she belonged to him.

Her heart pounded, hurting her chest. Her breasts heaved, drawing her eye. He murmured softly in Spanish against her painful skin, the touch of his lips drawing out the fire, the language beautiful, even hypnotizing.

Elijah took his time, even when her body trembled and she drew in ragged breaths. He kissed his way down to the small of her back, crouching low, and then, in the mirror, she saw him moving around to her side. His head was level with her panties, the little boy shorts that cupped her rounded cheeks and rode low on her hips.

His fingers curled in the stretchy band. "You shouldn't be wearing these, *mi corazon*. They'll aggravate that wound. The doctor told you he wanted you to expose these stitches to the air. No more covering up like this."

She cleared her throat. "I can't go around naked." She had no choice but to drop her hand to his shoulder to steady herself or she would have fallen face-first right into the mirror.

"Of course you can. No one is going to see you." There was a growl to his voice, as if having someone else see her was a sin. Not him, she realized, he *expected* to see her. He took it for granted that she was going to move in with him and stay with him because his child *might* be growing inside her.

She had refused to listen to the doctor when he came in to tell her he'd run another test on her. She couldn't hear it at the time. Denial was the only way she could get through seconds and minutes and hours. Now her gaze went to the mirror, looking at the uncontrollable, very thick hair, all the waves and whorls falling like silk down the back of Elijah's head. She could imagine a child with that hair. Hair so thick and inviting, she had to dig her fingers into his shoulder to keep from burying her fingers in it.

She closed her eyes when his mouth moved over the curve of her hip, her panties sliding down with the coaxing of his fingers.

"Elijah." She said his name in a warning tone.

"Let me, *carina*. I need this."

She swallowed hard. There was need in his voice. It wasn't his usual demand. Or command. His tone was soft, distressed. A note in there said this was essential, beyond his capability to stop. She didn't know why she gave him that. She just stood there, shaking, tears running down her face, burning along the laceration on her cheek as his mouth took the pain from her hip and leg. As his hands took down her cute little boy shorts to leave her completely exposed.

She told herself it wasn't anything he hadn't already seen. She told herself he was being impersonal, but having his mouth on her mottled flesh was the furthest thing from impersonal she could imagine. His lips felt like a kind of worshiping against her skin.

Siena forced her eyes open so she could see him. He was beautiful. That was all there was to it. So beautiful. She could look at him forever. She could dream about him. Fantasize. But she would never, *ever*, be so stupid as to allow her feelings for him to show again. It didn't matter how beautiful he was. She knew she could never match his sexual expertise. Heat crept up her body again, coloring her skin a deep rose.

She found herself mortified, his assessment of her skills reverberating through her mind. A single sound escaped. How did this happen *again*? Her stripped naked. Him fully clothed. She was an idiot when it came to him.

Instantly he lifted his head and blinked up at her, as if coming out of a deep fog. "Siena. Stop it." His hand circled her thigh. He brushed his fingers along her skin, right next to the long laceration, soothing the tightly pulled edges. "You have to let that go."

"I can't. I don't want to talk about it, but I can't. I need clothes on. And you have to stop." Her breath came in ragged, choppy gasps so her declaration sounded tattered and frayed and very, very weak.

His gaze drifted over her face and then her body. Her nipples, to her absolute horror, peaked under his possessive stare. He looked up at her with raw hunger on his face. She felt the answering hunger deep inside. Her leopard leapt toward the surface, as if she felt it as well.

"Please," she whispered softly. She didn't have the strength to fight him. She needed to shore up her defenses, and she didn't want to feel the things he made her feel.

Siena wrapped her arms around her middle, one hand sliding protectively over her womb. She knew the baby was there, but she still wasn't quite ready to admit it aloud. She didn't want him to say anything, not until she'd had a chance to process everything. Her mind still shied away from that. It was barely allowing her to manage her grandfather's death, let alone her guilt in how it all came about.

A knock on the outer door of the bedroom startled them both. Elijah stood and whipped around in one fluid movement, his body instantly between her and the door. He cursed under his breath. Siena realized he hadn't heard someone approaching. He'd been that caught up in what he was doing to her—feathering light healing kisses up and down the wounds on her body.

"I'll be right there," Elijah snapped, impatience in his voice. He took her arm, his grip gentle but very firm. "Let's get you in bed."

She moistened her lips. She detested being naked in front of him even though he didn't look at her like she was something out of a horror film. "I need clothes."

"Can you tolerate soft fabric against your back?"

She nodded, remaining perfectly still. She wasn't strutting around naked. Doc had told her she could expect that the lacerations would heal fairly quickly because she was leopard. There was a lot less pain. Especially on her face. That wound hadn't been quite as deep as the others. Even her ribs were less painful. The four furrows running down her back hurt, but not like the terrible wound that had almost been to the bone on her leg. Paolo had really hurt her. She'd run from him and he'd brought her down, slamming her facedown in the dirt and digging a claw into her hip.

She closed her eyes, feeling that terrible moment. The excruciating pain ripping through her body. The need to curl into the fetal position and protect her belly was so strong she'd done so, leaving her back and face exposed. She'd been more terrified than she had ever imagined possible, even more than when she'd been kidnapped as a child. A soft sound escaped. She jammed her fist into her mouth to stop the whimper of fear, of memory.

Elijah wrapped his arm around her waist and urged her back toward the bedroom. "You have shadows in your eyes, baby. Don't think about him. He can't get to you here. You're safe." He halted her by the walk-in closet and pulled out a soft, long-sleeved shirt. It was a beautiful slate blue. Very gently he wrapped the shirt around her, sliding her arms into the sleeves and buttoning it up himself. She felt the brush of his knuckles against her skin with every button.

"Elijah." Drake's voice was insistent. "We have a situation. I need you out here now."

Swift impatience crossed Elijah's face and she caught a glimpse of the man she knew best. The one who was in command. Rough. Tough. The man who was whispered about. If he truly worked for Drake—and she couldn't imagine him taking orders from anyone—then it was because he *chose* to follow Drake, not because it was in his nature. He was an alpha all the way, and she didn't have a single doubt that he had done things that crossed the lines of legality.

Still, for all the cold fury gathering in his eyes, his touch on her was very gentle as he pulled back the covers and helped her into bed. The bed was raised and she was short, so it was a stretch for her injured leg. The moment he saw that, he lifted her, sitting her on the mattress and helping her slide her legs beneath the covers.

"Take a nap. Do you need a pain pill?" He caught up the paper she hadn't written a thing on, glanced at it, then at her and tossed it aside.

She did need a pain pill, but Doc had told her not to take one unless she absolutely needed it. The laceration on her leg throbbed and burned, but not so much that she couldn't stand it. She splayed her hand over her stomach, rubbed the small pooch soothingly, not even realizing she was doing it until she saw his gaze drop to the movement. There was satisfaction on his face. Instantly she stopped.

"When you have a chance, Elijah, I really could use a cup of tea. Black tea. With milk. I haven't had a single cup of tea since I've been in the hospital and it's my go-to comfort drink."

"You've got it, *mi corazon*," he said, and leaned down to brush her forehead with his mouth.

He had to stop doing that. Every time he did her heart stuttered and stammered and she lost all control of her breath. She didn't want him touching her, let alone kissing her *anywhere* on her body. The moment he did, her entire body reacted to him. Melting down. Her brain short-circuited, and she couldn't even push him away. What did that say about her?

"Damn it, Elijah."

Elijah's head came up in a way that didn't bode well for Drake. He spun around and stalked across the room. Siena watched him the entire way, the fluid glide that made him seem invincible with his muscles rippling subtly beneath his tight shirt and the jeans cupping his butt so lovingly. She could read the dangerous fury in every line of his body as well as feel it filling the room so that the air seemed to vibrate with it. He yanked open the door.

Drake was there, framed in the doorway. Elijah put a hand on his chest and walked him backward, closing the door behind him.

"This couldn't wait," Drake said, ignoring the hand on his chest. "We've got cops coming up the drive. I informed Jake, and he's countered with a couple of cops he knows for certain are clean. It will take them a few minutes to get here."

"I have nothing to hide," Elijah bit out. "Do you think I would ever have anything in my home that would in any way be illegal?"

"You have Siena Arnotto. Paolo and Alonzo are with the police officers," Drake said. "Trailing behind in a second vehicle. We tried to stop them at the gate, but the officers claimed it was a well checkup and they had to physically see and talk to Siena."

Elijah cursed. "That bastard has balls coming here. He knows she can't point the finger at him. The word was a rogue leopard attacked her, but damn it all, he beat her. I just told her she was safe here. If I knew for certain the cops coming with him were dirty, on his payroll, no one would find their fucking bodies."

"Elijah, you might want to allow me to handle the cops," Drake suggested tactfully. "They can't take Siena against her will. I'll go in to her and tell her she has to let the officers know she asked to be brought here."

"She won't say that. She doesn't want any part of me or this house," Elijah admitted, rubbing the bridge of his nose. "Damn it. I should have been more careful with her. I should have recognized she was innocent." He wasn't going to use the excuse of his leopard turning savage and amorous on him, although that much was the truth. He had control and discipline. He'd learned it in a hard school, and he sure as hell should have had it with the one woman who meant something to him. He should have handled her with care.

"I'll talk to her. The boys have surrounded the house. Paolo and Alonzo will know they're there because they'll be able to smell them. The cops won't. Jake and Eli are on the way. Both have a great deal of pull with the police," Drake assured. "You get the door. Joshua will be right behind you."

"Protecting me or them?"

Drake smirked. "Them, of course. Keep it together, Elijah. Siena's broken. This goes wrong and you may lose her altogether. I can see how fragile she is."

Elijah hated to hear the truth. He'd contributed to breaking her. He nodded and swung on his heel toward the front of the house. Paolo and Alonzo wanted a look inside his home, hoping to get the layout and a feel for how much security he actually had. They also needed to see Siena and judge her state of mind. Elijah and Drake had managed to keep both away from him, but Paolo had to wonder how she was going to react to him.

Elijah had promised Siena that she was safe in his home. Now she was going to have to face the very monster that had ripped her body to shreds. He cursed again under his breath and stalked to the front door, Joshua falling into step at his side. He made them wait. The doorbell peeled melodiously several times before he got his fury under complete control and opened the door.

There was another long silence as he stared at the two officers in suits, rather than uniform, his eyebrow raised.

"I'm Detective Madison," one said, flashing his badge. "This is Detective Harrison. Elijah Lospostos?"

Elijah nodded curtly, ignoring Paolo and Alonzo as they crowded close behind the two detectives. Madison clearly didn't like it and turned his head to scowl at them.

"I'm Lospostos. I own this house." Outright. And the immense acreage surrounding it. The oil wells. And everything else on the land. Including Siena Arnotto, soon to be his wife. "What can I do for you?"

"These gentlemen are friends of Siena Arnotto's grandfather. They both work for him, and they've been very concerned about Miss Arnotto's welfare. They claim they were kept from visiting her in the hospital after she was attacked by a leopard."

Elijah nodded slowly. "She hired Donovan's security agency to protect her. Apparently she had concerns about her safety. Drake's in with her now. I can allow you both in to see her, but not the other two. They'll have to wait. You can ask her if she wants to see them."

Paolo shouldered past the detective to confront Elijah. His eyes were two pinpoints of blazing cat, the leopard obviously close. "I demand to see her."

Elijah deliberately—and slowly with contempt—looked him up and down, from his head to his elegantly clad feet and then shook his head. "Not unless Siena indicates to these detectives—and to Drake and me—that is what *she* wants."

"Her grandfather left me in charge of her," Paolo snapped. "I'm responsible for her. She's engaged to me."

Elijah's eyebrow went up. A slow, amused quirk was there and gone. "That is rather impossible. Siena ran from you, Riso. In fact we have you on the security tape outside Bannaconni's building forcing Siena into a car. We also have X-rays of her ribs." He looked at the two detectives. "Four cracked ribs, one broken. A black eye and bruising all over her face. Fingerprints on her arms. She told Drake you did that to her and that she was afraid of you. She was the one who refused to see you in the hospital."

"What the hell," Alonzo burst out. "*You* did that to her, not Lospostos?"

Both detectives swung around to confront Paolo. "You assaulted this woman?"

"Hell no. He's lying. Let me talk to Siena and she'll tell the truth. She's probably afraid of him. I'm telling you, she's been taken here against her will," Paolo said. He moved a little away from Alonzo, who continued to stare at him with ice-cold eyes.

"You'd better hope that's what she says," Madison snarled. He gestured toward Elijah. "I'd like to see her now. You two can wait here," he added to Paolo and Alonzo.

Alonzo pulled out a pack of cigarettes and immediately complied with the request, stepping off the porch and wandering away, as if he didn't have a care in the world. Elijah wasn't deceived. Siena had been correct when she insisted Alonzo was the far more dangerous of the two men. Paolo was clearly ruled by his emotions and those of his cat. Alonzo was controlled. Thinking all the time. He didn't have to appear to be top dog. He was content to slip into the background. Elijah had no doubt that he was sizing up the house and looking for weaknesses in the security.

Paolo swore savagely and began to pace.

"Evan, keep an eye on these two," he said softly to the watcher close by. Instantly Paolo and Alonzo tried to determine where the threat was. Smirking, Elijah deliberately turned his back on the men, knowing Joshua was there and would come out of the shadows like lightning if Paolo were stupid enough to make a move against him. Madison and his partner, Harrison, didn't seem under Paolo's thumb. Elijah led the two policemen through the house to the bedroom, where he knocked on the door.

Drake opened the door. "She's resting," he said softly, "but I let her know the detectives were here and she agreed to talk to them."

"We'd like to speak to her alone," Madison said.

"I'm sorry," Drake said. "I can't allow that, not without her consent. You came here with a man who attacked her. She's afraid for her life, and I'm handling her security."

Madison's gaze jumped to the bed. Elijah had already crossed the room and had taken her hand. Siena sat up in the bed, pillows supporting her back, but he could see she was sitting stiffly.

"Does it hurt, baby?" he asked softly. "You don't have to sit to talk to them." He glanced at the detectives. "The leopard injured her back as well."

Siena's free hand crept toward her face and the bandage there. He caught her wrist before she could cover the gauze with her palm. Deliberately he brought her wrist to his mouth, his gaze back on hers. She moistened her lips and then shook her head.

"You can do this, *carino*. This is Detective Madison and Detective Harrison. They would prefer to speak to you alone . . ."

She gasped and shook her head, her gaze jumping to his face and then to Drake's. "Whatever you want to ask me, you can ask me in front of them," she said.

Madison nodded. "Are you here of your own free will, Ms. Arnotto?"

"Please call me Siena," she said. Her fingers bunched in

the blanket. Elijah gently rubbed the back of her wrist and hand. "Yes," she said in a low voice.

"Are you engaged to Paolo Riso?"

A small squeak of alarm emerged. She shrank deeper into the pillows and winced, her face going pale. "No. Absolutely not."

"Did Paolo Riso assault you?" Harrison asked.

She turned her face away from the detectives. "I don't want to talk about any of this anymore. My grandfather was murdered and I was attacked by a leopard. I just want to be left alone for a while."

"We can put him in jail if you make a complaint," Madison encouraged.

She shook her head. "Men like Paolo don't stay in jail. I'm not giving any kind of a statement."

"Are you planning on marrying Elijah Lospostos?" Harrison asked.

Elijah's heart jumped in his chest. She had only to deny it and the detectives would be suspicious all over again.

"We haven't finalized plans," she dodged diplomatically, staring down at Elijah's hand.

Drake had coached her and apparently considered every contingency. Elijah leaned into her and brushed a kiss along her temple. "Her grandfather just died. She's mourning that loss and now has to cope with a leopard attack. It isn't the best timing."

Both detectives nodded their heads simultaneously. They stayed another ten minutes, asking Siena questions and coming back several times to the subject of whether or not she was there of her own free will. She insisted she was.

"Would you be willing to speak to either Mr. Riso or Mr. Massi?" Detective Harrison asked.

"I will not, under any circumstances, speak to Paolo," Siena said. "I don't want that man anywhere near me. If Alonzo needs to see for himself that I'm safe, well, of course he can, but I want Drake and Elijah with me."

Madison and Harrison exchanged a look. Harrison left the room, Drake trailing after him. They returned a couple of minutes later with Alonzo Massi. Ignoring everyone else in the room, Alonzo went straight to the bed, his eyes taking in Siena's face and the bandage there.

"Siena, I didn't know."

Elijah knew he meant he didn't realize Paolo had attacked her.

"Where else are you injured?"

"Four cracked ribs. One broken. Lacerations, four of them from her shoulders to the small of her back, fairly deep. The laceration from temple to the top of her cheek and the worst, a claw mark from her hip to her knee. That one was extremely deep," Elijah answered for her. "She got a massive infection from the bacteria in the leopard's claws."

Alonzo's face didn't change expression. Not at all. He looked as cold as ice. "You good here, Siena?" he asked.

She caught her lower lip between her teeth and nodded. "For the time being. I can't go home. It's a crime scene, and I don't want to be anywhere near Paolo. I don't trust him."

"Sweetheart," Elijah cautioned her. Alonzo was definitely not happy with Paolo attacking her.

Her gaze jumped to Elijah's face. She bit her lip again and then twisted her fingers together. Elijah gently laid his hand over both of hers, stilling the nervous habit.

"She's on the road to recovery, Massi," he said. "But it's a slow process. She had an enormous amount of stitches, and that isn't comfortable. She needs to rest as much as possible." He made it a clear warning that all of them should leave—and soon.

Alonzo nodded and then turned his attention back to Siena. "You have my cell number." It wasn't a question. She'd had his cell number since she was a teenager.

"Yes," she said softly, avoiding his eyes. "Thank you for arranging my grandfather's memorial service when I couldn't.

I really appreciate that you did that while I was in the hospital."

"This will be taken care of," Alonzo said. "You need me, I'll come running. Take your time, Siena, and get better. Your grandfather's lawyers are pushing to see you. They want to read the will."

She shrank back. "Not yet, Alonzo. Tell them I'm not ready."

He nodded. "You have any other orders?"

Siena blinked at him. What was he saying? She'd always been a little afraid of him. He was the coldest man she knew. Her grandfather often whispered to him in an aside and he'd be gone for two or three weeks and then come back. Her grandfather would seem very pleased for weeks afterward. After the kidnapping, Alonzo had watched over her more than any other of her grandfather's trusted inner circle.

Still, she was almost certain he had plotted with Paolo to murder Antonio. She tried to remember why she thought that. He'd fired his weapon, but could he have been firing at a shadow Paolo had pointed out? She honestly didn't know, but she didn't trust him. She didn't trust anyone. Not even Drake entirely. She sighed.

"Siena?" Alonzo prompted.

She shook her head. "No. I'm just trying to recover."

Alonzo turned to Elijah. "I'd like to be kept in the loop about Siena's progress. If she needs anything, let me know. Siena has my number." He waited, still, unmoving, his eyes focused on Elijah.

Elijah nodded slowly.

Alonzo switched his attention to Drake. "If you need help with her security, call me. I'll come myself."

A delicate tremor slid through Siena's body. She knew Elijah felt it because he shifted closer, drawing Alonzo's attention so that he missed her reaction. She was more confused than ever. Paolo at least reacted humanly to situations. Alonzo rarely showed emotion. More, it was Alonzo who carried out the discipline of anyone in her grandfather's employ who failed in his duties. Often that meant a physical retribution, and more than once she'd seen Alonzo dispassionately tear someone apart. He hadn't even broken a sweat and looked almost bored while he did so.

"Siena is tired," Elijah announced. "I think you got what you came for," he added to the detectives. "I think you can assure the lawyers and anyone else who is interested that Siena is recovering."

Madison nodded. "Ma'am, I appreciate you taking the time to see us. Are you certain you don't want to swear out a complaint against the man who beat you?"

Siena winced. The detective had slipped the question in so casually. She felt Alonzo's focused, unblinking stare, but she kept her gaze on her hands. More precisely, on Elijah's hands. He had strong fingers. Callused. A workingman's hands. Not at all what she expected from the head of a crime family. She closed her eyes, remembering the feeling of his hands on her skin. His fingers moving in her. His viselike grip when he threw her out. Around her, she heard the others leave the room, but she kept her gaze fixed on Elijah's hands.

He didn't hurt you physically, she reminded herself. Not like Paolo. But the emotional pain was so much worse. Far, far worse. She could almost take Paolo before Elijah because she would never feel about Paolo the way she had about Elijah. He couldn't hurt her that way.

"Stop it," Elijah said, his voice a growling command. "Seriously, Siena. Let it go." His hand settled in her hair, fingers sliding deep into the long, silky strands and fisting there. He pulled her head up, the little bite of pain startling her. His dark gaze blazed into hers.

"Do you really think I can erase the things you said to me so easily?" she hissed, wishing she were strong enough to push him away.

"I told you I didn't mean them. That should be enough."

She frowned at him. "That's arrogance, Elijah. Sheer

arrogance. You said it. You can't take it back." She ducked her head. "The worst part of it is, what you said was true. I didn't know what I was doing. I *was* there to distract you even if I didn't know it. The reason he sent me was so Marco could slip inside undetected. I confronted him and he all but admitted it to me." Bile rose and she pressed the back of her hand against her mouth.

"Baby, no way was it the truth. I'm telling you the truth right now. You're leopard and you can hear it in my voice. I have never once lost control with a woman. Not a single time in my life. You made me lose control. Hell, I was so far gone I didn't even realize you were a virgin. I needed to fuck you fast and hard. Rough. Get inside you any way I could. I was so damned hungry for you, I couldn't think straight. That's sure as hell not because you didn't know what you were doing, babe. It was because you made me crazy for you."

She shook her head, trying to hear what he said, wishing she could believe him. She'd had a lot of time while she was recovering in the hospital to go over every single thing that had happened between them from the time she drove up his drive until he threw her out. She'd been so hot for him—a fever of need—a hunger so great she couldn't think clearly. Once he'd touched her, lifting her out of the car and into his arms, she'd been lost. There was no going back. The fire burned too hot.

Had it been that way for him as well? He'd certainly acted as if it had. He'd seemed as far gone as she had been. He hadn't even taken his clothes off. He hadn't taken her to the bedroom. Still, he'd had a gun taped beneath the table in the foyer. Who did that unless they were expecting a hit man?

"You knew Marco was going to try to kill you." She made it a statement. Her eyes met his. She had to know. See. He nodded, and her heart took a plunge.

"When you buzzed the house from the gate and told me your grandfather had sent me his reserve, I knew then. I hadn't had a birthday recently. I had quietly carried out my own investigation of the four others you took the wine to. Don Miguel's son is a friend, and he asked me to look into it. He suspected Antonio because within days after his father's death, Antonio's men made a move on the territory. Still, I had no idea how he actually had gotten the hit man past security."

"Me," she said sadly. She needed to lie down. She was so tired. She hadn't gotten her cup of tea, but now all she wanted to do was sleep.

"You," he agreed. "So when you told me, I knew it was going to happen."

"And you taped the gun beneath the table in the foyer," she prompted.

"That gun is always taped there. I have several stashed throughout the house. I wouldn't have planned to seduce you in the foyer, Siena, if that's what you're thinking. That was no seduction. That was pure, honest need. I was so far gone, baby, that I forgot about a hit man. All I could do was think about you, and I almost got us both killed."

She couldn't help but hear the honesty in his voice. She wanted to believe him and maybe a part of her did, but that other part, the one that didn't know the first thing about hot sex, held her back. He hadn't come after her, not even when he realized she was a virgin.

He came after you and saved you from Paolo, her inner voice reminded when she wanted it to shut up. She didn't want to invest in him, or think he had any kind of a good side at all. It was just so much safer to view him as a complete player. Mean. Cruel. But she knew he wasn't. He had feathered kisses down her back. Down her hip and thigh. He meant every single one of them. She'd *felt* the sincerity. She didn't want to, but she did.

Pure, honest need. For her. For Siena Arnotto. She couldn't accept that, not with the blood on her hands. She closed her eyes again and leaned forward, silently asking him to remove the pillows so she could lie down for a few minutes.

She was supposed to get up and move around for ten minutes at a time and then rest for fifteen. But it hurt. Especially her leg. Right now, it was her emotions that hurt more than her body. She needed to turn everything off for a little while. Take a break from facing reality and just hopefully go to sleep.

"I'm tired, Elijah," she said, not lying. "Really tired."

"I know, baby," he answered immediately, pulling the pillows from behind her back and laying them flat for her. He helped her slide down in the bed and turn on her side.

His shirt was warm and comforting. She was very aware she wasn't wearing any underwear, but there was no material rubbing over her hip or pulled tight against her back, and honestly, the pain had been reduced mostly to a dull ache.

"Jake Bannaconni and his woman will be here shortly. His ranch neighbors mine. He wants you to meet Emma."

She touched her fingertips to the bandage on her cheek. She wasn't ready to meet anyone, least of all Jake Bannaconni's wife. She turned her face into the pillow and closed her eyes, surprised when Elijah pulled the cover up over her shoulders and tucked her in.

7

HEART pounding, Siena turned and ran, knowing she was fleeing for her life. Knowing the large, hideous cat with its evil eyes would run her down. It was faster and stronger and she was already injured. Her ribs hurt with every step she took. Her breath came in raw, burning gasps, but she tried anyway. She burst through the dense underbrush, branches scraping her naked body. She made it seven steps. Seven. That was all. In her mind she was counting, and she felt hot breath on her back at number seven.

A giant claw ripped down her back, taking off skin, the pain so excruciating she actually saw stars. Willing herself to pass out, she half turned toward the cat. A claw slapped at her face, knocking her sideways, tossing her body through the air as if she weighed no more than a feather. Her face tore open, a deep laceration, blood running into her eye, making it impossible to see.

She landed hard on her belly and curled into the fetal position as the cat leapt on her, sinking his teeth into her shoulder, twin ice picks driving deep, a savage move that held her immobile while those yellow, malevolent eyes stared down at her with fury. Watching her face, the cat raked its claw from her hip to her knee, the claw curving deep into her body, tearing through skin and muscle to try to get to the bone.

She screamed. She didn't want to give him that satisfaction, but the only release she had was the sound of agony pouring from her throat. She screamed and screamed.

"Siena." The door burst open and Elijah was there, gun in his fist, eyes tracking the room as he rushed to her side. He put one hand on her shoulder to reassure her he was there, and his body moved over hers, shielding her.

She was grateful as she jolted out of sleep and realized the room was filling with men. Drake. Joshua. Another man she didn't know. Jake Bannaconni hovering by the door. All of them with weapons. She turned her red face into Elijah's chest, hiding. She didn't care who knew either. She wanted them gone.

"I've got her," Elijah said, his voice a clear command. "We'll be out in a few minutes. She'll need food, she hasn't eaten all day."

He held her, one hand on the nape of her neck, fingers providing a soothing massage, the other arm around her bottom, low so that he didn't rub against the four long lacerations at her back. He waited until the door closed before he nuzzled the top of her head.

"Are you all right, baby?"

His voice turned her heart over. He sounded so gentle. Tender almost. He was definitely a man's man. He barked orders, intimidated everyone with his hard, piercing eyes, and the dangerous set to his shoulders. He held himself aloof from the others most of the time. She'd heard the men joking with one another even in her hospital room, but few of them ever spoke to Elijah that way. He didn't smile often. In fact, she'd never seen him smile at anyone else.

"It was just a bad dream," she admitted. Her pulse still pounded in her veins and every single place the leopard had attacked her ached with the memory so close.

He pulled back and looked down at her. "I need you to look at me, Siena."

She twisted her fingers in the front of his shirt and reluctantly obeyed him. Once her gaze met his, she couldn't look away. That was how powerful he was. He held her there, just with his peculiar mercury-colored eyes.

"I asked if you were all right. I expect an answer, not bullshit or a diversion."

She blinked. She would never win a stare-down with him. She couldn't defy him either, not when his commanding voice was so gentle. Not when his face was carved with real concern.

"I dream a lot about the attack. When I do, it's so real, it feels like it's happening all over again. Everything hurts." She glanced toward the window, afraid she might see the large head of the leopard appear there. Her gaze slid back to his as if drawn there. "I'm afraid all the time."

He leaned down and brushed his mouth lightly over the bandage on her face. "The team has the house surrounded. We have two men on the roof. Drake's in the house. So is Joshua. Jake's men are patrolling along his fence line, and Eli has men doing the same. No one is going to get through, baby. *All* of them are leopards, experienced in security work."

She swallowed. Nodded. "Intellectually, I know that, Elijah, but I can't seem to get my emotions to believe it." Her voice came out in a whisper. The attack felt too close. She didn't want to let go of him. She didn't know how it happened, but somehow, Elijah had become her anchor. She knew she would have to stand on her own feet soon, but for right now, she was going to set everything aside and just let him take over.

"You're shaking, Siena. Take a breath and let me hold you for a minute. Then I'll brush your hair for you."

Instantly she touched the wild mass tumbling everywhere. She'd always wanted board-straight hair, so at least it would look sleek and shiny. No, she had gotten thick waves. Big hair. Lots of it. The waves only added to the volume, and when she slept on it, the mass just got bigger. "It drives me nuts," she admitted.

"I love your hair," Elijah said, transferring his hold to her hips so he could scoot her forward in the bed. He got behind her, his back to the headboard, wedging her in between his thighs, but very careful of her back. "I could play in your hair for hours."

The way he said *play* sent a shiver through her body. She was instantly aware of his dark sensuality. Of the ruthless set of his mouth. His dark, hooded eyes. The way his gaze drifted over her. Brooding. Possessive. Hungry.

He took the brush from the nightstand and began to tug the bristles through the length of her hair. She twisted her fingers in her lap and bowed her head while the brush moved against her scalp.

"You don't have to do this," she said, not moving. Not wanting him to stop. Still, his sweetness was disarming and she didn't dare fall under his spell.

"I enjoy it, *mi corazon*." There was a smile in his voice. "We have company. We can't have you looking like I took advantage of you."

Her heart stuttered at the implication. She bit down hard on her lip, her mind shying away from the images his teasing provoked. Who knew a man like Elijah would enjoy brushing her hair? He didn't seem to brush his all that often—not that she minded the way his black hair fell in waves around his face and down his neck. He always looked—hot. Still, it didn't make sense to her that he would take the brush and smooth the tangles from her hair because they had visitors.

"Elijah? I would prefer not to get up." She wanted to stay

wrapped in her little cocoon, hiding beneath the covers, lying very still, feeling comforted by the soft material of Elijah's shirt.

"I'm well aware of that, baby."

He continued to brush her hair. He didn't seem in a hurry, although she knew Jake Bannaconni and his wife, Emma, waited in the other room for them.

"I don't want to see anyone," she persisted.

"I know you don't." He spoke gently. Matter-of-factly. He kept brushing her hair as if she hadn't spoken.

The action of the brush pulling through the thick strands of hair and massaging her scalp soothed her. She liked the feel of his hands in her hair. He took his time, as if they had all the time in the world and this was one of his most favorite things to do.

"I really would prefer to stay in here, Elijah." She tried to pour strength and resolution into her voice. "I don't think I'm up to meeting new people."

"You can't hide from the world, baby," he said, the brush continuing to tug at her hair. His voice was low, almost a purr. Mesmerizing. "You'll like Emma. You haven't had that many friends in your life."

"You don't know that."

"Siena." He said her name like a reprimand. "I've kept tabs on you ever since you were fifteen years old. All hair and eyes and gorgeous skin. You think I didn't notice you? Hell. I was a fucking pervert, dreaming about you."

Her stomach did a little flip at his admission, but she pushed down the warm feeling rising. "You preferred tall, skinny blondes." She blurted out the truth before she realized just how much it revealed to him—that she'd been watching him as well.

"I had no choice," Elijah said, leaning close as he swept the thick mass of hair from the nape of her neck. He pressed his mouth against her skin and then feathered kisses along her neck and her shoulder. His teeth scraped there, sending flames dancing through her belly. "I refused to be so much of a pervert that I dated women who were surrogates for you." He admitted the truth matter-of-factly.

She felt the burn of his mouth now, working at her skin, branding her. He invaded her space casually, as if she belonged to him. His hands on her body always felt intimate. He touched her the moment he was close to her. He had in the hospital, and he certainly was now. She knew she should put a stop to it, for the sake of self-preservation alone, but she couldn't help herself. She told herself it didn't matter, that she wasn't committing to anything, she just wasn't up to fighting with him. The truth was much more complicated, but she refused to think about it too much.

"No, you didn't." She had to deny that. She couldn't let it go. If it was the truth, he was even more of a danger to her than she thought, and she thought he was a *huge* red flag. She needed to put the brakes on, but he kept doing things like sliding his tongue just behind her ear so that small little flames danced in her bloodstream.

"I did, *mi amor*." His hands were back at her hair, dividing the mass into three sections. "Your braid is as thick as my arm, Siena. Can you imagine what our child is going to have in the way of hair? Mine is thick, and yours is even thicker."

She stiffened at the mention of her baby, one hand automatically dropping down protectively. "You can't talk about that. Not yet. I just can't go there." Elijah was right though—any child they had together would have a mass of hair. His was nearly as wild as hers.

There was silence. His hands stilled in her hair. She pressed her lips together and then looked over her shoulder at him. She couldn't read his expression.

"Elijah?"

He frowned, his dark eyes forcing her gaze to remain on his. "I guess I never asked you if you wanted the baby. I was happy we were having a child, so much so that I never once considered you might not want it."

She pressed her hand tighter against her stomach, as if she could shield the baby from the conversation. She didn't know how she felt, or how to react.

"Siena, talk to me. Be honest. This is important."

There was that note in his voice. A warning. Something lethal. She found herself shivering. She had the feeling that he would put a manacle around her ankle and hold her prisoner if she said she was considering getting rid of their child. *Their* child. That was the problem. Not the baby. She sighed. Elijah was right. They had to talk about it, and he deserved the truth. He was the father, there was no denying that fact.

"I want the baby," she admitted.

She caught the relief in his eyes before he leaned into her, brushing a kiss on her mouth this time. It was the first time he'd actually kissed her lips since he'd thrown her out of the house, and her heart nearly stopped. It wasn't sexual, but it was intimate. Just like sitting between his thighs was intimate.

"I want the baby too, Siena. It makes me happy that you do as well." He tugged at her hair until she turned her head around so he could continue braiding it.

"Elijah, I want the baby, but I don't like the fact that we made this child the way we did." There, she'd told him the truth. "I can barely look at you without hearing the things you said to me. Every word is branded on my soul. That may sound dramatic to you, but it's the absolute truth. I don't want to be here. I told you that when you said you were going to bring me here. I don't want you to be my baby's father. I don't know if I can ever get past what happened."

She bit down hard on her lip, afraid he'd be angry with her. He'd asked for the truth and she'd given it to him. She kept her head down, staring at her fingers, locked together so hard in her lap they were white.

"That's fair, baby. I don't blame you. I was a dick to you.

What woman wants to remember the father of her child being a *bastardo absoluta*?"

She drew in a startled breath. It was the last thing she expected him to say.

"That said, I *am* the father of our baby. I am your man. You're my woman. I know that's going to take some getting used to, but we're here and we'll find our way."

"I don't know who you are, Elijah. That man who said those things to me or this man, the one who's so sweet he makes me want to cry."

"Wish I could say I was only the sweet one, babe, but we're being truthful, and I have to admit I'm both. I can be a real bastard sometimes. You know the worst of me."

She shook her head. "I can't handle that, Elijah."

He tugged on the braid. "You think I don't know that, Siena? You think I don't know just how bad I fucked up? You think it doesn't eat at me night and day that I hurt you like that? I know you now. I know I have to protect you, and I swear, Siena, you give me that chance, you let me in, I'll take such good care of you, you'll never have to worry about anything again."

She didn't want the sincerity in his voice to break through the shield she was so desperately trying to keep up between them. Still, she couldn't stop the fluttering in her stomach or the curious melting sensation in her region of her heart. She recognized that she was very vulnerable where Elijah was concerned. She'd spent her teenage years dreaming about him. He had figured prominently in every single fantasy. In college, when she was so lonely, she had daydreamed about him.

"Elijah, I know you and everyone else thinks I came from a wonderful home, the princess everyone doted on. But that just isn't the truth. I loved my grandfather, but he sent me away when I was very young. I spent most of my childhood in boarding schools. Yes. They were private schools and I got a great education, and I had the best clothes and shoes money could buy, but I didn't have a home."

Elijah transferred his hold from her hair back to the nape of her neck, his fingers beginning a slow massage she was now very familiar with. He didn't interrupt her. He didn't remind her of their guests. He simply waited for her to continue.

"I didn't have friends at school. My grandfather made certain my bodyguards went into the classrooms with me. That didn't endear me to teachers, administrators, students or the bodyguards. I was different. I always was going to be different. I blamed his worries about me on the fact that my mother and father were murdered. Then I was kidnapped. I have to tell you, security was *much* worse after that."

"I do remember that," Elijah murmured. "Your grandfather went ballistic."

She nodded. "It was a terrible time. He didn't keep me home, although I begged him to. He sent me right back to school, but with different bodyguards. Alonzo was one of them and he practically didn't leave my side. Still, there was another attempt. After that, he made it clear I wouldn't be going on dates or to the home of any friend. I was even more isolated."

She sighed and made a move to inch away, to put some distance between them. The heat from his body had begun to seep into her, warming her. His masculine scent surrounded her until she felt as if she was breathing him in with every breath she drew. Instantly, his arms came up to surround her. He locked his hands over her waist.

"Stay put. I'm interested."

"I can tell you just as easily from a distance."

"Yes, but I want you right here. Close to me." His hands dropped lower until his palm was over her womb, his fingers splayed wide. "I like sitting here on our bed, you between my legs, my arms around you and our baby in my hand. Talk to me."

There it was. His bossy. It was natural to him. Before she could protest, he rubbed his face against the side of her neck, his lips leaving behind tiny flames with each kiss he gave her. Tiny ones. Barely there. She felt them all the way to her toes. She felt her sex flutter and clench, a slow burn starting. She sighed heavily, but he didn't loosen his hold on her, so she gave in. Like she seemed to be doing a lot of with him.

"Somewhere my grandfather got the idea that he wanted me to marry either Paolo or Alonzo. They ran things for him, carried out his orders, knew the business inside and out, he said. I thought he was talking about the winery and our other legitimate businesses. We own several, mostly to do with wine. We own several vineyards as well. I wasn't happy about it and I figured when I got my degree, rather than come home and face disappointing him, I would continue my education."

"You went clubbing." It was an accusation, and it came out like one. "I saw you. You were dancing and every man in the place was watching you. You wore a dress that clung to your body. *Dios*. So beautiful. I wanted my hands where that material was. All over you. It was all I could do not to carry you off that night."

"I didn't see you." And she usually had radar where he was concerned.

"I was so damned hard looking at you I could barely walk, let alone dance," he admitted. There was a definite edge to his voice. "I couldn't take all the men drooling over you, and I knew if I stayed, I'd end up hurting someone."

She glanced at him over her shoulder again. His handsome features had settled into hard lines and flecks of dark burst through the mercury of his eyes. It was fascinating to watch his eyes changing color.

"What did you do?"

He cursed in his native language, a rapid staccato of Spanish. "I took a woman home and fucked her brains out. It didn't help. I took a shower and jerked off. That didn't help either."

She blinked, shocked at his honesty. Reading his anger in

his darkening features. "Why are you upset with me, Elijah? I went dancing."

"In that fucking dress, without me to protect you."

"I had bodyguards."

"I don't give a fuck whether you did or not. You wore that dress. You look the way you do, and every bastard in the place had his eyes on you. Hell, half of them probably went into the bathroom and jerked off. I knew you were my woman, and I don't share with others. Not any part of you."

She didn't like a word he said. Conversely, she liked everything he said. That's what he did to her, confused her until she didn't know how to think or feel. She liked that he noticed her. She secretly liked that he was jealous, but the rest of it . . . Even that. She needed help. He was making her crazy. She decided the best course of action was to carry on with her story because she was making a point.

"I didn't date. Not ever. You know I hadn't been with anyone."

"Which is one of the reasons you didn't find yourself over my knee."

She started laughing. She couldn't help it, and the sound startled her.

"What's so funny about that?" he growled, his chin settling on her shoulder.

"That's such a *you* thing to say. If you're trying to convince me I'm safe with you, that's not the thing to say."

"You are perfectly safe with me. That doesn't mean I won't protect what's mine. You don't go anywhere in dresses like that without me right next to you."

She wasn't touching that. Not even a little bit. "The point I'm trying to make here, Elijah, is that I never had a home, and that hurt. My grandfather wasn't who I thought he was, and that hurt. The man he chose for me *really* wasn't the man I thought he was, and that hurt big-time. I've had enough of being alone. I've had enough of never feeling loved. I want that. I don't want to be hurt. You could hurt me. You *did* hurt me. The way you hurt me was worse than all the rest of it."

She knew what she was admitting. She'd had feelings for him long before she'd ever driven the wine over. She had known she was being ridiculous, but she'd still fallen in love with the mythical man—especially after they had ignited together. She thought he felt the same way—that what they had together was love burning so hot and bright they wouldn't ever be able to be apart. She'd been wrong. *Way* wrong. She knew she'd been naïve. It had been just sex. Raw. Hot. Over-the-top chemistry.

"Baby." He whispered it softly. Gently. His voice moved over her like velvet. "I'm telling you, what happened between us was something beautiful. The gift you gave me was precious. I didn't treat it like that after. I was so far gone, a dead body on the floor, and the shock of what I thought bouncing around in my head, nothing registered. That's totally on me. You have no part of that. I should have taken care with you. If I hadn't been so fucking selfish, I would have taken that care and I would have realized what you'd given to me. Never again. I swear to you, Siena, never again."

"You can't promise that, and I'm not strong enough to take what you're capable of dishing out."

"I'm not saying we aren't going to fight. Couples fight. The more passion they feel for each other, the greater the likelihood of it happening, but I know what I have now, and I'm telling you, I'll take care with you. I can give you my promise, my word on that."

Siena didn't know what to say so she didn't say anything, more confused than ever. She liked everything he said, but he wasn't asking. She wasn't so blinded by her fantasies of him that she hadn't caught that. He was a man in charge. He could be in control nice or he could take control rough. She liked that he wanted to take care with her, but she had no idea how to process everything that had happened to her, let alone that he wanted to claim her permanently. He hadn't actually said that. He wanted the baby, that much he *had* said.

"Siena? Talk to me."

"I don't know what to say. I don't know what you mean. Are you asking me to stay here with you until the baby's born?"

His hand reached around, caught her chin and pulled her head around and back until it was lying against his chest, turned toward him. His eyes moved over her face. There was a hard stamp of possession there. It was in every line and the hard set of his mouth. Possession burned in his eyes.

"You know what I'm saying. I don't want you until the baby's born. I'm talking us. Together. Raising our child. You in my bed. You're my woman. I'm your man. I'm talking, you don't wear that dress unless I'm with you."

That dress had really made an impression. She was going to have to go back and revisit that dress.

"I see." Because he'd made it so clear even an imbecile— like her right now—could see. "I don't know."

"You don't know about what?"

"You scare me, Elijah. I've been scared all my life. I don't want to be scared anymore."

"You feel safe with me, Siena," he corrected.

She started to shake her head but he stopped her.

"You're sitting here on this bed with me. You came home with me. You protested, baby, but you didn't throw a fit. You didn't tell the cops you wanted protection. You came with me because I make you feel safe. That's the truth."

She opened her mouth to deny it, but then closed it again. He had a point. The problem was, she did feel safe with him, it was her heart that didn't feel safe. There was a difference, but she wasn't about to tell him that, so again, she said nothing.

He nuzzled her neck again. "It's all right, baby. I'll give you time." He tugged her braid. "Let's go. I want you to meet Emma." He moved around her to slide off the bed and reach for her. "It's important for you to feel like you have a few female friends out here. Emma and Catarina both live on neighboring ranches."

"I can't go out there like this."

He tugged her to her feet. "My shirt's long enough on you to be a dress." His eyes darkened. "Longer than the dress you wore to the club."

"I was wearing underwear at the club."

His eyebrow shot up. "I didn't see any lines."

"Oh. My. God." She narrowed her eyes at him. "You looked that close?"

"I've got news for you, baby. Every man in that damned club looked that close. You're lucky I didn't commit murder that night."

She rolled her eyes and turned away from him. She had to have a long skirt she could slip on. One that dropped to her ankles and flowed around her so no one could tell whether she wore underwear or not. She rummaged through her bag and came out with a ruffled skirt that dropped to the floor.

He hadn't moved and she turned, skirt in hand. "Are you going to watch me get dressed?"

His white teeth flashed, reminding her a little of a wolf's. "Yes."

She bit back her protest. What was the use? Elijah did whatever he wanted, and clearly he wasn't going to leave her side. She liked that it was important to him that she meet Emma—that he wanted her to have a female friend. That was nice.

Siena pulled on the skirt without looking at him. She looked in her bag for a shirt that would go, but without wearing a bra, nothing really worked.

"You look fine in my shirt. Come on, baby, stop stalling."

She glanced in the mirror over the dresser and reached up to touch the gauze covering the laceration on her face. The stitches had been removed before she left the hospital, but she hated how red and raised the scar was so she kept it covered with gauze.

He took her hand and tugged until she was beneath his shoulder. "Seriously? You look beautiful."

She could hear the impatience in his voice. Mister Nice Guy clearly had a time limit on his nice. She hid a smile as she walked down the wide hall with him. Jake and his wife, Emma, were in the great room. The room was enormous and very comfortable with overstuffed chairs and warm tones, but the moment Elijah stepped into the room, he commanded it. There was no denying his presence.

He took her straight across the hardwood floor to Emma. She was at least seven, maybe eight months pregnant. Jake sat on the arm of her chair, holding her hand.

"This is Siena Arnotto, Emma," Elijah said. "Siena, Emma, Jake's wife."

Siena sent the woman a tentative smile. She'd never really had a female friend, not one who was real. A few girls had wanted to know her because of her name. Others had thought her bodyguards were hot. None of them got to know her as a person, and she knew she'd developed a shell, keeping others out to prevent herself from getting hurt.

"Finally," Emma said, her answering smile soft and beautiful. "I couldn't wait to meet the woman who has stolen Elijah's heart. Big, bad Elijah turned inside out by a woman. You have no idea how wonderful it is to meet you."

Jake grinned, looking at ease and relaxed, not at all like the man in his office. "She's brought him to his knees, Emma."

Siena blinked rapidly and glanced at Elijah, uncertain how to react. She didn't have his heart, and he certainly wasn't on his knees. That was one thing she knew for certain. He had told Detective Madison they were planning to be married. Was that the story Drake had come up with to keep her safe?

She realized Elijah still had possession of her hand and

she tugged, trying to get free. Instead, he brought her knuckles to his mouth.

"Since I can't deny the truth of what you're saying, I'll just kiss my woman and be happy she's in my home," Elijah said.

"I was sorry to hear about your grandfather, Siena," Emma said. "I know he raised you. Are you doing okay?"

Siena nodded. She wasn't thinking too much about it yet. Every day the reality of his death sank in a little more. "I haven't really processed his death. I was there that night, up in my room. We'd had a fight." Her throat closed at the admission. She didn't know why she'd blurted that out, but she couldn't take it back.

Emma's face grew even softer. "That makes it all the harder for you."

Elijah steered her to a chair opposite Emma's, put a gentle hand to her belly, and she sank into it. He snagged one of the beers Jake had brought, and perched on the arm of her chair just as Jake had done. Even she could see the very line of his body was protective.

Siena swallowed the lump forming. She didn't know how to take Elijah this way. She was completely unprepared for his dual personality. "I'm pretty certain I'm responsible for his death." She said it more to Elijah than to Jake and Emma.

Drake sat in the chair beside hers and he swung his head toward her, suddenly alert. Jake leaned closer to her. Emma shook her head as if denying the statement.

Elijah reached down and threaded his fingers through hers and pressed her hand to his thigh. "Why would you think that, *mi vida*?"

His voice was so gentle she had to blink back tears. How could he be so sweet to her? How could she believe he was real? She'd never had sweet before, not even from her grandfather, and she had no idea what to do with it.

She pressed her lips together, knowing they were all looking at her. Knowing she'd brought it on herself and she had to face the reality of what had happened that night. She had no idea why the sight of Emma, pregnant, with Jake hovering so close to her, had given her the courage to tell them, to tell Elijah, but she knew it was Elijah she was telling. It was Elijah she was confessing to. It was Elijah she needed absolution from.

"Paolo was Nonno's choice for me. He had planned that we get married. I came home that night, and Paolo was waiting for me and he was furious." She glanced up at Elijah. Met his eyes. He knew why. He would know his scent was all over her and Paolo would know they'd had sex.

Elijah pressed her hand tighter against his thigh as if he could shield her—shield both of them from what was coming. He took a long swig of beer.

Her eyes on Elijah, she continued. "Paolo beat me up. Not just slapped me. He used his fists on me. He kicked me."

Emma gasped. "Oh my God, Siena. That's terrible. Your grandfather must have been furious."

"That's what I thought." Siena soldiered on. "He wasn't. He called me names. Horrible names. I told him I would never accept Paolo as a husband. I told him to give the estate to Paolo if that was what he wanted, but I would never, under any circumstances, marry Paolo after what he did to me. Paolo was in the room. He heard everything and he knew I meant it. So did Nonno."

Drake leaned forward in his chair. She sensed the movement but she kept her gaze locked with Elijah's. His features had darkened, but it was impossible to read his expression. His eyes were flat and cold and so dark it took her breath away.

"My grandfather acknowledged my proclamation and indicated I would always be his heiress and he would accept my decision. I left the room and went to mine. I overheard Paolo arguing with him. A little while later I heard the gunshots, and I raced downstairs. Paolo was at the entrance of the sitting room and Alonzo was heading up the stairs toward me. My grandfather was dead."

She couldn't look away, waiting for condemnation. Clearly Elijah would understand what she was saying. She had made her declaration, her grandfather had accepted it, but Paolo hadn't. Rather than allow her to choose her husband, he had killed her grandfather.

"How was that your fault, honey?" Emma asked.

Still looking at Elijah, she answered. Truthfully. "Had I just accepted my grandfather's choice of husbands, I believe he would still be alive."

"Accept a man who beat you?" Emma said.

She nodded, still not looking away from Elijah. Her heart beat too fast. She still couldn't read him. *Say something. Anything.* She was terrified of his reaction. Of his judgment.

Elijah put down the beer bottle, framed her face with both hands, leaned down and took her mouth. He kissed her hard. Long. Wet. Deep. He kissed her possessively. His mouth demanded a response. *Demanded.* There was no coaxing. No gentleness. This was Elijah. Rough. In total command.

His kiss was unlike anything she could ever imagine. Just as it had the first time, his kiss ignited a firestorm in her. The world receded until there was only Elijah and his mouth. His perfect, unbelievable mouth and his extraordinary ability to kiss. She kissed him back, her mind melting. There was no thinking. No worrying. There was only the perfection of his mouth and the absolute ecstasy it brought.

He lifted his mouth first and when hers chased his, he kissed her again before pressing his forehead to hers. "Fuck, baby. I want to kill that bastard with my bare hands. You didn't do this. He did."

He whispered the words to her and her heart turned over. She shouldn't want to hear him say he wanted to kill Paolo with his bare hands, but somehow, his stark admission lifted some of the guilt that rode her so hard.

8

"SIENA. Baby. Open your eyes."

She heard the voice from a distance. Familiar. Warm. Sweet. That velvet heat cut through the cold terror forcing her heart to pound and her pulse to go wild.

"That's it, *mi vida*, open your eyes. Look at your man."

So sweet, that voice. Rough. Sexy. All man. Reassuring and solid. She felt the brush of his mouth over her eyelids. Her lashes fluttered as she made the supreme effort to lift them. To see his face. The remnants of the nightmare clung to her, so that her mouth was dry and her stomach hurt. Down the side of her leg, pain flashed, but already, it was fading, driven away by that mesmerizing voice and the brush of Elijah's mouth.

She opened her eyes and there he was. Close. So close. So beautiful. His jaw strong, dark with a two-day stubble. His cheekbones high. His dark features all man. His hair—she loved the wild, unruly hair that was so Elijah. He was wild, and his hair marked him that way.

His eyes were dark with concern, but he smiled at her, his teeth very white, his lips defined. "Sweetheart."

The single word turned her heart over. Without thinking she lifted her hand and traced his lips. "You have a beautiful mouth, Elijah," she whispered. Her heart pounded hard. From the nightmare, or from how close he was, how gorgeous he was. How much of a dream man he was. She tasted the echo of her nightmare in her mouth. The terror. The moment the leopard dragged her down. The sound of the gun. The sight of her grandfather. Paolo kicking her with his elegant, Italian, *pointed* shoes.

"No, baby." His eyes intent on hers, he pulled her finger into his mouth, his tongue curling around it, distracting her completely from the web of terror she'd been trapped in. He shook his head, releasing her, but his hands went back to framing her face. His eyes darkened even more. "He doesn't get any part of you. Not when you're awake and not when you're asleep. Give him to me, everything he said. Everything he did. Give *all* of it to me."

There was no looking away from the intensity of his eyes. He was wholly focused on her, his gaze holding hers captive.

"I don't know how." She wanted to. She was tired of being afraid. So very tired of it. She hated fearing going to sleep, knowing Paolo would be there. Knowing guilt over her grandfather's death would eat at her. Knowing fear would consume her.

"Look at me, *mi amorcita*, sweetheart. Really look at me. I'm not the kind of man another man messes with. I'm standing between you and anyone who wants to hurt you. I'm putting myself there."

God. *God.* He felt like he owed her because of what happened between them. He was the type of man who would do that too, put himself in harm's way because he felt he'd done something wrong. She let herself really look at him, taking in everything from the width of his shoulders to the heavy muscles of his bare chest. He was a man who looked invincible. Looked as if he could stop bullets. But he couldn't. Her grandfather couldn't.

"Elijah, you don't owe me anything. I was doing exactly what you accused me of doing when you threw me out. I was there to distract you so Marco could get in to kill you. I don't want you to put yourself in harm's way for me."

"I'm telling you to look at me, Siena. See who I am. I'm that man you're afraid of because I can be that scary man when I need to be. And I'll be him for you—to protect you any way I have to. I'm taking your nightmare. I'm *choosing* to stand between you and any enemy because I choose you. Every time, my choice is you, and it has been for years. I don't want you ever to feel fear again—not from Paolo Riso, not from anyone. Not ever again."

Just because Elijah ordered it didn't mean the fear would go away, but somehow, looking into his eyes, that terror inside her diminished. The tight coils in her belly unraveled. She found herself breathing easier. Looking at him. She didn't have a clue where the fear went, only that lying beside him, feeling his hard body surrounding hers, his arm locked around her, his gaze so intense and dark with real emotion, she knew she could let it go for the first time.

He must have seen the relief on her face, or felt her body relax. Satisfaction crept into the hard lines cut into his face. "Is it gone? The nightmare?" He closed the two-inch gap between their faces, his lips brushing back and forth across hers. Coaxing.

He didn't have to work hard to get her to open for him. The moment her lips parted, his tongue swept inside, and the last of the nightmare was gone. He could kiss. Seriously kiss. And he did. Her fingers found his hair and dove deep. She kissed him back, losing herself in him the way she always did. Melting so she didn't think. Only felt. Every cell in her body responded to Elijah's kisses.

His arm locked around her waist, pulling her tight against the front of his body. She felt him wrapped around her, so close. So hard. So hot. But careful. She had ignited, gone a little wild, a little out of control. His mouth did that to her. He *felt* wild. Out of control, but he never once brushed against her leg or hurt her back when he pulled her closer.

He lifted his head and stared down into her face, eyes intense as he studied her closely, looking for signs of distress.

"Thank you, Elijah," she whispered, her voice a thread of sound. Her heart was pounding all over again. Her belly somersaulted. All good. "Thank you for making that go away for me." Her nightmare. Not even a small aftertaste was left. He'd driven it away with his mouth, his tongue and his hand so tight in her hair. He'd driven it away by the strength of his will, and his beautiful declaration that he stood between her and Paolo.

"Are you okay, baby?"

The room was dark. The bed was warm. His soft, sexy voice, roughened with sleep, curled her toes and melted her insides. His body was hot, so tight against hers, and the leopard snarling and tearing at her had been driven back.

"Yeah. I'm good." She was and she wasn't. The nightmare was gone, but she was very, very aware of him. Her body had suddenly come alive and taken notice of the fact that he was hot. Sexy. And male.

"Then settle."

She had the unexpected urge to laugh. That was so the Elijah she was coming to know. Sweet as honey one moment and demanding the next.

"And if I can't?"

"Then I might have to do something about it," he warned softly. "You need your sleep. Doc said to make certain you give your body the time it needs to heal."

His soft warning sent a little thrill through her body. There was something very sensual about waking up next to him. He was hard and hot and smelled all male when she inhaled deeply. She silently cursed her back. The stitches were gone and the rake marks were healing, but lying flat on her back would be a problem because they were still sore.

She bit her lip and her gaze slid away from his. She was actually thinking about positions. Sheesh. Her body was beginning to feel the slow burn that had gotten her in so much trouble before. The burn that didn't allow her to think. Only feel.

"Stop." He breathed the word. "I'm not a fucking saint, Siena." Even as he ordered it, his hand moved up her bare thigh, proving to both of them that he wasn't.

His voice had roughened more. His gaze grew even darker and more intense. She moistened her lips with the tip of her tongue. Her body moved restlessly against his.

"I'm not looking for a saint, Elijah," she whispered.

He groaned and took her mouth again. She should have protested. She knew she shouldn't have invited his mouth or his hands or the slow, beautiful assault on her body, but the moment she had him back, she slid right into meltdown mode. Her brain turned to slush. Her body caught fire.

Elijah's hand continued to move up her left leg, her uninjured one, with exquisite languor, giving her plenty of time to protest. She didn't. She kissed him back harder, pouring herself into his kiss. Seeking his heat. Seeking oblivion. Bliss. She found it there in his mouth, in his touch.

"There comes a certain point, *mi amor*, where there is no turning back. I've been with you every day for nearly three weeks, and it hasn't been easy keeping my hands off of you," he warned.

"I wasn't asking you to turn back," she whispered, looking into his eyes. "Just to be careful of me. Don't hurt me, Elijah."

Elijah stared down at her. His face going soft. Tender even. She never thought to see that look on his face. When they'd come together before, both had been so hot, so out of control, the fire raging between them, that there'd been no time to look into his eyes, to see his face, to see him like this.

"You're safe with me, Siena," he reiterated, his voice stroking over her skin, very much like his fingers. He reached for her hair, the long thick braid that kept the mass of silk confined. She didn't protest when he pulled out the tie and used his fingers to unweave the strands, allowing her hair to cascade around her.

"Beautiful," he murmured. "Like silk." His mouth settled over hers again. He gave her long, lazy kisses. As if they had all the time in the world. His hands dropped to the buttons of the shirt she wore—his shirt—and, even with his mouth burning his particular brand and taste into her mouth, never stopping, he managed to slide the buttons open so that her breasts spilled out.

Elijah kissed his way from Siena's soft mouth to her chin. He liked her chin. He'd spent some time studying her chin. She lifted it whenever her eyes flashed fire at someone. She'd been doing that as long as he could remember. He'd dreamt about her lifting her chin at him. The last time he'd seen her do that was at the club when some man tried freak dancing with her. She'd done that little chin lift of absolute defiance. The gesture brought out the leopard in him. What self-respecting leopard wouldn't want to tame his female when she gave him that little chin lift?

He kissed his way over her chin and along her jaw. Under it. Down her throat. She nearly purred, and the sound vibrated through his body, through his muscle and bone straight to his cock. Her skin was soft, like satin, and he inhaled her unique scent. He loved the breathy little sounds escaping and the way her body went boneless for him. This time he was careful. Very careful. Her first time should have been perfect, not him slamming her to the floor like a savage animal. He should have worshiped her body. Memorized it. Showed her how much she meant to him, not taken her in a heat he couldn't control.

"I love the feel of your hair against my skin," he murmured softly. He kept her curled into him, off her back, off the injury to her right leg. Even so, her hair fell like a waterfall, pooling beneath them, rubbing along his bare shoulder and chest as he kissed his way along her collarbone. He wanted to bury his face in all that silk. He dreamt of that too. The way it would feel. The way it would smell. Perfection, and it was.

Her hands moved over his back. Slow. As if she was memorizing every muscle there, the line of his body. He reveled in that simple touch, and he hadn't expected to. Her fingertips and palms moving over him shouldn't have felt sensual, but it was, that slow, almost leisurely exploration. His belly did a slow roll and heat rushed through his body from every direction to center in his groin. He liked that too. The blood moving through his veins in urgent need. The heat pooling, filling his cock until he felt fully, completely alive, not living in the half world where he had nothing. No one. Where he was alone even when he was in a room filled with others. She was finally in his bed where he'd wanted her—even needed her—all along.

He lifted his head to look down at her. She was beautiful, her face flushed, her lips slightly swollen from his kisses, her breasts moving with every ragged breath. Such beauty, and she was giving it all to him. He knew she was afraid of him— afraid of his temper and his passion, but she still was willing to take that chance even though he hadn't yet earned it.

He nuzzled her breast, his tongue stroking her nipple. "You're so beautiful, Siena. So fucking beautiful I'm almost afraid to believe you're real. That this is real."

Her hands slid along his hips and down his butt. He felt her light touch all the way through his body as if she were using a branding iron on him. Branding her name into his skin. Into his bones. He could have told her, her name was already there, inside of him. It had been for a number of years. He held his breath as she pressed her fingers into him, over him, her palm sliding over firm muscle to slide along the crease between thigh and buttocks.

Lifting the soft weight of her breast, thumb stroking caresses over her nipple, he trailed more kisses over the creamy slopes of her breasts and between, in the deep valley where he felt her pulse. Soft. Gentle. Taking his time because he felt every shiver of her body. She was sensitive to his touch. To his mouth and hands.

He wanted her to hear him when he said she was safe with him. He was better at showing her than telling her. He couldn't resist the lure of her breast and he pulled her nipple deep into his mouth, tugging and rolling, using the flat of his tongue to stroke, the edge of his teeth to send flames dancing and the hard pull of his mouth to ignite a fire.

She was very responsive to him. A gift. Her soft, breathy moans set his pulse pounding, the blood roaring in his ears. His hand moved down her belly where she cradled his child while it grew. The child they'd made together. She didn't know it, but that child had been conceived in love. He had known the moment he had first laid eyes on her, sitting across from him at her grandfather's table, her eyes downcast, her hair everywhere, her soft voice doing things to him that shouldn't have been done, not when she was so young, that she was his other half, the woman who would make him a better man. The woman who could live with the man he was, the man his harsh life had shaped him to be.

"I knew," he whispered. "I should have given you that. I knew you were mine." He made the confession, his lips against that soft, perfect place where his child nestled.

Her fingers caught in his hair, sifted, then fisted. He felt the bite in his scalp and it transmitted straight through his body to his cock. Hunger grew. The burn became scorching. Searing him with urgent need. He pressed kisses over her belly, wanting them to go deep, deep enough for his child to feel loved. To know he or she was wanted by him.

He kissed his way down her injured leg, tongue moving over the raw ridges as gently as possible, and then back up the inside of her thigh. He lifted her leg and put it over his shoulder so his head was cradled on her good thigh.

She gasped and tightened her hold in his hair. "Elijah." His name came out raw. Sexy. Breathless. A moan.

He loved that. He loved the way she smelled, so welcoming,

honeysuckle and citrus. She tasted that way. He knew she did because he woke up every night remembering her taste. It was forever in his brain, just as addicting as her body was.

"Stay still for me, baby," he whispered into her damp entrance. "I want this to feel good, not hurt you."

He used his tongue first, a long, slow swipe to collect that honey and bring it into his mouth, savoring that first taste. "So good, Siena. You taste so damned good. You were made for me." He would forever wake up craving the taste of her in his mouth, on his tongue, and he'd never get enough of the unique flavor that was Siena.

He used his hands to open her, so he could feed on her. Sate his hunger. Drive her wild. He wanted her wild. He wanted her to need him, to feel the same urgent hunger consuming her until she couldn't take one more breath without him inside of her. He needed that from her. He wanted to give her that. He wanted to watch her face as he pushed her over the edge and sent her soaring.

He gave that to her twice, but really, he was giving it to himself, such pleasure, watching her eyes glaze, watching her breath grow more ragged, the bliss on her face. Such beauty, because he loved her so much, so deeply, and there was no other way he could show it to her like he could here, in his bed, taking his time with her the way he should have when he took her innocence.

The second time her body rippled and pulsed, he moved up her, holding her thighs apart, keeping her injured leg riding up over his hip as he pushed into her hot, tight sheath.

"So tight," he murmured. "Strangling me. Wet silk, baby, scorching. So good. So fucking good." He could barely inch his way through her tight folds, her muscles reluctantly stretching to accommodate his thick shaft. He took his time out of necessity, when everything in him wanted to slam deep, bury himself to his balls. If she hadn't been so slick from the two orgasms he'd given her, he doubted if he could have gotten her sheath to accept him.

When he was buried to the very hilt, feeling her cervix, knowing he couldn't get any deeper inside her, he waited, breathing deeply, feeling her body surround him, the slow yield to his invasion. Gripping him. A wet, silken fist wrapped so tightly around him, she stole his breath. Fire raced from his cock, up his spine and down his thighs, spreading like a storm of white-hot flames.

"You okay, baby?" he whispered, praying she was. Gritting his teeth, holding himself still when every cell in his body urged him to move. Fast. Hard. Deep.

Her hands slid around his shoulders, fingernails biting deep. "Better than okay. I need you to move. Now, Elijah. Please."

His eyes closed for just a moment, his heart turning over at that last little breathless plea. "You tell me if you're uncomfortable, Siena," he ordered.

"Just move," she pleaded again.

He withdrew and thrust deep, driving through her tight muscles, feeling the burn engulf him. Watching her face. Her eyes. Looking for signs of discomfort. He plunged deep again and again, rocking her body with every stroke. The breath left her in a rush. Her eyes glazed. Her lips parted. She was beautiful. Instinctual. Her hips moving to meet his.

The heat built. Tension coiled. He heard it in her ragged gasp. Saw it in her dazed expression. Her nails dug in, a bite of pain that added to building fire. His hand shifted to support the thigh of her injured leg, making certain not to jar that long, jagged wound while he picked up the pace. He kept her on her side, so that there was no pressure on her back, only the driving cock between her legs.

"Harder, Elijah," she said. "I need you to . . ." She broke off as he deliberately switched angles, using her legs to tilt her hips toward him so he could press down into her.

Her ragged gasp was music to him, adding to the pleasure threatening to overwhelm him. He stayed ahead of it, not wanting to end this. He could live there, connected to her, feeling her body squeezing until the friction seared him. He drove harder, giving her what she needed, watching her face as her orgasm raced over her. She gasped. Her eyes went wide with shock. She looked so beautiful he nearly closed his own eyes to lock that image in his brain for all time.

He kept moving, taking her back up fast, so fast her body didn't have time to rest before the next one hit, this time much stronger, this time taking him with her. He buried his face in her neck and let it take him, the burn. The fire. The pleasure spinning through him with such force he thought it might take the top of his head off. He buried his face in her neck and stayed still. Planted in her. Living in her. Feeling that burn pounding through her, spreading like a wildfire.

"Baby," he whispered, when he could breathe again. "Nothing like you in my life. Not. Ever."

She didn't answer, but her hands were buried in his hair, wrapping the unruly waves around her fingers. Letting the strands slide through and then fisting them all over again. He felt her fighting for breath, felt her body rippling around his, drenching him in honeysuckle and citrus. He lifted his head, fighting for air, careful of her injuries, holding her close to him, his gaze moving over her face to assure himself he hadn't hurt her.

"Siena?" he said softly. Insistently.

Her gaze jumped to his, eyes shimmering with tears. "You weren't fucking me." She sounded shocked. She looked shocked.

"No, *mi vida*, I was not," he admitted, because she looked so vulnerable, so confused, he needed to reassure her. It was as necessary to him as breathing.

She pressed her lips together. "I don't understand you, Elijah."

"I know, *mi amorcito*," he said. He kissed her chin and then couldn't resist nibbling. "But you will. Give yourself time and you'll understand me perfectly." He eased his body out of hers. "Can you sleep now? I'll get a washcloth and clean you up, but I need to know you can go back to sleep and not have nightmares."

She smiled at him, lifted a hand to the mass of hair spilling around her and then touched his mouth, tracing his lips. He liked that. He liked that she liked his mouth, and she did. That was clear.

"I think you chased my nightmares away, Elijah."

He flashed a satisfied grin at her, kissed her finger and exited the bed to get a warm washcloth.

Siena watched Elijah walk away from her, completely comfortable with his nudity. She was already pulling the edges of her shirt together and buttoning them. He came back, his eyes glittering at her in the dark as he sank down onto the bed beside her and carefully washed her thighs, pressing the warm cloth between her legs.

"I didn't hurt you?"

She shook her head. "Not at all. I think I'm definitely healing. The laceration on my leg is the worst, although I'm mostly self-conscious of the one on my face."

"Which is silly," he said, his attention on what he was doing.

She knew that. It was vain, but still. She bit her lip. "Um. Elijah, I'm starving. I didn't eat, remember?"

His gaze jumped back to her face. "You wouldn't let me get you food when Jake and Emma were here."

"I didn't want to eat in front of them," she admitted.

He sighed and shook his head. "Were you hungry when they left?"

His tone demanded honesty. She didn't want to try to lie, figuring he would know instantly she wasn't telling the truth, so she shrugged. He scowled.

"You were hungry and you didn't say anything. That's not acceptable, baby. You tell me when you need something." His eyes had gone diamond hard, pure mercury, glittering with menace. "I'm not bragging, but I know my way around a kitchen."

There it was. The Elijah she expected. Bossy. Intimidating. Only this time she wasn't afraid in the least. He was gently cleaning her thighs as well as other, more secret places, his touch tender even when his voice was scary hard. She hid a small smile, thinking it best she keep that knowledge to herself.

"I'll keep that in mind for the future," she said. "And I'll admit I'm really, really hungry, so if you have anywhere near the skills in the kitchen you have in the bedroom, now would be the time to whip them out and show off."

His glittering gaze drifted over her face slowly, taking in every detail as if ensuring himself she was perfectly fine. He touched her lips, his fingers pressing over them with the same gentleness he used cleaning her, but he dragged his fingers across her lips, tracing them, and then down, the gesture turning her heart over.

"You deserve the world, Siena," he said softly. "And I'm going to give it to you."

Everything in her went still. His eyes had gone all silver. Dark silver. Glittering silver, and so intense his gaze pierced her, went right through her, aiming straight at her heart and finding its target. She wanted to believe him. She did believe him. How could she not when he was looking at her with such raw, stark emotion naked on his face for her to see?

She knew no one else had ever seen that look. No one had ever seen him exposed the way he was giving himself to her. That look turned her inside out. He was a strong man, a dangerous one, and closed off from the world. His extremely handsome face was normally expressionless. He didn't give anything away, certainly not his emotions, but there it was, laid out for her.

"Elijah." She whispered his name because she could barely speak.

Everything in her life was gone. She was scared and confused, but there was Elijah holding out his hand to her.

Bringing her safely to his side. Wrapping her in his strength and protection. Offering the world to her. *His* world.

Siena's heart accelerated. She didn't know what his world entailed. She didn't want her child to grow up in her grandfather's world. What and who was Elijah Lospostos? The man sitting on the bed with her, so tender and sweet? Or the man who sat at her grandfather's table, commanding the room in spite of his age. Others had deferred to him. Even her grandfather had treated him with respect. Now he was working with Drake Donovan on Drake's security team. What did that mean?

"Baby, you should never play poker," Elijah cautioned.

She twisted her fingers together. "You're a good man, Elijah. What were you doing with my grandfather?"

She watched his face shut down. All that emotion swept away in an instant, and he was once again handsome, hard, scary and dangerous, giving absolutely nothing away.

"I'm not a good man, Siena. You tie yourself to me, you'll never have that. You'll never be free of the reputation and the rumors. The whispers. Cops will harass you. People will stare or look away fast. You're with me, that's what you can expect. I'll shield you always from the worst of it, but you have to know it will be there."

"That doesn't tell me anything."

"It tells you what to expect, and the rest of it, I swear, I'll lay out to you, just give me a little time."

"A little time for what?" she persisted.

"I'm asking for this, *mi amor*. A little time. Can you give me that?"

She studied his face. He was so beautiful, and maybe he was just as lost as she was, but he was a good man. She felt it. She knew it. She took a deep breath and nodded. She could do that, but they would have the conversation.

Elijah bent his head and kissed her. Gently. Turning her heart over. He moved then, up off the bed, back to the master bath to deal with the washcloth. Her gaze followed him, the fluid, easy way he moved. He was leopard. A shifter. She didn't—yet—know much about them, but she did know they shared the traits of the large cats that were so much a part of them. Leopards were jealous, temperamental creatures, with snarling bad tempers and the ability to strike hard and fast. All leopards were lethal, even those that were raised from baby to adult by humans.

He took her breath away just by moving. He turned her body into a place of sweet, exquisite ecstasy. She had no doubt he would protect her the instant she was threatened. She liked the way he always moved in close to her.

"You coming?" Elijah stood in the doorway, dragging on a pair of jeans. Barefoot. Hair unruly and a little wild. Silver eyes gleaming at her. Jeans riding low, barely buttoned.

She slid out of bed and went right to him, taking the hand he held out. She had no idea what she was doing with Elijah Lospostos, the man who claimed he wasn't a good man, who told her straight-out, but she liked the way he pulled her in close to him, tight against his side, under his shoulder, his arm clamped around her, but down low, avoiding the four lacerations on her back. That meant something to her. That he would take care even in the way he held her.

"Do you ever get lost in this house?"

He laughed softly, the sound startling her. He had a beautiful laugh. It was soft and warm and totally addicting. She could listen to that sound for the rest of her life.

"I don't know why you're laughing, because I'm going to get *very* lost. I have no sense of direction." That wasn't entirely true, but if it kept him laughing she'd be satisfied.

"I'll put up signs for you," he said. "Big ones that you can't miss." He dipped his head down, his chin sliding over the top of her head before he swept her to what obviously was the center of the house, a large glass atrium. "They're all going to point straight back to me."

She stopped dead, forcing him to stop as well. She looked

around her in shock. The atrium was filled with plants, trees even. Thick, beautiful bushes and flowering plants were everywhere. Water trickled over stones lined with bright green moss. It was a massive room that curved and twisted so it was impossible to see everything.

"Oh. My. God. This is why you bought the house." It was beautiful. The most beautiful thing she'd ever seen.

"Not exactly," he denied. "But a part of it. I told you about the exits in the bedroom. This house has many escape routes built in. Safe places for both human and leopard. The atrium has the best hidden exits for leopards. It's a labyrinth of underground tunnels."

She tilted her head to look up at him, her breasts pressed into his side. His gaze found hers, his eyes back to mercury, a glittering, *scary* look that meant they were on dangerous ground. There were reasons for needing escape routes. Reasons like Marco, a hit man sent by someone who supposedly was a friend.

The iron bar that was his arm tensed as he moved her forward around the huge glass room to the kitchen just beyond it. There was a small group of comfortable chairs where others could gather while the cook prepared a meal, and Elijah led her straight to the most comfortable armchair.

"You can curl up there." He slid the pad of his thumb over her lips. "I notice you like to pull your feet up onto any chair you're sitting on. This one has enough room to do that."

Her heart did that curious melting thing. He'd noticed the habit she'd had since as far back as she could remember. He'd noticed, and he'd found the perfect chair for her to relax in. It was much more difficult resisting him than she thought it would be because he really cared enough to notice everything about her.

Siena drew her knees up and rested her chin on top, her eyes on him as he moved around the kitchen—in the dark.

"You like grilled cheese?"

"Do you grill it in butter?"

His white teeth flashed and then disappeared. A small grin, but every cell in her body reacted. He was beautiful. Handsome.

"Is there any other way?"

"Nope." She could look at him forever. When she was a teenager she'd stared at pictures of him, spent hours studying him from every angle. She especially liked his wild hair and his exotic, unusual eyes. Silver. Gray. Dark. He had so many different colors to his eyes depending on his mood. Now she knew part of that was his leopard.

"Elijah? Why would my grandfather want you dead? Why would he want any of them dead? When I confronted him, he said he had to strike before you did. What did that mean?"

She kept her eyes on him, leopard eyes, using the sight that allowed her to see six times better than her human eyes in the dark. She used her leopard senses to listen for a lie. She wanted to catch every change in his body language.

Elijah sighed. "These are things you don't need to know or worry about, Siena. That life, that part of my life, should never touch you. It will, but I'd prefer to keep it to a minimum. You knowing anything puts you at risk."

There was honesty in his voice. She didn't hear the slightest hint of subterfuge, and she listened for it.

"I'm already at risk," she pointed out. "I'm sitting here with you, Elijah, in your kitchen. In your shirt. Your baby in my womb. Your cock was just inside of me. I'm already at risk, and I want to know what risk there is for my child before I make any commitment to you."

The moment the words came out of her mouth, his gaze jumped to hers. Glittery. Slashing. Silver this time. Dark silver. Cutting silver. His leopard was there, stamped on his face, a predatory animal, all male and very, very dominant. He had gone completely still. A statue, standing there on the other side of the aisle, frozen in place, a frying pan in his fist.

She didn't fool herself that she was safe. She knew what

a leopard could do. One jump could cover sixty feet easily. She was far less than sixty feet away from him.

"You're sitting in my kitchen. In my shirt. My baby in your womb. My cock was just inside of you, and deep inside, you've still got my seed. Make no mistake, Siena. None. You're already committed to me. You made that commitment when you gave your body to me. When I came inside you and your eyes went dazed and that beauty was on your face. Don't think you can give that to me and then take it back. Because, baby, that shit is fucking not going to happen. Not ever."

His voice was rough. Edgy. Harsh even. There was no hint of softness, or gentle or tender. She found herself facing the savage nature of the leopard. They stared at each other, and Siena refused to back down.

She lifted her chin in defiance, her hand coming up to cover her belly protectively. His gaze fastened on her chin and his eyes went darker. Sexy. All male. Uh-oh. She'd, without saying a word, made things worse. She knew that just by his eyes, and when he put down the frying pan and stalked across the room toward her.

9

SIENA didn't break eye contact. Her heart beat wildly as Elijah prowled across the room in utter silence. He didn't make a single sound. She could hear her own heart pounding and the roar of blood in her ears as he approached. He could intimidate from across the room, but up close, he was terrifying. She held her breath when, for a moment, he towered over her.

Abruptly he crouched low, catching her chin in his hand. "You. Do. *Not. Ever.* Look at me like that. I'm *not* Paolo. I would never hurt you. My leopard would never hurt you."

His fingers tightened on her chin and he bent his head until his mouth was inches from hers. "What I might do, you keep defying me like this, is tie you to my bed and fuck your brains out until you cry for mercy and beg me to put a ring on your finger. I'm not above doing that. Using sex to get my way. And baby, fair warning, I'm damned good at sex. I can get very creative. So you think to run from me and take away my woman because things get a little dicey, think again."

She sucked in her breath, mostly because she wanted to see how truly creative he could be and that meant continuing to defy him, and truthfully, he scared the crap out of her when he was looking so lethal.

Elijah's mouth brushed hers and just that light touch sent a jarring bolt of lightning straight to her core. His eyes didn't close. Neither did hers. They stared at each other, his gaze so intense she felt her resistance was melting.

Siena shook her head to try to break his mesmerizing spell. "You can't order me to stay with you, Elijah. I need to figure this out. I'm not just making decisions for me, but for my baby as well."

His eyes glittered ominously, and her heart sank. Definitely a mistake. A really, really bad mistake.

"*Our* baby. *Our* child. Not yours, Siena. That baby is mine as well. When you're making those decisions, it isn't just you and the baby. It's you, the baby and *me*. I'm part of that. Don't start by trying to cut me out, because I can tell you, and you'd better listen to me, I'm not getting cut out. Not from our child's life and not from your life. We're working this shit out."

She pressed her hand hard around her baby. His gaze dropped instantly, noting that small, protective, *minute* movement. His much larger hand covered hers.

"We're better together, Siena. Look at us. The two of us. Together, watching out for our child. I'm the shield. The armor. I'm the one standing in front of you both. *Shielding* you from anything. From everything."

God. *God.* She wanted him. She wanted him in her life. She wanted the crazy, macho, alpha leopard with his sexy eyes and velvet voice and hard, muscular body. She wanted his protection. She wanted all of it—except his lifestyle. Whatever that was. *Because she didn't know.*

"Elijah." She tried soft. Not defiant. She realized defiant

brought out the leopard in him. The dominant. "I'm not trying
to take anything away from you. I'm trying to understand.
Maybe I'm not using the right words, but I didn't know what
kind of terrible things my grandfather was into. My parents
were killed by a car bomb. I was kidnapped. I was used to
deliver wine so a hit man could sneak into houses and kill
people. I lived a lie for years. I will not do that again. I will
not have *our* child doing that. So you need to tell me what I
have to know."

She reached out her hand and cupped the side of his face,
running her thumb along his jaw. "Honey, I'd so much rather
not know, but I can't do that. I really, really can't, so if you
want me in your life, you're going to have to tell me what I'm
facing and let me make a decision."

He stared at her for what seemed an eternity, abruptly
pulled away and was on his feet, pacing across the room in
long, angry strides, swearing in Spanish. One arm lashed out
and for a split second she actually saw a paw as it swiped at
the frying pan on the counter and sent it flying. It hit the wall
with a loud crash and clattered to the floor.

She bit down hard on her lower lip and pressed her hand
tighter against her belly. She had really roused the leopard.
She curled deeper into the chair, grateful that Elijah paced
back and forth on the opposite side of the aisle, keeping it
between them. She knew he was attempting to make her feel
safe by staying on the other side of the room, but she could
actually *feel* the oppressive air, so heavy with his temper.

He didn't want to tell her anything. That was a really bad
sign. Still, she couldn't back down. She wanted to—for him.
For herself even. But she couldn't, for her child. She sat in
the chair, watching Elijah closely. He was angry, yes. She
could see that, but not at her. That took a moment to sink in.
He was angry with the situation and it dawned on her that
he was afraid of losing her. *He didn't want to lose her.* Her
heart melted even more.

She'd been honest with him. She couldn't have her child

living in a situation that wasn't safe. Or that was illegal and totally wrong. Drug trafficking? Gun-running ? What exactly was Elijah involved in that he didn't want her to know about? What had her grandfather been involved in aside from having their friends murdered?

With a little sigh she got to her feet, took a deep breath and padded barefoot across the room, to the other side of the island where Elijah stood. She moved in close and wrapped her arms around his middle, leaning her weight into him. He stood stiffly for a moment, every muscle locked in place, his body feeling like a steel wall. Very slowly, almost reluctantly he put his arms around her, locking her to him.

"Honey, I'm asking for an explanation. You said to me you weren't a good man. When you said it, I thought . . . I'd hoped you meant you were dangerous. That you were capable of doing things to protect your family, not that you did something illegal such as selling drugs. I need to know what my grandfather was into because I have the feeling that I inherited his businesses. I have the feeling you know *exactly* what he was into. He didn't have a reputation, not like your family has always had. So I need to know what you're into so I can make an informed decision."

His hand came up to the back of her head, his palm fitting there, holding her to him. She felt the tension coiled so tight in him.

"I can't lose you, Siena." His voice was raw with emotion.

When she tried to lift her face away from his chest so she could look into his eyes, he held her still.

"Don't. Not yet. You have to understand. Never in my life have I had someone who was mine. Who looked at me the way you do, as if I was worth something. Me. The man. Not a Lospostos who might do something for them. Not a man to be seen in public with. You see me. I see it in your eyes, Siena. I've always seen it. A leopard doesn't tolerate a female—the wrong female—for very long. I needed sex. I walked around as hard as a fucking rock and I needed a body to get rid of that ache, but I never felt a fucking thing other than relief. Not until you. Not until I saw you sitting across a table from me with your beautiful eyes, so green a man could get lost forever there. That hair, wild, baby. So wild I knew the wild was in you. That the moment I touched you, you would go up in flames and take me with you."

His arm locked around her lower hips, pulling her body into his until it felt as if he were imprinted on her skin, in her bones.

"Suddenly sex wasn't just sex. Suddenly it mattered who was with me. It's always been you, Siena. You're the one who got to me. Got inside me. You're in so deep, and I know that sounds crazy because you've only been with me a couple of weeks, but really, it's been years. As sick as that is, it's been years."

"That doesn't sound sick to me, Elijah," she protested. She had to give him the truth. "For me, it's always been you. Ever since I sat across from you at that table, I never looked at another man."

"I know that, baby. I know you gave me that. You gave me your body, something no one else had. Mine. For me. A gift beyond anything I could have ever imagined. Do you think I want to risk losing that?"

Siena pressed her uninjured cheek tight against his chest. She couldn't help but hear the raw honesty in his voice. He didn't attempt to hide it from her. He hadn't hidden his temper, and he also didn't hide how much he wanted her.

"Elijah, fix me my grilled cheese and start with my grandfather. You know if he's some kind of crime lord and I'm inheriting his businesses, I'll need to know what I'm in for. Those businesses are what Paolo is after."

"He's after all of it. You included. A leopard doesn't go that crazy unless he thinks someone is fucking with what's his."

"You have to stop dropping f-bombs before the baby's here, honey." She tipped her head back, and this time he let her. "I'm not Paolo's. I never was."

"No. But you're mine. You were born to be mine. Siena, I'm asking you, baby, don't take that away from me."

Siena closed her eyes, trying to block out the sight of his face. It had been a mistake to look at him, look into his silver eyes, darkened now with a kind of fear she never thought she'd ever be capable of putting on someone's face, let alone a man as strong as Elijah. There was raw pain there. She'd done that.

"I'm a lot stronger than you think I am," she said.

He was silent a moment, studying her face. She felt him take a breath, and then he nodded. "All right, baby, how about we do this. I'll lay it out a step at a time. Not all at once."

She liked that idea. A lot. "Give me time to process and don't push at me."

His thumb came up to rub across her lips. "I can do that. But you promise me that you won't run. We talk things out. You don't understand something or you're afraid, you talk it over with me. I'm not losing you because you get scared, Siena."

She nodded her assent. He'd asked for time, and she'd pushed him, scared for her child, but she could do one step at a time. She could do that.

"I need your word. Say it to me. You give me your word and I'll know you'll keep it. No matter how scared you get or whatever fucked-up thing is whispered in your ear, I know you'll come to me first if you promise me. I swear to you, *mi amorcito*, no matter how bad it is, I'll tell you the truth."

She searched his eyes for a long time. She was in there. Inside of him. Wrapped deep. She could see that on his face— he let her see it. She was slowly becoming more and more aware of the gifts her leopard gave her—and one was the ability to hear the truth. She heard it in his voice.

"I promise I'll talk to you first and get the answers I need, always." She could give him that. She *wanted* to give him that, because she wanted, more than anything, to have it work out between them. He was the man she'd waited for.

She knew it in her heart. But it wasn't just her she had to think about.

He reluctantly released her, and she curled up in the chair, propping her head up with one hand, studying him as he leaned down to pick up the frying pan.

"You might consider, Elijah, before the baby's born, that you should get that temper under control."

His gaze cut to her, and then he rinsed the pan in the sink. "That's never going to happen, *querida*, so don't hold your breath. I'm leopard. I stay in control, but I have to release it somehow or my male gets so edgy it's nearly impossible to hold him back. I think we feed on each other's bad temper. But you, and certainly our children, will never be in danger."

Our children. She liked that he thought of a future for them. She didn't respond, because she didn't want to have to ask him again to explain what he did. How he came to work for Drake's security company when he was a major player in the underworld. She had said one step at time and he'd told her he'd lay it out for her. She was going to give him the opportunity to do it.

Elijah deftly buttered bread and placed it in the frying pan, adding slices of cheese and then putting on the second piece of bread. "A man by the name of Rafe Cordeau disappeared a few weeks ago. Cordeau was a major player in Louisiana. He ran everything from drugs, guns and a very large stable of—um—prostitutes to business protection there. He had his hand in just about everything, and he made a fortune at it. No law enforcement agency was ever able to bring him down, and they tried. Over and over. He was known for his violent retaliation. He had no qualms about torture and murder. Every witness that ever thought about testifying against him disappeared, and most turned up dead. They died hard. The others simply disappeared."

Her grandfather had mentioned Rafe Cordeau. She nodded

her head. The butter sizzled and the scent of melting cheese reached her. Her stomach growled. She was definitely hungry. She rubbed her chin on the tops of her knees and waited.

"When Cordeau disappeared, he left a huge, very lucrative territory up for grabs. Everyone made a move on it. Some were willing to divide it up and share, others wanted it for themselves, and a couple of Cordeau's men were making a bid for it as well. Your grandfather was one of the bosses who wanted to keep it all for himself. He had Luigi Baldini and Angelo Fabbri taken out because he feared they'd fight him for it. Angelo was making noises in that direction. Antonio went after me for the same reason."

She closed her eyes and shook her head. "And Don Miguel and Carlo Bianchi? That was months ago, *before* Cordeau disappeared. Carlo was his friend for *years*. He spoke at his funeral. He cried. I had to finish his talk for him."

"Don Miguel was always a threat to him. It was no secret he wanted to expand his business, and your grandfather refused to allow it. Carlo Bianchi had formed an alliance with Don Miguel, mostly because Carlo had grown weak and Don Miguel was eating away at the edges of his territory. By cementing his relationship with Don Miguel, Carlo could keep his territory together. Or so he thought."

"So it was all about power plays. They weren't really friends at all, after what? Fifty years? Sixty? For money?"

"Mostly for power," Elijah said. He slid the grilled cheese sandwich onto a plate, added a few chips and took it to the table. "Come eat, sweetheart."

"Why would my grandfather use me to deliver the wine?" She uncurled her legs and seated herself at the kitchen table. She'd seen the long, gleaming oak table with inlaid wood as they'd passed the formal dining room. This was much smaller, but no less beautiful. She ran her hand over the glossy surface before she slipped into the wide, padded chair.

Elijah sighed. Went silent.

Her gaze jumped to his face. "Elijah?"

"How much do you remember about the second kidnapping attempt?"

She swallowed hard. Shook her head. "Not much. I remember more about the first one. The second one I think I went into shock. They stabbed a needle in my arm, and everything was fuzzy after that. Not much," she repeated lamely, because she really didn't and it bothered her a lot.

"Don Miguel was always suspected of that attempt on you by most of the bosses."

Siena gasped and went still. She'd known Don Miguel all of her life. He had been friends with her grandfather. Close friends.

"He convinced your grandfather that it wasn't him. Truthfully, your grandfather, being leopard, would hear a lie. So if Don Miguel was guilty, and I'm fairly certain he was, your grandfather would have known. It would be very like Antonio to want revenge on Don Miguel—and no one else would ever suspect you of distracting someone while a hit man entered their home. Because you truly were innocent, you wouldn't give off anything that would tell the mark he was in danger. Antonio would like that. You delivering his reserve while Marco enters the house. What a sweet revenge."

"That's *awful*." But she could see Antonio waiting patiently for years for her to grow up. He would do that. He liked his petty revenge on anyone he thought had slighted him. It would be just like him.

"The other very real reason is if you were part of the murder, he could force you to do what he wanted because you would be tainted. Your grandfather liked to control everything and everyone in his world."

The air left her lungs in a long rush. More than anything, her grandfather had wanted her to marry Paolo. She had always laughed, brushing the idea off because she wasn't the least physically attracted to the man. He hadn't asked her out, or acted interested in her until a couple of years earlier when he began watching her closely. The way he watched her lately had actually creeped her out, so much so that she had taken an additional couple years of schooling just to avoid going home. Paolo hadn't worried about trying to court her because he believed he had her no matter what. Now she knew why.

"Once he sent you in, and he probably figured he'd only do it that one time to exact his revenge, it worked so well that he kept doing it."

She pressed her lips together to keep from crying. Everything Elijah told her made sense.

"What would you like to drink?"

His voice was soft. Gentle. She had to blink back tears. "Water," she answered, without looking up. Absently, she traced patterns in the tabletop. "He wanted me to marry Paolo. He talked about it all the time. Ever since I turned eighteen. I thought he was joking at first. Paolo never even looked at me then. Even that night, after Paolo beat me and Nonno saw what he'd done to me, he still wanted me to marry him."

"Baby," Elijah said softly. "Don't. I told you I didn't want to share this shit with you. It hurts. I don't like being the one to cause that hurt."

"You aren't, Elijah. I need to know this. It was my grandfather who hurt me. He couldn't love me for some reason, and I guess I'll never really know why."

"Never for one minute think that he didn't love you, Siena. Your grandfather loved you."

She lifted her gaze to his face. "He didn't though, Elijah. I'm not certain he knew what love was."

"He loved you, *mi amor*. No one could have you in their life and not love you. He lost sight of what was important. Once your grandmother died, he lost himself. My uncle and aunt used to talk about it. How different he was. How hard he became. How focused on being at the top. Before, when she was alive, he laughed all the time. He had parties and opened the winery to his friends. He was very closed off after she died."

His hand swept down the length of her hair in a caress. Gentle. So gentle her heart did a curious little melting around the edges and her stomach fluttered as if a million butterflies had taken wing.

"I was lost too, and he sent me away."

Elijah put a glass of water in front of her and then pulled out the chair beside hers. He sat down, his thigh pressing against hers. Close. Staying close to her. For comfort. To make her feel safe. She realized it was the little things that mattered. He did those little things. He'd done them in the hospital. Braiding her hair. Noticing her lips were dry and smoothing on lip balm. Each time the pain got too bad, he'd already called the nurse. If anyone opened the door, his body had glided between the door and the hospital bed, shielding her from sight.

"You're not eating, Siena," he reminded softly.

She picked up half of the sandwich. "It's very thoughtful of you, trying to convince me that my grandfather loved me, but he didn't even want me home with him."

"Baby, I was there. In your home, having dinner with you. Do you remember that? He sat at the head of the table. He was laughing then. The only times I ever saw him laughing was when you were around. He had a great booming laugh that could make everyone in a room want to laugh with him. He looked at you so proudly, and he talked about how well you did in school. Do you remember him telling everyone that you already knew everything there was to know about growing grapes for the wines? That you'd been following him around the vineyards since you were first able to walk just absorbing information like a sponge. He bragged about you, Siena, all the time. Your name came up in any conversation and he was smiling and bragging."

She bit her lip hard. She did remember his laugh. The board games he would play with her after dinner when she was home on her short visits from school. She hadn't wanted to remember because then it would hurt too much, and she had to acknowledge her part in his death. She'd driven Paolo over the edge.

Her eyes burned and tears spilled over. "If I'd just kept my mouth shut," she whispered. "Elijah, I shouldn't have tipped my hand like that. If only I'd not said a thing. But it was such a betrayal that he hadn't fired Paolo on the spot. I wanted to hurt both of them. I knew it was his dream to have me marry Paolo, and I knew Paolo wanted the inheritance."

His hand caught her chin and he turned her head toward him. "I need you to look at me, baby," he said softly. "I need you to hear me. Can you do that for me?"

"You have to stop being sweet to me, Elijah." A fresh flood of tears tracked down her face. Embarrassed, she tried to turn her face away, but his hand, firm but gentle, prevented movement. She had cried in front of him too many times, but her brain had simply refused to process her grandfather's death until that moment. "I can't pretend I didn't say those awful things to him. I can't pretend Paolo didn't shoot him because he was going to change his mind and let me choose someone else."

"You aren't thinking this through, Siena," he said, his thumb moving through the tears on her face. "He couldn't dictate to you who you would marry. Both of them knew that. Paolo didn't court you because he was certain he didn't have to. We aren't in a country where there are arranged marriages. All you would have to do is say no. Both of them had to know you could do that, yet Paolo felt confident enough to beat you and then calmly walk downstairs and talk to your grandfather. He didn't act remorseful. You told Drake he didn't even say he was sorry."

Had she said that? Drake had asked her a lot of questions

when she was there in the hospital and she'd answered all of them as honestly as possible. Elijah had been in the room because he never seemed to leave. He'd heard everything she'd said—and clearly he remembered it.

"I don't understand what you mean."

"Paolo has something on you, something to connect you to the murders. He's counting on that to force you to marry him. He's so certain you'll do what he wants that he hasn't bothered to court you or pretend that he's going to treat you decently."

Her heart stopped and then began to stutter in her chest. Hard. The blood drained from her face and she tasted fear in her mouth. Stricken, her eyes met Elijah's. "Oh. My. God. He does." She shook her head. "But he can't. I didn't even know they were killing anyone. What could they possibly have on me?"

"The wine. It connects you to all of the murders. You show up with the wine and within hours the man you visited is dead. Drake checked into it with his police friends and there was never a case of wine at any of the houses. Marco had to have brought the wine back with him."

She chewed slowly, not tasting the delicious cheese sandwich. "If the wine wasn't there, how could it possibly throw suspicion on me?"

"Babe." His voice went soft. Gentle. "Everyone these days has security cameras, and you can bet anyone in our business has them. Marco had to have removed the tapes. He must have brought them back to Paolo, so Paolo has evidence of you arriving with your case of wine. The case of wine that was never found at any of the crime scenes."

Her heart thudded again. The sandwich tasted like cardboard and she forced herself to swallow. "Anyone in our business?" she repeated. "You're in the same business my grandfather was in?"

She'd dreaded asking the question. All along she'd been dragging her feet, avoiding it, hoping that a miracle would happen and he would be anything but what he appeared. The Lospostos name was associated with crime. With murder.

Elijah's gaze turned diamond hard just that fast. The soft lines in his face disappeared and he looked . . . intimidating. Dangerous. Very, very scary. His hand slid along the back of her chair and then into her hair.

"Baby, I grew up in a family so deep in that shit we bathed in it. Every relative I had was or is involved. I cut my teeth on enforcing and then gunrunning. I told you from the beginning I wasn't clean. I wouldn't have been sitting at your grandfather's table if I had been."

The blow was much harder to take than she expected. She found herself hunched over, the cheese sandwich a stone in her stomach. She couldn't look at him anymore because he would see how that piece of news affected her—she didn't have a poker face. His admission shouldn't have stunned her, but it did.

"Mi amor," he said softly. "You know my name. You hear or read the news. I'm not going to hide what my family is. It would be ludicrous to try. I didn't know any other way of life. I didn't know there was any other way of life."

She twisted her fingers together in her lap beneath the cover of the table, keeping her head down, allowing her hair to fall around her face, hiding her expression. She'd promised him she'd give herself time to process, but how did anyone process what he was admitting?

"Finish eating, Siena, while we talk."

She pushed away from the table. "I'm not hungry anymore." If she could have, she would have run from him. Run from the room with her hands over her ears. It was so much easier to be the girl coming home from boarding school believing her grandfather owned a winery and just didn't like having little children around.

Elijah didn't argue with her, rising with her as she stood up. Instead, he leaned down and lifted her into his arms, cradling her against his chest. Her stomach fluttered. Her heart somersaulted. He'd held her so carefully after he found her, running with her to the helicopter. She remembered the feel of his arms and his hard chest. The steady sound of his heart beating. He made her feel safe when her entire world was collapsing around her. The very strange thing was, she still felt safe in spite of the information he'd just disclosed to her.

Siena sighed and slid her arms around his neck, buried her face against his shoulder and hung on, her mind racing as he carried her back through his beautiful, perfect house. She loved his house. She loved being in his arms. She loved his wild hair and his rock-hard body. She didn't love what he was telling her, but she did love that he told her the truth.

He moved with a fluid, casual elegance, his muscles rippling subtly, suggestively beneath his skin. "Thanks for not judging me, Siena."

It wasn't about judging him. It was about having a baby with him. Raising a child with him. She tightened her hold on him and pressed her face deeper into him, breathing him in. She even loved the way he smelled. She was so far gone on him she could barely separate her dreams of him from the reality.

"Growing up in a home like that, with the violence, the guns, fists, expected to be that person because you're the head of the family's grandson and then son, you have something to prove all the time. Hell, baby, my own family expected it of me. My leopard made me fast and violent. Strong. I excelled, and my family pushed me to really excel. To be that man. The punisher. The enforcer. The killer."

Siena shook her head. She couldn't imagine being a child in those circumstances. She'd been devastated when she'd lost her parents so violently, but she hadn't known why. She didn't understand that her grandfather's world invited violence. That someone had retaliated for some move her grandfather had made.

She stiffened. Of course. She hadn't put that together. "My

grandfather made a move against another family and that's why my parents were killed." She made it a statement.

"My uncle murdered his own brother," Elijah said. "I was a kid, but he wanted to groom me properly to take over the family business. He was extremely violent and he enjoyed hurting others. I have a sister. Rachel. My uncle threatened her. If I didn't do what he wanted me to do, she paid the price."

She lifted her head and looked him in the eyes. His eyes were so unusual. Quicksilver. Mercury. Dark antiqued silver. Passionate. Intense. Deadly. The stare of the leopard. He was all those things, all those moods. He was Elijah, opening himself to her. Giving her a priceless gift and in doing so, risking her turning away from him.

His glittering gaze searched hers for a long moment and then his mouth descended on hers. He poured himself into his kiss. Gave her who he was. Commanding. A takeover. Savage. Brutal even. So good. So hot. She kissed him back, giving herself up to him. Uncaring that no one would ever be able to match his kisses and she was risking everything.

He needed her. She felt that in his kiss too. He. Needed. *Her*. Siena Arnotto. No other women. She shifted in his arms to kiss him back just as deeply. Just as passionately. Her breasts felt swollen and achy. Her nipples hardened and rubbed against the material of the shirt she wore. Her body went boneless, pliant. The smoldering deep inside became a slow, hot burn that threatened to consume her just as it had the first time she drove up to his house.

"Siena." He whispered her name, a combination of husky and velvet. So sexy. An urgent need.

"Yes," she answered softly, because there was no other answer. It would be yes every time with him.

"Unbutton your shirt." He carried her through to the bedroom with long, ground-eating strides, as if he couldn't wait one more moment for her.

The blood rushed through her veins and roared in her

ears. Her hands dropped to the buttons and she fumbled as she tried to get them open fast. The moment she had them open, she slid her hand down his chest as he put her feet on the floor, his hands at her waist, steadying her. She kept sliding her hand down until she found the thick bulge in his jeans, rubbing, needing.

"Get it done, baby," he whispered as his hands came up to cup her breasts, his thumbs sliding over her nipples.

She found herself fumbling with the buttons of his jeans, her breath coming in ragged gasps as his fingers rolled and tugged and then his mouth closed over her breast, pulling it deep into his mouth while his hand did all sorts of delicious things to her other one. It seemed to take forever to free him from the confines of his jeans.

"Get them off of me right now," he urged, his mouth still working, sending more flames dancing through her body.

She shoved the jeans from his hips and tugged to bring them down his thighs. His hands went to her hair, fisted there while she bent to strip him. He kicked the jeans aside and dragged her back up, tipping her head back so he could take her mouth.

He caught her bottom and lifted her easily. "Wrap your legs around me, baby," he ordered softly. "Hurry, sweetheart. I need you right now."

She loved the urgency in his voice. The way his fingers bit deep. The rough gravel to his velvet voice. She wrapped her legs tight around his narrow hips and hooked her ankles as she locked her fingers behind his neck.

Then he was in her. Filling her. Driving her body down over his, impaling her with the thick, long length of him, and she'd never felt so full, or so hot. She cried out, the soft sound accompanying his deeper voice. She loved that too. The sound of their bodies coming together, so urgent, almost desperate, along with the sound of their ragged breathing added to the absolute beauty and excitement of the moment.

She pushed her face into his neck as he pounded into her. Hard. Hot.

"Fucking amazing, baby," he whispered hoarsely. "Scorching hot and so damned tight I'm not going to last two more minutes."

"More," she urged. "Harder."

Every jolting stroke was glorious, sending fire streaking through her. Feeding the burn. She wanted all of him. She wanted him to give her everything he was.

He swore in his language, a deep soft string of curses that should have blistered her ears, but it only added to the urgency of the moment, to the storm that grew inside of her. He tipped her body, going deeper, taking her breath. Her soul.

"*Dios*, baby, so fucking good."

The deeper he drove into her, the more her breath burned raw in her lungs, in her throat. She curled her fingers into the waves of his thick hair and bit down on his shoulder to keep from screaming out her pleasure. It was building and building and she knew when it came, it was going to be amazing. Perfection. The biggest and best.

"Ride me, Siena. Hard." His fingers bit deep into her bottom, urging her up and down the length of him as he pounded into her. "That's it. Like that."

She had the rhythm now, and she ground herself onto him, and kept grinding, the friction so hot she thought they might both burst into flames, but it didn't matter, not when she could feel so good. "Elijah." She whispered his name, her talisman, because she needed an anchor when her entire body was going to fly apart.

"Hold on for me, *mi vida*," he urged, his voice so sensual she felt her entire core pulse with the need to let go. "Give me another minute."

She couldn't. There was no way, but she did, grinding down, wanting him with her. He gripped her hair and yanked her head back, his hooded eyes completely silver, intense, his face dark with passion, lined with such sensuality her breath hitched in her throat.

"Give it to me now, Siena. All of it."

God. *God*. That was so sexy. The way he stared into her eyes, the way he watched as the orgasm rushed over her. He continued thrusting. Hard. Driving right through her fragmenting body, his eyes never leaving hers. She felt him take her there, right out into subspace, where she floated in bliss. He kept pounding into her, keeping her body right there, over and over until one orgasm slid into another.

Then he buried his face in her neck and let go. She felt him swell, that steel shaft, already impossibly thick, pushing and stretching her tight muscles, and then blasting her with hot, hot seed, triggering a third orgasm. His body settled into a sweeter, much more gentle rhythm, gliding in and out of hers, while her sheath convulsed and gripped him.

"So beautiful, *mi amor*," he whispered against her neck. "Did I hurt you?"

She hadn't thought so. She felt only beauty, paradise, but now that she was floating down, she felt the burn in her leg. It hurt, but not enough for her to want to change positions.

Elijah lifted his head. "Baby? Talk to me."

"I can't talk. I can't think. Let's go to bed," she suggested. "I want to sleep with you curled around me. I want to wake up in your arms. I'll take my time processing, and we'll talk when I can handle more. Is that okay with you?"

His hand tightened in her hair. His fingers dug deeper into her bottom. "That sounds perfect to me, but you didn't answer my question."

She sighed. "You've got your bossy on all over again."

"Siena." There was warning in his voice.

"My leg hurts a little bit, but it would anyway."

He carried her to the bed and very gently laid her down as he slipped out of her. She had the urge to reach out and grab him, to pull him back inside of her. Instead she reached up to trace the line of his jaw.

"Stay with me, Siena," he said softly. "Keep looking at me like that. Always. I'll always need that look you have right now."

She wanted to give him that. She wanted to stay with him. Her free hand went to her belly where their child was already growing. "I want that more than anything," she answered honestly, because it was the strict truth.

10

THE pool sparkled a deep blue. Siena had never seen a swimming pool quite like the one in the courtyard of Elijah's house. It was extremely large, included a high waterfall with a slide and a smaller cascading waterfall that poured into a hot pool. A narrow lazy river surrounded the entire pool where one could float with the current. She'd been at Elijah's home for two and a half weeks, and the stitches on her hip and down her leg were gone. Even her ribs had mostly stopped hurting.

She was excited that she'd been given the okay to swim and she'd been doing laps every morning and evening in an attempt to stretch out the skin on her back and legs. She loved the pool. She didn't love the fact that her hair was always wet or drying, or that already, even though she knew exactly when she got pregnant, there was already a pooch. Her waist wasn't thick yet, but there was a definite pooch already, she threw up often and she wasn't more than seven weeks along. But she *loved* the pool.

The afternoon sun poured down on her as she floated in the little river, one hand trailing in the water. Emma Bannaconni and Catarina Perez floated just a few feet from her, each in their inner tube, heads thrown back watching the clouds as they drifted through the current. Emma's belly moved, and Siena touched her own with her fingertips.

The sound of children's laughter turned her head. Jake, Emma's husband, lifted his son out of the water and sent him flying. He landed with a splash, and his daughter yelled excitedly to be flung through the air.

"It's sort of a revelation to see Jake Bannaconni playing with his children," Siena observed. "If anyone saw this, they'd be shocked."

Emma smiled. "Jake is an amazing father. Even when they were first born. He sat up at night and rocked them or watched me rock them."

"But completely different in public or at his work," Siena said, remembering the steely-eyed man she'd faced when asking for Drake's location.

Emma nodded. "Jake is the best father I can imagine for our children, and he treats me like a princess . . . well . . . most of the time. He's got a temper and he's bossy."

Catarina burst out laughing. "You think your man is bossy, mine patented bossiness. Ever since he's known I was carrying a baby, he's been Mr. Protection and double the bossiness, which, by the way, I didn't think was possible," Catarina continued.

Siena's heart jumped and she rubbed her hand over her growing tummy and swung her head around toward Catarina, who was behind her. She nearly tipped her tube over craning her neck looking at Catarina's flat stomach. "You're pregnant too?"

Catarina was married to Eli Perez, and they owned the bordering ranch. Siena had caught a glimpse of Eli when he'd dropped Catarina off. He'd looked tough and hard, and when he caught Catarina's hand as she started up the stairs, he'd jerked her back around and pulled her body tight into his. His mouth had come down on hers in a gesture so intimate, Siena had turned away.

"Yes, I'm three months and then some. Eli is beside himself. He thinks he's the coolest man in town." Catarina burst out laughing.

Siena closed her eyes, absorbing the sound. She'd never done this in her life before. She didn't have girlfriends to float in the water with and just gossip about everyday life and the husbands they loved. It was surreal. Perfect. The lazy clouds floating by. The sound of the children and Jake's laughter in the background. The deep blue of the water in the pool. Most of all, sharing with two women who seemed to understand what her life was like without judging her.

"I'm pregnant too," she announced. Her eyes flew open at the admission. It had just slipped out. "And it's a little embarrassing that I'm already beginning to show and you don't even look like you could possibly be pregnant."

Catarina grinned at her. "Oh, that's just great. Eli thinks he knocked me up fast; Elijah didn't wait at all. What was it, your first time together?"

Siena blushed. Turned the color of a ripe tomato. Both Emma and Catarina sat up straight, rocking their inner tubes.

"It was," Emma said. "He got you pregnant the first time he ever touched you. He probably did it on purpose."

"We were a little heated," Siena said hastily, defending Elijah. "*Both* of us. I didn't think about using protection either."

Catarina exchanged a look with Emma, and both burst out laughing. "Honey," Emma said, "we're leopard. Our men are leopard. You don't have to try to explain or defend yourself. We both know what it's like."

Siena rubbed her hand down the long puckered, ridged skin along her leg. "When are you due, Emma?" She'd noticed Jake hovered close to his wife and never seemed to lose sight of her.

"Doc's going to take the baby next month," Emma said.

"It's a little early, but they don't want me going into labor. Jake's insisting on a million doctors being present, but I just agree with everything he demands since he agreed to let me have another baby. I nearly died when Draya was born and he's never gotten over that. I go on bed rest in another week as a precaution only."

"Eli thinks Jake was nuts to agree to let you carry the baby," Catarina announced with a small sigh. She splashed water up over her dangling legs. "That's how bad he is." She wiggled her fingers in Siena's direction. "What's Elijah like? He never smiles. In fact, he looks scarier than Eli or Jake. Is he good to you?"

Siena felt Emma's gaze center on her and knew immediately it was no idle question. Both Emma and Catarina were worried about how Elijah treated her. "He's the sweetest man I've ever known. Arrogant. Bossy. But so sweet he makes my heart melt." She sighed and turned her face back to the water.

"But?" Emma prompted. She reached out and caught Siena's tube, linking them together as the current took them around a bend. "What's wrong? I can tell something is. We both can. Are you afraid of him?"

Catarina reached out as well and caught the other side of Siena's tube. The two women hitched closer, keeping their voices lowered.

"No. Elijah would never hurt me," Siena defended immediately. "He might not show that side of himself often to others, but he's incredibly sweet to me."

"I've known him a long while," Emma said. "He's always been respectful but distant. Jake really likes him and I know Drake does as well, but he doesn't laugh—not ever that I remember. The mess his family created for him is just plain scary." She tipped her head back to look at Siena. "Is that what worries you?"

Siena didn't have girlfriends, but she knew they talked to one another. She wanted to be friends with these women, but Elijah was alone. Too alone. He only had her. She might not feel she could stay in his world, but she was planning to try. She'd promised him she would talk to him. That didn't mean sharing anything he said with the rest of the world, not even the women trying to be her friends.

"I have a lot of problems I'm bringing to the table," she said quietly. "My grandfather was murdered, and I think the man who did it will try to kill Elijah." She'd thought about what Paolo's next move would be and she was fairly certain he would go after Elijah, unless he decided to take the chance of killing her before he established himself as her grandfather's successor. She'd tried to have the conversation with Elijah, but he simply told her not to worry about it, like that would stop her.

"Elijah takes everything on himself." She chose her words carefully. "He doesn't want me worrying, so when I bring things up, like I believe someone will try to kill him, he sort of blows me off, expecting me to just not worry my empty little head."

Catarina snickered. "I think that must be a leopard trait. Eli doesn't want anything to touch me. I was raised in Rafe Cordeau's home. He was my guardian. He was a big crime lord in Louisiana. I escaped, but he followed me along with some of his men. I nearly got Eli killed, but he doesn't want me to even listen when he's talking about Cordeau's network and who might be taking it over. By the way, that scares me, because I'm afraid they'll send someone else after me and that would put Eli back in harm's way. He won't listen to anything I say though."

Emma nodded. "Definitely a leopard trait. Jake would put me in an insulated, bulletproof bubble if he could get away with it."

Siena found herself laughing. The women understood. She secretly hugged herself because she was certain Elijah was the sweetest out of all three men, although the sound of Jake's laughter was truly appealing, so maybe he ran a close second.

She felt eyes on her and knew before she turned her head that Elijah was close. He stood just inside the shaded part of the patio. His wild hair was as unruly as ever, curling in a riot of waves and out-of-control swirls, spilling over his forehead and around his ears. His eyes were pure mercury, so liquid and intense her heart beat faster. His white tee stretched tight across his chest, defining his muscles rather than hiding them. As usual when in the house and casual, he was barefoot and wore his old blue jeans that rode low on his hips and shaped his body deliciously.

"You ladies ready for something cold?" he asked, but his gaze moved over Siena as if making certain she was having a good time. He did that a lot, just checking her. She knew with absolute certainty that his question was a ploy to allow him to ensure she was comfortable with the two women.

"Water," Emma called instantly.

"Same here," Catarina said.

"Make that three, honey," she said, pouring affection into her voice. She claimed him in front of the others. She wanted them to know she had his back, that they were together and whatever Elijah was—or wasn't—was hers and she accepted him.

At the tone of her voice, his eyes went dark. His gaze moved over her again. Hungry this time. The stamp of possession on his face. He didn't smile, but his look seared her. Branded her. The slow burn began all over again, smoldering deep in her core and between her legs. Her nipples peaked into two hard pebbles. The pads of her fingers itched to feel his skin beneath them.

He nodded to her, indicating he heard her, but he didn't move, holding her gaze for a long time before turning and walking away. He looked just as good from the back as he did from the front.

Emma and Catarina let out their collective breath. "Holy cow," Catarina said. "I'm in awe. That man smolders with sex."

Siena kept her silent agreement to herself because she was afraid if she opened her mouth nothing would actually come out. Maybe a croak.

"He's sinful," Emma said. "Totally sinful. And that's saying something, because I have Jake."

Siena nodded. Silently. Pressing her lips together, still staring at the spot where Elijah had been.

The flat of Catarina's hand sent a plume of cold water cascading over her. "Snap out of it," she ordered. "You're in a trance."

Siena burst out laughing. "He makes me that way."

"I can see why," Emma agreed. "He *smolders* with sex."

"You're not making it better," Siena pointed out, shifting in the inner tube so she could put her sizzling, burning, *needy* body deeper in the cold water, hoping to put out the fire. "I wake up in the morning to that man."

He was careful with her most of the time. Gentle. Almost reverent. Not always, and when he forgot to be, she loved it the most. The look on his face, the starkly sensual hunger in his eyes, made her think he'd gone beyond gentle right to full-out hot in the blink of an eye. Maybe it was the fact that he'd talked her into wearing the two-piece suit, which he bought for her to "sun" in.

She knew his real reason was he wanted her to get over being self-conscious of the four long rake marks down her back and the really, really ugly one on her leg. She'd managed to stop hiding the smaller, much more refined scar on her face. It was still red, but the line wasn't thick and jagged like those on her back and leg.

She was *very* curvy, and the halter top he chose revealed more cleavage than she'd ever shown before. It was black, stretchy material. A very thin ruffle of the same stretchy material framed her breasts in a wide vee and tied in a knot beneath them. The same ruffle stretched across her hips, very low, the material encasing her bottom. She'd noticed along with a little pooch that was growing fast into a bigger pooch, her already generous breasts were growing as well.

She'd put the bikini on at his insistence and would have taken it off right away, but Elijah had wrapped his arms around her and whispered how proud he was of her. Then he'd kissed her neck and she forgot all about being self-conscious. She still had a strawberry there, reminding her of how he, while biting her neck, slid the bottoms right off of her, bent her over the bed and pounded into her, holding her hips back so her leg wouldn't accidentally brush against the mattress.

She had her eyes glued to the door so she saw him the moment he returned, the three bottles of water dangling casually from his fingertips. He looked yummy. Good enough to eat. She especially liked that bulge in the front of his jeans showing he thought she looked as if *she* was good enough to eat.

She allowed the other two inner tubes to slide away from hers as she caught the edge of the pool and held on against the pull of the current. He leaned down to her, handing her one of the bottles.

"Baby, you're going to have to stop looking at me like that," he whispered. "You're killing me."

"It's good for you." Deliberately she removed the loosened cap and tipped a little of the contents down her throat, and then poured some down the front of her so it ran in a little river over the swell of her breasts and into the deep valley.

His breath hitched in his throat and his eyes darkened with lust. "You're playing with fire, *mi amorcito*. I have no problems throwing you over my shoulder and carrying you off to the bedroom right in front of our guests."

She wanted to dare him, but she knew he'd do it. She'd totally love it, but she'd never be able to face Emma or Catarina again without blushing. She bit her lip and let her fingertips answer him, sliding over his denim-covered leg, indicating yes, but no at the same time.

His hand fisted in her hair, pulling her head back, tilting her face up to his. He bent low and took her mouth the way he often did. Pure hunger. Uncaring who saw him. She tasted love in her mouth and the moment she did, she gave him everything back, pouring herself into his kiss like a gift. Just as hungry, hoping he could taste what she felt for him.

He broke the kiss and pressed his forehead tight against hers. "You still with me, baby, or are you processing?"

"Both," she answered a little breathily. She processed slow. She knew that, letting in a little bit of information at a time. He'd given her a lot, but there was so much more she needed to know. He'd told her about the past, not the present or the future. She needed all of it before she could make a decision.

It wasn't lost on her that he was courting her every minute of every day. With his sweet side. With his kisses. With his body. He was determined to make it difficult for her to ever leave him, and he was doing a really, really good job of it.

"You going to give my woman her water," Jake demanded, "or are you two going to take it inside?"

Siena couldn't help but smile as she buried her face in Elijah's throat. She heard the teasing note in Jake's voice, but Elijah had instantly shifted, nearly pulling her out of the water to wrap her up in his arms protectively. He didn't like her the least bit uncomfortable—unless he was the one making her that way.

"You okay?"

"Perfectly. Your friends are really nice. I've never had the chance to have friends, Elijah, so this is awesome," she assured him.

He settled her back in the inner tube and shot Jake a glare. Jake erupted into loud laughter, not in the least intimidated by an Elijah scowl. She *really* liked his friends. She liked that they knew Elijah well enough to occasionally tease him. He needed that every bit as much as she did.

She couldn't imagine what it would have been like for him growing up with the violence and controversy in his family. Other children were forbidden to play with him because their fathers were afraid if there were a childish fight, his parents would retaliate. That was how bad the Lospostos reputation was.

She let the current take her away from Elijah, all the while keeping her gaze on him as he walked around the pool until he caught up with Catarina and Emma. She loved looking at him, at the fluid, easy way he walked. He did look like a leopard padding so silently around the pool, danger in the very set of his shoulder and the rippling of the roped muscles beneath his white tee.

He turned his head and looked at her, his eyes meeting hers, and for the first time, in front of his friends, he smiled. Really smiled. The kind of smile that reached his eyes and lit them up, turning them from dark mercury to dazzling silver. The burn between her legs grew hotter. Company was definitely going to have to leave soon if he kept looking so good.

She held on to the side of pool, waiting for Emma and Catarina to make their way around it as Elijah disappeared back into the house. She lay back, closing her eyes, her long, thick braid in the water, her fingers clutching the water bottle. She felt lazy and happy, completely relaxed for the first time in months ever since she'd come home and found Paolo's eyes on her every time she moved.

Paolo didn't look at her the way Elijah did. There was something sneering and perverted about the way Paolo stared at her. She felt her stomach shift into knots. Just that fast, the thought of Paolo could take away the beauty of the afternoon. A shadow seemed to slip into her mind, coloring the blue of the afternoon gray.

She opened her eyes quickly to look up at the floating clouds. The sky was still blue. Very blue. A slight breeze pushed fluffy formations across the sky. The pool gleamed, and the children still laughed in excitement as Jake carried both from the water to wrap towels around them.

She took a deep breath and let herself float away, trying to escape the sudden suffocating feeling that gripped her. She'd been plagued with panic attacks since she'd woken up in the hospital. Elijah had managed to keep most of the nightmares at bay, but sometimes, during the day, she suddenly couldn't breathe. Mostly that happened when she let herself think about Paolo and what he might be doing.

The more time passed without anyone laying eyes on Paolo, the more worried she grew. She knew he wouldn't let things lie. She turned her head toward her left, looking over the high wall toward the rolling hills where the trees were. She knew Drake's men patrolled regularly through the trees and brush, and that they were all leopard and able to use their leopard senses.

She hadn't let her leopard out since she was injured. Her ribs and lacerations needed to heal first, but the little female was growing restless and Elijah had indicated several times that his male was becoming irritable and hard to control. She hadn't asked the doctor how shifting would affect the baby. Maybe that was a good question to ask Emma. She certainly would know.

She started to turn her head when she caught sight of one of Elijah's personal bodyguards, Joaquin, running across the yard in the distance, a gun in his hand. Elijah and Drake burst from the house, shouting at Jake to get under cover and for the women to get out of the pool.

"*Dios*, Siena, move it, now," Elijah shouted, running toward her.

Emma and Catarina were close to the house and both bailed out of their inner tubes. Drake reached an arm down for both of them and hauled them out of the waist-deep river, curved his arms around their waists and ran with them toward the house, Jake closing in behind with the two children.

Siena was on the far side of the pool. She leapt off the inner tube and dragged herself up onto the cement. Elijah's arm went around her and he lifted her right off her feet and ran with her away from the house and toward the protection of the wall. Several gunshots rang out, the sound echoing across the water. Something spat at the cement, and she saw three trails of silver in the water.

Elijah wrapped his arm around her head, shoving her to the ground and covering her body with his. "Stay down, baby."

"It's Paolo, isn't it?"

"I don't think so. The team's got this. Joshua spotted someone creeping up on the house. Paolo wouldn't be so stupid. He knows Drake is your security. I think this is Cordeau's man," Elijah said grimly. "His name is Robert Gaton. He's trying to stake his claim and tie up loose ends."

"Catarina? Is she considered a loose end?" In a way it was a relief that maybe she wasn't the cause of the danger to Emma, her children and Catarina.

"I think we were his target," Elijah admitted. "Gaton would perceive us as his biggest threat. You've inherited your grandfather's territory. Paolo may act like he's running the show, but you're the princess. You're living here with me. In everyone's eyes, that makes us partners. Gaton, as well as several other bosses, believes we're joining forces."

His voice was matter-of-fact, as if he wasn't delivering really, *really* bad news. In fact, his voice was devoid of all feeling. She hadn't even considered what the outside world might believe about the vacancy on her grandfather's throne, but it was his voice that sent a chill down her spine.

"Elijah," she whispered softly, her fist bunching in his shirt.

"I don't know for certain, *mi amorcito*, it's just a gut reaction. We'll know more when we find out who's out there." He didn't look at her. His gaze fixed on a point above her head and his features were cut deep with lines, carved with something dark and very dangerous.

She pressed her face against his chest, listening to his heartbeat, trying without words to bring him back to her, because, although he held her, he wasn't hers. She felt him moving away from her, his mind going somewhere she couldn't follow. His fingers burrowed beneath her long braid to find the nape of her neck, massaging gently to ease the tension out of her, but he did it absently, as if she barely registered.

He suddenly lifted his head and looked toward the house. "We've got the all clear. I need you inside. Now."

She winced at the edge in his voice. His tone cut, lashed, a crisp command delivered impersonally.

"Elijah," she began, running her hand up his chest, trying to find their connection. Feeling suddenly very afraid.

He caught her hand and brought it down to his thigh, still not looking at her. "I'll want Drake to explain to me how someone got close enough to the house to fire on us."

"It sounded like a rifle to me." She tried placating him, diverting his anger from Drake and the others. Because he was angry. She got that, not from his voice, but from the heavy, oppressive feeling coming off him in waves.

"It was, but no one should have gotten close enough even for that."

She shivered at his cold tone. Yeah. He was seriously pissed. She didn't think it was fair to Drake or his team. The ranch was huge. No one could cover the entire acreage.

"They got him, honey," she reminded softly, as he pulled her to her feet.

He didn't reply, keeping her hand against his thigh and pulling her across the open area fast. He didn't say a word to Drake as he passed.

Once in the house, she tried to pull away, but he tightened his grip on her and turned her away from the great room.

She protested, trying to come to a stop. "We have company, Elijah. I need to check on everyone."

"You need to do what I say, Siena," he growled. "I want you in our room where I know you're safe."

"But . . ."

He didn't listen to her, all but dragging her right through the house straight to the master bedroom.

"Take a shower and get dressed." His voice was clipped.

"Elijah," she protested.

"You're shivering, Siena." His hands settled on her shoulders. "I promised you safety. You didn't feel fucking safe. I want to know why, and by God, I'm going to find out what the hell happened and who shot at you."

He dropped his hands and stalked from the room, leaving her standing there with her mouth open, a little shocked at the abrupt way he left her. She stood there a long time, shaking, rubbing her hands up and down her arms, as panic took her. She didn't even know why she was suddenly so scared, but she was.

The hot water didn't drive the cold from her belly. That cold was like a snake, slithering through her, leaving devastation in its wake. She knew she was living in a dream world of her own making. She didn't want to process anything Elijah said because she'd have to face the reality of his life. Of what and who he might be. There was no escaping it now, and it wasn't the rifle firing bullets at them or their guests—it was the look on Elijah's face.

He had gone so distant. So remote. So deadly. The sweet man she had come to rely on had disappeared altogether and a stranger was there. His eyes had gone diamond hard, as cold as ice, yet there was such a gathered fury there, as if all of it was concentrated deep in his soul. If his eyes revealed what was inside the man, she knew she was looking at hell. She saw the real Elijah Lospostos, the man born and bred to rule a world of violence. He lived outside the law because he was his own law. The man she saw in her bedroom was capable of extreme violence, and he wouldn't hesitate to use it if he decided he needed—or wanted to.

She washed her hair, taking her time, her hands trembling, the terrible cold sinking so deep into her bones, she feared she'd never get it out. She felt still inside, as if she held herself together by sheer willpower and if she moved too far one way or the other, she'd shatter from the cold.

Siena dressed with care, needing to feel as if she had armor when she faced Elijah again. She wasn't certain how best to approach him. She'd promised she'd talk to him if anything upset her, and seeing him like that, well, not only was it upsetting, it was terrifying. He had gone so remote, she wasn't certain he was even the same man. He'd felt—and looked—like a total stranger.

She tugged on her softest skirt, the one that fell to her ankles and made her feel taller. She hated putting on a bra, because the strap rubbed along the four rake marks, but she did it so she could wear one of her favorite blouses. It was a beautiful silky material, almost, but not really see-through. It hinted at what was beneath it, but was very classy. No sleeves, but tiny pearl buttons down the front, it came to a vee at her waist and hugged her narrow rib cage. It went perfectly with the skirt and gave her confidence in her appearance, even with the scar on her face.

She stared at herself for a long time in the mirror, her heart beating fast. She didn't want to lose the Elijah she'd had for the last month. She wanted to find a way to bring him back to her. Taking a deep breath, she smoothed her hands down her thighs and moved barefoot out of the master bedroom.

The house seemed silent, and she knew, while she'd been in the shower, Jake had whisked his family home and Eli must have come for Catarina. That embarrassed her a bit. Wasn't she supposed to be the hostess? Still, there was movement in the house and the low murmur of voices. The voices didn't sound happy and the atmosphere, as she moved through the hall, seemed tense and oppressive.

Two men, Joshua and Joaquin, came out of a room at the end of the hall and closed the door behind them. She knew that was Elijah's private office. When they opened the door, the two voices got a little louder and she knew Drake and Elijah were arguing. The two men walked toward her, and she pressed herself against the wall to allow them past. Joshua jerked his chin at her. He didn't look happy. She didn't blame him. She could tell by the voices, Drake's and Elijah's drifting from the large office off the hall to her right, that neither man was happy.

She waited until Joshua and Joaquin had turned the corner of the hallway before she approached Elijah's office. She stopped abruptly as Elijah's words penetrated. His tone was low. Furious. *Scathing.*

"How far do you expect me to take this fucking charade, Drake?" he demanded.

Her breath caught in her throat and she pressed her back into the wall as if she could become part of the house. Everything in her stilled. A charade? What charade? What was Elijah talking about? Even outside his office, the air vibrated with anger.

"You take it as far as you can before you're so sick you can't take one more minute. That's how far," Drake said in a quiet, steady voice.

"That's easy for you to say. I've got her in my house. In my fucking bed. What more do you want? A ring on her finger and a target on her back?" Elijah snarled.

Siena bit down hard on her lip and pressed a hand to her mouth to keep any sound from escaping. A charade. *She* was the charade. She was in his fucking bed. How could she have let herself be that stupid? *The worst I ever had. Don't know how to suck cock.* Never once had he indicated he wanted her to go down on him. Not one single time. Didn't all men like that? He hadn't, because he knew she was terrible at it and this was all a charade. A terrible, deceitful charade. A sob welled up and she choked it down, but tears swam in her eyes. So many she couldn't see for a minute.

"The idea is still sound, Elijah. Nothing's changed."

Elijah erupted into a string of Spanish. There was silence for a brief moment. "The world sees we're forming an empire and this was retaliation."

"What the hell did you think was going to happen? You knew."

The world sees we're forming an empire. He was talking about her grandfather's business. Rafe Cordeau's disappearance had left a vacancy in the underworld and now, with her grandfather's death, there was another *huge* vacancy. Elijah Lospostos had made the world believe *he*, as the head of the Lospostos family, was taking over that vacancy. He had done that so easily by bringing her into his home and into his bed.

"Yeah, I knew what was going to happen, but you were supposed to handle it." That was pure accusation. Snarled. Elijah's voice had gone so low he sounded like he was growling. The hair on her body rose and she shivered.

"I didn't say it was going to be easy. Everyone has to make sacrifices for this to work. You know that."

Drake knew. The man she had hired to handle her security was part of the charade. Oh God, this was getting worse by the moment. Her breath caught in her chest, her lungs fighting for air. There was no controlling the tears tracking down her cheeks. Elijah didn't care about her. He was no different than Paolo, wanting whatever it was her grandfather had. He'd played her. *Played* her, and she'd been so desperate for him she'd believed every single thing he'd said to her.

Her face burned with humiliation. Her heart felt shattered. So many pieces there was no recovery. She'd lost everything. Her legs trembled and she was terrified they wouldn't hold her up. She pressed one hand to the wall and kept the other firmly over her mouth to keep the sounds of her shuddering breath from escaping.

"Easy for you to say, Donovan, you aren't the one making the sacrifices."

Sacrifices. That was the worst. The absolute worst. Elijah was making sacrifices by having her in his house. In his bed. He'd told her. Straight up he'd told her how awful she was. The worst. She didn't even know how to suck cock.

Siena flinched, and this time, behind her hand, muffled, a small sound of absolute pain managed to break free. Elijah's betrayal ran deep. So deep she was afraid she might vomit right there in the hallway. She became aware of the sudden silence. Both men had heard the sound and they knew.

The door flew open and Elijah strode out, his face a mask, eyes so silver they gleamed in the darkened hall. Sheer predator.

"Siena," he said, his voice rough. Raw. He took a step toward her.

Siena stepped back, holding up one hand. The shame was so acute, she could barely stand it. "You *lied*, Elijah. *God.* How could I be so stupid, believing every word you said to me. Telling me you'd always tell me the truth. So, so stupid."

His face darkened. The silver eyes slashed her face, cutting deep. Deeper than Paolo's leopard had ever cut her. So deep she felt that cut in her soul.

"That's enough, Siena," he cautioned, his tone a whip.

She flinched under that lash, but it didn't stop her. "You didn't fuck me because you wanted me. Because I meant something to you. This was all a *charade*." She threw his words back in his face. "You made the ultimate sacrifice, didn't you? You had to have me in your bed. The worst you ever had." Her face flamed, but she kept doggedly on. She couldn't stop herself. "Let's see if I can remember this right, because there was a moment when you were so angry you told the truth. My amateur performance, I believe you called it. The worst cocksucker you ever experienced. Those words are branded on my brain, but I was stupid enough to let you make me forget them for a moment."

"Siena, damn it . . ."

"If I'm going to whore myself out, I seriously need a few lessons in fucking. Is that what you've been giving me, Elijah? Or did you just plain fuck me?"

He erupted into a string of Spanish curses, and she turned and ran back to the master bedroom, slamming the door and locking it. She never wanted to see him again. She wanted to disappear. She *had* to disappear. She couldn't face anyone ever again.

11

"OPEN the fucking door now, Siena," Elijah demanded.

His furious voice galvanized Siena into action. She ran to the closet and pulled out the small backpack she'd used before to make her escape. Rolling a pair of sweats, underwear and a tee, she jammed them inside along with her cell phone, license and credit cards. There was no going out the front door. Hell. She was *paying* Drake's men to help make her a prisoner and they were crawling all over Elijah's estate.

"Damn it, Siena. Open the door before I break it down."

He would too. She didn't have much time. Ignoring the patio doors, because it might draw the attention of one of the men patrolling around the house, she stripped as she raced to the window and raised it quickly. She called a little desperately to her little female. She'd only shifted on two occasions and was a little hesitant on remembering how it was done, but clearly the leopard knew. She was eager for freedom.

Siena barely managed to fashion the backpack around

her neck before her joints cracked and ached. Fur slid under her skin, the wave causing a terrible itch, and then it burst from her pores as she went to the floor on all fours. Her jaw ached. Elongated. Pain gave way to satisfaction as the little female leopard stood on the bedroom floor right beneath the window.

Her fur was beautiful and thick, a gorgeous gold with black rosettes covering every inch of her. The piercing green of Siena's exotic eyes was even more striking on the cat. With a flick of her long tail she leapt through the window, ignoring the loud crash as the door sprang open across the room. The moment her cushioned toes hit the ground, she took off running across the open area toward the tree line and heavier brush, avoiding the smell of man.

Siena directed the leopard to take toward the main road leading to the front of the Lospostos estate. It was a distance away, but if she made it, she could call a taxi to pick her up. Once she was away, she could find a place to hide from everyone until she could get out of the country.

It was a good plan. A solid one. But for one thing. The moment her little female hit the trees and sprinted through the brush, she heard the heavier male coming after her. He let out a husky, sawing roar that sent her heart pounding. The female shivered and chose the path of least resistance, rather than trying to hide.

Leopards were built for stealth, not sprinting, and she grew tired very quickly. The female had only been out on a couple of occasions and she hadn't built up her ability to run, play or fight. She slowed her pace at Siena's urging, even though she knew the much larger male was gaining ground.

He came out of the trees in *front* of her. Clearly he was far faster and much more experienced. The female's only encounter with another leopard had been Paolo's male, and it had attacked her. Siena's female skidded to a halt and watched the male carefully. He approached slowly, and she hissed and batted at him with one paw, claws out, a clear message to stay away. The male backed off patiently and circled around to try to get behind her.

The female turned, keeping a leery eye on him. The moment she had a clear pathway to move forward, she took it, leaping forward and sprinting once again. The male fell in beside her, although keeping his distance, pacing along, not trying to stop her, but every now and then, he moved up, forcing her to turn off course.

Siena realized, after a time, what Elijah was doing. He didn't use brute strength, but rather cunning, his male herding the female away from the road and freedom. He kept her moving, or, when she tired and sank down to rest, he harassed her by continually circling her, looking for an opening to claim her.

He was patient. Too patient. The female began to entice the male rather than simply run from it. She extended her claws, spit and rebuffed him, taking off to leap over several fallen trees and then stopping to crouch in a beguiling pose. The male approached cautiously and she instantly was up, growling and spitting at him, swiping up a plume of dirt at him and then leaping away again.

The male followed her. Siena tried to induce her to head for the fence, but the male stayed firmly between the female and the fence line, turning her back every time. The more exhausted the female became, the more solicitous toward the male she was. Vocalizing her acceptance of him as her mate, the last thing Siena wanted, the female began to rub seductively along the tree trunks and occasionally roll and stretch.

The male watched over her, keeping her moving, not allowing her to stop. Siena knew shifters mated for life and she tried to keep the female away from the male, but he was persistent and the female had already begun to bond with him. Siena could feel the bond growing stronger and stronger with every dance the two leopards made around each other.

She couldn't believe how patient Elijah and his male

were. They kept following and turning her female away from the road for half the night. Finally, the female was so exhausted she crouched in submission. Instantly the male was on her, covering her, his teeth sinking into her neck to hold her in place.

Once Siena realized the female was accepting of the male, she disappeared as best she could, retreating to give her leopard the freedom to be a cat. The male kept at her, over and over, all through the night. He mounted her, holding her in place to ensure neither got hurt during their rough sex. Once finished, he lay beside her, panting and resting until he was ready to go again.

As dawn broke, Siena's female curled up to sleep. The male refused to allow it, pushing at her with a hard shoulder to get her back on her feet. Siena knew exactly what Elijah was doing, and she tried to resist. Her female tried to resist. The male was much larger and his stamina was greater. He kept her moving until she was stumbling with fatigue, and he made certain to move her back in the direction of the house.

Siena cursed under her breath, despising the fact that Elijah had all the control. She didn't want to shift back to human form, because he was bigger and stronger and she was far too humiliated to *ever* face him again. Her little female was so exhausted she couldn't pick up her feet and actually dragged her paws in the dirt as she staggered back toward the house. She was so fatigued, she stopped directing herself and allowed Siena to take over completely.

Over and over Siena tried to stop to allow her cat rest, lying curled in the grass or dirt. The male pushed at her, driving her forward with his shoulder. When she refused to get up he sank his teeth into the thick fur at her neck and dragged her several feet until she began to walk again out of sheer desperation. He stayed close. The female's fur was dark with sweat and she trembled continually. Siena was just as exhausted, worn out from the long night of fighting Elijah's will.

The male leopard continued to be patient, never hurting

her female, but never allowing her to rest. It was a matter of time before she couldn't keep trying to circle back toward the road. She walked a few steps forward, dropped to the ground panting and shaking while the male stood over her protectively. After a few minutes he nudged her, warning her with a low growl to get to her feet and move.

The house loomed up. Siena smelled several of the men patrolling but none of them came to her aid. She knew they wouldn't. They didn't work for her. They worked for Elijah. She stood under the window, trembling. Terrified. Tears burning. The male crowded her until her female made the leap inside. She landed on the gleaming hardwood floor, paced forward three steps and collapsed.

Siena curled up inside her. Hiding. Ashamed. Humiliated. Trying to form another plan. She couldn't—*wouldn't*—call Paolo, but maybe Alonzo. She didn't have anyone else. The thought was terrifying. She had no idea how long a shifter could stay in the form of a leopard, but she was going to find out. She would refuse to shift back to human.

The male landed so silently she barely realized he was in the room with her. He nuzzled the female as she lay trembling. Then she felt a hand move through the damp fur. Elijah's hand. She'd know his touch anywhere, even when she was in her leopard form.

"Siena, shift."

Screw you, she thought, so exhausted she couldn't even lift the female leopard's head to threaten him. She could barely keep her eyes open. Suddenly his fingers were pushing down ruthlessly on several pressure points she hadn't even been aware the female leopard had. Hard. Brutal. It hurt. The female squirmed, trying to get out from under his hands. When she couldn't, the animal, exhausted and completely done in, gave up and slipped away, deserting Siena.

Siena found herself curled on the floor, naked, the backpack around her neck and Elijah's fingers digging into the small of her back. The moment she shifted, he lifted her in his arms, his face close to hers. She turned her face into his chest, refusing to meet his eyes. She'd never been so tired in her life. She couldn't fight him, no matter how much she wanted to. She couldn't lift her arms. She could barely turn her head.

He took her to the bed and, placing a knee in the middle, dipped down to deposit her there gently. She felt his hands unsnapping the backpack from around her neck and she turned her face into the pillow.

Light spilled in from the window, the sun already climbing in the sky. She squeezed her eyes shut. He had to be as exhausted as she was, but he didn't show it. He set her pack on the end table beside the bed and went to the window, closing it and then pulling the heavy drape to block out the sun.

Her gaze immediately touched on the backpack. Her phone was in there. Elijah padded barefoot and naked through the bedroom, blocking all light before heading for the bathroom. He was very comfortable without clothes, while she dragged the cover over her and held it over her breasts. Elijah didn't close the door, but the moment he disappeared, she reached for the backpack, nearly knocking it to the floor when her shaking hand caught the strap.

Jerking it to her, she hastily unzipped it and yanked out her cell phone. She had no idea whether or not Alonzo had betrayed her grandfather, but she had no one else and she *couldn't*, *wouldn't*, stay with Elijah any longer than she had to. Better to take a leap right into the fire; at least she knew who she was dealing with. She hastily scrolled down her list of contacts to find his number.

"What the *hell* are you doing?" Elijah demanded.

Of course he heard the zipper. He was leopard. She cursed under her breath as she found Alonzo's number and hit it with her thumb. Elijah was on her instantly, leaping across the room with the ease of his leopard, landing on the bed, his much larger and heavier body pinning hers down while one hand closed over her wrist and the other tore the phone from her.

"Alonzo *fucking* Massi?" he snarled. "That's bullshit, Siena, and you know it." He hurled the phone against the wall so hard it came apart in pieces.

"Get off of me," she snapped, furious. She pushed at his chest as hard as she could. "I want you off of me."

"You're going to listen to me."

"I *did* listen to you. I heard everything you said. It's such a *sacrifice* being with me, isn't it, Elijah? Poor man to have to have such an inexperienced *whore* in your bed." She closed her eyes, ashamed. In pain. He'd *gutted* her. Torn out her soul.

"*Dios*, Siena, I thought we were past that bullshit. How many times do you want me to apologize? I said it and I didn't fucking mean it. You know that. And what the hell do you mean, it's a sacrifice to be with you?"

She opened her eyes to glare at him. "I *heard* you. With Drake. I heard you." She shoved at his chest again. "Get off me."

"Baby, take a breath. We'll sort this out."

He watched her with the focused, unblinking gaze of the leopard. His silver eyes moved over her face as liquid as mercury. Intense. She wanted to block him out, but he was everywhere. She breathed him in with every breath she took. There was no way to get away from him, and she needed to. Desperately.

"You promised me, Siena. You promised you'd talk to me." His voice was rough with emotion. Raw. Worried.

"That's before I knew you were such a liar. I've had enough of your lies." She wanted to shout at him, but her voice came out a whisper. "It hurt. What you did to me hurt. At least Paolo was honest. He didn't try to make me believe he would ever be good to me. Protect me. He didn't ever tell me I was safe with him."

He frowned down at her, shaking her head. "I don't know what you thought you heard, *mi vida*, but whatever it was, it wasn't what I said."

"Elijah, please get off me. *Please*." She wasn't above begging. She couldn't stand his touch. She didn't want to smell him, or feel him, or even see him. She tried her best not to hear his lying voice. He sounded torn up. Not angry, but hurt. As if she'd done something wrong, not him.

"You'd go to Alonzo?" he asked. He sounded tortured. "*Mi amorcito*. That doesn't even make sense. You're so mixed up, and until I know what you think you heard, I can't make this better."

"You can *never* make this better because I don't believe you. I. Don't. Believe. You." She enunciated each word, biting it out between her teeth for emphasis.

Elijah stared down into Siena's face, seeing the stark hurt there. He'd put that look in her eyes and caused the terrible pain that was evident. She wasn't good at hiding her emotions, and he could see the pain was very real. Somehow, and he wasn't certain how, he'd made her doubt him all over again.

He wanted to curse. To hit something. Someone. He knew he was a violent man. He'd been raised in violence and he knew he would always have that reaction, but not with Siena. She got his gentle. She got his heart and soul. He'd shredded something important in her, taken her self-esteem, her confidence, with the things he'd said to her after the first time they'd had sex.

He couldn't take it all back, and he wanted it done between them. Over. He'd apologized more than once. He'd explained. He *couldn't* have blown this. Siena was too important. There was no one else. There had never been anyone else. He was a fucking robot, and he knew if she left him, he was lost. Not even Drake would be able to pull him back from the edge. That was how far gone he was.

He dropped his forehead to hers, pressing into her. Breathing her in. Needing her. What the hell did a normal man do when he'd ripped out his woman's heart? She was alone. Pregnant. Emotional. He'd clearly gutted her, but he didn't know exactly what he'd done. What he said. He tried to go over the conversation with Drake in his mind, replaying it, but he'd been furious. He'd wanted to strangle Drake with his bare hands.

He hadn't wanted to lay his life out in front of her. Or their future life. Not until he was absolutely certain she would stay with him of her own free will. He'd been so close. What the hell had happened? He felt lost. He'd never been in a relationship, and he didn't know the first thing about them. He was floundering and Siena was far too important to him to be taking chances with saying something wrong. Still, he had nothing to give her but the truth.

"All right, baby, let's start at the beginning. I know you're upset. I see that. I promised you that you would be safe with me. I gave you my word and I meant it. That shooter shouldn't have gotten anywhere near the property, let alone within distance to fire on us. On you. I was angry. Furious. I wanted to rip Drake's head off. You should never have been in any danger. Not even a little bit."

She didn't reply. She kept her eyes closed. Her body was stiff. He wasn't getting anywhere. But he wasn't giving up. Nothing was more important than this moment in his life. He had to take away the hurt. For both of them. He didn't know a human being could hurt so much. He felt raw on the inside, just as gutted as she was. Maybe more so because he'd caused this. The ugly, hurtful things he'd said to her had contributed to her believing he was playing her. How could she have gotten that from his conversation with Drake?

"Baby, please. I need a little help here. I need you to look at me. I need you to talk to me. I say things when I'm pissed. I know that. And I was royally pissed at Drake. By bringing you here, I put you in jeopardy. *Hell*." He spat the last word and rolled off of her to lie on his back, both hands pressed to his eyes. Eyes that burned like a son of a bitch.

She didn't move. He took a deep breath and tried to control the fear snaking through him, knotting his belly and putting bile in his throat. He tried to remember every single thing he'd said to Drake, but all he could hear was her accusations.

You didn't fuck me because you wanted me. Because I meant something to you. This was all a charade. You made the ultimate sacrifice, didn't you? You had to have me in your bed. The worst you ever had.

He groaned softly. He was never going to live that down, no matter how many times he apologized to her.

Let's see if I can remember this right, because there was a moment when you were so angry you told the truth. My amateur performance, I believe you called it. The worst cocksucker you ever experienced. Those words are branded on my brain, but I was stupid enough to let you make me forget them for a moment.

What had he said to Drake that would have brought all of that back when they'd been doing so great together?

"What did I say, Siena? What did you hear that set you off? That made you believe I lied to you? Baby, you have to tell me. I swear to you, I don't know what I said that you could have misconstrued."

Beside him, she stiffened, a small sound escaping, as if she wanted to yell at him, or hit him. Scratch his eyes out. He wished she'd try. At least he'd have something to work with. He turned on his side toward her, his arm locking around her waist, dragging her resisting body into his. He caught her hand and forced it down to his cock, holding her palm over the thick erection there.

"Do you really think I could fake this? Do you, Siena? Never in my life have I walked around with a permanent hard-on—until you came into my life. I can't look at you without wanting you. It isn't possible."

He studied her face, her averted eyes. Closed off. Hell. She wouldn't even look at him. But there was genuine pain there. She wasn't faking that. This wasn't some little manipulative tantrum she was throwing. Whatever she thought she heard had ripped her apart.

Siena tried to pull her hand out from under Elijah's. His erection felt huge, hot. It pulsed with life. She couldn't help but feel the velvet-soft flared head and the thick steel spike of a shaft, the way it throbbed with need, calling out to her for attention. She didn't know if men could fake that kind of thing. She heard the raw pain in his voice, and his tone rang with truth. But she'd heard him. It wasn't idle gossip she'd listened to—she'd heard him with her own ears. She hated the look on his face. So torn up. If she looked at him, she'd burst into tears and throw herself into his arms. She couldn't be that stupid. She'd already humiliated herself twice for him.

"Baby."

She closed her eyes. When he called her baby in his gentle, rough-with-need voice, everything in her responded. Melted. He was getting to her, because she heard the ring of truth in his tone, she heard the genuine pain.

"You have to stop, Elijah," she burst out. She struggled to get her hand back again. His hold tightened, both on her hand and the arm locked around her waist. "I *heard* you." He might sound truthful now, but he had then as well.

"All right, I'll accept that you heard something, *mi amor*, something that has really upset you. Something that made you *think* I was lying to you." Elijah's voice was soft, almost stroking caresses over her skin. "Tell me what I said, because I swear to you, I don't have any recollection of a conversation with Drake that could possibly make you believe I'm lying about wanting to be with you."

She bit her lip hard and maintained her silence. If she moved she was afraid she would shatter. She had already made herself so vulnerable to him, she feared if she let him in even a little more, if she cracked that door again, she would be lost. Already she felt broken, and she knew she couldn't take any more.

His hand rubbed hers over the thick bulge, and her heart nearly stopped. That bulge had grown, gotten even harder.

"Siena, you can't offer me the world and then take it away from me. Do you have any idea what my life was like before you came into it? Bleak. Lonely. Violent. One of my earliest memories was of my grandfather blowing a man's brains out. I saw it. The blood spattered everywhere, all over the walls. All over me. I was there when they beat a man to death. I think I was about six when that happened. When I threw up, my grandfather beat me while his men all laughed."

Her entire body jerked. She gasped, her breath catching in her throat. She'd been lonely as a child, but she'd been happy.

"I was trained from the time I was a boy in the use of guns, knives, martial arts, boxing, kickboxing and good old street fighting. I knew I was going to be an enforcer in my family's world. That was my job, and I did it from a very early age. You don't have friends. You don't dare care about a lover. You keep to yourself. If you're the son or grandson or nephew of a Lospostos, you're always a target."

He was killing her. He couldn't tell her this. She didn't want to feel anything at all for him or for that little boy growing up. She'd been safe in boarding school with bodyguards all around her. He'd been fighting to stay alive. She heard the truth and knew what it meant. He didn't have to spell it all out for her.

"Stop," she whispered, because already her fingers, of their own volition, wrapped around his thick cock, holding him tight in her fist, as if she could hold him close and keep him safe that way. "You have to stop, Elijah."

"My uncle murdered my parents. He wanted to be the sole power in the Lospostos family, and my father was taking us in a direction my uncle didn't want to go. He threatened to kill my sister if I didn't cooperate with him. He turned me into a killer, Siena. For years, that's all I was. That was my life."

"Stop," she whispered again. She couldn't stop her body from turning into his. She wanted to be strong. She sternly told herself to be strong. Where was her sense of self-preservation? She was an idiot for listening to him. For letting him tell her these things. So personal. So deep, so real she knew no one else had ever heard the things he was saying to her. "Elijah, don't."

"I'm not going to let you go." He moved suddenly, his body rolling back over hers, his chest pressed to hers, his hips wedged between her thighs. One hand spanned her throat and his beautiful, exotic molten eyes moved over her face, a brooding, hooded perusal that stole her breath.

"I *can't* let you go. I brought you here instead of locking you in a safe house until all this shit was over because I believed Drake and the team could protect you. I *believed* that. I know Drake. He's the best there is, and he was certain this was the best place to keep you safe. I agreed with his assessment, but maybe I wanted you so much I didn't think it through."

His tone was a sensual rasp. His hard cock pressed tight against her mound, and against her will she felt an answering heat in her core.

"You have to know who I am, Siena."

His hands framed her face, forcing her head around until she had no choice but to look at him. That was a mistake, just as she'd known it would be. He looked ravaged with pain. So much. Her heart broke for him, compassion and caring slithering through her own heartbreak and humiliation in spite of her desire to stay strong and hard against him.

She tried to shake her head, to stop him from telling her things he should never tell anyone. He should never *ever* say aloud.

"I'm a killer. Straight up. That's who I am. That's what they made me. My own flesh and blood. My grandfather. My father. My uncle. I was never a little boy playing baseball with my friends. I was the little boy learning how to beat the brains out of someone with the baseball bat. I was learning the ropes of the family business and how to defend it. How to hurt others and scare and intimidate them into doing whatever the family wanted or needed. So you have to know, baby, you're in my bed and I'm touching you, you're in bed with that man.

The hands touching your beautiful body are hands that beat people. That hurt them. That killed."

"Elijah." Her voice broke. Tears blurred her vision. "You have to stop."

"I can't say any one of those I was sent after was innocent, because they weren't, but still, that's what they made me into, my own family, that's what they made me into."

She could barely breathe with the pain she saw in his eyes. On his face. It was raw and terrible. "Honey." She breathed it, trying to find balance. Trying not to wrap him up in her. She needed to help him, but she was terrified of losing herself again in him and being torn apart. She didn't think she could put herself back together.

"I live in hell, Siena. That's my world and I have no fucking right to drag you down with me, but I can't stop myself. You're the one thing in my life that's worth anything. I can't let go of you, no matter how much I know I should. I'm not that strong. I can't come to you as an innocent. You are innocent and beautiful. Your body is. Your mind is. Your heart and soul. You think I don't feel the weight of that every fucking minute I spend with you? You gave yourself to me, Siena. You *chose* me and I'm going to do everything in my power, with everything that I am, to protect you. To cherish you. To keep you exactly the way you are. Innocent and beautiful. But I can't give you up. Don't ask that of me, because, baby, I swear, I'm not that strong."

There were tears in his eyes. He blinked them away, but she *saw* them. He couldn't take that back any more than he could take back the things he'd revealed to her. She was more confused than ever. Her arms slid around him, holding him to her and already, her body had softened, melting a little so that he sank into her. She took his weight because she needed to.

"So, I'm *telling* you, baby. I'm not fucking asking. Tell me what the hell you overheard that has you this upset. Right now, before I lose my mind."

She took a breath. Let it out. "You're asking me to put myself in your hands all over again, Elijah. You hurt me."

"No, baby, you're still not getting it." He ground the words out between his teeth. His body moved against hers and there was nothing subtle about what it was saying. "You're already in my hands. I'm holding you to me and I'm *never* letting you go. It isn't going to happen, so we work this shit out now. You promised me, Siena, and you're going to keep that promise no matter what you hear, what you think you hear or what kind of bastard you think I am."

She stared up at his face, her heart beating fast. His mask was back, the tortured look gone. He was back to hard. Implacable. He meant what he said. "Do you think scaring me is going to make me want to stay, Elijah?"

"I don't care how I get you to stay. Just that you do. You're the only good thing I have in my life. The *only* good thing. I'm not letting you leave because of bullshit. You have to know that about me, baby. I don't deal well with bullshit. We're gonna fight. That's what happens to couples occasionally. We're both leopard. That means we're passionate and have tempers. You're going to have to be able to deal."

She frowned at him. "You're acting like what you said wasn't huge, Elijah. I have every right to be upset."

"I'm not saying you don't *think* it was huge. I'm saying learn to deal. You leave me, I'm coming after you."

"Elijah," she warned.

"No, baby. This is me. Telling you. Getting through to you what kind of man your man is. If I didn't know how you feel about me, it might be different, but you want me the same way I want you. I wouldn't be able to rip your heart out if you didn't. So I'm saying, as long as you feel that, you're staying and we're working it out."

She didn't want to talk about it or think about it or relive it. Her gaze slid away from his.

He caught her chin. "No, *mi vida*. We deal with this now. Tell me what the hell happened from the time I took you to the bedroom to when I walked out of my office and saw you look like someone had ripped your heart out."

She jerked her chin out of his hand, wishing she could find anger again. She didn't know what she felt, but it wasn't anger. "You said it was a sacrifice to be with me," she whispered. She couldn't keep the hurt and shame from her voice.

He scowled. Fury gathered in his eyes. "The hell I did."

"I heard you. Drake said everyone had to make sacrifices, and you said it wasn't him making it. That was *after* you said I was in your bed." Just repeating it made her heart ache and her stomach rebel.

Siena didn't take her eyes from his. She wanted to see what kind of reaction he had, and there was no mistaking the dawning of realization as well as genuine relief. He shook his head. "Baby." He whispered it softly and then leaned in to bury his face between her shoulder and neck.

She felt the rasp of the shadow along his jaw. She felt his lips moving against her neck. She felt something damp against her skin. Her hands slid into his hair, fingers sifting through the dark, thick waves as he held her tight to him.

"I guess I took something out of context?" She felt still inside, but hope had blossomed, and there was no turning it back.

"Yeah, *mi amorcito*, you definitely took something out of context," he answered. His mouth moved to her earlobe, his teeth gently tugging. He slid his tongue along the smooth shell and then dipped behind it, sending a shiver through her body. "You must have come in on the end of all our argument. I was furious at Drake. I still am."

"Elijah," she said softly. "What did I get wrong?"

"*You* were the one making the sacrifice. Not me. *You*. You're the innocent caught up in all this. In the hell that's my life. From the beginning, I wanted you protected. We knew what the others would think and we knew some of them would make a move against us, but Drake assured me this place was impenetrable and that his men would be able to keep all of it from you."

"All of what?" They were in dangerous territory now and she knew it. She was about to learn things she would have to take time to process.

"If your grandfather's businesses are aligned with mine, we would control more territory than any other boss. We would have unparalleled power. None of the other bosses want that. Most will back off, but a few are going to try to stop it. Drake wanted to draw them out."

"What does Drake have to do with crime lords?"

"He and Jake take apart their businesses. We have to identify each family and then figure out what they're doing and then take them apart."

She smoothed his hair. He'd said *we* have to identify them, as if he was part of Drake's operation and not a part of the underworld, but she didn't ask him. Not yet. Not when he needed to explain what she'd heard.

"How could you think I would say that, Siena? *Dios*, I can't keep my hands off you. I wanted to climb in your hospital bed with you. If I had my way, we'd have anointed every room in this house as well as every piece of furniture. The rugs in front of the fireplaces and the floors as well. You wear those skirts and I want to lift the hem and see if you're wearing panties. If you're not, I want to claim what's mine. If you are, I want to see how sexy they are."

"You could be a little obsessive." She couldn't keep the smile out of her voice, because really? Every room? The furniture? The idea sent a shiver of excitement down her spine.

"You think?" He nuzzled her throat. "Get used to it, baby, because now that you're feeling better, I intend to make certain you know just how much I want you." He lifted his head again. "When you hear or think you hear something, you *have* to come to me, Siena. You have to get how much you mean to me."

"You were so different, after the gunshots, I didn't even recognize you. You scared me," she admitted.

"I wanted to strangle Drake with my bare hands," Elijah admitted. "Baby, it's going to happen. I lose my temper, but not at you. I'm not ever going to come at you that way. I'll walk away and let loose somewhere else where I know I'm not going to scare the hell out of you."

She realized that was what he'd done. He'd taken her to the bedroom and he'd removed himself. He didn't want to scare her. He had no qualms about showing Drake his temper, but he hadn't wanted her to see him like that.

"This is really about the things I said to you when we first came together, isn't it?" he asked softly, pushing the hair from her forehead. "You lost confidence in yourself, and I did that to you. I have to find a way to give it back to you, because there is no other woman for me. There never will be. You have to know that in your heart and soul, Siena. You have to feel that so this kind of thing never happens again. You get me? When we fight, it can't be about whether or not you think I want you. Because, baby, there's no question. You're the one. The only. There has never been another woman I let in and there isn't going to be."

12

SIENA sucked in her breath. He'd laid it all on the line for her. Everything about his family. His life. Maybe he hadn't touched on their future, but he told her things he'd never told anyone else. Given that to her. She needed to give him something back.

"I don't have any confidence in myself as a lover, Elijah. None. And for you, because of the way I feel about you, I want to be able to please you. Sometimes I want to touch you, or explore, and I'm afraid I'll do something wrong." Like right at the precise moment. The slow burn that had smoldered had become something hotter. Something scorching her. Driving her. She began to feel the way she had when she'd driven up to Elijah's home for the first time. Edgy. Needy. Restless.

Elijah groaned softly. "That's on me, baby, not you. I made you feel that way."

She shook her head. "It's more than the things you said. I won't pretend that didn't contribute, but honestly, I was already feeling that way. I wasn't like the other girls in boarding school. I didn't look at men, not even celebrities, and want them. I didn't feel anything at all until I saw you."

His eyes went molten. "There isn't a man on Earth who wouldn't be excited to hear that, Siena. I won't pretend it doesn't make me happy to know no other man has touched you. I want you for myself. I've never had that. Anything at all for just myself, let alone a woman. My life was never about me. It was always about the family and what I was supposed to do for it. Later it was about staying alive and keeping my sister that way. Then I just didn't give a fuck. I did what I had to do, but I didn't feel much. Until you. So you saying there wasn't another man you burned hotter than hell for, that's gold for me. That's fucking perfection. That's everything, Siena. The fact that you gave that to me, I'll treasure you until the day I die."

She dared to run her hand up his chest, over those defined, rippling muscles. He had a chest filled with power, and it showed. She tested the feel of his hot skin, of the muscles running like ropes beneath them.

"You said I was the worst cocksucker you'd ever had," she whispered. "I don't want to be your worst, Elijah. I want to be your best."

Silence followed her admission. His eyes had gone all cat, dark and almost glowing. Heated. Filled with a dark lust. A terrible hunger. His hunger stirred her own rising one, so that a shiver crept down her spine and her sex went damp, clenched and pulsed, and deep inside that burn began to coil hotly.

"Baby." He nearly groaned it. His voice sounded raspy, sexy, a lure as dangerous as his eyes. "If you had ever been with a man before, you would have known I was full of shit. I nearly came in your mouth. I nearly lost all control. I don't lose control. I've never once—not once, Siena—lost it like I did with you. A man wants his woman's mouth on him because she wants it. She enjoys it. She sucks hard. She's eager to please him. And she looks at him like he's her world. Baby, you did that. I was in fucking paradise."

He rolled over, taking her with him, so she sprawled on top of him. "But, *mi amorcito*, you want to practice, just so you're feeling confident, I'm all for helping you out. Have at it. Your body belongs to me, so that means my body belongs to you. I'm never going to feel another woman's hands or mouth on me, so I'd be obliged if you want to practice a lot."

She kissed his throat and then looked up at him. "Would you have finished in my mouth? Do you like that?"

"*Dios*, baby, yes. Most women don't like that sort of thing."

"But you do?" she persisted. She drew the letters of her name on his chest with her tongue. Licking him like a cat. Tasting his skin. All that hot male skin. Her mouth found his flat nipples, sucking gently, feeling the muscles of his belly bunch, and she explored each with her tongue, outlining them.

"I do, Siena, but you don't have to take it that far." He bunched her hair in his hand, forming a tight fist around it, pulling her head up so he could look at her. "I'll be happy with whatever you give me."

She smiled at him and rubbed her breasts along his chest, needing the contact with all that delicious heat. The burn inside had turned to a pounding pressure, hot and beginning to spiral out of control.

His hand tightened until she felt a bite of pain, and her gaze jumped back to his. "I've got to tell you this, so you know what I like, baby. Right now, I'm giving you this play because you need it and I'm yours, but in bed, when I say enough, I want your mouth or I want a position, anything at all, I get it. That's my way."

She felt the laughter bubble up from some place deep inside. She didn't smile, but she held his eyes. "That's your way?"

He nodded. Serious—*very* serious—which made her want to laugh all the more.

"Another thing: when I want you, I don't care where the hell we are, I get you."

She rubbed her palm along his flat belly, but she stayed where she was because he wasn't through. "Anything else?"

"Just laying it out there for you, baby."

"I have a little newsflash for you, Elijah, that maybe you aren't aware of, being all macho and scary dangerous."

He heard the laughter in her voice and that liquid silver darkened even more, sending another thrill of excitement down her spine. She was teasing a leopard and she knew it. She liked doing it, and she was going to be doing it a *lot*. Just to put that look on his face. Just to feel the thrill of danger. The bite of pain in her scalp when his hold on her hair tightened.

"Your newsflash?" He used a tone. An ominous one. His gaze narrowed.

"You like control all the time, honey, not just when it comes to sex, and you're not all that good at hiding it, if that was your intention." She did laugh then. She couldn't help it. He might be sweet when it suited him, but his sweet included him getting his way. She would have been blind not to see that trait in him.

"Woman, now you need to get that mouth of yours working somewhere important," he ordered, sounding irritated. "Before you get yourself in trouble."

Laughing softly, happy, she started to bend toward his chest again. The hand in her hair didn't move, making it impossible. Her gaze jumped to his.

"Kiss me, *mi amor*."

She had no problems with that. The man could kiss. He could ignite fires with his kiss, detonate fireworks or even cause towering firestorms. She was all for kissing him. She let him bring her head to his, his fist nearly relinquishing its hold. Maybe she liked the way he was in control, because that burn inside burst into a roaring hunger. She felt the heat inside her increase.

Deliberately she took her time when his fist urged her to hurry. She lowered her head slowly, holding his gaze, watching him as she bent her head to his. She'd never felt so sexy in her life. The hunger built so fast, so intensely in his eyes and was carved in the lines on his face, that she felt the intensity deep inside her core.

She brushed her mouth over his. Once. Twice. The hand in her hair tugged hard and held her firmly in place. His mouth took over. The fire in her belly exploded, and she melted into him, her mouth devouring him, just as he devoured her. It was beyond what she remembered. She was lost in him immediately. He kissed her long. Hard. So rough it bordered on brutal. Delicious. Perfect. She felt as if fire consumed her. Raced inside of her, radiating a scorching hunger.

His hand in her hair loosened, and she kissed his chin, along the hard sweep of his jaw and that bluish-black stubble she loved. Down along his throat. Her hands joined her mouth in her exploration, smoothing over his hot skin, loving the muscles she found there.

Elijah lay still, but she felt his pulse jumping and the tension gathering in his body. He liked control, but he was giving it to her. She loved that and she planned on taking her time, mapping his body—the body that belonged to her.

His fingers sifted through her hair, and he trembled when she licked over his nipples and then sucked gently.

"I've spent my life alone, Siena. Dreaming about you. About a girl I saw with hair down to her waist, hair I wanted to see spread across my pillow and feel sliding over my skin. Knowing what I was. Knowing I didn't deserve her and I never was going to deserve her."

She looked up at him, her eyes meeting his. "Don't, Elijah," she warned, and dropped her head to nip him in the belly. He had more than a six-pack. She didn't think that was possible, but he had more muscles in his abdomen than she could conceive. She didn't know it if was the leopard in him, but if it was, her leopard had shortchanged her.

He ignored her caution. "You gotta know, baby. You have to see exactly what you mean to me. Those eyes of yours. *Dios, mi amorcito.* Those eyes. I dreamt about your eyes. I love looking into them. I knew I wanted to be looking into them when I made you come apart. You have no idea how many times I jacked off, thinking about your lush body and those fuck-me eyes of yours. My dream girl. Still can't believe you're here in my bed."

She loved that. *Loved* it. She loved that he thought those things about her. The sincerity rang in his tone. Her leopard heard it and she heard it and knew he was giving her the truth. She smoothed her hands down his thighs, felt the muscles there tense and shudder beneath her wandering fingers.

"I'm big, baby. Always feels like I'm too big when I get inside you. Stretching you. Does it burn, I wonder. And then I can't think anymore because you feel so fucking good I can't breathe. You do that to me, Siena. I can't get air in my lungs because you grip me so tight and you're scorching hot. Strangling me. Milking me. I feel that. Fucking paradise, baby."

She lifted her head, not to look at his face, but to examine the beautiful, perfect portion of his anatomy he was talking about. He was big. Intimidating. He looked all man, just like his face and body. Nothing soft about Elijah. He was hard and unashamed about it. She curved her palm around the thick shaft and one by one added her fingers to form a fist.

His cock was long and thick and pulsing with heat. With life. It jerked in her hand and she leaned down to breathe air over the flaring head. Her tongue tentatively licked along the shaft and settled just beneath the crown. His breath exploded from his lungs and she nearly pulled back, afraid of doing something wrong. But then he was talking again, his voice so rough with need, she knew she was on the right track.

"Alone all my life, even in the midst of my family, baby. Couldn't show my sister affection. Hell, couldn't show a dog affection. They use that shit. After a while you don't feel anymore, you train yourself not to. You do what you have to do to survive and then you wake up one morning knowing that's all you're doing. Existing. Surviving. No reason to live. You got nothing, and you're ashamed of what you are because all the good in you has been siphoned out. You're left with what you are when you look in the mirror. What you see. And baby, what I see isn't good."

She hated that he felt that way about himself. *Hated* it with every breath in her body. She needed him to know he was more than what his family had taught him to believe he was. She saw so much more in him. She always had. She saw the good.

She closed her mouth over that pulsing, velvety head and sucked hard, her fist tightening around the thick shaft because his hand curved around hers and clamped down. It was sexy. Hot. His hips rose just a little. Just enough to know he liked what she was doing to him. A low groan escaped his mouth. Guttural. Sexy.

"Then you see her driving up in her convertible, sexy hair, fuck-me eyes, body made in heaven. She looks at you like you're the only fucking man in the world. Those eyes. Looking. Seeing something else beside a killer. Seeing a man. So hungry for him. You know you shouldn't touch that. You know, but there she is. The damn world right in front of you. Making you see yourself as a man, as something worthwhile, not the fucking killer they shaped you into."

She couldn't stand it. His voice was so raw with truth, with what he believed of himself and of her, and he made her out to be something so special, so perfect to him she wanted to cry. Instead she did her best to show him what he meant to her. That she'd dreamt of him. Of being with him exactly like this. In his bed. Giving him something special, a gift from her to him.

"*Dios*, baby. That's right. Right there. Fucking heaven. I knew you'd be heaven. That mouth of yours."

Her gaze jumped to his face. He was staring down at her, his eyes hooded. Sensual. Filled with lust and something else entirely. Something warm and soft and beautiful. Her heart nearly stopped beating and then began to pound. She didn't stop, her mouth moving on him, her tongue sliding up and over him. Dancing. Licking. Mouth engulfing. All the while she looked into his eyes.

His breath exploded out of him. His face darkened. He was beautiful. Gorgeous. Hers. Power was a heady thing, and she knew she was getting to him. His voice changed subtly. That smooth, velvet rasp became a little more hoarse. A little harsher.

"I know better. I know you're too damned good for me, but there you are. And I'm not man enough to send you on your way because you're the reason I survived that shit. You're the reason I stayed alive and protected my sister. You're the reason, Siena."

Her heart beating hard, melting at the things he told her, she sucked hard and fluttered her tongue against the underside of that crown. His breath left his lungs. She heard it as her tongue swirled, shaping him, caressing him. Exploring. Taking her time.

She moved over him now, body undulating restlessly, making its own demands, her breasts sliding over his thighs, the hair rasping against her nipples. Her mouth worked him. She was intimidated by his size and tentative at first about trying to take him deeper, but he let her do all the work, set the pace, and he never pushed her.

His hand left hers to settle in her hair. She liked that. Liked that he loved the silky mess she could never quite keep under control. She found she liked her mouth on him. The way he tasted. Hot. Masculine. Salt and spice. Maybe it was the leopard in her, because she hadn't thought she would enjoy giving him pleasure unless she was so wild she was out of control, not like this, a deliberate seduction, but she did.

Watching him watch her as she took him deeper was just plain erotic and sent little streaks of fire darting to her sex. Damp, liquid heat pulsed between her legs. The burn was so hot now she began to lose her own control. There was nothing tentative about the way she used her mouth or her hand on him. The way her other hand strayed to his balls, rolling gently, loving the velvet feel of him.

Part of it was the things he told her about himself. He made her all the hotter, and she knew he had managed to distract her from being self-conscious or afraid of doing something wrong. How could she do anything wrong when he was baring his soul to her? Telling her what she meant to him. Letting her know she was his everything?

He groaned. His hands tightened in her hair, the bite of pain sharp. His hips jerked, pushed his cock deeper so that he touched the back of her throat. A thrill shot down her spine. He looked lost in the sensations she created. The look on his face was more than enough for a reward. So beautiful. So masculine. Lines of pleasure carved deep, so sensual and just plain hot.

There was no denying she felt incredibly sexy. The burn in her sex had gotten out of control, the tension coiling tighter until she thought it was possible she could have an orgasm just watching his face.

"Baby," he groaned softly. "You're about done."

She loved when he called her that. But she wasn't about done. He was thicker. Harder. Longer. A treat. Hers. She clamped down tightly with her mouth, hollowing her cheeks and using her tongue. He was a man who had never had love. Never had care. He had given himself to her, and she wanted him to know she could take just as good care of him as he did her.

His body shuddered. "That's it. Come here to me."

She wasn't through. She *loved* what she was doing. She loved how it made her feel to bring that look to his face. She loved that she could give him so much pleasure. He took care of her, saw to her every need, and she was determined to do the same. He needed it. He needed to know that to her, he was worth every second she spent bringing him pleasure.

He reached down and caught her beneath her arms and hauled her up his body with his enormous strength. Before she could protest, he rolled her, her back to his front and then rolled both of them, so she ended up belly down in the bed, his body covering hers. He sank back on his calves, caught her hips and yanked her to her knees, one hand sliding up her back to settle between her shoulder blades. He pushed her head to the mattress, holding her still with one hand.

Excitement flared. She secretly loved the growls rumbling from his chest and the way his eyes turned from molten mercury to quicksilver. She loved the feel of his hands, so hard, fingers gripping, digging into her.

"You kept that up, *mi vida*, I would have finished in your mouth." Now his voice was a growl too.

Siena was glad her face was pressed into the mattress because there was no way she could have hidden her smile from him. She wouldn't have minded. He thought he was still protecting her, but she was so far past that now. He'd handed her confidence, and she wasn't going to *ever* go back to being uncertain. He'd given her too much of himself for her not to realize what she meant to him.

One hand transferred to the nape of her neck, holding her in the position he wanted. The other moved over her bottom, rubbing gently. He traced the indentations in the small of the back, slid over the curves of her firm cheeks to the junction between her thighs.

Siena shivered. His fingers moved to her inner thighs, stroking little circles just beneath her pulsing sex.

"Spread your knees for me, baby," he ordered softly. "As wide as you can."

She liked that too. She complied immediately, spreading her thighs as wide as possible. His fingers never stopped dancing along her skin. Everywhere he touched, he left behind flames. His caresses were so light that at first she barely felt them, but then they began to sear right through her skin to her core. Her sheath wept for him. Grew hotter. Tension coiled tighter. She pushed back, seeking more.

His hand went away and her breath left her body in a long rush.

"Elijah," she wailed.

"Behave," he ordered. "You had your fun. I get mine."

She supposed that was only fair, but he was torturing her, and she had the feeling he was *way* better at it than she was. She forced her body to be still. The moment his hand came back, she closed her eyes and drifted on that tide, allowing the sensuality of his touch to take her higher.

"Oh, God, honey," she gasped. "I need more."

He didn't reply right away, at least not verbally. He sank a finger into her tight heat, and the air rushed from her lungs. He pushed deep and it took everything she had not to push back.

"Just so you know, baby, a man like me *never* forgets protection. Never forgets to wear a glove. *You're* the only woman in my life who managed to make me forget everything but losing myself in your body."

He pushed a second finger into her, stretching her tight muscles. At the same time he leaned into her and bit down gently on her left cheek. The shock of pain mingled with pleasure bursting through her so that her head swam, brain short-circuiting instantly.

"Not only did I not wear a condom, I forgot all about the fucking hit man I knew had to be making his approach. I was so far gone in you, Siena, both of us could have been killed. You know damn well all that shit I said to you was just plain bull, because it was."

The fingers withdrew and then pushed deep again. She heard her breath come in a ragged sob. His mouth moved over her buttocks, tasting the silk of her skin, moving down the curve so his tongue could trace along the crease between her thigh and then back to that firm swell of her butt.

She could barely think when his teeth bit down a second

time while his fingers continued to plunge in and out of her. She gasped. Pushed back. Ground down desperately on his fingers, a sob of need escaping.

Just like that his fingers were gone. "Don't move, baby," he hissed. "You stay still and let me play. I'm going to leave my brand on you."

Heat scored through her. The blood rushed hot through her veins. She *loved* his voice, loved the way his hand smoothed over her skin, and his mouth went to the inside of her thigh and the stubble of the shadow along his jaw rasped over the inside of her legs. Then he was sucking. High. Close to her sex. She knew she'd have a strawberry there. It felt sexy and hot. Very hot. She could barely breathe, her breath coming in ragged gasps.

"Elijah." His name came out a plea.

"Have we erased the major fuckup of the century, or do we need to do some more work to make you put that shit to bed *permanently*?"

His teeth scraped along her inner thigh. Close. So close to her heated center. Her sex spasmed. She felt almost desperate.

"I never want you to feel a lack of confidence again, Siena," he went on, his voice dark with hunger and lust. "I never want you to think about that shit again. And I sure don't want to hear about it. No man wants to have that big of a fuckup thrown in his face. You get me?"

She got him. She would have smiled at the edge to his voice, but her brain could only focus on the need pulsing in her. Every cell in her body ached for him. She felt moisture on her inner thighs. His tongue licked up her leg in a sexy, hungry gesture that sent more damp liquid pulsing through her channel.

"Elijah." She sobbed his name, pleading with him.

"That's not what I want to hear, baby." His tongue stroked across her entrance, collecting the taste of honeysuckle spilling from her body.

Her brain was scrambled but she managed to pull herself together enough to get the words out. Her voice shook, but she gave him what he wanted. "I think it's safe to say it's been put to bed permanently, Elijah."

"About damn time," he growled, and then his mouth was on her.

She heard her own keening wail as his tongue thrust deep and he suckled, devouring her. Not gentle. Not easy. A man starving. Ravenous. The contrast between the way he had played so gently with her, his fingers light on her skin, barely there, and now his tongue and teeth and mouth ravaging her sent her spiraling out of control.

Her body clamped down, rippling, the breath-stealing orgasm rushing over her before she had a chance to even know it was there. He didn't stop. He consumed her, claimed her body for his own, ate at her, drawing out the hot cream and demanding more. She didn't have a chance to catch her breath before the second one overtook with even greater force than the first.

She chanted his name. Sobbed as pleasure took her, fragmenting her body and sending pieces of her in a million different directions. If he hadn't clamped his hands around her hips, she would have collapsed onto the bed. He didn't stop. Not even when the bliss threatened to drive her right out of her mind and she pleaded with him, gasping out his name and fisting the sheets in her hands on either side of her head.

"No, baby, I want more," he whispered against her entrance, his tongue licking at the cream in between each word.

His teeth scraped at her sensitive bud, and her sheath convulsed. Her head thrashed back and forth on the mattress, facedown, side to side, hair spilling around her until she couldn't see. That only intensified the sensations. His hand was suddenly in her hair, gathering the silky mass into his fist and yanking her head up even as he knelt up behind her, the flared head of his cock burrowing into her entrance.

For a moment her heart seemed to stop beating in

anticipation, but the orgasm ripping through her continued to pulse and throb. He drove forward hard. Slamming home, burying himself to the hilt. In the position he held her, he could go even deeper, his thickness burning and stretching her as he took her hard and fast. The orgasm increased in strength, gripping him, milking, until the fiery friction sent her reeling into subspace.

His fingers dug into her hips and he yanked her back into him as he surged forward again and again, sending whips of lightning through her body straight to her core, up her belly and into her breasts. He rode her hard, an endless, dazzling ride, brutal and rough, pushing her high again.

The tension coiled so tightly inside her, she feared her mind would unravel with her body this time. Fear skittered down her spine, but that just seemed to add to the building need burning inside her. He seemed insatiable, demanding more of her. He swore in his language, his voice a rough rasp over her skin, the sound stroking her insides.

"So. Fucking. Beautiful." He bit the words out. "You're killing me baby. Scorching hot. Strangling me with fire. Fucking beautiful. Give that to me again."

"I can't . . ." She couldn't. Not again. But he was relentless, pounding into her, forcing her body to build and build. Coil tighter and tighter. Soar higher and higher. "Elijah." Again she sobbed his name, her fingernails digging into her palms through the sheets. She was going to come apart, and this time there would be no putting her back together because each orgasm had gotten bigger. Stronger. Lasted longer.

"For me, baby. Give that gift to me again," he whispered.

She felt him, already so big, thickening more. Stretching her, the relentless pounding increasing in strength. Her body shattered. Clamped down hard on his, dragging over his steely shaft, bathing him with hot liquid, but so tight the friction threatened to set both of them on fire.

She screamed, the sound tearing up from her core, through her belly and breasts and out her throat. She turned her head to muffle the sound in the mattress, terrified her cries would bring the security guards running to save her. Elijah's body swelled even more, stretching her through the force of her orgasm, the fire streaking around him. Hot jets of seed rocketed deep.

It took forever for her body to quiet, to calm, to settle into rippling aftershocks that kept his body shuddering right along with hers. Elijah pressed kisses down her spine, his arms locked around her hips.

"You okay, baby?" he asked when he got his breathing under control.

"I don't know," she answered honestly. "Don't move."

"No worries, *mi amor*, that would be impossible right now. You drained me of everything. My brain is fried right along with my body."

Even as he assured her he wouldn't move, he was slipping out of her, his heavy cock dragging over her sensitive bud so that another violent quake burst through her. She would have collapsed forward, but he rolled her to her side, tucking her to him, his head at her breast. The slide of his hair on her skin sent a burn rushing through her veins.

She lay staring up at the ceiling, her breathing ragged and labored as she tried to draw air into her burning lungs. Her body felt as if it was floating. Her mind was somewhere else. She turned her head slowly to look at Elijah. His features, always tough, always closed down, were an open book.

Her heart somersaulted. Her stomach did the same. She had almost escaped, and if she had, she would never have seen that look. Soft. Loving. So beautiful. All for her. Instinctively she knew no one other than their child would ever get that look. He would reserve it for her and any children they had.

She managed to roll over, keeping one hand on his belly to prevent him from moving. She crawled down his body. So strong. All those roped muscles, all that hot, hard skin. Hers.

"Baby," he breathed softly. "What are you doing?"

"Hush," she ordered. She could find her bossy when she needed it. "I'm seeing to my man, taking care of him."

She loved taking care of him. No one else had ever done it. He had never had care. Or loving. She was going to give it to him. Spoil him like no other man had ever been spoiled. Siena had no idea what drove her, but she *needed* to take care of him. Clean him. Curl up beside him, into him, so he knew she was there—that she'd always be there—for him. It was important he understood what he had—what they had—in their world.

His hands immediately went to her hair, stroking caresses, sifting through the silky strands as he waited to see what she would do. She liked that too. That as bossy and controlling as he could be, he let her do what she wanted, what obviously was important to her.

She kissed his belly, using the pads of her fingers, taking her time as if memorizing his body. She kissed her way along the path of his hip bones and then began to lap at him gently, almost reverently, her mouth and tongue bathing him, cleaning their combined scents from his body. Her gaze went to his face as she pressed kisses along his thighs and lapped with her tongue.

Elijah closed his eyes, his face that of a contented man— or leopard. She loved that she put that look there. Warm. Moist. She bathed him with love. She hadn't told him, but she tried to show him. Using a velvet rasp. Sucking and lapping as she cleaned him, paying attention to details, his shaft, the underside of the crown, his heavy sac, the front of his thighs. She took her time. Was thorough. Was loving. Wanting him to go to sleep knowing he mattered. And feeling loved.

She crawled back up his body and his arm tightened around her, locking her to him. When she tilted her head to look at him, his eyes were open, moving over her face in the way of a leopard. All silver. Molten. Possessive. Soft with love. Her stomach fluttered and then did a slow roll.

"You shatter me, baby. *Shatter* me. I don't know what I ever did to deserve you, Siena, but you can't do this, give me this beauty and ever walk away from me."

"Does it feel like I want to walk away, Elijah?" She had thought she was the one without confidence. The one who would always wonder if she was good enough and if he really wanted her, but she realized he felt that way. He didn't think he was good enough for her.

He took her mouth. Hard. Aggressive. She gave him their combined taste, and he stripped it from her, holding her to him, his fist bunched tight in her hair.

"So fucking beautiful, Siena," he whispered against her throat.

He moved then, sliding down in the bed, onto his side, turning her toward him on her side, front to front. One thigh slid between hers.

He locked his arm around her waist and pulled her tight against him. "I've wanted to do this since the first time I saw you sleeping, Siena," he said. "You have beautiful breasts. I love to look at them. To know they're mine." His tongue licked at her nipple, and deep inside her sex, her body convulsed again. "I want to go to sleep like this. You in my mouth."

The idea of it sent heat spiraling through her bloodstream again. There was no way for her body to settle, not when he talked like that. One hand cupped the underside of her breasts, and then began to move down her body until his palm found her softening belly.

"My baby is right here. Growing inside you, *mi amorcito*. Do you know what that does for a man like me? To know that I have a family? Want to put a ring on your finger, baby, give you my name, but we have to sort through a lot of shit first." His hand slid farther until it came to rest on her mound.

His mouth stayed at her breast so she could feel the heat from his breath. "I want you sleeping with me inside you. My baby. My seed. My mouth on your breast. My fingers inside you."

"I'm not certain I can go to sleep that way, honey," she said honestly, "but if you want that, I'll try."

His mouth nuzzled her breast as his fingers sought her entrance. Two slipped inside of her. Instantly her tight channel clamped down, holding him to her. Her entire body reacted to that intimate closeness. Every cell.

"Tonight I want to fall asleep inside in you," he whispered.

She reached up and tangled her fingers in his hair. "Go to sleep, Elijah," she whispered, already drifting. Exhausted. Happy.

13

ELIJAH woke, his leopard snarling. Someone was close. In the hall. He listened and knew by the padding of the feet that one of the men was patrolling close. He'd asked for that, worried that Paolo might find a way inside.

Siena was close. Naked. Her body soft. Lush. His. Sound asleep, she was just as beautiful as when she was awake. He studied her face. She looked like a Madonna, the long sweep of her lashes dark against her pale skin. She took his breath away when he looked at her like this.

He especially loved her face. The oval shape of it, her high cheekbones, her lush, kissable mouth. Inviting. She looked sexy when she wrapped her luscious lips around his cock. So sexy. Her large exotic eyes looking up at him and her hair falling in long waves all around her, brushing his skin. She was beyond any fantasy he'd ever had of her, and what she'd done afterward . . .

Her mouth and tongue on him. The care she'd taken. He

hadn't asked, nor would he have ever asked for such a thing, but she'd made him feel as if she worshiped him. As if he was the greatest thing in her world and she took her time caring for him. She hadn't rushed it, lapping at him with her velvet soft tongue. Little kisses up and down his shaft, on the insides of his thighs.

He closed his eyes, his body stirring with the memory. So beautiful. So shocking. Completely unexpected. The fact that she would treat him like that, initiate it and *enjoy* it, left him shattered inside. She would forever be inside of him. Every preconceived notion he had about the intimacy between a man and woman was gone. She'd made him feel like a good man. A man worthy of an incredible woman.

Her body was close. He wrapped himself in the faint wild, exotic scent that was uniquely hers. Her body was as lush as her mouth—full, soft curves—a body a man could get lost in—would want to get lost in. He leaned down and pressed a kiss into her belly, right where his child was growing in her. A small miracle. Siena was the real miracle. She seemed to be able to accept him as he was. She hadn't even told him to watch his language. She just . . . *loved* him. She hadn't said it. She hadn't used those words, but he felt it in every stroke of her tongue. As if that wasn't enough, she'd given him more. She'd let him drift off to sleep, his mouth on her, his fingers in her.

A leopard chuffed just outside the door, and he stiffened. He was needed. He knew the morning was gone, along with most of the afternoon. He wanted to be alone with Siena, without the security team. Without the threats to her life. To his. He shook his head as he slowly, with great reluctance, pulled his thigh from between hers. He probably wouldn't know what to do with normal. Without knowing every second of his existence, someone was plotting against him. That was normal, but he didn't want that for Siena or his children.

The moment he moved, her arm tightened around him

and she murmured a protest. His heart shifted. "Go back to sleep, *mi amorcito*," he said softly.

Her long, feathery lashes lifted, and he found himself staring into the piercing emerald green of her eyes. "What's wrong, honey?"

He knew his expression hadn't changed. He didn't blink. He simply stared down at this woman who so easily had taken his heart and soul. Still, she knew. His heart fluttered when she called him honey. He loved the way the word rolled off her tongue and the soft look in her eyes when she said it.

"Nothing for you to worry about, baby," he said, and ran his finger over her nipple, watching it form a hard peak. Distracting her.

She shivered, drew in a breath, but sat up, shoving at the long hair neither of them had braided before they'd fallen asleep. "Tell me, Elijah."

"I said not to worry about it," he repeated. This time he used his rough, leopard voice, the one that no one defied.

She lifted her chin at him. *Lifted her chin.* The little defiant chin that made his cock harder than a rock and made his leopard snarl and leap for the surface.

He shook his head, eyes glittering, more cat than human. The leopard roared with savage, brutish need to dominate. "Back the fuck off, Siena. This shit isn't touching you any more than it already has. This is my mess. *Mine.* Drake's. Your grandfather's. You have no business being caught in the middle of it, and if it's the last thing I do, I'm making sure you're out of it."

Her mouth opened and then closed with a snap as her green eyes darkened from emerald to a dangerous forest. Her face flushed. "Did you just tell me to back the f-word off?"

She sounded incredulous. Pissed. Adorable. His body, already painfully hard, began to burn. Heat rushed through his veins. Little jackhammers began tripping in his head. He tried to breathe away the need.

"The f-word? Baby." There was no stopping his grin. No way. He wanted to lean down and kiss her mouth.

"Don't you *dare* laugh at me, Elijah," she snapped. "For your information, this *shit* is *my* shit. I brought it with me. It was never yours. So I have every right to know what's going on and help figure out what to do about it." She leaned closer, tilting her head to his. "Do you get me?"

That lean. That head tilt. She was fucking finished and she didn't even know it. "Yeah, babe, I get you, but you'd better fucking get me." He framed her face with both hands, and his cock jerked hard against his stomach. His body moved aggressively into hers. "My woman doesn't have shit touch her, hers or mine. I'd give you the world, walk on water for you, give you whatever the hell you think you want, but not this. This *shit* doesn't touch you again."

He slammed his mouth down on hers, using his weight to drive her back to the mattress. Her body was soft, all lush curves, and he ran one hand over them, stopping to tug at her nipple, rolling it between his thumb and finger hard. She gasped into his mouth, arching her back.

"Open your legs," he instructed against her mouth. Kissing her. Devouring her. Claiming her.

"Elijah." She put one hand on his chest, trying to push at him.

He caught both wrists in one of his hands and slammed them above her head, holding them pinned there while the other continued to travel over her body. "Right fucking now, Siena. Spread your legs for me."

His mouth was back on hers, capturing her shocked protest. Taking the taste of her into him, that sweet honey she never withheld from him, not even now when she was finding him bossy and annoying. She spread her legs. He rewarded her with a nip on her chin and a bite on her neck that turned into a nice strawberry.

"Wider, baby, wrap your legs around mine." He bit at the swell of her breast. Left another strawberry, loving to see his marks on her.

She complied, hooking her legs around his hips.

"You wet for me?" He knew she was. He knew she liked his bossy. More, she loved his kisses. His rough. His sweet. His woman liked it all. "You ready, baby? Because I'm burning up."

"Let go of my hands. I want to touch you." Her hips bucked under his.

"No." He left a string of strawberries across her breasts and then suckled. Strong. Used the flat of his tongue. Her breasts were sensitive, and her entire body bucked. Her breath came in ragged gasps. She tried to free her hands, but he kept her pinned. "You didn't earn that, baby. You argued with me first thing."

She went still, fury gathering in her eyes. He loved riling her. Loved that beauty, and she was easy to rile. Passionate. She might say he scared her, but she had no hesitation going up against him. Even as she glared at him, her hips pushed against his.

"I didn't *earn* that?"

She hissed it, her leopard just as close as his. He guided his cock to her hot entrance, to the paradise he knew was there. She was dripping. Slick. So scorching hot there was no way he was waiting. And he didn't. He slammed home. Hard. Brutal. The way he needed. The way she needed.

Her sheath clamped down on his cock, strangling him in slick, living silk, a brutal, beautiful fist that worked him as he hammered in and out of her. Her hips rose to meet his every thrust, her body jolting, breasts thrust up and moving with every deep stroke. Her face was a mask of sheer beauty, sensual passion in every line, eyes dark with lust and a little dazed, just the way he loved to see, as if he took her mind and filled it with him.

"More, honey. I need harder," she whispered.

"Earns you back your hands, baby," he managed to bite out between his teeth. He let go of her wrists, wrapped his arms under her knees and yanked her bottom up, nearly folding her in half, giving himself more leverage.

Instantly her hands went to his buttocks, fingers digging deep. He felt the sharp nails sinking into him, urging him to take her harder. Yeah. She liked his bossy. She liked his protection. She liked her man in charge. She might not know it, but she definitely responded to his commands.

He lost himself in her, burying himself deep in that haven of sheer bliss. He let her sweep him into another place where he wasn't covered in dirt and shit. Where he was clean and his woman worshiped him. Where he could live free and feel like a man instead of a fucking killer with blood on his hands. She gave him that.

She held him to her, wrapped him up, he felt that gift even when she was consuming him, the fire raging hotter than it ever had. He could hear the little noises she made in her throat. Frantic. Sobbing his name. Music. Sweet. Sexy. He stared down into her face even as he increased the brutal thrusts. Savage now. He couldn't get enough of her. Couldn't bury himself deep enough. Rocking both of them.

He felt her building. Coiling. Her sheath gripped hard. Clamped down. "Wait," he hissed. "You wait for me."

"I can't, honey," she gasped.

"Damn it, fucking wait," he growled, increasing the pace, slamming harder. Giving himself up to her. Burning from the inside out.

Her fingers dug deep, but she held on for him. Fought back the tsunami as it built and built. He felt it then, coming at both of them, a tidal wave, throwing them both high, consuming them, burning him clean, so clean he didn't recognize himself. She did that to him, turned him inside out until he was in pieces scattered at her feet.

He buried his face in her neck, his teeth in her skin. His heart pounding as the earth moved all around him, shaking him up. Deep inside, where no one could see, he let fear sweep through him. He had lost everything good in his life practically before his life had even started. Now there was Siena. Now there was a priceless gift, a treasure so unexpected and beautiful, he knew if she were taken from him he wouldn't survive intact.

Her arms went around him, hands sliding down the sheen of sweat on his back. He allowed her legs to drop to the mattress, the action sending ripples of aftershock through both of them. He closed his eyes and breathed in their combined scents, feeling sated. He knew it wouldn't last long, but with her scent surrounding him and her soft body crushed beneath his, his cock softening inside her heat, he felt content.

"Honey, roll over," she whispered softly. "You're squashing me."

He was. He knew it. He had given her his weight, but he needed to. He needed to feel her there beneath him—his. He licked at the bite mark on her neck and then complied, rolling them both so she was sprawled on top of him. She lifted her head, her green eyes moving over his face. Seeing too much. He couldn't give her any more or he'd be so lost in her he'd never find his way out. He had a job to do, one that required the bastard. The killer. Not the man he saw in her eyes.

He moved his hips, allowing himself to slide from the haven of her body as he rolled off of her. "Gotta go, baby. Drake's waiting."

She pinned him with her green eyes. Cat eyes. Focused. Glittering. "You can stay right there until I'm done, Elijah." She sounded every bit as bossy as he did, although on her it was rather adorable. She moved down his body, keeping a hand on his belly, fingers splayed wide. "You are such an ass sometimes." She hissed the accusation, bending her head to his hips, licking up the indentation along his bone. "You had your fun and you aren't moving until I say so. Got that?"

He sank his hands into that thick sweep of hair meaning to pull her head up, to keep her from undoing him more, but he couldn't actually take that away from her. Or take it away from him. He just lay there, both hands sifting through the mass of her hair, all that silk. It moved over his skin as she began to clean him. Using her mouth. That warm, soft mouth, that velvet rasp of a tongue.

"*Dios, mi amorcito*, I got it." She was killing him. Bringing him beauty when his entire life had been a fucking nightmare.

Emotion welled up, threatening to choke him. He felt the burn behind his eyes and he nearly pulled her off of him, his body going rigid. She was stripping him bare. Removing, layer by layer, the armor he'd spent a lifetime growing around his heart and soul. She saw him. Deep where he hid. Where that small, tiny piece of humanity he guarded was cowering. Protected. She had that. She saw that. Anyone else he would have killed. But Siena . . . He belonged to her. Heart and soul. That last piece of him was in her hands. He'd given that to her without knowing it, and it was far too late to take it back.

"Honey?"

She whispered the soft inquiry against his shaft. He felt the vibration right through his body. Her fingers stroked caresses there and then lower, to his suddenly aching balls. Taking her time. Paying attention. The insides of his thighs, her mouth following her hands. He shuddered. Still tense. So vulnerable he feared he would shatter into a million pieces and he would never be the same.

"What is it? Tell me." That was whispered against the base of his shaft. Her tongue curled. Lapped around the base of his cock, finding every crease and sending waves of heat riding up his shaft. Blood pooled low. Wicked. Sinful. His personal miracle.

"I can't ever let that vile shit touch you, baby. Not ever. I don't want you angry with me because I am who and what I am. I have to protect you. Keep you like this. Keep you safe and protect that innocence in you. I *have* to." God. His voice was so raw his throat burned.

"All right." She licked up his shaft, curled her tongue

around him and then pressed a kiss to the crown. Her tongue tasted the pearly drops waiting there.

"All right?" he repeated, whispering because he couldn't find his voice. Not believing his little spitfire would give that to him without a fight.

"I won't be angry, Elijah," she promised, pressing kisses up his shaft. "Just relax and let me show you how I feel about you. I want you to hear me when I'm talking, saying what needs to be said." She pressed another kiss on the flared crown and then her mouth engulfed him. Took him. Swallowed him.

His entire body came to life. Every cell. He'd been semi-hard and he instantly swelled. Thickened. Lengthened. She was talking all right, and he was hearing her. He'd just come and he'd come hard and suddenly he was on fire. Burning. Her mouth worked him, tongue stroking and dancing, curling around him, rubbing the underside of the crown in that sweet spot.

He opened his mouth to caution her, but nothing came out. She took him up fast and he could already feel his balls drawing up, hard as twin rocks, boiling with need. She devoured him, suckling hard, rubbing with her tongue, her hands moving over his thighs, cupping his sac, pressing between his buttocks. He found himself thrusting into her mouth, and he didn't honestly know who had the control. He didn't feel in control. He felt insane with lust. With love. With everything a man could feel for a woman and more. His fists tightened in her hair, holding her head to him. That didn't scare her or deter her.

He hit the back of her throat and felt her choke, and then she breathed deep and took him deeper. Swallowing. Massaging him with the muscles of her throat. Giving him that. Giving him something so beautiful he could barely comprehend. He was dazed, shocked, pumping into her mouth, guiding her with her own hair.

Her mouth was hot and tight and she didn't stop. She made

little desperate noises, as if she couldn't get enough of him. As if she was so hungry for him, she was frantic. Every sound she made vibrated through his cock, adding to the fire scorching him. Her fingers dug deep into his buttocks, urging his hips to move into her. Her mouth tightened as he moved in and out. Then he was there. He felt it moving through him, shattering him. Hot jets of his essence pouring into her, down her throat, and the suction softened, gentled, became tender and sweet.

Elijah lay there, one hand covering his eyes, breathing deep, unable to process what she'd just given him. What she was still giving him. His eyes burned like a son of a bitch. His throat felt raw. For the first time he knew what real love felt like. Intense. Scary. Painful. So fucking painful. He was Elijah Lospostos. Just about every member of his family had been nothing but brutal and vile. There was no sweet. There was no clean, and there was no woman loving and adoring.

"I don't deserve you, Siena," he choked out.

She licked up his shaft, over the sensitive crown, and then pressed kisses over him, kissing her way up to his belly where she laid her head. Her hair slid over him like a cover of silk.

"You deserve me, Elijah. You're arrogant and bossy and I'm going to have to kick you once in a while, but your sweet takes my breath away."

He sifted his fingers through her hair. "Baby, I really have to go. Take a hot bath or you're going to be sore. I don't want you sore for very selfish reasons. As soon as I take care of whatever it is Drake needs me for, I'll fix us dinner."

She turned her head, chin digging into his belly, her eyes on his face. "I like that you cook."

"I'm a good cook." He enjoyed cooking. It reminded him of his grandmother, the one person in his life who had been really good to him.

"I'm not. But I want to learn. Will you teach me?"

"I don't mind being the cook."

"I'd like to learn at least how to make a few dishes. You're mine, honey," she said softly, pressing a kiss on his belly. "You take care of me however you need to, but know that I'm going to take care of you my way—the way I need to. You have to give me that. That includes in the kitchen and in our bed."

"Siena. Woman, you're killing me." Because it was true. The absolute truth.

She lifted her head again, chin back against his abs, her green eyes moving over his face. "Can you do that, Elijah? Let me have this. Let me have all of you." She stretched her body over his, sat up, straddling him. She leaned into him, kissing the hollow of his throat as her hands swept over his chest. She trailed kisses down the middle of his chest to his belly button.

"That means talking to me when you're angry or upset. Giving me that guidance so I can give you whatever you need." Her gaze jumped back to his face. "Can you give that to me?"

His heart nearly stopped in his chest. She sat astride him, her sex pressed to his. Her body was straight, breasts jutting toward him, full and enticing. His. Her narrow rib cage and small tucked-in waist emphasized the curve of her hips. All his. Her expression was soft. Tender even. Soft like her skin and her lush curves.

"I can do that, *mi vida*," he agreed. He could barely choke the words out around the lump in his throat.

She *was* killing him and she didn't even know it. She was peeling away the man he'd been and letting out the one he wanted to be—for her. He knew she was wrapped so tight around his heart there was no escaping. He'd do anything to keep her. He didn't dare show that to the rest of the world. He was going to have to walk a very thin line to keep her safe.

She pressed another kiss to his belly, slid her hand up his chest and shifted off of him. "I'll go take a hot bath and then join you in the kitchen for my first cooking lesson."

"Wear that long skirt of yours for me. The one that has all the ruffles falling to the floor." He loved that skirt on her.

She embodied feminine. From the first time he'd ever met Siena, she had loved girlie things. She wasn't a jeans kind of girl. She owned them and wore them, but she definitely preferred skirts.

She smiled at him. Soft. Her expression taking his breath, her eyes teasing. "You can wonder whether or not I'm wearing panties under it while you're cooking for me."

He caught her wrist as she slid off the bed, stopping her, looking up at her from where he lay. She was naked. All bare skin and lush curves. Beautiful. "Who do you belong to, Siena?"

Her green eyes drifted over his face. Over his body. Touching him without actually skimming her fingers over his skin. He felt that look. It seared him. Claimed him. Along with the soft there was possession. Tenderness. Things that knotted his belly more. That sent fear curling through him—the ugly snake that said any enemy could slay him, using her.

"I ask you a question, baby, I expect an answer," he said quietly, but with an edge to his voice. She had to know. She had to *always* know.

"I belong to you, Elijah."

"You get that we're leopards. Shifters."

She frowned, uncertain where he was going.

"Yes. I don't know much about that part of who I am, but yes, I know we're both shifters."

"What you need to get, *mi amorcito*, is that leopards don't like other males around their woman. Around their mate. My male is bonded to your female. He's going to need her regularly, and he isn't going to want any other male close to her. I don't want any other male close to you. Don't touch any of the men."

He saw her shut down. Her green eyes glittered and she took a step back. He didn't relinquish his hold on her wrist. His fingers tightened, shackling her to him as he sat up. "Don't get all pissy on me, Siena. I'm telling you a fact we both have to live with. I've got a male that rides me hard and I'm part of that. I feel that. You're mine. You belong to me. I need you safe, and I need other men to back the hell off. That means you don't encourage them . . ."

"*Encourage* them?" She spat the words out. "Let go of me. I'm going to take my bath, and I suggest you go soak your head in a bucket of water. I don't flirt with other men. I certainly don't *touch* them and I don't care for the implication you're making."

"Who the fuck were you calling earlier, then, because I'm pretty damn certain that was another man. Another leopard." He spat the words at her, knowing each time she got close, shattered him, *owned* him, he used his temper to pull himself back together. And there was always something he could get angry about. His leopard leapt for the surface. Savage. Fierce. Demanding to bring her back to his bed and force her to acknowledge that he *owned* her. Because, by God, she wasn't owning him without it going both ways.

She turned her head to look at the bits and pieces of her phone lying on the floor beside the opposite wall. "You broke my phone. You threw it."

"Who were you calling?" He knew damn well who she had called and he knew she knew he knew. Still. He wanted her to acknowledge that it had been another man she'd turned to. Another leopard.

"Let go of me before I smack you over the head."

"Who. Were. You. Calling?" He bit out each word, his temper rising.

Siena didn't seem intimidated. She reached down with her free hand, picked up a pillow and hit him in the head with it. Yeah. He lost control of her. She knew she'd reduced him to a marshmallow. Self-preservation was an ugly need rising like a tidal wave. A leopard's fury mingled with his own, both determined to dominate. To control. He needed control. It was the only way he survived. She had stripped him bare, and now she was defying him.

He yanked her down onto the bed so that she sprawled

across his lap, facedown on the mattress. Before she could move or speak, his hand came down hard on her ass. He smacked her five times in rapid succession. Hard. Making it count. Letting her know he wasn't going to be led around by his cock. Snarling. Growling even.

She began to struggle and he held her down, his hand on her red ass, smoothing over the handprints there, realizing his fury was about fear. Helplessness. She hadn't only stripped him bare and exposed that only soft spot, the place he could be killed; now he was terrified of someone hurting her. He needed complete control over all things in his life, especially Siena, and he feared there was no controlling Siena.

"You *hit* me. You bastard. I can't believe you hit me."

She stopped struggling and lay across him, shaking, her body soft and pliant, no sound emerging. He thought she was crying but he couldn't tell. Then a small sound, muffled by the mattress slipped out. Quiet. He was certain soft little sobs shook her body, but her face was turned away from him.

Remorse hit him hard. It wasn't about Siena at all; it was about him. His fears. His needs. His desire for complete control. No. It was even worse than that. He didn't want her to know just how far she'd gotten in. He continued to rub her bottom, trying to soothe away the hurt he'd caused.

"Baby," he began. There was nowhere to go with it. He wanted to kill Paolo for hitting her. This hadn't been an erotic spanking leading to other things. It wasn't about bringing her pleasure in any form. This had been a punishment. For what? What had she done but show him love? She'd done that. Given him a precious gift, and he'd thrown it back in her face because he was terrified. What the fuck was wrong with him?

He moved her body off of him. She didn't turn over. She didn't look at him, but kept her face averted, the long hair effectively hiding her from him. Hiding her expression. Hiding her tears. His stomach knotted more. Brutal. He was disgusted with himself.

"You aren't fucking leaving me over this, Siena. You're not leaving me. You're going to get past this fuckup too." His voice was harsh. Strangled. Savage, just like the savage beast raging inside him. He made it a dark decree. "You aren't leaving me. You try running and I'll hunt you down, bring you back and tie you to my bed until you see reason. Don't think for one minute I won't find you."

He didn't care if he sounded like the stalker man from hell. She gave him nothing. Siena was always an open book, but she just lay there, body shaking, spread across his bed like a fucking gift, a miracle, and he'd broken her because he was scared shitless of loving her so much it hurt. It fucking hurt.

He'd forgotten fear. He'd forgotten the taste of it in his mouth. The way it crawled up his throat and lived there. He hadn't felt fear since he was six years old and his grandfather shot one man, beat a second man to death in front of him and then when he cried had turned those fists on him.

Before he could utter another word, the muffled sounds grew in strength. She jammed her fist into her mouth, but they kept coming. Her body was really shaking now. Strangely, the noises she made, even muffled as they were, didn't sound like tears. At. All. He scowled and reached down to slide the veil of hair away from her face.

Siena rolled over. She was laughing. *Laughing.* At him. She sat up, pushing at the heavy fall of hair, still laughing. "Did you just try to spank me? Like as really a spanking, or was that some attempt at an erotic spanking, because I tell you, it didn't work. It was too funny. Really, Elijah? You spanked me? Like I was a child?" Using both hands, she moved them down the length of her body. "Newsflash, genius. Woman right here. Not child. *Woman.* All grown up. Spankings went out a few centuries ago. And another newsflash, you won't be spanking me for some erotic kink you have going, or for some misguided attempt to punish me or our children because, right now, I can tell you after that, it wouldn't work."

She burst out laughing all over again. "Seriously, Elijah,

you have to get over these little tantrums you throw. I feel as if I'll be raising two children, not one. You act out again, and I'll be putting you on time out."

Relief mingled with his anger. She wasn't planning on leaving him. Still, having his woman laugh at him wasn't a good sign. Seriously, the entire world was afraid of him. His name made grown men shake. If he couldn't control his woman, all that would change and the vultures would begin to circle and then he couldn't protect her . . .

"Elijah."

She said his name softly. Tenderly. Wrapping him in love. So much he had to close his eyes. He heard her move close to him, and her hand went up his chest to his neck. Her fingers curled around his nape.

"Honey. I get that you're a macho man. I totally get that. I get that you're having a hard time with this, but you solving our problems with your temper isn't going to work. It just isn't. You promised me you'd talk about things that upset you. Going off like an idiotic savage, beating your chest and declaring your woman is going to mind you, isn't going to work. Not with me. You want me to know what I'm getting. You were honest about who and what you are—well, you need to see the real me. I'm not a woman who would for one second put up with a man who won't share himself with me. Not just his body, but all of him. You have to be able to talk to me."

He dropped his head to push his forehead against hers. "Baby, you terrify me." He made the admission without thinking. Before he could examine the words, before he could think what she might read into that.

"I know," she replied.

Just as softly as before. Just as gently. Making his heart turn over.

"You have no idea the danger you're in. Because of me. Because of my lifestyle. I can't have that. I can't have anything happen to you. You have to get that, Siena. It can't happen. I've only got so much decency left in me. That's all you now.

All for you. You get taken from me, I got nothing left and I'm one of them. I'm dark and ugly and not fit to live. But I would, baby. I would live and I would be a monster."

"Elijah."

Just his name. He couldn't look at her. "I'd kill them all. Whoever touched you. I'd wipe them out. Not just them, everyone they loved would die first. I'd take everything and everyone from them before I killed them. I'm capable of that." She'd better fucking believe him. She'd better take what he said seriously. Did she think he wanted to admit that shit to her? Hell no. He didn't want to see her look at him and recognize that killer in him.

"You have to know me, Elijah. I'm not the kind of woman to ever put my man in jeopardy. I won't flirt with other men. I would never defy you in front of others, although I might kick you hard under a table. I will have your back always. If I don't understand what you're doing, I'll wait until we're alone and ask you, but honey, you have to know I'm going to ask. You can't pretend I've got an empty head, because I don't. I lived with secrets all my life, and I don't want to live that way any longer. So you make up your mind to talk to me."

"You strip me bare." What the hell was he going to do with her? He'd just handed her that last little piece, the one that she could use against him.

"That's a good thing, Elijah," she said.

His gaze jumped to hers. His heart pounded. He tasted the bitterness of fear in his mouth.

"Because you strip me just as bare. No one else in this world could tear me up the way you could. But I trust you won't. I'm safe with you. You have to know you're safe with me. I get that you have never trusted anyone in your life. That you couldn't. Everyone you loved betrayed you. I get that. But you have to get to a place where you know you're safe with me if what's between us is going to work."

"Not 'if,' baby. It *will* work. We don't have a choice anymore." He took a deep breath and gave her more. "I told you

I have a sister. I don't talk about her much because she's safe now. She's married and happy. And she's finally safe. I don't like anyone to remember she exists. She never betrayed me. Not even when she thought I put a hit out on her." There was pain in his voice.

Siena put her arms around him and lay her head on his chest. Over his heart. Holding him close to her. Her body fit into his as if born for him. And she was, he was certain of that. "I've got you, Elijah. I'll always have you."

"All right, baby," he murmured, and brushed a kiss on top of her head. "Go take that bath. I'll take care of business and then fix you dinner."

She pressed a kiss over his heart and dropped her hands, turning toward the bathroom while he reached down to snag his jeans from the floor.

"You know, baby," he said, just to see her catch fire, "I think we should try again with the spanking. I could make it erotic. Make you love it."

"I could hit you over the head with a frying pan in your sleep too," she said. "Make you love that."

He laughed as he dragged on his jeans, and listened to her soft laughter coming out of the bathroom. Then the water was running and the scent of honeysuckle and jasmine drifted through the open door. He figured he'd love just about anything she did to him. Even the fucking frying pan.

14

"WE'VE got a visitor, Elijah," Drake announced. "He's been cooling his heels for a while, and I can tell you, he isn't happy. He's been pacing, and he's dangerous. He's leopard, no mistaking that, and he's pushing the edge of his limits."

"Name," Elijah demanded tersely.

"Alonzo Massi. He's big and powerful. Be careful, Elijah. I've come across some very dangerous leopards and I can tell you, this man is extremely lethal."

"Yeah. I've met him."

"Not like this. Not with his leopard riding him hard. You okay to do this, or you want me to take care of it?"

Elijah knew Drake was telling him he needed to keep his leopard under control. Was he that edgy now that he had Siena in his home? Out of necessity, he'd learned to stay in complete control, expressionless, an enigma, his features sheer stone. Now his woman was laughing at him and his friend was warning him.

"I can handle Massi."

"We don't know if he's an enemy yet," Drake pointed out.

"He worked for Siena's grandfather, and she suspects that he covered for Paolo killing him."

Drake shrugged. "I got genuine concern, that he was looking out for her, but he shut it down fast, so who knows?"

"How'd he get inside the compound?"

"Came over the fence as a leopard. My men swept him up but it wasn't easy. In the end they used the threat of putting a bullet in the leopard's head to make him shift. To his credit, he didn't kill anyone, and he could have. He let that be known. He could have. He doesn't look worried, Elijah. He didn't then and he doesn't now."

Elijah nodded and headed down the hall to his office, Drake flanking him. Joshua dropped into step behind Drake as they entered the room. It was empty, but the door hidden in the wall was cracked open. Drake took the stairs down to the small interrogation room. The room had no windows, thick walls that were soundproof and was clearly built for intimidation.

Drake hadn't bothered to cuff Alonzo, and the man paced back and forth in the small room. Joaquin and his brother Tomas, Elijah's personal bodyguards, both were leaning a casual hip against the wall, neither saying a word, not unusual for them. Joshua closed the thick door softly and leaned against it. Drake stepped to one side, taking the spot by the wall so Alonzo was surrounded. Elijah walked right up to Alonzo.

"Heard you invited yourself to my home," Elijah greeted.

Alonzo stopped pacing and turned toward him. Up close, the man was scary dangerous. He was built solid. All muscle. Elijah was fairly certain he didn't have an ounce of fat on him. He'd lived hard, fought hard. It was there in his face, although he was fairly young. Maybe even younger than Elijah, but he'd grown up in a hurry and he'd been around violence all his life. Elijah recognized that trait. Alonzo was comfortable with it. Violence was a friend. He knew that. He lived with it. More, he was aware that all five men in the room with him were leopard. That didn't appear to faze him in the least.

"Where is she? She tried to phone me and then she didn't answer when I called her back. I texted her. Nothing. For hours. She wouldn't try to call me unless she was in trouble."

He had known Siena had tried to call Alonzo before he got to her and he'd thrown her phone, breaking it. He didn't blink, his gaze fixed on Alonzo with the focused stare of a leopard. "What exactly is your interest in Siena?" He didn't ask a question. He was giving a warning, and the way Alonzo's head came up, his eyes going cat, Elijah knew he got it.

"What the fuck kinda question is that?" Alonzo demanded. He took a step toward Elijah.

Instantly Joaquin and Tomas straightened, the room filling with dangerous tension. Elijah held out his hand, palm up to warn them to back off. His bodyguards had been at his side, growing up with him, and they were more than bodyguards to him. They'd tear Alonzo apart if he tried to lay a hand on Elijah. And they'd do it before Joshua and Drake moved.

"It's the kind of question a man asks when his woman has been beaten so badly she had to be hospitalized. It's the kind of question a man asks when his woman has been betrayed, raked over by a leopard so fucked-up and out of control, it would tear a woman's flesh from her body. That's the kind of question I'm asking you and that's why I'm asking, so fucking answer the question."

Alonzo stared at him for several long moments. He was as good at keeping all emotion from his expression as Elijah was.

"She matters to me," Alonzo answered. "I've been looking out for her since she was fifteen years old. She's a good woman, and she got hurt on my watch. It isn't going to happen again." There was a hard edge to his voice. "You keep saying your woman, but I need to hear that from Siena."

"You saw her in my bed. Did she look like she wanted

to leave? The cops were here. She didn't tell them she wanted to leave."

"I need to hear that from Siena. I want to see for myself she's safe and happy. Calling me like that means maybe she isn't. Not answering my calls jumped that possibility. You putting me down here in this room tells me that probability just got higher. So no, her sitting in your bed doesn't make her your woman. I need to hear her say that to me without a hint of coercion."

The man didn't have any back-up in him. More, he didn't appear in the least bit concerned about being locked away with Elijah and his men, and that meant he had all the confidence in the world that he could take them down, which was another thing Elijah knew about. Elijah never had much to lose so he was never very worried about what could happen to him in any given situation. Alonzo clearly didn't feel he had much to lose. Elijah knew that made him doubly dangerous.

"Your man, Paolo, he wants her in order to take over Arnotto territory. You looking to do the same?" Elijah watched him closely for any signs that suggestion hit a nerve.

"Is that what you're doing?" Alonzo countered, his eyes every bit as flat and cold as Elijah's.

Yeah. Alonzo Massi recognized exactly what he was facing, but he wasn't going to back down, and that said a lot about him.

"I have enough territory to worry about," Elijah said. "I'm looking to keep her safe. I don't think being with you is going to do that."

"I think you're right about that," Alonzo agreed unexpectedly.

His expression didn't change, nor did the cold eyes. They didn't blink and Elijah could see the leopard staring at him. Sizing him up. Judging him. Alonzo didn't like the idea of Siena anywhere near him, but then, Elijah couldn't blame him for that. He'd built his reputation carefully. Preserved it. He'd earned it. Elijah waited. He'd learned the value of silence, and most leopards had patience, but they didn't like silence when they were fishing for information.

"I'm hunting Paolo. He's in strong right now and has surrounded himself with Tonio's soldiers. They believe him that you murdered their boss and you've got Siena here under duress. He says you beat her into submission."

That didn't surprise Elijah in the least. He'd expected it. After the visit from the police, he knew the direction Paolo was going. He would have insisted Siena make out a formal complaint, but Paolo was leopard and he couldn't live after what he'd done. The laws of the shifters were very different at times from the laws of civilization.

"You thinking you'll take his place once you take him down?"

For the first time Alonzo looked annoyed. He glared at Elijah. "You're a king. You know what that looks like. And that isn't me. I don't aspire to be king. I'm not the kind of man who wants to be noticed. I live in the background, and I'm good with that. My leopard is difficult and makes life a living hell sometimes. I get up in the morning and I do what I have to do to get us both through a day. I'm a soldier. I didn't like the fact that Siena was afraid of me, but she's intelligent enough to know I'm not a nice man. My leopard would never accept her and more than that, she's always going to be the granddaughter of a famous winemaker. That puts her in the spotlight."

Elijah wasn't certain he liked the man so focused on Siena. He kept fishing. Kept his voice matter-of-fact, easy when he didn't feel at all easy inside. "Right now, you're a soldier without direction."

Alonzo's eyes went pure amber. "Siena's my direction. I'm *her* soldier. She may only have one at this point, but I'll get to Paolo. It's just a matter of time."

"And then?"

"And then I'll keep making certain Siena's safe." His eyes went glacier-cold. Pure undiluted cat. "From anyone threatening her. She doesn't have to like it—or me—but I'm taking care of her."

"You need a paycheck," Elijah pointed out.

"I've got money. Live off the grid. Don't spend. I can get by."

Elijah studied his face. The man gave absolutely nothing away. If he was lying about wanting to make certain Siena was safe, he was the best actor on the planet. His voice rang with honesty. Even Elijah's cat had a difficult time objecting. He glanced at Drake, who nodded subtly, both actions so slight most wouldn't have caught it.

"You ever think about a different way of life?" Elijah asked.

Alonzo's eyebrows shot up. "What other way of life is there for someone like me? Like you? We need this. Our leopards need it. We aren't human. We've got that prey drive, some more than others. My leopard would go insane and drive me that way if I tried to live normal."

Elijah nodded. "Yeah. I get that. So how do we solve this little problem we've got going on right now? You coming onto my land and trying to sneak past the guards I have on Siena?"

"You let me see her. Talk to her. Alone, so I know she's where she wants to be and not doing what you're forcing her to do." Alonzo didn't change expression. "I might even try to tell her what kind of man you are if she insists on staying with you."

Elijah stared at him for several long moments. "You don't think by saying that, it might lower your chances of seeing her?"

Alonzo shrugged. "You can try killing me. I'll take one or two of you with me. But that's the only way you're going to keep me from seeing her."

"I don't mind killing." Elijah told him the stark truth and let the honesty ring in his voice so there was no mistaking it.

"I knew that the first time I ever laid eyes on you."

"Still. You're here."

"I'm here."

"You love her." Elijah made it a statement, and watched him closely.

Alonzo shrugged, not bothering to deny it. "Not like you think," he said. "I told you, my leopard is a savage bastard. Wants to kill anything that comes close, even women, and don't tell me you don't know what that's like or what it means. Doesn't accept Siena's leopard. Don't have family. She's it. I made her it when Tonio assigned me to keep her safe. She was a good kid. Sweet. Turned into a fine woman. Not like Tonio. Not like anyone I've ever known. I'm her soldier."

Elijah had to agree that Siena wasn't like anyone he'd ever known either. So Alonzo claimed her as family. He got that. "She's my mate." He didn't take his eyes off the soldier so he caught the wince, the slow closing of the eyes. "See you're not happy about that."

"You got a sister?"

His life was an open book. Alonzo knew he had a sister. He also had to have heard the rumor that he'd put a hit out on her. Rachel had even half believed it. That had about crushed him.

"Yeah, I got a sister." His tone was strictly neutral.

"Would you want her mated to a man like you? A man who would kill her protector right in the same house while she was upstairs?"

Elijah shrugged. "Hell yeah, I would, he was taking care of her, seeing no one harmed her or upset her in any way. She's not in this."

Alonzo gave him a hard stare. "Long as Paolo is alive, long as that territory is open, she's in this."

Elijah couldn't argue with that. He'd had that exact argument with Drake. "You think Paolo's the only man who is going to consider that if he has Siena, he reigns over the Arnotto territory?"

He didn't want to kill Alonzo Massi. It wasn't that he

minded killing. He knew the man was dangerous. He also was fairly certain, if he was reading him right, he would lay down his life for Siena. If he had no other choice, Elijah would get the job done, but he didn't want this to come to that.

"No. I think she's in this shit until it gets sorted."

"I'm sorting it for her," Elijah said. "You can believe that or not, but she's mine. My leopard's mated with hers. She's carrying my baby. You can read anything you want into this, but I'm not letting her go. I'll do everything I can to keep her out of it, but there are going to be others coming at her whether I'm with her or not. My name is protection. I'm protection for her."

"She want you?"

"Yeah."

"I need to hear that from her—alone."

Elijah shook his head, his hand curling around the nape of his neck. It suddenly felt tight. "See, that's where we have a problem. You're leopard. You could kill her in seconds. *Seconds.* We both know that."

Alonzo shrugged. "You're well aware that I could kill her with you standing right by her side. I knew coming here I was taking a chance. If you caught me—and you did—then you were either going to let me see her because you believe me, or you would kill me. The only way I'm *not* seeing her is dead."

That put it right back on him. Keeping his features blank, Elijah swore to himself in his native language. He liked the tenacity of the man as well as his loyalty. He wouldn't have continued to press all that time had it not been for the fact that the person who was most at risk was Siena. He could take care of himself. If Alonzo were looking to kill him— hell—he'd give him that shot. But to allow him into a room with Siena alone, or even close to her . . . He swore again.

"You're not giving me a lot of choices here," Elijah said. He dug his fingers deep into the knots in his neck. "I'll ask her if she *wants* to see you," he offered.

Alonzo shrugged. "Ask away. Better do it where I can hear her answer. I'm not taking no."

A hard-ass. Elijah would give any amount of money for Alonzo to be his soldier rather than Arnotto's. The man took loyalty beyond comprehension. He wasn't even getting a paycheck. Paolo probably had a hit out on the soldier in spite of the fact that they weren't yet at open war. Paolo had worked with Alonzo. He knew *exactly* what kind of man he was and where his loyalties lay—probably better than Antonio had.

"Why is she so afraid of you?" Elijah asked. Elijah had a reputation. It was out there for the world to speculate over and add to the rumors.

For the first time, Alonzo looked uncomfortable. He actually ran his finger around his collar as if loosening it. "Made a big mistake. My fault. She saw something she shouldn't have. She doesn't remember, at least I'm fairly certain she doesn't, but it started her nightmares. I know because I broke into the office of the counselor she was seeing just to make certain. She changed the way she looked at me."

"Tell me."

"There was another kidnapping attempt. When she was fifteen. She has this laugh, like the sun pouring down on you. Her face lights up and the room . . ." He shook his head. "They came at her on my watch. I'm ten years older than she is, and there was the dream you have before your leopard takes it all. Because you never had anything good. She's good, Lospostos. No matter what you think about her grandfather, she's everything good."

Elijah waited. He didn't dare open his mouth. Alonzo thought he had nothing to lose and everything to gain by telling the truth. In a way, he was pleading for Siena, trying to convince Elijah to let her go.

Elijah knew Siena was too good for him. He already knew that. He knew it with every fucking cell in his body. He knew that laughter. That sunshine lighting the room. He knew the way she cared for her man. Gentle. Sweet. Showing him care in a way few women ever would love their man. She tore his heart and soul right out of his chest.

"I killed them, shot two of them, but the others were on her, put a gun to her head. I shifted. On the run. Shifted into a fucking leopard, and my male is fast and he's vicious. He took them both down, before either could even pull the trigger. It was a bloodbath. All over her. She checked out. Just checked out." Alonzo scrubbed his hand down across his eyes as if he could wipe out the memory. "Scariest thing I ever saw. She woke up in a hospital and didn't remember a thing or how she got there or why. But those nightmares started and sometimes, late, I could hear her screaming."

His woman had been through hell, and Elijah couldn't say he hadn't contributed. Now this. She had nightmares for a reason. "Fuck." He spat the word. Alonzo had also revealed a huge piece of information. He carefully avoided glancing at Drake. Elijah could shift fast—very fast. But to shift and take down two men who had guns to a fifteen-year-old girl's head, that was saying he was lightning fast.

For the first time, Drake spoke. "What lair are you affiliated with?"

Alonzo shut down. His eyes, already amber, slipped closer to the leopard. "Don't have a lair. I'm a soldier."

That meant he had gone rogue—at least he'd gone off on his own. If he had been born outside a lair, he wouldn't have known what one was. There was a story there, Elijah decided. He respected the man. Abruptly, he turned on his heel and stalked out of the room, knowing he might have to kill this man if Siena refused to see him.

He wasn't going to tell her Alonzo's life hung in the balance, but he was going to ask her if she'd talk to him. If she said no, he'd kill the man fast. It would be something he would regret for the rest of his life, but he wouldn't have that dangerous of a man hunting him and he didn't have a single doubt that Alonzo Massi would never stop coming at him to get to Siena.

He opened the door to the master bedroom. Immediately her scent hit him. Surrounded him. He breathed her into his lungs. Took her deep. The door to the bathroom was open, but there was no sound coming from inside that room. For one moment his world went black. Completely black. The air left his lungs and his heart pounded in his chest. He heard a roaring in his head. Pure thunder. Had he been wrong about Alonzo? Had the man distracted his team enough that someone else had gotten through the security lines?

He moved fast, using his leopard's speed, his stealth, leaping across the room to the door, his gun out and ready, his heart in his throat. She was there. In the bathtub. Her head was back against the slope of the tub, eyes closed. Her hair was on top of her head, and in spite of the knot, a riot of waves cascaded down around her face.

Air rushed back into his lungs. He pushed the gun into his waistband at the small of his back. For a moment his legs felt like rubber. Clear water lapped at her breasts. She was sound asleep. Still exhausted. The leopards had gone at it all night, and then he'd claimed his woman. He hadn't been particularly gentle. She wore his mark all over her body and he was dick enough to love the sight of his brand on her skin.

He padded across the room, eyes on her. That beautiful, *gorgeous* sight was his. His heart settled into a more natural rhythm, but it beat hard and the lump in his throat still refused to go away. He'd had nothing in his life. Nothing clean and good. No sunshine when he walked into a room. No woman who didn't give a damn that his name was Elijah Lospostos and his family was pure shit.

When she'd come to his front door he'd thrown her out. *Dios. Dios mio*, he was such a fool. He knelt beside the tub and tested the water. It was growing cold. Too cold. He swept his knuckles down the side of her face gently.

"Baby, wake up. You can't sleep here."

Her long, feathery lashes lifted slowly and his already hard cock went from aching to painful when those green eyes took him in. Turned soft. Loving. *Dios, Dios mio*, he was the luckiest bastard on the face of the earth.

"Hey," she greeted softly, blinking sleepily.

He loved the drowsy, sexy look on her face. He could wake up to that every morning. He loved looking at her face when he made her come, the pure, sensual *dazed* shock she got on her face, the way she got lost in his eyes and his body. Gave herself up completely to him.

He nuzzled her throat. "Come on, baby, let's get you out of there," he said, and his voice had gone husky, dropping an octave, a little hoarse around the edges.

Instantly she frowned, one hand lifting to his face, finger tracing the bottom edge of his lip. "What is it, honey?"

Her voice, the look on her face, so loving. Seeing him. Not the monster in the room, not the killer with a victim waiting for him downstairs. Seeing him. The man he had tried so desperately to hang on to. The one no one else saw. So damned small there was almost nothing left of his humanity, in spite of how he'd tried to guard it, yet Siena Arnotto, she could see him.

He reached down and unscrewed the plug and then pulled her to her feet, standing at the same time. He reached for a towel. "Out."

She stepped out and he wrapped her up, feeling the little shiver.

"Elijah, what's going on? You're upset."

How the hell did she know that? He could guarantee Alonzo Massi didn't know he was conflicted about killing him. But Siena, just like that, realized he was upset.

"Not upset, *mi amorcito*," he lied. "You're just so far out of my league. I see you and something inside me . . ." *Breaks apart*. He couldn't say that. Leopards didn't lie to each other because they could hear honesty or deceit. She turned her head and looked at him over her shoulder and he knew she'd heard the lie, but judging by the softness in her eyes, she was giving him that.

"We've got a situation and I need your help." His hands moved over her gently, taking the beads of water from her skin as he dried her off.

"Anything, Elijah, you know that."

She turned straight again, allowing him to dry her body. He didn't know why it meant so much. The trust she gave him. The intimacy. Standing still for him, not asking, just waiting. He leaned down and brushed a kiss on her shoulder, then into the sweet spot where her neck and shoulder met.

"I need to know why you're afraid of Alonzo."

His hands were on her—through the towel—but they were on her and he felt her stiffen. It was subtle, but his leopard reacted with a protective leap toward the surface. That was enough for him. Damn it. Just damn it. He brushed another kiss against her skin, this time behind her ear.

"No worries, baby, get dressed. I'll meet you in the kitchen in a few minutes." With blood on his hands. Probably the blood of a good soldier, but one that would keep coming at them.

She caught his hand when he stepped away. One hand caught the towel, the other, her fingers tangled with his. "I don't know why I'm nervous around him. I honestly don't know. I liked him a lot when I first met him. He's very quiet. He keeps to the background, but for the longest time I felt safe around him. And then suddenly I didn't." She frowned, turning toward him. "It's weird, Elijah. I have nightmares about him. He's there and he's got a gun pointed toward me and suddenly there's blood all over me and . . ." She trailed off, her hand going to her throat.

Fucking Alonzo. He wrapped his arms around her. "It's all right, don't think about it if it's upsetting to you. Nothing touches you here. I'll take care of things."

She turned in his arms, pressing close, sliding her arms around his neck, the towel held up in the front by the tightness of her body against his. Open down the back. He couldn't stop himself from running his hands down her back and over the curve of her very fine ass. He loved her ass. He loved watching her walk. She had a sexy sway that called to him. Called to any man watching, but that was his.

"Elijah, is Alonzo here? Is he the situation?"

She was smart. Her eyes were on his. Steady. She'd tilted her head to look up at him and close, that face was so beautiful it hurt to look at her, and his hands, full of her soft skin and perfect ass, pressed her even closer.

"He's the situation, baby. You tried to phone him when you were so scared and wanted to run from me." He saw the realization dawning in her eyes.

"I did," she whispered, astonished. "I was so hurt and needed help. But why would I call him of all people? That doesn't make sense."

She shivered again, and he didn't know if it was because Alonzo—or the thought of him—frightened her or if she was cold. He ran his hands up and down her back, rubbing heat into her. The towel had to go because it was damp and didn't need to be against her skin. He was a hell of a lot warmer. He tugged at it and tossed it aside.

She pressed closer. "Why would I call him?"

"I don't know, *mi vida*, but when the phone went dead, he risked coming back here, knowing he might get shot in order to make certain you were okay." He kept his voice strictly neutral, not wanting to sway her one way or the other.

The fingers of one hand curled in his hair, making him glad his hair grew long and thick and he detested taking the time for haircuts. Her other hand slid up his chest, *inside* his shirt, tracing patterns with the pads of her fingers. It took him a minute to realize she wrote her name on his skin, over and over in invisible ink. She did it often. The thing was, that signature sank through the skin straight to his soul.

"He did that? Came to check on me?"

"Right through enemy lines. Got him downstairs. He refuses to leave without talking to you. Says he has to see you're staying here because you want it. Says he's *your* soldier, and Paolo—or anyone else—isn't going to get to you." Again he kept his voice neutral. He believed the man, but if she didn't . . .

"Wow. I remember him before the nightmares as always staying close. I knew he was my bodyguard, and I felt safe. I really did. Until the nightmares. And then Nonno started acting as if I had to choose either Alonzo or Paolo as a husband. I really watched Alonzo because I didn't like the way Paolo looked at me. I realized how dangerous Alonzo was, way more than Paolo. The other men steered clear of him. Paolo bullied, using threats, but Alonzo never threatened. If something happened, he went into action and he was always cold, Elijah. Stone-cold."

There was nothing cold about the way she was pressed against him. Or the movement of her hand. It had slipped lower. Caressing his hip bone. Moving over the material of his jeans to rub the thick bulge there. He became acutely aware of the gun tucked into the waistband at the small of his back.

He strove to keep his mind on saving Alonzo, but her hands both had dropped to the buttons of his jeans. "Baby, you're making me hard as a fucking rock. I got that man downstairs and he wants to talk to you."

"I know," she replied softly, without looking up at him.

Her hands stayed busy, forcing him to reach around and withdraw the weapon.

"Can't walk around with a hard-on, Siena."

"If you'd stop talking and cooperate, I'm pretty sure I can figure out a way to take care of that for you, Elijah. You need to take care of me."

Hot blood rushed through his veins, drove out thoughts of anything but her body. He bent to her breast, wrapping his arm around her, keeping the gun at his side, his mouth pulling strongly, tongue stroking her nipple. He suckled hard. The moment he did, she gave him her weight, the air leaving her lungs in a gasp. Her breasts were that sensitive.

"Love these, Siena. Can't wait for you to start producing

milk. Not sure I'll be leaving much for the baby." He began walking her backward, toward the bedroom, his fingers finding her nipple and tugging. Hard. Rolling. Watching her face. Watching the beauty of the pleasure he was giving her build.

"You might not like how it tastes," she warned.

She hadn't protested that he wanted to drink milk from her breasts. She hadn't thought it was bizarre or freakish. "I want everything from you. *Everything*. Nothing off-limits, and *Dios mio*, you give me that without batting an eye. You taste good everywhere, Siena. Your skin. Your mouth. Your unbelievable mouth. So good. And when I go down on you it's a fucking feast I never want to leave. I could eat you all day, like candy, baby. So good. Can't imagine that your milk isn't going to be just as good."

He opened the drawer beside the nightstand and shoved the gun inside, pushing the drawer closed.

"I don't know why that makes me burn all the hotter, Elijah, but it does," she confessed, her hands continuing to pull open his jeans.

He tasted her in his mouth and suddenly he was starving for her. Talking about devouring her wasn't enough. He stepped back, shoving a knee in between her legs to widen her stance. He crouched low, both hands at her waist, then moving to the inside of her thighs to force her legs even wider.

"That's it, Siena. Spread for me. I'm so hungry for you and can't wait another minute." Not even to get his damned pants open and get some relief. "You're an obsession, baby, an addiction and I've got to have my fix." She was. The taste of her was a drug in his system, the fire spread like a storm through him.

Not only was he addicted to the taste of her and that way her sheath clamped down so tight she strangled him in all that wet silk, but he was just as hooked on the way she caught fire for him, going off like a stick of dynamite.

He caught her very fine ass in his hands, fingers digging deep as he pulled her to his mouth. There it was, his wine.

His nectar. All his. All for him. He loved that she was slick and hot and giving him exactly what he wanted.

She threw her head back, her hands going to his shoulders to hold herself up. "Elijah."

He felt the whisper of his name in his cock and his erection nearly burst through the heavy material of his jeans. He lifted his mouth away from her, his hands tearing at the buttons to free himself. "Brace your left foot up against the bed," he instructed.

She did as she was told, giving him better access. His throbbing, pulsing cock free, he resumed his feast, bringing her back to his mouth, tongue pulling out the sweet, sweet taste of her. Hot and sweet. He suckled, using his tongue ruthlessly. Growls rumbled in his throat. One of her hands transferred to his hair and she fisted bunches in her palm, crying out, grinding down on his mouth.

"That's it, baby. I want it all. Give it to me." He covered her hot little button and used suction, the edge of his teeth and the flat of tongue. Her head fell back, her fingers dug deep into his scalp and she gave him everything.

"Elijah."

His name. Wrapped up in her pleasure. In sheer bliss. So sensual. All his. All for him. He looked up to see her face, that expression, sexy as sin. *"Dios. Hermosa,"* he whispered, and caught at her once again, lapping up the nectar spilling from her body.

"I can't stand up," she panted.

"Again," he demanded.

"I can't," she repeated, her fingers digging deeper into his shoulder, into his scalp.

He refused to stop, needing more. Needing that sweet, sweet taste of her. Needing to feel the powerful orgasm ripping through her body and hearing his name vibrating right through his cock. He knew he was losing control and it didn't matter. He didn't need to be in control. Siena took him as he was, wild, savage, brutal even. She gave herself to him. Gave herself up to him.

He took her up fast, using only his mouth, devouring her, lapping at her, plunging his tongue deep, loving the heat and fire she gave him. Loving the taste. Her legs trembled, threatening to give out on her. Her hips bucked. She didn't have any more control than he did, grinding down on his mouth. Little gasping sobs escaping. Pleading with him for release again. Or to stop. Or to never stop. She came fast, the tidal wave taking her hard so that he had to catch her before she fell.

Hands at her waist, he turned her, belly down, bending her over the bed and yanking her hips back and into him. He didn't wait. Couldn't wait. The fire was burning through him, and as he jerked her hips to him, he thrust. As always he met resistance. No matter how hot, how slick, how ready, her channel was tight around him.

"Pure fucking heaven, baby," he managed to bite out between his teeth. The ecstasy of her body was incomparable. Once inside her, he never wanted to leave. He never wanted it to be over, but she was so hot. So tight. The friction so great, he knew he couldn't last no matter how hard he tried.

He wasn't gentle. There was nothing gentle about the way he took her. Savage. Brutal. He couldn't stop the hard slap of his body against hers. It was too good. His hands moved over her. Possessive. His. All of her.

"Baby." He said it softly. Her back was to him. She couldn't see his face when he made the admission. "I'm loving you the only fucking way I know how."

Her hips bucked back. Hard. Meeting his. Over and over. The sound of her ragged breathing, the soft little sobs of pleasure, all of it, every little whimper and plea, was music adding to the beauty surrounding him.

"Elijah."

There it was. She was with him. He felt the wet, silken clasp of her body bite down hard, scorching hot, surrounding him with fire, gripping and milking, taking him over the edge.

Taking him to that place only she could take him. He thrust several times and then collapsed over her, burying himself to the hilt. Holding her. Fighting for breath. So full of love for her he didn't know what to do with it.

He kept her there, holding her soft body to him, her face turned from his because he had to get himself under control. She hollowed him out inside. Poured herself into that space and filled every crack in his damned soul. Gluing him back together.

"Honey," she said softly. "Lie on the bed for me."

He closed his eyes for a moment, not certain he could take any more from her, but he was incapable of denying her. The need was in her voice. He pulled out of her and rolled, laying his back and butt on the bed, his jeans down around his knees, shoes still on. He even had his shirt on.

There was something very decadent and sensual about being fully clothed when his woman was totally naked. When she lifted her head, all that messy hair falling out of the thick knot at the top of her head, her eyes were sultry.

She slid from the bed, not bothering to turn over, just going to her knees, and then her mouth was there. Exquisitely gentle. So good. So beautiful, just like everything she did. Her fingers caressed him. Her hands cupped him. Her tongue lapped at him. Her mouth was hot and felt like velvet.

"You hear me, Siena?" He needed her to confirm she got him. She understood what he was telling her. What she was doing to him, not just his body, but he felt her mouth, her care, right in his fucking soul. She had to get him. He had to give her that.

She finished what she was doing, pressing a kiss on the crown of his cock and lifting her head, still kneeling there. Expression serious. "I heard you, Elijah. Did you hear me?"

There it was. *Dios.* Did other men feel this full? So full he could barely stand it. He hadn't known a man could love a woman so much.

"We need to get dressed so I can talk to Alonzo," she said, and held out her hand.

He sat up and pulled her to her feet, standing as he did so. He reached down and yanked up his jeans. He could still feel her mouth. Her hands. He was going to be feeling that for hours.

"You don't have to do this, baby, not if you're afraid of him."

She tilted her chin at him. "Elijah, you would never have woken me up and even talked to me about this if it wasn't important. It's important in a way I can only guess at. You were upset when you came into the bathroom. I could see it in you. You try to hide that from me, but I see you."

She did. Too clearly.

"So I'm going to go talk to Alonzo, and I'm going to make him realize once and for all that you are *my* choice. No coercion. I'm staying with you because I want to be with you. I'm leopard. You're leopard. I'm guessing he is as well, or my grandfather wouldn't have had him in the running for my husband. I'm going to walk into that room with you inside of me, with your scent all over me. Our combined scents. He'll know. Just from that and from the way I look, he'll know. I won't have to do much to convince him with that evidence in his face."

He liked that. Too much. He fucking loved the idea of his woman walking into the room with him inside her. With him all over her. He shouldn't have allowed her to clean their combined scents off of him. He loved what she did so much he hadn't even considered giving it up for a moment.

"You *seduced* me." He wanted to laugh. The little minx. He was going to have to work hard to keep ahead of her.

She gave him a satisfied smirk. "It wasn't that difficult, honey. You're easy."

15

SIENA was acutely aware of Drake, Joshua, Joaquin and Tomas standing in the corners of Elijah's office. She'd practically bathed in Elijah's scent because he gave her courage, but she hadn't thought about anyone else smelling Elijah all over her. In her. On her. It was sexy though. She *felt* sexy. She knew she looked thoroughly taken. Her lips were still swollen. Her face and body flushed.

She wore Elijah's favorite skirt, the one with the cascading ruffles and the matching camisole that did nothing to hide the strawberries and fingerprints on the swell of her breasts, so she added a light sweater that at least gave her a little modesty. Now she was glad she had.

The moment she'd opened her eyes and looked at Elijah's carefully expressionless face, she'd known something was wrong. He hadn't shown it. She couldn't tell even when he'd spoken to her, but she'd known. She just knew. And she knew it was bad. Something was riding him hard, and the moment he told her Alonzo had penetrated their security she feared she knew what was happening.

If she didn't talk to Alonzo and get him to stand down, Elijah would act and something very bad would happen. She was afraid to think what he would do, but she was fairly certain Alonzo would never come around again. Elijah didn't want to do whatever he was going to do if she didn't talk to Alonzo. She got that. But he would. She made up her mind to find the courage to face Alonzo, and instead of acting like a child, hiding from her fear, she planned to confront it, to find out why she was so afraid of him. Whether or not she could put that nightmare to rest didn't really matter. What mattered was keeping Elijah from doing something he didn't want to do.

She walked into his office with her chin up, eyes sweeping the room, Elijah at her side, his hand on her back. His hand felt like a flame, burning through her clothes like a brand. Alonzo was leaning against the opposite wall to the entrance—the four men close, but not looking like threats. She knew they were. She knew Alonzo was in trouble.

His eyes came to her immediately, moved over her face, her body. Inspecting. He inhaled, and she knew he caught the scent of sex and Elijah imprinted over and in her. His expression didn't change. Not in the least. His eyes were as cold and dead as ever, his hands rock steady, but he knew.

"Alonzo," she greeted, and moved away from Elijah straight toward him.

Elijah caught her arm. "Baby, I want you to keep a safe distance from him."

"Is there a safe distance?" Alonzo asked.

She lifted her chin. "I'm sorry I worried you, Alonzo. I did try to call you but then the phone broke and I forgot. I honestly didn't think the call had gone through."

He folded his arms across his chest. "You got a price on your head, Siena. Paolo is an asshole, but he didn't put it there.

He's still thinking he's got a shot at marrying you and cementing his empire. You need protection, and I'm it. I'm all you've got right now. Until you or your man step up and take back what your grandfather built, you got one soldier to look after you."

Elijah snarled. Audibly. A low rumbling growl emerged from his throat. The room suddenly was electric with danger. The air went heavy. Oppressive. Elijah's rage was almost tangible. "Leave, Siena. Go now."

She glanced up at his face. His dark features were carved with danger, but his eyes were alive with strange liquid silver that glittered with menace. His entire focus was on Alonzo. She wasn't certain why, or what Alonzo said to set him off, but she wasn't having this.

"I think I need to talk with Alonzo . . ."

His fingers bit into her arm, jerking her to a halt when she took another step forward. "You *fucking* will do what you're *fucking* told," he snapped, his tone low. Furious. Dictating. So close to his leopard she could feel the wave of fur slide for a moment against her skin and then it was gone.

She took a deep breath and let it out, tilted her head as she swung around to plant herself right in front of his body. Showing Alonzo she wasn't afraid of Elijah Lospostos or his *foul* mouth. She met those glittering eyes with her own narrowed and challenging and all green.

"And you can just f-ing stop saying that f-word to me when you want your way. Because I'm f-ing not going to leave when Alonzo came all this way to deliver a warning and maybe help us out. I would like to hear what he has to say."

They stared at each other for a long moment. Someone snickered. She thought it might be Joshua, but she wasn't certain. She refused to break the stare, which was a good thing because she saw it in his eyes first. Warmth spreading through the danger. Amusement. Smirking, arrogant *male* amusement, but still, it was there. Something deep inside her that had coiled tightly and formed hard knots in her belly she hadn't even recognized earlier released the tension and she was able to breathe normally.

Elijah framed her face with his hands. "The f-word, baby? What exactly is that, because I don't have a clue? F-word? F-ing?"

"You have a clue. And stop laughing at me. You have a dirty mouth."

He leaned down, his mouth against her ear. "You like my dirty mouth."

She did. But she wasn't going to admit anything. She glared at him. It was difficult to keep that glare in the face of his amusement.

He straightened. "Baby. Really. It's just a word."

"It's a *foul, dirty* word."

He leaned down again and pressed his lips right against her ear. "I love *fucking* you. The dirtier the better."

Her eyes went wide, she knew it. Shocked. Hot. She felt her body get damp and her nipples get hard. Seriously. This was so not the time, when she was trying to defuse a bad situation and make a point.

His amusement grew as he watched her face flush with color and the heat hit her eyes. She glanced at the other men and saw they shared his humor. She shared her glare with all of them, including Alonzo.

"Apparently it is a prerequisite to be able to drop the f-bomb to get into the men's club around here." She gave them all her haughtiest, nose-in-the-air look. Princess to peasant. "I have no desire to join your club. Alonzo, since you're my only soldier and I don't even know what that is, could you tell me exactly who wants me dead?"

Elijah cleared his throat. "Babe. This is my jurisdiction. We talked about this. I keep you safe, and you live free, not having to deal with this crap. Alonzo and I will be civilized and he'll help me sort it out."

"You didn't look civilized," she accused. "Either one of

you. And just this once, because it really is upsetting to me, I would like to know what's going on. Paolo scares me to death, and earlier, when those shots were fired, I thought maybe it was Paolo trying to kill you and I felt *horrible*. Emma and Jake and the children were here. Catarina was here and she's pregnant. That would have been my fault." She ducked her head, her voice dropping an octave. "Clearly I was right, just not about Paolo."

"Siena."

Elijah and Alonzo both said her name simultaneously. Elijah sounded sweet, so sweet her heart melted. Alonzo sounded as if he were reprimanding her.

"Paolo has always wanted the kingdom," Alonzo said. "As far back as I can remember since signing on he was determined to get in good with Tonio. He knew you didn't have a clue what your grandfather did other than his legitimate businesses. He knew, and he thought Tonio would just hand the reins over to him when he died. He made certain he was in position to be the natural successor. But Tonio wanted you to have it all. He wanted your husband to run things and keep you out of it, but he was determined that you inherited everything."

"So he didn't think Siena was part of the deal?" Drake asked.

Alonzo glanced at him, shaking his head. His gaze swung back to Siena, and then jumped to Elijah's face. "You need to declare your intentions and soon, or there's going to be all-out war. Paolo put out a hit on you, not Siena. A man by the name of Robert Gaton, one of Rafe Cordeau's lieutenants, is going after Siena. He wants her territory and believes if he kills her, he has a better chance."

Elijah's face was a mask. "He better look to his own territory before he decides to declare war. He hasn't cemented that yet."

Alonzo's gaze flicked to him, and Siena's stomach dropped at the knowledge there. She took a deep breath, replaying Elijah's words and what they meant. There was no mistaking that meaning. She didn't want to live in a crime family. She didn't want her children to do so either. She wanted to raise her children clean and normal, whatever that was. She'd never had it.

She pressed her hand protectively to her stomach. Instantly she felt the heat of Elijah's gaze. She should have known he wouldn't miss even that small of a gesture. More than anything, she didn't want this life for her husband. And Elijah Lospostos was going to be her husband. She knew that. She knew what they had together she'd never have with anyone else, and he needed her. He needed her because without her, he would be just like Alonzo, cold and dead inside. Well, she amended, sneaking a quick glance at Alonzo, something in the way he looked at her told her she was important to him. If he were truly dead inside, he wouldn't be able to feel one way or the other for her.

"What happened, Alonzo?" she asked softly. "I remember feeling safe and comfortable around you. I was never scared. And then I was and I don't even know why. Do you know?"

He sighed. For the first time he looked uncomfortable, but she could see that he was going to answer her. He didn't want to, but he had declared himself her soldier and that meant when she asked him something, he came through.

"You saw me shift and kill two men who were threatening you at gunpoint. You were so traumatized you never remembered it."

Her breath caught in her lungs. Of course. Her nightmare. She'd had blood all over her, but it wasn't her blood. Alonzo hadn't killed her, he'd killed two men to save her. Why had she blocked that out? She knew. It was the leopard. To have seen that meant she was insane. There was no such thing as a shifter, a man who could turn into a leopard.

It hadn't been the violence of the moment that had traumatized her so much, but the sheer impossibility of a man turning into a leopard. The leopard had been snarling, covered in blood just as she was. Terrifying. Close. Those eyes glowing with the drive to kill. She shivered, and wrapped her arms around herself.

"I'm sorry you saw that, Siena," Alonzo said quietly. "You had nightmares after that, and you wouldn't come near me."

She had hurt him. She hadn't even realized he could be hurt. That shamed her. "Alonzo, I don't know the first thing about what my grandfather was doing or what he wasn't doing. I love that you're protective of me and that you're looking out for me, but I have no idea what to do."

"Your man does."

"My man doesn't need to be involved in my mess." She stuck her chin up.

Elijah caught at her arm. "That's it, baby. You're done here."

"You can't tell me I'm done here. I have to sort this out."

"Your man sorts it out," Elijah said, and dipped down, his shoulder hitting her belly gently, and he stood up.

She found herself upside down, over his back, hair hanging down in her face, his arm across her buttocks holding her in place. Before she could get more than a squeak out, he was striding from the room, using long, purposeful steps, slamming the door behind them. She was *not* giving him the satisfaction of being so undignified that she struggled.

Elijah carried her through the house, past the atrium without going inside it this time, which meant there were more ways than one to get to the various rooms on this side of the house. He set her on the counter and kept one hand on her belly.

"Baby, I'm going to say this once more because it's important. I know what you were doing in there, and I appreciate it. I do. But this business does not touch you. I know you think you're responsible, but your grandfather is, not you. You are mine now. My woman isn't touched by shit. Not ever. *Mi amorcito*, this business is shit. I was born into it and I know how to handle it. You are not to go near it again. Are we clear?"

She studied his face. He meant every word, and there was

a warning, as sweet as he was trying to say it, as subtle as he was making it. Elijah wasn't the kind of man to be crossed, not even by her, not when he laid down the law. When she'd accepted him, made the decision to be his, she'd gone into it with her eyes open about him. She saw him. She saw the dominant in him. If she was his woman, the one for him, she had to accept that in him as well.

"Elijah," she began carefully.

"I asked you if we were clear on this."

His voice hardened and she winced. She put her hand on his chest, tipping her head up to his. "Honey, we're clear," she agreed, "but I'd like to say something."

"Say it, then."

He didn't give an inch. She realized she'd been very, very lucky he'd taken her into his office to confront Alonzo. He really didn't want her anywhere near his family's business. Or her family's.

"I don't want you to have deal with any of that, Elijah. Clearly it's distasteful to you. We're thinking about being a family together . . ."

Both hands went to her skirt and he pulled it up to her thighs. Then his hands dropped to her waist and he yanked her toward him, so that she was right on the edge of the counter, his body wedged between her legs. Close. Close enough she felt the heat of his anger.

"*Don't* piss me off, Siena. You're already skating on thin ice. We aren't thinking about being a family. We *are* a family. My baby's in your belly and my fucking seed is so deep inside you you're never going to get it out. What more do you need before you admit we're together and we're going to stay that way?"

The room got scary. Tense. The air thick with his anger. Fury had gathered like pinpoints in his eyes. Before she could formulate a suitable apology for not wording her protest correctly, he heaved a frustrated sigh. His fingers flexed at her waist. Dug in. He gave her a little shake.

"We're fucking getting married. Immediately. I'm calling Jake now and asking him to find us someone and get the paperwork done. We do the paperwork, wait the seventy-two hours and then get it done. My ring's on your finger maybe you'll get it through your head you belong to me and . . ." He stuck his head close to hers, his eyes so silver they were pure liquid. "You. Aren't. Going. *Fucking*. Anywhere." He spat the last five words.

She felt the answering anger start in her roiling stomach. Pressing a hand there, she glared at him. "Do you think that's the marriage proposal of my dreams? Because . . ." She leaned into him, her eyes narrowed, just as focused as his. "It. *Isn't*." She yelled the last two words.

His hand moved up to the nape of her neck, fingers curling there. "You need to get this, Siena. You don't talk about leaving. You don't think about leaving. You got something sticking in your gut, you fucking talk to me about it."

"Which," she snapped, "I was *trying* to do. You are *such* a hothead and I hope to God you are not going to be this crazy when we have children. Because I'm the type of person who believes parents should be on the same page. You fall off that page with your *nasty* temper, Elijah, we will have words, quite possibly in front of the children."

He studied her face. One eyebrow went up. "Words? We're going to have *words*?"

She nodded. Solemnly. "Yes, Elijah. You lose your temper like this with our children we will most definitely have words." She folded her arms across her chest, indicating in no uncertain terms she meant business.

He reached out and very gently brushed strands of hair away from her face, tucking them behind her ear. His mouth quirked, and she narrowed her eyes even more because just for one moment, it looked as if he might be finding her funny, which would get him in even more trouble than he already was in.

"You have words with me in front of our children, baby,

and I'll express myself in a very different war of words in the privacy of our bedroom. You won't like it and then you will."

His dark tone made her shiver.

"You can't threaten me with . . . with . . . um . . ."

He leaned close, and this time she most clearly saw the glint of humor in his quicksilver eyes. "Baby, the word you're looking for is *sex*. My kind of sex. The kind where I keep you right on the edge for as long as I want to play. Maybe tie you up and play for hours until you beg me and I'll remind you of you having *words* with me."

She blinked. Her breath caught in her lungs. She felt damp heat gathering between her legs and just for one moment, her sex actually spasmed. "Why do you keep using that *tone* when you say *words*. And before you answer, let me explain carefully, in grown-up language, that if you are in the least bit finding something funny about this conversation, that is only going to get *you* in more trouble."

He framed her face with his hands, pushing closer with his large body, wedging himself between her thighs so that her legs were spread wide. Too wide. Her skirt, although long, was moving up around her hips. Exposing the fact that she hadn't worn panties. The cool air actually teased her suddenly heated sex. She didn't make the mistake of squirming, although it took a lot of control.

"If I laugh, *mi vida*, do you plan to have *words* with me?" He dipped his face down toward hers and she totally lost her breath. All of it. Air rushed out in a long, slow trail as she stared up into his handsome face.

For Siena, it had always been this man. Always. He filled her dreams, her fantasies. There had never been another man and there never would be. She couldn't help herself, she had to trace that shadowed jaw. He always looked like he had a shadow, that wonderful abrasive stubble that felt so incredible between her legs. His lashes, so dark and long, framing his amazing eyes. He was handsome, so much so that she couldn't believe how masculine he looked at the same time. All hard lines and planes. He looked dangerous, and every time he came close, her heart pounded and her stomach did a slow, delicious roll. Every time he came close, deep inside, fireworks went off. How did she hide that from him?

"Yes." She managed to get the affirmation out, but just barely because she had no air in her lungs.

His lips brushed hers. "Baby, you're so fucking adorable, sometimes you just take my breath away and I don't know what to do."

It was the last thing she expected. Especially when his mouth was so close, distracting her.

"You need to take me seriously, Elijah. Especially when I'm trying to tell you something important."

He nodded. His hand dropped to her bare thigh, circling there. She was acutely aware of his palm burning a brand in her skin.

"Tell me what you wanted to say before I lost my nasty temper," he prompted.

Back to gentle. He could disarm her with his gentle. She took a deep breath because she needed air desperately. His fingers weren't still against her skin. He moved them in subtle patterns. She felt each one sink deep into her. Inside. Right at her deepest core, where she grew hotter. Where the burn settled and smoldered. She tried not to squirm so he wouldn't know that his touch, although on the inside of her thighs, burned through to the inside of her body. He'd take advantage of that. She just knew it.

"I didn't mean to imply I wasn't fully committed to our relationship," she began. Needing him to know. Still, he deserved a kick for his outburst, especially the crack about marriage. As if she would even consider such a *ridiculous* proposal. "What I need to say, Elijah, is that I don't want this life for you. For us. But mostly for you. You don't want it either. The problems I've brought to your door are only miring you deeper in the muck."

He stared at her for what seemed an eternity. His gaze was wholly focused. Intense. Finally he shook his head. Slowly. *"Dios mio, mi vida."* His silver eyes moved over her face. "'Miring me deeper in the muck'?" he echoed. "You don't want that for me?"

She shook her head. "No, I want you happy, Elijah. Not worried. Not in danger. Not doing things you hate with every breath you take. I want you free."

His gaze burned her. His eyes were so silver they glowed. Gleamed. She could see his cat close.

"I don't get free you going to leave me?"

She studied his features. So still. So expressionless. A mask. But his eyes were alive. Liquid. Burning over her and into her. The hand on her thigh had gone still and he held himself like a statue. No, not like a statue. Like a leopard. Freeze-frame. Completely, utterly still. Focused.

"I'm here, Elijah. Your seed deep inside me. Your baby growing in me. You're not free, and I'm here." She leaned into him, laying her hand against his jaw, looking into those liquid eyes. "I'm *here*, Elijah."

"Like knowing my seed's in you, baby, but right now I want to eat you, and I can't do that. So you're going to go clean that up and I'm going to deal with the problem and then you're back in our kitchen while I fix you dinner."

He didn't move. He kept looking at her. Making her heart pound. Making her stomach melt and that burn deep inside grow hotter.

"I still have to know we're clear on this, *mi amorcito.* This business doesn't touch you. I'll handle things. You live your life sweet and clear and I'll handle the . . ." A slow smile softened the hard edge of his mouth and crept into his eyes. "What word did you use? *Muck.* I'll handle the muck."

She tried not to smile, or feel the heat moving through her veins. "You are definitely finding me amusing and that is so not cool."

"Siena, you say things like you're having a word with me

when you're supposed to be angry or that I'm mired in muck, yeah, it's fucking adorable, but it's also amusing. You have to get that."

"I get that you're not taking me seriously."

The smile was gone and she instantly missed it. He leaned close, his fist bunching in her hair. "I take you seriously, baby. Very seriously. I'll watch my foul temper around our children. All six of them."

The air was gone again. Not just from her lungs, but from the entire room. She stared up at him, mesmerized by the look on his face. By his eyes and voice. By the way his fist tugged at her hair. By the things he said to her.

"Thank you," she whispered.

"Go clean up for me." His hands settled around her waist and he lifted her to the floor, allowing her skirt to drop to her ankles. "And Siena, keep those panties off. Cooking for you, knowing you're right there, waiting for me, available to my hands, my mouth, my cock—I like that, a fuck of a lot."

Her womb spasmed right along with her feminine channel. She felt the rush of damp heat and sent him a smoldering look. "I'll just go clean up. I can't wait for my first cooking lesson, so hurry, Elijah." She walked a few steps from him, feeling his eyes. She stopped and turned slightly, heart pounding. "Honey, I know you don't want me to interfere, but I need to know Alonzo is safe."

His face turned to stone. Absolute stone. Her heart stuttered. He stepped close, curled his hand around the nape of her neck and pressed his forehead to hers. "I thought we were clear."

She swallowed—hard. "I know, Elijah. I thought we were, but he's mine. He feels like mine, and I didn't do right by him. He saved my life and I didn't treat him right. I need to know he's safe."

His hands went to either side of her neck, his thumbs sliding along her jaw. "*You're* mine, Siena. That means I do right by *you*. That means you've got to trust me to make

certain your life is good. You got my baby in you. You're
mine. Understand what that means, *mi amorcito*. I need to
know you trust me. People are going to say things. You'll
hear them. They'll treat you a certain way. You have to hang
on to me. You have to know I'm doing right by you. That
always, you're my first priority. Learn that now, Siena."

She searched his liquid silver eyes. They burned. Took her
breath. She read honesty there. She read the fierce, driving
need of the male shifter to protect and care for his woman,
his mate.

"I've trusted you this far and you still haven't told me
everything, Elijah. I'm waiting for that. I know you will
because you gave me your word. So I've given you my trust
on sheer faith. I'm not taking that away." She had committed
to him. She had chosen him even knowing she didn't want
his life. Even knowing he was outside the law. She'd still
chosen him, and he was right, she had to trust him.

"Consider it learned," she whispered.

He took her mouth. Hard. Wet. Long. Owning her. Pos-
sessing her. Then his mouth gentled and he was loving her—
tender—sweet. Giving her something indescribable that tore
at her heart and sent tremors through her body. He lifted his
head slowly, his eyes on her, checking. Making certain she
was all right.

"Hurry, Elijah," she whispered, and turned away to head
back to the bedroom.

She went by way of the atrium. The house was a labyrinth
of rooms. She knew why. She knew the house was built for
leopards to escape. She knew Elijah's family, one by one,
had been murdered or died a violent, bloody death. This
place was designed to allow him to get out when attacked.
To get his mate and his children out safely. She was determined to learn every route, so she could do the same.

Her body felt sensitive, breasts achy and swollen, nipples
hard, pushing against her camisole. The burn that smoldered
so deliciously was hot. Not so comfortable. More delicious,

but much more demanding. She felt her pulse pounding between her legs with every step she took.

She loved him. *Loved* him. She didn't know how it happened or even why. She wasn't in love with the fantasy man she'd dreamt of for so many years. She loved Elijah with his dirty mouth and his sinful hands and his dangerous edge and unbelievable temper. She loved him with every cell in her body. With her heart and soul. She wanted to be his woman. The woman he spent every waking minute loving. Wanting. Needing.

She washed carefully, and every pass of the hot, wet cloth sent shivers through her. She changed. She couldn't help it. She chose another skirt, this one long, with more flow, falling from her hips rather than her waist, hugging her bottom, but swinging out in folds like a handkerchief around her legs to her ankles.

She removed her bra and found another camisole. She needed to go shopping soon because all the clothes that had been sent over from her house were getting a little too snug. Still, the little form-fitting camisole with the lace-up ties in the front, cupping her breasts, seemed just perfect, even if her breasts were more generous than they had been. She tightened the laces, and admired the marks Elijah left behind on the tops of the curves. Just looking at the smudges sent a thrill down her spine.

She wrapped herself in her sweater just in case any of the men were patrolling the halls, although she was fairly certain Elijah would get them out of the house after his meeting. He seemed pretty certain no one would interrupt them in the kitchen.

She put her hair up. Took it down. Braided it. Took the braid out. Her hair was beautiful, she couldn't deny that, but there was so much of it. If she wore it down, it would be everywhere. He didn't like it up so much. Still, she settled on pulling it back in a loose ponytail, keeping it off her face. She wanted to be able to see him every second.

* * *

ELIJAH entered his office. The atmosphere was just as heightened as when he'd left. He got straight to the point. He wanted to be with his woman, not fucking around with crap. "You good with where she wants to be?" he demanded.

Alonzo nodded. There was the slightest glimmer of humor in his flat, cold eyes. "She is going to be a handful. You have no idea."

He had more than an idea. She was going to have *words* with him. *Dios mio.* Words. She was fucking adorable and it was impossible, when she was pissed at him and about to have *words*, to do anything but rip her clothes off and take her hard and fast wherever they were. *Dios.* Words.

He kept his features a blank mask. This was important. "You still her soldier even though she belongs to me?"

Alonzo nodded slowly, not blinking, his amber eyes focused, his cat close. "You need to take over for Tonio. You don't, there's going to be all-out war and she'll be caught in the middle. You're respected. The council will accept you."

"You willing to work for me?"

Alonzo studied him. Didn't just jump right in and grab at the chance. He took his time deciding, turning the idea over in his mind.

"You going to keep her out of this? Really keep her out, not like Tonio, having her deliver fucking wine to distract his marks so his man could slip inside to take them out. Really keep her out of it."

"That's the plan." Elijah didn't like explaining himself—not to anyone. But the truth was, soldiers like Alonzo were worth their weight in gold. He would be loyal, and more, he would work his ass off to keep Siena safe. Siena and his child.

Alonzo nodded slowly. "I'm in."

Elijah held up his hand, glanced at Drake, who nodded and then turned back to Alonzo. He gestured to the comfortable high-backed leather chair. "Take a seat." He slipped behind his desk. Drake took one corner of the desk. Joshua, Joaquin and Tomas remained leaning against the wall.

Alonzo didn't like sitting in the chair. That left him more vulnerable to an attack than ever. Still, after a moment's hesitation, he did it.

"You know anything about Drake Donovan?" Elijah asked, waving a hand toward Drake.

Alonzo nodded. "He's leopard. Fast. Skilled. Know enough to be surprised he associates with Elijah Lospostos. Don't mean that in a bad way, just a fact. He's got a reputation. Hard man. Not one to cross. Tonio warned us to back off anything he was involved in."

"I'm warning you now, we go any further, I tell you much more, you want out, or you decide to betray us, you're a dead man."

"Always been leopard. Always been family. I know the rules. I said yes, and my word is binding."

Elijah studied his face. "You ever consider a different way of life?"

"I told you, don't know any other way. I was born for this. Can't live normal."

"Didn't say normal. Didn't say easy, Alonzo. Some time ago, I decided I didn't want the life of Elijah Lospostos. I ran into Drake, and he taught me a better way. The underbelly is always going to be there. Always. We take someone out, someone else fills that void. That's just the way of things. But that doesn't mean we can't control that shit. Who is in power. What they do. It's all based on money. On deals. We control the money and deals and we control who's in power."

Alonzo sat very still, turning the information over and over in his mind. Elijah already had recognized that the man was intelligent. He was also careful and thoughtful. He didn't jump to conclusions. He might say he wasn't material to be a king, but with a little training and experience, Elijah could shape him for that role. More than ever, he wanted the soldier committed to their work.

"Dangerous," Alonzo mused.

Elijah nodded. "Particularly so with those who are leopard. We have to get them out first. They can hear a lie. Around the others, we have an advantage, around shifters, no. Shifters can read us as easily as we read them. So it takes work to get around that."

"Siena know you doubled the danger to yourself?"

Elijah's features hardened. His eyes went pure cat. "No. And she's not going to know unless I see fit to share. You don't give a woman all the shit you're in all at once if you intend to keep her, and I intend to keep Siena. We keep her safe and we take apart the underworld and build it back in a way we can control. At least our part of it. I'll take over Siena's territory at least long enough for the council to agree. We'll have to find Paolo and kill him. In the meantime, we have to discredit him with Tonio's soldiers."

"And Robert Gaton?"

"He tried to kill her. I'll hunt him to the ends of the earth, and when I find him, I'll tear out his fucking heart," Elijah snapped.

Alonzo nodded slowly. "Wanna be there for that."

Elijah sat back in his chair. "You in all the way?"

Alonzo got to his feet and moved around the desk to Elijah's side. He reached for the outstretched hand. The ring indicating the head of the Lospostos family. The ring indicating Elijah was a leopard. A shifter. A king. And Alonzo swore his fidelity. Meaning it.

16

"MY man can really cook," Siena said, inhaling the amazing aromas filling the kitchen. She leaned over the counter, half coming off the barstool to closer inspect what he was doing. "That not only looks wonderful, but it smells that way as well."

Elijah looked up from where he was expertly rolling the dough for tortillas, flashing a grin that took her breath away. His hair was messy and he looked handsome, relaxed. Happy.

"Siena."

He said her name, and her heart melted and the butterflies in her stomach took off when it did a slow roll. Even her sex reacted to that soft, velvety reprimand.

"Did you doubt it?"

She leaned her chin into her hand, elbow propped on the counter, totally fascinated with this side of Elijah. She *loved* watching him. She knew she was devouring him with her stare, but she didn't care. Didn't care that he could see how she felt right on her face. She knew he could because he looked happy. Not just happy, relaxed and happy.

"You keep looking at me and we won't be having dinner. We'll be eating, baby, but not this delicious food. Something else delicious. *Both* of us."

"That sounds just fine for dessert, Elijah," she replied, using her most demure voice. "I think this food needs to be eaten, as you spent such time and effort preparing it for us, and our baby even knows all about it. So we'll wait on the other and have a long, leisurely dessert."

His eyes went dark mercury. Sensual. Hooded. He liked the idea of dessert. She decided a little teasing was in order. Her man liked food. He loved sex. The two joys were definitely not equal in his book. She waited until his tortillas had his full attention.

"Still, now that you've got me thinking about it, I do like the taste of you. A lot."

His gaze jumped to her face. She flashed a dreamy smile. "Well, I do. A lot. You're hot and spicy and I kind of love rubbing my tongue up and down that delicious shaft of yours. Like an ice cream cone, but scorching hot. And then there's that little spot that if I rub just right . . ."

He groaned. "Woman, you're going to get yourself in trouble you keep going like that."

She widened her eyes in innocence. "I'm just reliving the joys of your body belonging to me, Elijah. I think, when it's me that gets to possess that fine of a body, I should spend a little time thinking about it before I make hasty decisions."

His grin was slow and sexy. "You need to eat food, *mi amorcito*. You don't eat nearly enough and you've got a baby inside you taking all your nutrients. You're going to eat. Dinner. After we'll think about other things."

She sulked. Deliberately. Squirmed a little on the barstool. Deliberately. "You've got me thinking how delicious those other things are. Some people do eat dessert *before* dinner."

His gaze flicked to her. "You're eating dinner first."

She pouted. "Just saying."

He turned back to his work. Stirred the spicy meat in the skillet. Checked the rice and tomatoes. The aroma honestly made her mouth water. She was hungry, no doubt about it. But that burn had been on her for a while now. Always with her. Craving him. Talking hadn't helped much; in fact, her banter had really made her squirm. It hadn't been altogether pretend.

"Honey." She couldn't keep the need out of her voice. The hunger. "Maybe dessert's the best idea. So I can enjoy the food you prepared properly."

His gaze slid over her again. Hot. Sensual. Her man was super hot. Super gorgeous and altogether sexy. She loved that she could put that look on his face. That he could stand in his kitchen, burden free, even if for a few minutes, intimately barefoot, hair wild, looking handsome and so very sexy. And so happy. She'd done that. She'd given him that.

"Dinner's ready, baby. How about you go on over to that table you set so beautifully and sit down and wait for your man to serve you."

"You're really going to make me wait?"

"Food's hot. You don't eat enough. Settle, honey. I'll take care of you after. And I promise to be thorough about it."

That just heightened the burn. She was supposed to be teasing him, and it seemed as though he was in complete control and she was the one out of control. She sent him one emotion-laden look that should have said *everything* to him, and she slipped from the barstool to walk to the table. She knew he was watching so she put a little extra sway in her walk. When she got to the high-backed, gleaming cherry-wood chair, she pulled it out and walked around it, as if studying it from every angle.

"What are you doing, Siena?" he asked, placing bowls of steaming food on the highly polished wood of the table. She was surprised to see he wasn't typical in that he put hot pads beneath each bowl.

"I'm considering the best way to sit without getting my skirt damp." She caught the sides of the material and began to slowly bunch it into her hands. Inch by slow inch. Brought it from her ankles to her knees. "I really like this skirt and I don't have very many clothes that are a comfortable fit for me anymore."

She drew the soft, silky material right up over her thighs. Watching him watch her. She saw the gathering lust there in his eyes. The hunger. She kept talking. Kept working the skirt up. She had a surprise for him. That had set the burn in her off. The thought of her surprise and the look on his face. She'd walked all the way from the bedroom, through the house, knowing he would love what she did. She'd taken her time in the bathroom, cleaning every inch of her.

Siena kept pulling up her skirt, letting the feel of the soft material against her thighs heighten her need. She knew the exact moment he saw her smooth, completely bare sex open to him, to his every touch, his tongue. His breath hitched in his lungs and his face went dark. Sensual.

"Turn the chair toward me."

She did so and immediately sank down onto the seat of the chair because, really, the look in his eyes destroyed her ability to even stand.

"Open your thighs for me," he ordered.

And it was an order. He wasn't fooling around. Or teasing. He was a hungry alpha male and she was his prey. Deliberately she moved her knees apart, but only a few inches. Just enough to give him a glimpse of her damp, pulsing flower.

"Slide your ass forward, right to the edge of the chair, lean back and widen your thighs, Siena."

She *loved* that hard edge to his voice. Rough. Hungry. Demanding. A fresh flood of liquid heat pulsed deep. She obeyed him, leaning back and widening her thighs. At once, the cool air hit her and she swore steam rose. She dropped hand to her thigh, sliding her fingers up the inside, need- o be touched.

"That's mine," he said. And he said it softly. "Open the front of your camisole, baby, I want to see your hands on yourself, on those beautiful nipples. Don't go easy either. You like it rough. I want to see it rough. I want to hear you, all that music you make when I'm eating you."

He opened the front of his jeans, allowing his cock freedom. Her heart jumped. Stuttered. Her mouth watered. He was beautiful. Large and thick and all hers. His fist surrounded the shaft in a casual, sexual way that sent more liquid heat pulsing through her core. She had gotten the idea to go bare because he was always clean of hair around his hard cock, and when she took him in her mouth it always felt so good.

He went to his knees on the floor, sliding his shoulders under her legs, pressing close, forcing her legs farther apart. Her heart pounded. She could barely breathe. She felt him there. Right there. His breath. The whisper of his mouth, yet he didn't move. Her brain slipped, going from thinking to chaos. To need. To hunger. To absolute lust.

"Elijah," she pleaded.

"What did I tell you to do?"

She felt every word against her bare lips. She had never been so sensitive. Never. He was killing her. She brought up both hands—*shaking*—to the lace-up front of her camisole and slowly pulled the ribbons apart. The material immediately gaped open, and her breasts spilled out.

She looked down at herself, leaning back, sprawled out, legs around Elijah, his head between her thighs, her skirt around her hips and her bare breasts exposed over the top of the lacy material. She felt the rush sliding into her—over her—a mini-orgasm before he'd actually touched her.

"Cup your breasts for me, *mi vida*. Play with your nipples. Pinch them. Roll them. Hard."

She gasped, but did as he instructed. Her nipples were extremely sensitive. The moment she touched herself, the moment her thumb and finger settled over the tight, hard little buds, he swiped his tongue through her aching entrance and a sob escaped. It was so good. *So* good.

Once Elijah started, there was no his escaping his hands and mouth. He devoured her. Deep rumbling growls escaped whenever she squirmed and she was squirming, sobbing, pleading, hips bucking. It was impossible to stay still, not when he was so ravenous, not when he was in the mood he was in, his rasping tongue a weapon of destruction. Soul-destroying. So beautiful and so incredible, she could barely breathe.

He drove her up again and again. He knew how to use his mouth and tongue. His teeth. His fingers. He obviously enjoyed what he was doing. He went fast. He went slow. He savored her. She lost count of how many times the earth moved and her body went up in flames. Maybe it was all one very long, strong quake, maybe one orgasm rolled right into the next. She felt shattered. Blown to pieces. Floating. Screaming. Amazing. His. Thoroughly, totally his.

When he finally lifted his head, the strong shadow along his jaw gleaming with the liquid honey spilling from her body, she could barely stay in the chair. If it weren't for his strong shoulders, she just would have slid straight to the floor.

Watching her, he licked at his fingers and slowly stood. "You taste so fucking good, baby, better than any dessert I could whip up."

"I want mine," she said, forcing her body under control. "Right now, honey." Her body still was rippling and pulsing from the strong, powerful tsunami he'd created. Her breasts ached. Her nipples were tight and hard, and every movement of her fingers continued to send streaks of fire straight to her spasming core.

She pushed herself up into a sitting position and reached for his hips, dragging him closer. He let her, his eyes on her breasts spilling over her camisole.

"Fucking beautiful," Elijah whispered. "Wild. My wild cat."

e cupped his heavy sac in her palms, her fingers gently g the soft velvet. "I think you're beautiful, Elijah," she said, her eyes on his cock. It was full and hard and very erect. Pulsing. Pearl droplets spilled along the crown temptingly. "I love that you belong to me."

Just the touch of her fingers and the look in her eyes, so hot and excited, so hungry, had his cock jerking hard. She licked over his balls, her tongue swirling little circles. He realized she was once again signing her name on him—on his heavy erection, this time with her tongue, and that was fucking hot. She licked up his shaft, all around the base, taking her time. Enjoying it. He could see the eagerness. The hunger. The craving. She was addicted to his cock and she didn't care that he saw that. She loved going down on him. Knowing she had all the power when she did.

He'd never had a woman give that to him. When she took him in her mouth, it was all about him. Every thought in her head was about pleasing him. Giving him pleasure. She couldn't wrap her fist completely around his shaft, and when she took him in her mouth, it was a tight fit. Still, she got him wet, really wet, and that tight fit felt like pure heaven.

Her hair was in a ponytail. He liked it down, but the ponytail gave him something to grip. And he needed something. She was working him. Using her mouth. Her tongue. That very talented tongue. All the while one hand continued to massage his balls while the other slid over his shaft with her mouth. Tight. Hot. Perfect. His brain began to shut down.

He stepped even closer, forcing her head back to tilt it up, using her hair to guide her, he began to use his hips, slow at first, pushing deeper into her mouth. No way could she take all of him, but she was willing to try and he loved her for that alone. He had gone from having nothing—no one— to being in his kitchen with the woman of his dreams, her mouth wrapped tight around his cock, her eyes on his face, watching his every expression, taking him as deep as she could because she loved him like that. Gave him that gift.

"Baby," he breathed. Warning her.

She didn't stop. If anything she took him deeper, her

fingers moving from his balls to his hip, urging him to her. She suckled hard, hollowing her cheeks while her tongue danced and stroked him toward oblivion. Every single time she did that, every single time she gave him heaven, he felt a burn behind his eyes and his throat went raw. Worse, that fucking emotion, that love he had for her was so strong, so powerful, he knew he would do anything for her. Give up anything. He knew she could so easily be the weapon that would destroy him.

When he thought she'd given all she had, she always gave more, taking him down her throat when she didn't have to. When most women wouldn't give their men that kind of paradise, she did. She didn't come to him with experience, but she sure as hell learned what pleased him. And she did it willingly and happily.

She finished gently. Loving him. Taking care of him with her mouth and tongue. On top of paradise she gave him fucking heaven. He leaned down and ran his finger across her lower lip. His breath came too hard. His legs were made of rubber, but it was his heart that wasn't going to recover.

She licked her lips, catching the last droplets, her eyes anxious. She sat up slowly, her hands going to her camisole as if she might pull it up. His hands covered hers, stopping her.

"Leave it." His voice came out harsh. Edgy. His leopard close. So close. He had to breathe deeply to keep the animal at bay.

Anxiety crept into her eyes. She didn't look away from him, still with that expression on her face. His fingers curled around the nape of her neck.

"Honey," she whispered softly. "What did I do wrong? You have to tell me, and I swear, I'll learn."

He stared down into her face. That beautiful face. In a deeply perverted way, he even loved that apprehension because it said so much. It told him she cared enough to be _____s. To want to please him. That maybe, just maybe, she could love him enough to see past the killer in him and want to stay even if she learned the absolute worst about him. He hoped so. He hoped he sucked her in deep enough to accept his life. To stay with him in spite of what he could never get out of—because he couldn't. He knew that. Not alive.

"You stay if they tell you I killed people?" His fist gripped her hair harder. Involuntarily.

Her gaze didn't waver from his. "Elijah. You might not have said that to me, but you certainly implied it. I heard rumors. I'm here."

"You going to stay no matter what I ask for in the bedroom? Even if it scares you?"

She blinked. Drew in a breath. "I trust you, Elijah. I imagine that if I were really scared you would help me get past that. Having said that, I'm willing to try anything you want at least once. Then I trust you to hear me if I say it didn't work for me."

His heart actually stuttered in his chest. In his life, other than Rachel, his sister, who he had to pretend he didn't care about, and Joaquin and Tomas, his bodyguards, he didn't have a single soul who stuck by him. Not one he could trust. Not a single other family member who didn't want something from him.

"What do you want from me, Siena?" he demanded.

"I want you to be happy, Elijah." Her voice was soft. Her face was soft. Her eyes, intensely green. "Honey, share with me what's going on. Let me in."

She was so far in he was totally fucked, but she didn't see it. She didn't see what she meant to him. He didn't understand how that could be when he felt the earth shake under his feet and his lungs burning with the need for air every time he tried to take a breath around her.

"Here's me sharing, Siena. You didn't deserve a fucked-up grandfather who put your life in jeopardy, or a father who followed in his footsteps and got your mother killed. You sure as hell shouldn't be anywhere near a man like me. If I were any kind of a man, I'd let you go, but it's not going to happen. Ever. You get pissed, we talk about it. We work it out."

"Honey, we had this conversation. You're skirting around what's really bothering you. Earlier, you had that same look on your face right after I . . ." She trailed off. "The same one after I had you in my mouth tonight. If I'm doing something wrong, you have to tell me."

Siena tried not to think about the words Elijah had said to her when he'd thrown her out of his house. He'd proved time and again that he hadn't meant them, but they still reverberated through her mind when she caught that particular look on his face. For the first time her gaze slid from his, and she looked down at her body. Her breasts exposed, her skirt around her hips, exposing her bare skin to him. She had to look slutty.

Siena shifted in her chair, drawing her legs back so she could sit upright. The problem was, he didn't move back. Not an inch. Not one single centimeter. She put a hand to his belly, trying to shove him back.

"Are you fucking kidding me right now?" he demanded. "Fucking get a clue, Siena, the way you touch me, the way you work me with your mouth. The way you give that to me undoes me every single fucking time." The admission burst out of him.

Siena looked up at his gorgeous, masculine face, the hard features even harder than usual. The silver eyes burning brighter than normal. Intense. Focused. Close to leopard. He looked aggressive. Dominant. Standing over her like a conqueror.

The truth hit her then. Her man, the supremely confident, arrogant, powerful Elijah Lospostos, head of the Lospostos crime family, feared by everyone, was insecure when it came to her. Siena Arnotto. A virgin who knew nothing about sex. Who brought him trouble—the kind of trouble that could get a man killed. He was the type of man who reacted with anger and intensity when he felt threatened. *She* was the threat to him. More precisely, the way he loved her.

She *loved* that. She also detested it with every breath she took. She realized that one woman, his sister Rachel, had been his Achilles' heel all his life. His love for her had made him vulnerable. He'd been forced to do vile things, things that shaped him into the dangerous killer who stood in front of her, staring down at her with a kind of fury gathered in the centers of his eyes. Rachel had made him vulnerable. What would loving Siena do to him? And he loved her. He wanted her in his life. He needed her.

The thought of just how much he wanted her took her breath away. She understood. In that moment, she realized she mattered more to him than she ever had to her grandfather in all the years of her life. To anyone. Elijah loved her. *Loved* her. She'd never had that. Not like he loved her, with that intense, focused, single-minded purpose. It was the reason he was so protective. So determined the life they were both caught in, through no fault of their own, would never touch her.

"Fucking look at me when we're talking about this, Siena. I thought we put this crap to bed."

"I am looking at you, Elijah," she said gently. A whisper. Her hand slipped over his abdomen, tracing the defined muscles there.

"You aren't looking where I want you to look."

"Then you shouldn't be distracting me," she accused.

He caught her chin and yanked it up, forcing her to look into his eyes again. His gaze burned over her face. Fierce. Possessive. "I love when you go down on me, baby. I dream about it. The thought of it and the way you do it, the way I feel you loving me, giving me that gift, and enjoying giving it to me, distracts me a million times throughout the day. I get hard thinking about the way you love me. And you fucking love me, Siena. I feel it every time your mouth is on my cock."

His tone was just as ferocious as his expression. As the

heat in his eyes. Her heart fluttered. Her stomach went into a slow roll and damp heat bathed her sex. "I do love you, Elijah. It's fierce and hungry and with me every second. It's also about taking care of what's mine. You take care of me in your way and I have to do the same. For me. I want to care for you better than any other woman ever could. Is that what puts that look on your face? The one that says you love me and you hate me at the same time? Do you feel I've trapped you in some way?"

His face softened. Instantly. "It would be impossible to hate you, *mi amorcito*. I'm so grateful for that baby I put inside you. It means you aren't going anywhere."

She shook her head. "You aren't getting it, Elijah. I *choose* not to go anywhere. I made a mistake earlier, just in my unfortunate choice of words. I have no intentions of leaving you. Ever." She added a little pressure to his belly. "But seriously, honey. I'm hungry and the food is getting cold and I really need to clean up. I get lost so can you please point me in the direction of the nearest bathroom?"

He studied her face for a long time before he stepped back, drawing her up with him, so that she stood on her feet, swaying a little while her long skirt dropped to her ankles. "I love this thing you're wearing, baby. Do me a favor and wear it for me just like this while we have dinner. I love seeing what's mine."

"I feel just a little exposed."

"You live dangerous, baby, you want it or you wouldn't be with me, you wouldn't have chosen me. You're *my* wild cat. Your man wants to sit across a table from you seeing the candlelight play over your skin, I know you're up to that. You were up to letting me take my dessert and giving you yours right here in the fucking kitchen."

Her heart accelerated. She not only had done that, but she'd been the one to initiate it. Worse, she hadn't even considered if someone might walk in on them. "What if someone comes in?" But she knew she was going to give him whatever he wanted.

"No one will come in. They know better. The bathroom is there," he gestured toward a door. "Right off the kitchen. You can clean up in there." His hand cupped the soft weight of her breast, his thumb sliding across her nipple giving her another rush and a little aftershock. "Do me this favor, right?"

She moved around him because he didn't move. He said things like that. *Do me this favor, right?* She had never considered that she might be the type of woman who would want to have crazy hot sex in the kitchen, or sit across from her man half naked just because he asked her, but she was. She loved his voice, velvet over steel, rough and yet so sexy, his voice took her there every time.

Elijah watched her disappear into the bathroom. He stood a long while looking at the closed door, his heart beating too fast. She had become his world, his reason for existing, and that wasn't a good thing for a man in his position. There was protection in his reputation, but there was also a great deal of danger. Mostly, he didn't know how to be loved like that. He was rough. He'd grown up rough. He was violent. He'd known no other way of life. He could find his way around the criminal world blindfolded, but a relationship with Siena wasn't going to be easy.

He had sex with women and sent them on their way. He didn't spend a lot of time trying to impress a woman—truthfully he'd never had to. He tended to look at a woman and she went to bed with him, and then it was over because he wanted it over. He was in new territory—he loved Siena to distraction, and he had no clue what to do with her.

He had heated the food and lit the candles when she returned. The moment she entered the room, his gaze was on her. It would always be on her. He would know if she was close. Not only did every cell in his body react, but so did his leopard, the male leaping toward her female every time. The large cat was just as enamored with her little female as he was with the human.

He took a deep breath, watching her walk to him. She

looked ethereal and very feminine in that long skirt, the way it clung to the curve of her hips. The camisole was tight through her narrow rib cage and tucked-in waist, but she hadn't done up the laces, given him just what he'd asked for. Her breasts, so beautiful, full and creamy spilled from the top, the material framing them.

He took her hand, threading his fingers through hers, bringing up her knuckles to his mouth. "You're so fucking beautiful, Siena, sometimes I'm afraid to look at you."

He was. He was afraid if he looked too long, if he believed too much, she'd be gone, and the monster inside him, crouched and waiting, would swallow him completely.

She stepped in front of him before he could lead her to the table, blocking his way. He halted and found himself looking down into her piercing green eyes. Those eyes that always seemed to find him. The man. To see him. The man. Never the monster. She could keep the killer at bay so easily.

Her hands slid up his chest, she went up on her toes and her hands locked around his waist. "Look at me, Elijah," she whispered.

He was looking. There was nothing else in the world for him but this woman and the child she carried in her body. His woman. His child. His own family. Right there in his arms. He locked her in place, holding her close to him, sheltering her with his body.

"I see you, baby," he whispered.

"Do you? Do you see how much I need you?"

His heart clenched. Hard. Stuttered. He shook his head without thinking, an involuntary response to her question. How could she need him? He was a Lospostos. That name alone left a bad taste in anyone's mouth. Unless they were looking for a favor or a thrill, good people gave him a wide berth. She was good people.

"I do need you. Just to breathe, Elijah. I've been holding my breath for so long. I have nightmares all the time. I'm always afraid. Since I woke up in that hospital bed, with you there, even when I was embarrassed to look at you, I wasn't afraid. Not in the same way, not that deep-down fear that any moment my life is going to end. You give me that. I'm not afraid to bring our child into the world. That's from you. That's big, Elijah. Huge."

He shook his head. She continued, never taking her gaze from his.

"I've never had girlfriends. You bring me two women who were nice to me. Good people. They didn't want anything from me, just to be my friends. You gave me that. I'm so in love with you, Elijah, I sometimes can't even contain it all."

His hand came up to find the silk of her hair as his mouth found hers. She tasted like heaven. Like she always did. She'd rinsed her mouth, maybe even brushed her teeth because she tasted like mint. She didn't realize how she could twist him up and wrap herself so deep inside him he didn't know where he started and she left off. When he lifted his head she was smiling at him. Giving him the world right there on her face.

"You have to eat, baby," he said softly.

"So true. I'm starved," she agreed, and released him, turning toward the table.

He held her chair for her, making it formal. He'd lit the candles and brought the lights in the room down low. He was right about the candlelight. It loved her, dancing over her skin and hair, casting the most beautiful glow over her.

He watched her face when she tasted the dish, one of his favorites. He'd been careful not to make it too hot. He liked his food spicy but she was a novice. He didn't want to start out burning her mouth.

"It's wonderful," she said, "perfect. Where did you learn to cook like this?"

"My grandmother." His voice went tight, and he forked a mouthful of food.

He felt the impact of her gaze. He'd been young when she'd

died. Right after his seventh birthday. He knew his grandfather had taken her from her home when she was fourteen and married her. He knew that because his grandfather liked to brag about it. She'd been a very quiet woman and she'd stayed in her kitchen. He'd sought refuge there many times.

The spices, the smells in a kitchen were comforting to him all of his life. When he was particularly upset, he always headed to the kitchen to cook. He could work out his problems when he cooked. He hadn't thought about the influence his grandmother had on him. He'd spent too much time thinking about the lives his grandfather, uncles and father had destroyed—ultimately, the lives he'd helped to destroy. None of them were good people, but that didn't matter. He had lived in the underbelly of the world so long he had come to realize there were layers of scum. Layers of bad. His family had been one of the worst.

"Honey, you're going far away from me," Siena said softly.

His gaze jumped to her. She was beautiful. All his. "I'm never going to be far from you, baby," he replied honestly. "I was just remembering my grandmother. I thought I just had my sister, but I had her. She gave me this." He gestured at the food, at the kitchen.

"Do you use her recipes? Because this is really delicious."

He nodded. "I have them all. She kept them in a book. I like looking at her handwriting. Some of the recipes were her mother's."

"I want to learn to make them for you. For our children."

"I can teach you. I don't mind trading off cooking. Although, Siena, you want me to bring in a chef . . ."

"No. We don't need that. I always wanted to learn to cook. I'm good at picking things up fast. I'll try a few recipes out of the book."

"It's in Spanish," he pointed out. "But I'll get it translated for you."

"Thanks," she said softly. "I have to get to the winery and

see what's happening with that. I can't neglect that. Too many jobs are at stake. I grew up around the grapes and the winery. I went to school for it. I don't want to lose that business because of the rest of it."

He didn't hesitate answering her, but inside his gut coiled into hard knots. "We'll take care of that, *mi corazon*." He didn't want her anywhere near her grandfather's estate, not until he'd ferreted out Paolo and buried him deep. The man was never going to lay a hand on Siena, and he was going to pay for what he'd already done to her. And he was going to pay hard.

She flashed him a smile. "Just thought you should know. My leopard is pretty eager to see her mate. I thought maybe they could run this evening."

He nodded. "Sounds good to me. Keeping my male mellow helps."

Her green eyes jumped to his face. "Is it difficult?"

"I've been controlling him all of my life, baby. I'm used to the way he snarls."

She laughed softly. "I can't believe I'm sitting here talking calmly about our leopards. It's kind of insane."

"It's just a fact. Who we are."

"Elijah, if we have a girl, she has to know. I don't want what happened to me to happen to her."

He winced. Cursed himself for not realizing what was happening the first time he took her.

"Elijah?"

"You give me a girl and I'm putting you across my knee."

"That didn't work out very well," she pointed out, her eyes laughing at him.

His breath caught in his lungs. He loved that look on her face. He loved that he put it there. He leaned across the table toward her. "I just need a little practice."

Her fork was halfway to her mouth and she stopped. He saw the passion rising in her eyes. Yeah, she liked his brand of sex, no matter what he gave her. She was with him every step of the way. The moment they were finished, he was picking her up in his arms, carrying her back to his bed, and he was going to take his time, loving every inch of her body.

He saw the answering burn in her heated gaze. The hunger that matched his own. Yeah, she was made for him. His woman. His wild cat.

17

ELIJAH woke abruptly as he always did. Fully alert. Listening. His leopard reached out into the dark room and beyond, looking for trouble. Finding none, Elijah buried his face in the thick silk of Siena's hair. He'd woken her twice in the night and both times she'd given herself to him exactly how he asked. She never hesitated. Trusting him. Loving him.

The way she loved him brought him to his knees. She kissed him every single time as if she were giving herself to him. When her hands and mouth were on him, she did so lovingly, wildly and possessively. He loved that about her. She had two more visits from Emma and Catarina and after each, she'd been more than wild in bed, almost as creative as he was, thanking him in her way for the friendships.

She'd told him Emma was on bed rest for the next month before the baby was taken by C-section and she wanted to go to Jake and Emma's to visit. Today was a good day for that because he had shit to do. Really fucked-up shit. He didn't want her anywhere near him when he was doing it.

He brushed kisses along her temple and trailed more to the corner of her mouth. His hand slid over her breasts, which he swore were already fuller, down to the soft pooch that was her belly. He loved that pooch. It was forming fast. His baby. His child. He wanted a son only because he was certain if he had a daughter she would make him as crazy as her mother already did.

"Baby, wake up for me, *mi vida*, just for a minute."

She murmured sleepily, and the drowsy note hardened his cock, but then just about everything about her managed to do that. She didn't turn away from him, although she had to be exhausted. Her arm slid around his waist and her hand slipped down his hip. He loved when she did that. As if she was wrapping him up with her.

"Tell me what you need, honey," she whispered, her voice soft and husky with sleep.

"You give me whatever I want?"

Her head tilted and her long lashes lifted. He felt the impact of her green eyes piercing his heart. "Anything, Elijah."

The absolute conviction in her voice turned him inside out. He caught her wrist and inspected it, there in the dark, using his leopard's vision to make certain there were no bruises. He hadn't used soft scarves like he should have. He hadn't thought to keep them handy, in the drawer beside the bed. He'd had metal handcuffs, not comfortable, and he'd been a little feral. They had been letting the leopards out nightly and his male was ravenous for the female, feeding his own desire for Siena.

He brought her wrist to his mouth. "Gotta go, baby. I've got all kinds of shit to do. I've got a couple of boys taking you over to Emma's and they'll bring you home whenever you want. I need you resting. I kept you up, and the leopards were out a long time."

"Where are you going?"

He ignored her question. "If you want to try your hand at cooking, I'll be home for dinner. I had my grandmother's recipes translated for you and I left the book on the island in the kitchen. Groceries are in as well. If you don't feel up to it, that's all right, call me on my cell, leave a message and I'll pick something up on the way home." He brushed another kiss along her wrist. "You feeling all right?"

She'd been sick a lot lately. She didn't ever complain. She just went into the bathroom, and he could hear her as her stomach rebelled every single morning and several times throughout the day. She was fairly pale. He was careful not to have her go down on him anymore. He didn't want to make her morning sickness worse.

"I'm good. Don't worry about me."

"Baby." How could he not worry? When he called her *mi vida*—my life—he meant it. She was his life. "Don't like you sick, *mi amorcito*. Want you to stop."

She laughed softly, her breath warm against his ribs. She moved her head to cushion it on his belly, her long braid sweeping over his body, tangling for a minute with his cock. His body shuddered with pleasure. With contentment.

"I'll get right on that, boss-man."

"Glad you finally recognize what I am to you," he said. "You sleep in this morning and eat something. Even if it makes you sick, baby. Doc says you have to eat. Small meals. A lot of them. And take those prenatal vitamins."

She traced her name with the pad of her fingers into his chest. She did it often, her way of claiming him. He marked her body to brand her his. Her claiming was invisible but no less binding.

"Where are you going, Elijah?"

"*Mi vida*, I've got business to attend to." Setting up a king-pin in Rafe Cordeau's territory. Hunting down Robert Gaton and Paolo Riso. Killing them. Burning their carcasses. Bury-ing them deep. The usual business men attended to.

She kept her eyes on his stomach. "I'm carrying twins."

For a moment he thought he heard her wrong. She just said it straight-out in a low, whispery tone as if she was responding to his statement. He was thinking about killing and she was thinking about life. Bringing more life into his world. Giving him two children. More *familia*. Above her head, he closed his eyes. She gave him beauty. Too much. Almost more than he could handle.

"Doc tell you?" Because Doc hadn't told him. They were going to have words about that. He needed to know how to take care of his woman. Doc had no right to keep anything from him.

"No. I don't think he knows yet. My female told me. Last night. Before we went to bed."

She knew, and she'd still come to him every way he wanted, giving herself to him. Wild. And she'd been wild. Begging him to be harder. Rougher. Matching the primitive savage need in him.

"Should have told me right away, baby. I need to talk to Doc. Find out whether our kind of sex is going to have to wait until they're born."

She pressed kisses into his belly. Swirled her tongue in his belly button. Nipped him with her teeth. "Don't you dare talk to Doc about our sex life. I'd be embarrassed to ever look at him."

He laughed softly. He couldn't help it. Her wild belonged only to him. He loved that, but it didn't negate the fact that he needed to know how to protect her and his unborn children. He was rough. He liked his sex rough. He was wild. He liked his sex wild. And he liked it often. But not at the expense of his woman and children.

"Baby, if I ever hurt you, you need to tell me."

"If Doc ever says we can't have sex . . ." She trailed off.

He bunched her braid in his hand and tugged until her head turned and she looked up at him. Reluctantly. "Where the hell did that come from?" he demanded. He was going to *kill* Doc if he wasn't communicating.

"Emma can't. You know. With Jake. It's hard on him, she says. Catarina's not having a difficult time. Doc doesn't think she's going to have any problems carrying her baby. She's having one. But what if, down the line he says we have to stop. I'm carrying two. You like . . ." She hesitated. "You *need* sex."

His gaze moved over her face. Her beautiful face. Anxious eyes. So worried. She still didn't get it. She still didn't understand. Her grandfather had never made her feel important. No one had. She couldn't possibly understand that when he told her she was his life, that was exactly what she meant to him.

"You think I could touch another woman after you? Loving you the way I do? Never going to happen, *mi amorcito*. Fucking never. Doc says you can't have sex we'll get creative. Your mouth is paradise. That's off-limits then I guess we'll get really good at hand jobs. Kind of like the idea of you learning how to do that for me."

He felt her shiver. Her face was soft. Sexy. Eyes slumberous. *Dios*, but he loved this woman and he wanted her all over again. He was greedy when it came to her. So hungry for her he never seemed to get enough.

"I have to go, baby. I want you to sleep in," he reiterated. "Go see Emma and Catarina, have a good time, but if my boys tell you to do something, you do it, no argument. You get me?"

Her gaze fastened to his. Stayed there. Intelligent. Far too much intelligence. He didn't give a damn. She might suspect all kinds of things, but he needed to know she was going to do what he told her.

"They say you leave, you get your ass home, no sassing them. They'll have orders to carry you out, you don't cooperate. And, baby, you make them do that, you'll be answering to me."

There was no erotic note in his voice. He wanted her to know he wasn't playing around. Not with her safety. She needed to know there were certain lines she couldn't cross with him. They were hard lines. And he would do something about it. She'd be uncomfortable and not laughing when he got through with her, and she'd never forget the lesson.

"Elijah, do you think I'm stupid? Brainless?" Her tone was ominous. She lifted herself up on one elbow. "Because I'm not. You don't need to threaten me to get me to use good sense. I know you're doing something dangerous. You wouldn't be doing it if you didn't have to. I know I brought this storm down on you. I want to keep our babies safe as much as you do."

She had that tone. That attitude. The one that teased his cock into one hell of a hard-on. Painful even. Perfect. She looked pissed, but adorably pissed. How the hell did she think he could take her seriously when she was propped up naked next to him, one soft breast pressed deep into his side, the other resting on his abs?

"Sorry, baby. You going to have words with me over this?" He couldn't resist, because seriously, who said that kind of thing? *Words.* He loved that.

"Yes we are," she said. "More than words." She leaned down and bit him. Hard. Right on his belly.

The bite of pain arrowed straight to his cock. He yanked on her braid, to bring her head up, but her tongue was already soothing the ache. He heard her muffled laughter.

"You do that again and you'll make me late. Won't like that, baby."

She turned her head, her lips whispering against his belly, sending little flames dancing over his skin. "Yes, you will. I'll make certain of it. But . . ." She pushed herself up into a sitting position. "I think, unfortunately, our babies have other ideas."

With that, she flung back the covers and rushed into the bathroom. He lay there, one hand over his eyes, listening to her, wishing he could figure out how to stop her morning sickness. Hating it. Hating he couldn't take it away for her. She didn't complain. Didn't blame him. Didn't in any way act as if carrying his child—his children—was a burden. He loved her all the more for that.

He heard the water in the sink. Her scrubbing her teeth. She did that a lot. He moved then. Because if he didn't move, he was going to be late, and they needed to be on the road. In truth, he should have left hours ago. They were headed to New Orleans. Jake had given them the use of his private jet. He needed to establish a new boss in what very soon was going to be open territory again. Joshua Tregre was going to be that boss.

Drake Donovan had married into a family of law enforcement. None of them could take that title with any believability. Elijah dressed slowly. He'd given a lot of thought to whom he could set up in that position and make it work. He had discussed it with Drake, Jake and Eli before approaching Joshua and laying it all out to him, laying it out that from the moment Joshua took over Cordeau's territory, he'd live a shit life. It would change Joshua's life. Forever. He would lead a double life, the same way Elijah was leading one. The same way he was going to ask Alonzo to lead one.

Joshua would have to do things he didn't want to do, things that would cement his role and title in the underworld. Their network would grow—was already growing if they could just keep from being killed. Soon, Elijah knew he would have to sit down with Siena and have the conversation he'd been avoiding.

What did one say to the woman he loved? How did he ask her to do that kind of shit with him? To put her and his children through that? He kept it from her as long as he could, hoping he could find a way to make her so into him, so in love with him that there was no other choice but to stay. Now, because of his decision, Joshua would have to have a similar conversation if he found a woman. And Alonzo.

He pulled on his clothes, clothes he could remove fast

when he needed to shift. Everything from his jeans and shirt to his boots had been specially made for that purpose. He could strip and shift on the run, and he was fast. He had to be. He didn't want the others to be responsible for the things he knew he had to do. Robert Gaton had put out a hit on both him and Siena. He'd sent a sniper to his home. He was sending others. He was leopard, and he was a criminal.

Gaton knew Elijah's reputation and he knew that wasn't going to fly. Still, Gaton was dumb enough to do it and that meant he had a plan in place. Elijah suspected Gaton aligned himself with Paolo. Elijah had already taken steps with the council to let them know he was taking over the Arnotto territory on Siena's behalf and Alonzo would be running it. He had even intimated that when the time was right, the territory would be Alonzo's alone and he would remain as a consultant and friend, a business partner, but Alonzo would have complete control once he knew the ropes.

He'd announced his engagement to Siena and the papers for the license were waiting for her to sign. The notary would be there that evening and they'd both have the papers signed so in seventy-two hours they could be married. He'd arranged for that too. In Jake's home. Emma and Catarina there, Jake and Eli with Drake as well. He was putting a ring on Siena's finger, and the rest of the world could deal with it.

She wasn't having his babies without a ring. And he didn't want to go five minutes longer than necessary before it was done and she was irrevocably his. He heard her come back into the room and he turned. Somewhere she'd found his shirt. He didn't like her wearing anything to bed. He knew he never would.

He loved feeling her soft body, with all those lush curves pressed tight against him. He liked to put his mouth on her breast and feel the way her body went damp for him as he drifted off to sleep. She always gave him that, but when he left their bed before her, she always put a shirt and panties on.

"Have fun with your girls, baby," he said, turning to her. Taking her into his arms. Holding her close. He loved holding her. She was small and perfect against him. He'd never in his life considered he'd have someone like her as his mate. Someone decent. Someone innocent. Innocent and wild. He brushed a kiss on her head. "I love you, *mi vida*. More than life. I love you that much. Never forget it."

She went up on her toes and pressed kisses along his jaw. "Come home to me, Elijah. You stay safe and come home to me. I need you. *We* need you." She narrowed her eyes. "You get me?"

His own words. He smiled down at her. "Yeah, baby. I get you. Get in bed and let me tuck you in. I like knowing you're in our bed and sleeping peaceful. Keep your cell on you."

"Um, just in case you don't remember, my cell is toast. You threw it. Broke it to bits. I haven't replaced it because—well—I haven't thought about it."

"I'll call my boys. One of my men, you know Tomas Estrada, is taking this shift with you. He and his brother Joaquin have been with me since I was a kid. Tomas will look after you with Trey Sinclair. They'll have their cells on them, and I'll see about getting Jake's secretary to pick one up for you."

She lifted her chin at him. The way she did it always made his leopard go a little crazy. That little defiant attitude always made his cock hard and his alpha nature go ballistic. She hadn't figured that out yet.

"I can get my own cell phone."

He brushed his mouth over hers. "Of course you can. I'm the one who broke it, though, baby, so I'm the one replacing it. Yeah?" He didn't give her a chance to answer. Jerking back the covers he motioned her in. "Get back to sleep and I'll see you this evening."

She slid in and waited until he tucked the blankets around her before she caught his hand. "You'll come back to me. Safe. Intact. *You*."

He knew what she meant. Whatever he was doing, she didn't want him to suffer from it. He knew he wouldn't. Leopard law was the law of the jungle. They had strictly enforced laws. They had to. Leopards could kill easily. Leopards weren't allowed to hunt humans in the swamps as Rafe Cordeau had allowed his male to do. His lieutenants had joined in his hunts. Robert Gaton had been one of his lieutenants. He was a vicious killer, and he'd put a hit out on Siena. That was unacceptable. He wasn't going to get the chance to take over Cordeau's territory. He'd run it in the same bloody, cruel way his predecessor had.

"I will," he said. Meaning it.

She still didn't let go. He was patient. He didn't care that the others were waiting. That Jake's plane was waiting. Siena's gaze clung to his face, moving over his features, seeing him. Seeing the killer in him this time. He endured that. For her. He took it, but he hated it.

He watched her just as closely, his leopard close, but quiet. Both recognized this was a defining moment. Elijah detested that she was so damned intelligent. There was no hiding from her. No hiding from those see-all eyes of hers. She'd always been able to penetrate his armor. She'd found that little piece of him hidden deep, protected from the rest of the world. There was no doubt she saw everything else.

"Elijah." Her voice was whisper soft. "I've trusted you. Believed in you. Let myself fall, not just in love with you, but so deep, I don't know how I'd survive without you. I'm looking at you and I need you to give me the truth."

He braced himself.

"Is this necessary? Are these really bad people?"

"You sure you want this, Siena? I don't want it for you. I want you to live your life free."

"You're mine. I can't watch you go, knowing what's going to happen, without you telling me what our lives are going to be like. I've been patient, waiting. Now you're going and it's . . . bad. I can see that. So give me that much. I have to know."

"I wouldn't go after an innocent, baby," he assured her. "Hold on to Drake's reputation, not the one that was mine. Is mine. I promise we'll have that talk when I get back if you still want it. I'll lay it out for you."

"All of it."

He closed his eyes. Knowing she saw. He *fucking* hated his family, what they'd made him, what they'd given him.

"Honey." Soft. Beautiful. Loving. She kissed his hand and his heart turned over.

Elijah opened his eyes and nodded. "All of it."

"Then go, but be safe. And come back to me." She rubbed her palm over her belly. "To us."

He put his hand on her soft pooch where his children lay safe and snug inside his woman. "I'll always come back to you."

He got the hell out of there before he lost his resolve. He would come back to her with blood on his hands. He swore with every step he took, furious at himself, at his life—a life he'd chosen when Drake had proposed it—and furious at the people who had taken a little boy and shaped him into a monster.

The men with him on that plane were good men. All of them. He trusted them when he didn't trust very many. Joshua sat alone, face turned toward the window, looking like stone. Part of him wanted to go to the man and talk him out of his decision. It was easy enough to make when you didn't have a woman, when you didn't have decent, when you were alone with nothing and wanted to do something with your life.

"You okay?" Drake asked, dropping into the seat across from him.

Drake was one of the few people who could read him—or dare to ask him questions. Elijah had never been friendly. His leopard rode him hard. His upbringing had never allowed for friendship. He liked his brother-in-law, Rachel's husband, but when he first met him, Elijah still had major trust issues.

He didn't like someone that close to his sister, not when he didn't know him. Still, the man made her happy and Elijah had learned, over the years, that Rio was a good man.

"She saw me tonight," he admitted. He pressed his fingers to his eyes. "She saw who I am. What I am."

"What you *were*," Drake emphasized. "Even then, it wasn't you, Elijah. That was never you."

"Don't kid yourself, Drake. It's me. It will always be me. Whatever I could have been was gone the moment I was born into that family. I am what they made me. And I chose to do this work, believing in it. I didn't know the gods were going to hand me Siena. She's my miracle and my punishment all rolled into one. I can't let her go and I have to live with the knowledge of what I am, what she has in her bed, every fucking minute."

He didn't give a damn if he sounded bitter. Siena deserved a normal life and she wasn't going to get it.

"You knew when you made the decision there was no getting out. You laid that out for Joshua, and you emphasized that. More than once. This kind of thing, Elijah, the only way out is death. They would hunt you to the ends of the earth. I'd try to protect you, but sooner or later, they'd get you. Your best protection is to be stronger than anyone else, have enough allies. We're building that. We're almost there."

"I know that," Elijah said. "Doesn't make it any easier when she's looking at the monster and not seeing the man."

"She still in your bed?"

Elijah's gaze hit Drake's. He nodded slowly.

"Then she saw the man. She's not going anywhere."

"She did, I'd go after her," Elijah admitted. His voice was dark. Ugly. The killer, not the man. He wanted Drake to see the worst of him. "I'd drag her ass back home so fast she wouldn't know what hit her. That woman has no idea what's in her fucking bed."

"Yeah, she does," Drake said. "She knows. She climbed into it with her eyes open, Elijah. She's smart, that one. Like

Emma. Like Catarina. They know what they got. They love their men and accept them."

"Jake's clean."

Drake burst out laughing. "You know better than that."

"He's clean to the rest of the world."

"He's dangerous. Eli's dangerous. Their women know."

"Lot of difference between being dangerous and dirty, Drake. Siena lives with knowing her man heads a crime family. Her man beat the shit out of other men to force them back into line. Her man killed. She doesn't just get to pretend we're living clean, because the neighbors are always going to look at her like she's filth."

"Siena is in your bed, Elijah. Right now. She knew your reputation before she ever made that choice."

Elijah shook his head, his eyes going pure cat. "Did I give her a choice? A real choice? I forced her to come home with me . . ."

"That was me," Drake said. "Not you. Your home was the only safe place for her. *You* were the only safe place for her. She was under your protection the moment she entered your house. No matter where she landed, someone was going to go after her. With you standing between her and everyone else, that threat was minimized. You have Cordeau's heir and Paolo and no one else to deal with because of your reputation. That's what saved Siena. You think she doesn't know that? She can't very well get too righteous if she's hiding behind that strength."

"Shut the fuck up. She's not hiding behind anything, and she can get as righteous as she wants to. What the hell does that mean? You think she knew her grandfather was dirty? He was a winemaker. She went to school to take over his business."

"You really are a hothead when it comes to that woman," Drake said. He didn't even bother to hide his grin. He sure as hell wasn't afraid of Elijah or his anger. "She should take over her grandfather's business. Waltz right back home and announce she's the boss. And no, I don't believe she knew about her grandfather. Even the Feds weren't certain. There's never been a shred of evidence. The man was brilliant at hiding his activities. If he hadn't associated with known criminals, he wouldn't have even been on their radar."

"Eli told me the Feds believed he was friends with them because of their American-Italian connection. His wine is considered among the best in the United States, and naturally the families would gravitate toward it."

Eli Perez was on the plane as well. An ex-DEA agent, he was tough as nails and good in a fight. He was a recent addition to Drake's team, and he was assisting Jake in coming at Cordeau's business partners from another angle. Jake was famous for buying up companies and taking them apart. He was ruthless when it came to business.

They'd brought Alonzo with them. They needed to see him in action. Make certain before they brought him further into their fold. Most of Drake's team had come from his home lair in the Borneo rain forest and Drake had known them from his childhood. Any new members were also men he'd known and worked with on his rescue teams from various rain forests around the world. They didn't have to worry about their loyalty.

Bringing Alonzo in was dangerous. All of them knew it and were willing to take the risk. Like Elijah, Drake and the others thought he would be a good asset, a man worth saving. Still, one wrong move and he wouldn't make it back. Elijah sighed. He was leopard. He knew the rules of living in the world of leopards. The rules were even more rigid and ruthless, more primitive and savage than the rules of his family.

Joaquin Estrada was there as well. He kept to himself, although he'd met Drake a few times when Elijah had pulled him in on a rescue job they needed. There was no way Joaquin or Tomas would ever allow Elijah to go too far without one of them.

"Siena wants to take over her grandfather's winery," Elijah

confirmed for Drake. "But I can't let her go back there until Paolo is dragged out into the open and I can take his ass down."

"You take Siena to that winery, I guarantee Paolo will come out of the shadows," Drake said. "He'll have no choice. He's made his brag to her father's army. They see the princess and she tells them Paolo beat the crap out of her and murdered their boss, they aren't going to welcome him."

A snarl erupted before Drake could finish. Growls rumbled deep in Elijah's chest, and his eyes banded with heat. His leopard rose fast, angry, vicious. There was instant silence on the plane. Elijah fought back his male. Cleared his throat several times to try to stop the raging beast from coming up any farther. He felt the itch of fur. The ache in his joints. The need to shift.

Drake didn't move a muscle. He didn't back away. He didn't try to shift in order for his leopard to combat Elijah's. He simply waited for Elijah to get himself under control, as if he had all the faith in the world that he would. If he didn't, Drake was dead. Elijah's male would kill him instantly, and no one, not even Elijah, would be able to stop him.

Elijah breathed deep, forcing his leopard under control. Breathing away the need to shift. The anger remained. "I should rip your fucking head off," he snarled, his voice low, dark with his rage. "You already put her out there as bait once, against my better judgment, and someone got close enough to take a shot at her."

Drake nodded. Calm. Elijah recognized instantly why he'd always admired Drake. He took responsibility. He never passed the buck. And he remained calm. He got the job done. It was how he could lead so many, clean up and run a very difficult lair and run so many jobs with dangerous leopards following his orders. Elijah could be that calm over everything and anything—unless Siena was involved.

"I get that, Elijah. I'm just saying, you want that man out in the open, you have the way to do it fast and easy."

"Not going to use my woman as bait, Drake. I don't need

fast and easy to bring that fucker down. I'll get him. And when I do, you don't want to be anywhere around. He ripped her to shreds. He put his hands on her. He hurt her. He doesn't get to do that and die clean."

"I don't think you're going to get any arguments over how the man should die, Elijah," Drake said, shrugging his shoulders. "He's rogue. He knows the rules of our world. The boys are standing in line to teach him a lesson. To make him a lesson. No one is backing away from taking him out or teaching him that lesson."

"My woman isn't bait."

Drake grinned at him. "Get a handle on it, Elijah. You're a crazy fuck when it comes to her. Where's your famous cool? If I didn't know better I'd think you just came out of a cave for the first time."

Drake, damn him, was *teasing* him. Looking to get a rise out of him, and he'd managed to do it in a very dangerous way.

"I still ought to rip your fucking head off," Elijah groused, but the anger was gone, replaced by something else altogether. Affection. It wasn't just respect he had for Drake Donovan, it was affection.

Alonzo slid into the seat across the aisle. "You hitting them in broad daylight?"

"That's the plan," Drake said.

"He's leopard?" Alonzo prompted.

"He's a big son of a bitch too," Elijah said. "I didn't see his leopard, but he's a big man. Walks like a cat. He's going to be expecting us to hit him at night. He knows he blew the hit, and all this time he's been waiting for retaliation. He's on edge, knowing it's coming but not when or how. He's probably locked his place down and thinks he's got a fortress. We've made him wait, get anxious. Made his boys stretch their nerves out. He's in meltdown mode by now."

"So why daylight?" Alonzo reiterated.

Elijah wasn't used to anyone questioning his decisions. He sized Alonzo up. The man wasn't questioning the decision so much as trying to learn. Elijah liked that. He was certain Alonzo was far more than the soldier he claimed to be. He was comfortable in that role because he was used to it, but he could be a king. He needed to learn the ropes and become comfortable in his decision-making. The very good thing about Alonzo was that when he gave his loyalty, he didn't take it back. That meant he would always give his allegiance to Elijah and Siena, even if he were crowned the new king.

"He knows I'm leopard," Elijah said. "It won't occur to him that I'm going to hit him during the day, so his security won't be as tight. At night, he's going to have every soldier he can muster, especially the leopards, guarding him. During the day, he'll want to take care of business. Let everyone know he's the new boss. He'll be working at shaking down everyone Cordeau had on his books and cementing his relationships with the gangs running his drugs and guns for him. He's got a prostitute ring that goes through four parishes. He can't afford to keep all his soldiers home with him during the day."

"You have someone on the inside?" Alonzo asked. "Someone feeding you information?"

Elijah smiled like the leopard he was. Hungry. Cunning. "In every family, Alonzo. That man is your bread and butter. You keep him happy. You protect anyone he loves. You build him up. You make certain that whatever he gets from you is far more than he can ever have where he is. You don't ever ask for anything but information. Nothing that ever can blow back on him or anyone he cares about. They have to come from that territory, not yours, because there can never be a tie back to you. That's a protection for them. So always, take the time to do homework. Know everyone low, mid and high level. Low level moves up. High level is usually very loyal."

"Do you have the layout of his compound?"

Drake nodded. "Down to the last bush. We've got aerial. We've got blueprints. We've got the contractor who did the work fifty years ago and his son who added a few new escape routes since then. Talked to the painters, the electricians and even the plumber. All a very long time ago, back when Cordeau was alive and getting a stranglehold on the territory. Elijah's uncle was very thorough finding out about every boss connected to his business. But more than that, when Gaton moved his ass to Rafe Cordeau's mansion, he made the mistake of his life. We've got Catarina Perez, and she was raised there. She knows every inch of that property and she drew it all out for us."

18

RAFE Cordeau had bought one of the oldest plantations existing near New Orleans. The huge rambling house with its elegant white pillars and large wraparound verandah spoke of decadence and affluence. It hid the secrets of those who had lived before, although Elijah thought Cordeau's ownership was fitting.

The property was large. Great cypress trees with barreled trunks lined the water lapping at the lawn on two sides of the house. Great shawls of Spanish moss dripped down toward the water, swaying in the slight wind. The swamp crept up toward the house on the other two sides, threatening to take back the property at any moment.

The air smelled musty. Old. The farther Drake and Joshua moved through the swamp, the more often they came across the old slave cabins Cordeau had renovated for his men to use for various activities. It was where Cordeau's lieutenants took their women so screams couldn't be heard.

It was where they took enemies and tortured or beat them into submission or to death.

As they got closer to the main house, they ran into razor wire strung through the trees and brush. The motion detectors in the trees were much more frequent here, and the guards were used to animals setting them off. Drake and Joshua didn't. They moved with ease through the dense vegetation, not making a sound, closing in on the plantation, the sniper rifles flat against their backs, avoiding every single motion detector and camera along the way.

The road leading to the plantation had never been paved and Cordeau had kept it that way. He liked looking at the tracks and recognizing who drove what vehicle. Once he'd learned to identify tire tracks of each, he always knew who had come close to his property.

The plantation had been outfitted with a surrounding high fence, the top three strands razor wire, and a guard shack. The propane truck rumbled up to the guardhouse and the driver leaned out. He was sweating. The morning was already hot and humid, the air heavy with moisture. His shirt was wet under the armpits and down the front. His cap was pulled low over his eyes and he chewed on his toothpick.

"Danny."

"Pete," the guard answered, even more bored than the driver. He'd been on duty 24-7 since Cordeau had disappeared with several of his lieutenants. At night, Robert Gaton insisted everyone stay alert. Mostly the plantation was visited by deer and other wildlife. They set off the motion detectors and the floodlights every so many minutes. Danny was sick of it, just like most of the other soldiers. Gaton treated everyone like shit. He liked being the boss and knowing everyone had to jump if he told them to—and he told them to often.

"Gonna be hotter than hell today," Danny observed. "And it's gonna rain."

Pete glanced up at the sun, squinting. "Yeah. Maybe in an hour or two. I got a heavy schedule today. I'm going to get wet."

Danny grinned at him, revealing crooked teeth. "You ever find that niece of yours? When she disappear? 'Bout three months ago?"

Pete's face closed down. He pulled his hat lower. "Nope, we never found her," he said. "Funny thing, that. You and your partner, Bart, spent a lot of time talkin' to her every night at the bar."

"Didn't get anywhere." Danny shrugged. "Legs were tight, man. She wasn't givin' anything up."

Pete's mouth hardened. His hand closed over the small caliber gun tucked down the side of his seat, but then he relaxed. He had a little surprise for Gaton and his crew. He knew Danny and Bart had taken his niece from the bar when her shift ended three months earlier. Hell, everyone knew it. Danny liked to taunt him about it. Pete also knew she was dead and that she'd probably died hard. Women tended to disappear if any of Cordeau's men took a fancy to them. Gaton was every bit as bad, but everyone feared them and no one dared to challenge them. Until now.

Danny waved him through, laughing softly. Knowing he'd had Pete's niece and he was going to keep on having her until he used her up. He and Bart had been having good times for the last three months. They enjoyed putting on shows for some of the other boys. She didn't seem to enjoy it, but then she wasn't into receiving pain as much as they liked dishing it out. He especially enjoyed taunting Pete to his face, because he thought Pete—and no one else—would ever stand up to them.

Pete drove the truck around the main house, back behind the shrubbery that hid the large propane tank. He'd been there hundreds of time. No one ever paid any attention to him anymore. Still, even though he was certain his niece had been taken here, somewhere on the property, he'd never dared to look around. The men all were armed and they thought nothing of killing.

Like most people who had to deal with Rafe Cordeau and

his men, Pete kept a low profile. But he heard things. He certainly had heard of Elijah Lospostos. There was nothing low profile about him. He was a devil. Worse than the likes of Rafe Cordeau it was said. His name was whispered by Cordeau's men and they looked at one another uneasily when they said it. Since Rafe's disappearance, the name came up much more often. Everyone knew a war was coming. Everyone including Pete, so he had tried, like his neighbors, to stay under the radar.

He was shocked when Elijah Lospostos's men approached him. They were civil. Respectful. They didn't threaten. They didn't treat him like he needed to bow down before them. They had a plan and they laid it out. They needed a ride onto the property. They would use one of the propane tanks to get in. They'd construct a place in the belly of the tank to hide their men. He'd drive in, fill the tank as usual and drive away. Seeing nothing. Saying nothing. In return they would pay him very well and find out what happened to his niece. They would also avenge her. Nothing could be traced back to him.

Pete liked them. More, he liked their plan. It was a good one. He wouldn't know that the gas smell would mask their scents from the shifter guard. He liked the idea of the Trojan horse, driving right onto their property, under the nose of Danny the guard.

Pete's older rig, one he rarely used anymore, had been completely reconstructed inside. There was space—although cramped quarters—for five or six men and their equipment as well as a smaller tank that he could use to actually pump the gas into Gaton's propane tank. He liked being part of taking Gaton and his men down. It hadn't taken much convincing to put him squarely in Lospostos's camp.

He drove into the deepest brush, where he knew it was difficult to see from the house or any of the outbuildings. Cordeau hadn't wanted to have a propane tank visible. Gas made him nervous. He liked it hidden so no one would get the idea of using it against him. Pete parked and got out, walking around to the hose. As he did so, he hit the side of the truck hard to indicate they were undercover and this would be the best chance the men had of getting out of the truck without being seen.

Pete should have been tense, but he wasn't. All he could think about was Danny's taunting smirk. That voice. The one that told him his niece had suffered and there wasn't anything he could do about it. He went about his business pumping the gas and trying not to see the five men moving silently out of the belly of the truck. He didn't recognize any of them, and none of them looked at him until the last man. He turned and saluted Pete, as if respecting him. That meant a whole hell of a lot when he'd spent the last three months feeling less than a man.

Elijah smelled the air. Somewhere close, an outdoor barbecue was going. Steak, if he was any judge. Steak and pork. He signaled the four others with him to go easy. They had to slip in and take over the control room. If whoever was on the cameras was sharp, they'd eventually spot something wrong. So, the control room had to be theirs first.

Alonzo and Eli split off, moving around toward the back of the house where the large barbecue pit was. Joaquin, who had always remained Elijah's ally throughout the war with his uncle, stayed close to Elijah. Elijah knew the man would lay down his life for him. That was Joaquin. He tried not to use him too often, because Joaquin had seen too many battles and, like Elijah, killing came too easy, but this one was necessary.

Evan would be their man in the control room. He was fast and silent and knew his way around computers, cameras and just about any technology possible. He had come to Drake straight out of the rain forest. In the beginning, Elijah had confused him a few times with Jake's worker, Evan. Jake had a habit of picking up strays. His Evan didn't talk, but used sign language and was as tall and muscular as a tank. He wasn't leopard and was totally loyal to Jake and his family.

Evan Courtier was a little leaner, a lot meaner and had eyes that never stopped moving. He worked with Drake in the bayou a lot, but Drake had called him in to help.

Evan broke off from Elijah and Joaquin, dropped to the ground and rolled beneath the wide verandah while the other two skirted around the porch. According to the very detailed plans Catarina had drawn out for them, the control room was located on the left side of the house, on the first floor. There were two windows, both with bulletproof glass. One man stayed inside the room at all times.

Elijah and Joaquin had studied the cameras and the angles. There was one spot, just along the southern corner of the verandah, where the roof dipped a little lower to meet a pillar and a large live oak tree blocked the camera. Cordeau had left the enormous tree because he was leopard and the compulsion to keep the tree was too strong. No self-respecting leopard would cut down part of a personal highway.

Branches stretching across the forest, in the jungle, rain forest or the bayou—it didn't matter where—that was the leopard's ultimate highway. Glancing up, Elijah could see that Cordeau had escape routes from every direction of his home. Gaton had moved into the mansion, eager to become the boss over the territory. As a leopard, those private escape routes were now his.

Elijah crouched low and sprang up, catching the edge of the roof and easily pulling himself up. As a shifter, he had the same enormous strength as his leopard. And leopards could take several times their own weight right up a tree when they needed to do so. He gained the roof and, staying low, made his way along it until he was in position by the door closest to the control room. Joaquin was close behind him.

He never heard Joaquin. No one ever did. Most shifters were silent on their feet, but Joaquin was a ghost. He always had been. He rarely spoke, and it was far rarer to get a laugh out of him. He avoided Drake and his men, although he stayed close to Elijah. Elijah had laid it out for Joaquin and

Tomas, all of it, before he'd ever made the move to kill his uncle and get out from under the brutal monster of a man who had murdered his father. The brothers had simply shrugged, and said, "I'm with you, *mi hermano*." That was Joaquin and Tomas.

Elijah purposely didn't expose them too much. Not to anyone. Joaquin and Tomas were his personal bodyguards and the closest thing he had to men he trusted until he met Drake. Joaquin touched his shoulder, and instantly Elijah dropped down flat on the roof. He heard a twig snap as a man walked up to the door.

The newcomer was short, but had the familiar roped muscles of the leopard. He yanked open the door. "Food's almost done, Terry. You hungry?" he shouted.

There was the sound of movement almost directly below them. The man in the control room opened his locked door. "Starved, Bart. What took so long?"

"Fuck you, Terry. I'm getting you food first. You think it's easy cooking for so many? Gaton brought in a whole new crew he's so paranoid."

Elijah lifted his head, did a quick sweep of the surrounding yard and he leaped, driving Bart into the house with both feet. Joaquin was right behind him, going over the two rolling figures on the floor of the entryway to hit Terry in the chest like a battering ram. Terry fell back into the control room.

Bart began to shift, clearly unaware that Elijah was leopard as well. Elijah was there before him, his huge male coming eagerly to the fight, head and arms already shifting, slashing, a silent kill as the claws ripped out the throat. He didn't need the suffocating puncture his male wanted to add. Elijah controlled him, controlled the need for blood. His male was difficult to control when fighting. He liked it. Elijah liked it.

He shifted completely back to his human form and dragged the body into the control room. Terry lay dead on the floor. Joaquin's work was always fast and efficient. He had the body dumped in the corner, and Elijah tossed Bart on top of Terry, out of the way.

"Blood in the hall. Too much to hide. We got to do this fast," Elijah informed Joaquin. He touched his earpiece. All the men were wired. "Evan, we're good."

Evan responded immediately, rolling out from under the verandah, and was in the house so fast he was almost a blur. He didn't even glance at the two bodies in the corner or at Elijah and Joaquin. He was already in complete control, reaching for the wide board to shut down the recording equipment. "I've got this. Go."

Elijah and Joaquin went, closing the door behind them. It locked automatically. "We're sweeping the house now," Elijah informed the others, signaling Joaquin to go left. Joaquin didn't like it. Didn't like having Elijah out of his sight, but he went.

The plantation house was enormous, a tribute to the elegance and decadence of days gone by. Cordeau had modernized the home, updating the wiring and plumbing, but the house retained the old-world feel. Elijah could smell and feel the call of the swamp. He was leopard and he would always want the freedom of the wild close. This would be Joshua's home. He would take it over, and they would clean up the lair Cordeau had allowed out of control. It wouldn't be easy. Drake was cleaning up the lair close by and he'd had several challenges to his leadership. No doubt Joshua would as well.

Elijah moved in silence, slipping through the hallways, clearing each room thoroughly, using his cat's acute senses to tell him far in advance if danger was close. The downstairs rooms were empty. Even the large poolroom. He started up the stairs and immediately heard activity as he neared the top of the landing.

Elijah went to the floor, moving in human form in the way of the leopard. Stealth. Freeze-frame. Slow inch by inch. He moved in silence. He knew a cat could steal into a room full of people, grab a man and drag him out without anyone aware of his presence. He knew it, because he'd done it more than once. He knew it, because even as a man, he'd done it.

He heard the heavy fall of boots on the carpeted floor and froze, his body exposed. All the man had to do was take a few more steps and he'd be on top of Elijah. Elijah took a deep breath, scenting the air. The man with the boots was alone. He took another step and Elijah came up off the ground, already shifting, using just his upper body, but this time his entire upper body. His shirt shredded as his male leopard's head and chest emerged.

The soldier was no leopard and the shock of seeing one was his undoing. He had his gun in his hands, but he didn't even aim. He just stood there, his face frozen in fear as Elijah took him down. There was no sound, although the man opened his mouth to scream. The cat's wicked claw stopped him with a swipe across the throat. Elijah eased the body to the floor and then moved into the room he'd come out of to clear it.

From the vantage point of the window he could see a telescope had been set up. Beside it, a pair of binoculars rested. He bent to peer into the telescope. A cabin leapt into view. Through the window, he could see a woman, back to him, hands trapped over her head, wrists in manacles. Her head was down, hair falling around her face. She was naked. There was blood running down her back. Her legs had given out and she was hanging from just her wrists.

Elijah swore. The man had been watching the show someone had provided. "Drake, the first cabin on the southern end of the house. A woman's in there. A prisoner. She's in bad shape. Get her out."

"I'll take your back and then we'll get her," Drake responded into his ear, his voice as calm as always.

"Get her the *hell* out of there. She needs medical attention."

"We'll get her medical attention. You've got five men in

there against who knows how many. You need backup. We'll get her, Elijah, just get this done."

Elijah swore at him in Spanish. When Drake made up his mind to do something, nothing could budge him. Besides, Elijah knew he was right. He pushed down his temper. "Gaton brought in a new crew. They're probably resting in the bunkhouse. Joaquin and I are going there next the moment the house is clear. No sign of Gaton yet."

"We'll find him." Drake was confident.

"Alonzo, you locate the leopards yet?" Elijah asked, as he began to sweep down the hallway of the upper story. Joaquin was clearing the other side and so far he'd been silent, but that didn't tell anyone much. That was Joaquin's way.

"Two factions," Alonzo replied tersely. "I'm watching the ones who need killing. Three of them, and they love to hurt people. I caught part of the show with the woman. Man named Bart beat her with a whip. These three laughed and did a lot of crotch clutching. One jacked off. I'm killing him as soon as you give me the word. All I could do to stay put. Give me the word. I'll take all three of them."

"You wait. I'll join you in another minute," Elijah ordered. He understood. He would have wanted to kill the bastards after witnessing them torturing a woman and getting off on it. "Bart's dead, if that makes you any happier."

"Yeah. Makes me downright fuzzy. Eli's following the other leopards. They weren't happy with the show and left. Five of them."

Elijah wasn't surprised that the leopards weren't mixing with the fully human soldiers. The shifters didn't want to accidentally make a mistake and give themselves away. They'd have to kill the soldiers, and that didn't make for good business. He was thankful that not all of Cordeau's shifters allowed their savage natures to overcome their humanity.

If Joshua challenged for leadership of the lair and won the battle, defeating and killing Gaton, those five leopards would follow him. That would help immensely. Drake and

Elijah were already spreading their own crew thin trying to cover all the bases, and Alonzo would need help when he took over the Arnotto territory.

Elijah stopped just outside the door right in the middle of the wide loft area overlooking the first story. There were two staircases, one to his left that he'd used and one to his right that Joaquin had crawled up. Joaquin had cleared every room on his side and found no one. He met Elijah at the middle door. The double door itself was ornate. According to Catarina's plans, this was the master bedroom. Gaton's room. He would have moved in the moment he was certain Cordeau wasn't returning. Cordeau's body—and those of his four leopard lieutenants—had never been found. Shifters were always burned and the remains buried deep.

Elijah smelled the leopard inside the moment he was close to the door. His male rose fast, so fast it was difficult to contain him. He glanced over his shoulder and saw Joaquin's chest and arms contorting. He was already silently removing his clothes, fast, as he shifted, so they would remain intact, not shredded as Elijah's shirt had been. Elijah signaled to stand back, to the side of the door, and he stepped aside as well.

The blast put a hole straight through the center of the door. The wood splintered around the edges of the gaping opening. Instantly the barrel of a shotgun was pushed through, moving first one way and then the other. Elijah's boots and jeans were gone in seconds. He reached for the barrel, wrenched it from Gaton, pulling it all the way through the gap, reversing and firing blindly inside the room.

The answer was a roar of rage and Elijah knew the man was shifting, allowing his cat to take over. He jerked the door open to see Gaton at the window, his large male leaping for a tree branch. Instantly Elijah followed.

"Incoming," Evan said softly. "The soldiers from the barracks. Stay away from the verandah. It's rigged all the way around."

Evan was also an amazing specialist when it came to

making bombs. Few people could put together the type of charges he did, directing the blast exactly where he wanted it to go. The crew Gaton had hired were green, greedy men willing to do anything for money, but not used to the kind of war they were going into. They were disorganized and had no real leadership. The leaders were the leopards and Gaton.

"My three are on the move and I want them," Alonzo reported.

"Coming to you," Elijah said. His big cat swung his head around to Joaquin, indicating he go after Gaton and *not* kill him if at all possible.

Joaquin vaulted from the windowsill to the branch as Elijah leapt to the ground, already running to Alonzo's aid. Eli, with the help of Joshua and Drake, would herd the five leopards they wanted to spare away from the kill zone, but Alonzo was tracking the cruel ones—leopards who had hunted humans with Cordeau in the swamp. Men who enjoyed and got off watching a woman being tortured.

Elijah's male rounded the corner just as Alonzo's big male brought down a tall, heavy, tawny leopard. Alonzo's male was huge and heavily muscled. His coat was golden, with darker rosettes. He hit his target hard, coming in from the side, giving the other leopard no chance to get away. He drove him off his feet, and the other leopard rolled and tried to get up.

Alonzo was so fast he looked a blur as he leapt, coming down on his prey, going for the kill, going for the throat, claws raking the exposed belly while his teeth bit deep to hold and suffocate his prey.

The two other leopards turned back to aid their fallen companion. Before they could reach Alonzo, Elijah was there. His male launched himself into the air, using his flexible spine to twist, hitting first one and then the other, knocking them away from Alonzo.

He landed between the two males and their fallen friend. They split off to come at him from two sides. He remained utterly still, his male used to battle. He'd been fighting since he was six years old, life-or-death struggles, and he had come up against multiple attackers many times. The sound of explosions tore apart the day, the noise hurting his ears. He was expecting it and held his leopard steady. The other two whirled toward the sound. Elijah was immediately on the closest cat, raking him viciously from the side of his neck, shoulder to his hind end.

As his opponent tried to turn to face him, Elijah knocked him off his feet and opened his belly, spilling the contents onto the ground. He whirled to face the second rushing leopard, rearing up on his hind legs, teeth and claws meeting the big male. The two leopards grappled standing on their legs, clawing for a hold, both going for the other's throat while more explosions rocked the ground.

Elijah knew immediately his leopard was far more experienced. The other male didn't know to protect his underbelly or exposed genitals. The leopard had grown lazy living with Cordeau and hunting human women in the swamp for sport. Elijah was brutal in a fight. Vicious. Using every means possible to kill his opponent quickly so there was far less damage inflicted on him.

The best—and worst—was that he felt nothing at all when he won. Human or leopard. There was no triumph and there was no remorse. It just was. He'd been at it too long and knew the need for violence, the need for combat, was never going to go away. He accepted that as well. That had been the reason he'd thrown in with Drake in the first place. He'd tried to get out of that life, found it impossible and switched directions one more time.

His leopard reared back and lunged again, this time using his teeth, tearing through the softer exposed parts on his opponent. The leopard screamed and tried to turn, desperate to get away. Elijah was relentless, following, taking him down with a hard drive to the shoulder, sending the heavy male to his side. Then he was on him, teeth going deep into the throat. Holding. Waiting. He turned his body just enough that he could see Alonzo and the big cat he was fighting.

Alonzo's opponent, unlike Elijah's, definitely had experience, but it didn't matter, because, like the two Elijah had fought, his leopard was out of shape and Alonzo's leopard wasn't. Alonzo took good care of his cat and it showed. He was fast and deadly, spinning on a dime in midair, twisting and raking and leaping away. He had absolute purpose and deadly concentration in spite of two more explosions sending birds screaming into the sky.

The other leopard finally realized he had no hope of winning and tried to run, but Alonzo cut off all escape and kept at him, wearing him down, ripping and clawing, using his teeth until the other leopard was standing, head down, sides heaving, coat dark with sweat and streaked with blood. Alonzo's leopard took him down hard, teeth to the throat.

Elijah dropped the carcass of the leopard he'd killed and turned to the one dying just a few feet away. The leopard lifted his head and snarled, hatred and fear in his eyes. Elijah ignored the warning and was on him fast, delivering the suffocating bite. There were no more explosions, but the scent of gunpowder and death was heavy in the air.

Birds began to settle in the treetops and insects started their incessant droning. Elijah and Alonzo stared at each other through their leopards' eyes, and as if by mutual consent, dropped their respective opponent to the ground and turned to help Eli and Joshua with rounding up the other leopards.

As they approached the five men standing in the clearing surrounded by a grove of cypress trees, Elijah shifted enough to talk to Evan. "Need a report," he clipped.

"What I didn't get with the charges, Drake took down with his rifle. It's quiet here. Neighbors might have heard the explosions, although we're out a ways and my guess is no one wants the kind of trouble this crew can deal. I'll let you know if anyone shows up. The guard at the gate, Danny, took off into the swamp when the explosions hit. Drake took his ass down. When you're burning bodies, don't forget him."

"You have the girl?" Elijah asked Drake.

"With her now. She's nearly comatose. Terrified out of her skull. Pete's niece, the one he thought was dead. She's been living a nightmare for months. Whenever he showed up to deliver the gas, the men would torture and rape her while he was here, thinking it funny." Drake's voice was harsh. Furious. Not the calm they knew so well.

"We need to know if any of these other men participated," Elijah said, staring at the five shifters under Joshua's and Eli's guns. He shifted all the way and caught the jeans Joshua threw him, tugging them up over his hips.

"Any of you touch that girl you had there in the cabin?" Elijah demanded.

They shook their heads.

"Say it. Don't be shy. I'm leopard too. You lie to me, I'll know it," Elijah snapped, fury riding him hard. He couldn't imagine how Pete was going to feel knowing his niece was tortured and raped while he was on the property. He knew if someone took Siena from him and held her captive, he'd be on a killing spree to end all sprees, taking down everyone connected to whoever took her.

Each of the five men denied their involvement aloud. Elijah heard the ring of truth in their voices.

"Any of you go with Cordeau or Gaton, letting your leopards hunt humans in the swamp, prostitutes or enemies?" he demanded next.

Again there was a shake of heads before each one declared that no, they hadn't participated.

"Joaquin's headed your way and he's got himself a live one," Evan announced.

"There's going to be another change of leadership," Elijah said. "Gaton's been challenged. The crew he brought in is dead. You're going to do cleanup, burn the leopards and get rid of the bodies. Take them out to sea. Scatter the leopard ashes. Do you understand? There are going to be some changes around here."

"Gaton's not an easy leopard to defeat," one said. "If he was, we would have gotten out a long time ago."

"Joshua, you hear that?" Elijah asked.

The five men shifted their attention to the silent Joshua. Joshua nodded. "I heard."

"Scary son of a bitch. Gaton must come from one of the families from Borneo."

"Nope. Right here in the swamp. His grandfather and mine made moonshine together just like every other family in the bayous. Difference was, both were insane. They liked hurting people and they surrounded themselves with others just like them," Joshua said. "Sadistic sons of bitches."

"Who are you?" one of the shifters asked.

"Joshua Tregre," Joshua replied. His gaze moved to Gaton as Joaquin herded him through the cypress grove and the branches with the long strands of Spanish moss.

Gaton looked worse for wear, which didn't surprise Elijah in the least. Joaquin got the job done and he wasn't delicate about doing it. Gaton was streaked with blood, his clothes gone, but he'd shifted back to human when Joaquin had raked the crap out of him and then shifted, pulling the weapon from the pack around his neck.

Gaton's fierce gaze swept over his men and then rested on Elijah. "Should have known you were behind this."

"Shouldn't have come after me," Elijah said. "Might have left you alone. Now you've got yourself a challenge to leadership of the lair and everything that goes with it."

A derisive sound issued from Gaton's throat. "You think you can take me?"

"Not me who wants this mess. That would be Joshua. He's feeling left out of the killing today, so you're it for him."

The moment Robert Gaton was told he wouldn't be fighting Elijah, his eyes lit up. The shifters formed a loose circle around the two men. Joshua didn't take his eyes from Gaton. Gaton all but pounded his chest, certain of victory. His smirk taunted the challenger. "You think I haven't already defeated every soldier here?" Gaton snapped. "Elijah Lospostos endorsing you doesn't mean a damn thing. Not one thing. He can't take this territory without the leopards, and they're *mine*. My crew. They can kill any soldier coming up against them. Lospostos is too chicken to face me himself so he puts a pansy ass in his place."

Joshua didn't reply. With one hand he whipped his shirt over his head and flung it aside, eyes on Gaton. Cool. Calm. So Joshua. Elijah kept his eyes glued to Gaton's five leopards. None of them made a move to aid their boss, as was the way of the leopard. Anyone could challenge for leadership if they had the balls. The telling factor was their silence. None of them were verbally backing Gaton. Elijah had the feeling they *wanted* him to go down. If he was as brutal as Cordeau had been, it was easy enough to see why.

Gaton didn't wait for Joshua to strip all the way. He shifted, his leopard leaping at Joshua. Joshua's clothes were gone and he was already shifting, leaping, meeting Gaton in midair. Fast. Drake had drilled it into them—that practice of stripping, shifting and moving all at once—and it paid off.

The two leopards came together with a terrible roar, twisting and ripping at each other before they even hit the ground. No one in the circle moved or spoke. The swamp once again went silent as the two male leopards fought not just for supremacy, but for life. One wouldn't walk away from the battle and both leopards knew it.

The fight was vicious and ferocious. It became clear, quite early on, that Joshua's leopard was faster and much more skilled and experienced than Gaton's. The knowledge wasn't lost on the five shifters watching their boss get torn to shreds. They exchanged long looks. Each of them had challenged Gaton and none of the five had defeated his leopard in battle, leaving him to rule the lair.

Joshua's leopard was patient. Cunning. So fast he was a blur when he sprang in, ripped Gaton to the bone and sprang away. Usually the loose skin and roped muscles prevented the kinds of wounds Joshua's male inflicted, deep, punishing lacerations that left the other leopard panting and desperate to escape. There was no way to get away from Joshua's leopard, and in the end, the big male closed in for the kill.

There was a long silence while everyone watched the life go out of Gaton's leopard. Elijah studied the faces. "Does anyone want to challenge for leadership of the lair?" he asked quietly. "Joshua will spare your life even if you challenge him."

The five men all took a step back simultaneously as if by standing where they were, that might mean Joshua's leopard would come for them.

"Then you need to swear your allegiance to him or leave now. That woman will be returned to her uncle and cared for. Money from this lair will be given to the family for her counseling and medical care," Elijah said. "That means if he wants it to come out of your salaries, it does. You knew what was going on and you didn't do a thing about it."

"Gaton would have killed us," one said.

"Then you should have gone to Drake. You know his reputation. You know he would have done something. Leopards aren't allowed to act this way. We have our own rules and we follow them, even in this business."

Joshua shifted, caught the jeans tossed to him and tugged them on. "A lot of things will be changing around here. Starting with our neighbors. No more shakedowns. No more ruling them with fear. We keep our lair and our neighborhood clean. You want to stay in, all to the good. If not, get the hell out now, but you won't be coming back."

The men looked at one another and then nodded. Each of them, one by one, in front of witnesses, swore their allegiance to Joshua.

"I want all the bodies burned and the ashes taken out to sea. Even the humans. I don't want any evidence of this battle.

So when the bodies are taken care of, and there are a few in the house, get out your tools and repair the damages to the house. I'll bring in some men to help us get set up. When we're ready, we'll do some recruiting, both human and leopard. I'll need your input because all of you know the men around here. We don't want killers. We want soldiers who are loyal and who will get the job done."

The five nodded and immediately went to drag the bodies of the four fallen leopards closer together.

Elijah and his crew stalked up to the house. Evan had set the charges to do the least amount of damage to the building and the most to anyone trying to enter. There were bodies strewn on the ground, but little damage to the actual house.

The men gathered in the front room. Elijah was anxious to end this thing and get back to Siena. Every fight jacked him up. He always wanted sex after a battle, and the adrenaline coursed through him. Still, they had to get everything in order. That meant bringing Alonzo in the rest of the way and setting Joshua up.

"You go to Pete, Joshua, tell him how sorry you are about his niece. You offer to pay for her care, for the counselors she's going to need. Tell him you hate that shit, and none of your boys will ever do anything like that. Then you tell him he, his business and his family are under your protection. No, you don't want money. He's in your neighborhood. No one fucks with your neighbors or your friends. You spend some time building relationships with the businesses. Use them. Feed them money. Get your crew under control and have them always treat the neighbors with respect."

Joshua nodded. Elijah's gaze cut to Alonzo. "You listening to this? Because you're up next. You're going to take over the Arnotto territory. I'm standing for you in the council. Siena is naming you as her business manager."

Alonzo shook his head. "Not my gig, brother. I told you. I'm not a king."

"You will be when we finish with you," Elijah said. "Look

around you. This is our lair. We're *familia*. The people in this room are the people you can trust. A few more. Jake, his crew. The rest of Drake's crew. Tomas. We stick together and we've got this. You're needed, Alonzo."

"I told you, I'm Siena's soldier," Alonzo reiterated stubbornly.

Elijah nodded. "I get that. She gets that. This is what her soldier needs to do to keep her safe. You're that man for her, Alonzo. She needs to name a business manager. She'll take over running the winery. I'll give you lessons in running everything else. We'll all help you."

Alonzo shook his head. "My cat needs to fight sometimes, Elijah. Don't like to admit it, but so do I. I don't want to end up like those men we destroyed, their animals ruling them. I'm a soldier."

"You think I'm not like you? Or Joshua? Or Joaquin? Even Drake? I can give you more, Alonzo, but you need to know the further in you go, the deeper you're in and you can't ever walk away."

"I can't walk away, Elijah. I'm trapped. Not because I'm afraid you'll kill me, but because I don't feel anything anymore. Not when I kill. If I choose to be a decent man, I have to decide on some morality, and Siena Arnotto is my morality. She's a good person. She deserves a life. I'm going to do whatever I can to keep her that way."

"Then you're in. I'll explain in the plane on the way home. Joshua, call Pete now. Tell him his niece is alive but needs medical care immediately, that you'll meet him outside the gates. Don't let him onto the property until everything is fixed and bodies have disappeared. I'm leaving Joaquin and Evan with you. Eli needs to get home to Catarina, but the others will stay a few days until we can bring in a crew from Borneo."

Joshua nodded, and Elijah glanced at his watch. If they left now, they could get back in time for dinner. He'd have his woman before that. And then again after. His cock was already hard, hungry, needy. Thinking about Siena and her sweet, talented mouth didn't help him at all. When he tried to stop thinking about her mouth, his cock jerked hard, urgently, reminding him how it felt to be inside her, that tight clasp of scorching-hot silk, fisting him.

He groaned softly and concentrated on walking out of there without making a fool of himself.

19

"I really, really hate bed rest," Emma admitted. "Jake hovers. He's always watching over me, but now it's a million times worse. I can't move my little finger without him glaring at me. And it's really just a precaution."

Catarina put her bare feet up on the leather ottoman and leaned back in the plush golden brown leather chair. "Jake is *not* as bad as Eli. I think, if he could get away with it, Eli would tie me to him."

Emma laughed. "Could he get away with it, Cat?" she teased.

Catarina joined in the laughter and winked at Siena. "Probably. Okay. Yeah. Absolutely he could." Eli could, and she meant it.

"How do you do it? Handle it? The bossy?" Siena asked.

Emma fluffed her pillow and lay her head back down. "The rest of it is worth it. The things they do for us every single day make the bossy worthwhile. I wouldn't trade Jake for anything. He's so thoughtful. I don't ask for anything. I don't have to. He just provides me with it. Sometimes he's so off-the-charts sweet I don't know how to handle it. Jake makes me feel beautiful and loved. He makes me know I'm important to him. The most important person in his life. He gives me that every single day."

"My relationship with Eli is much newer," Catarina said. She took a slow sip of iced tea and then raised the glass to her forehead. "We didn't start out very well either. I was on the run from Rafe Cordeau. I was raised in his home, and he was waiting for my leopard to emerge. I had no idea I was leopard, but I knew whatever he wanted from me, I didn't want to give him. So I ran."

Siena didn't know a lot about Cordeau, but she'd heard some of the rumors, and none of them had been good. She was beginning to think leopards had a penchant for living outside the law. And some of them were savage. Maybe most of them.

"Eli was undercover, and he . . ." Catarina took a breath. Clearly it still hurt. "He got close to me. Really close. I was falling in love with him even though I knew I shouldn't. He was the first person I let in, and when I found out he was DEA I was devastated."

Siena couldn't imagine what that must have felt like. Catarina looked vulnerable and fragile all of a sudden. "The first time I ever had sex with Elijah, and it was my very first time *at all*, he threw me naked out his front door and said horrid things to me. Really, really humiliating and horrid things. I can't think about it without it hurting."

She blurted the truth out because she couldn't stand the look on Catarina's face. The naked pain there. She had to give something of herself to these two women who had opened up their friendship to include her. She mostly sat back while they talked. She enjoyed their company and wanted to be a part of their circle, but she didn't know how. She clapped her hand over her mouth, stricken that she'd told them something so awful. She didn't want them to think badly of Elijah.

Catarina's eyes widened. "Naked? Threw you out?"

Siena nodded. "He thought I'd come there to distract him with sex so a hit man could sneak in and kill him."

Emma burst out laughing. "You have got to be kidding me. Oh. My. God. That's priceless. He must rock in bed or you wouldn't have given him a second chance."

"Well. He does sort of rock in bed," Siena admitted. Elijah had said it was safe to talk to Catarina and Emma, that Eli and Jake worked with Drake Donovan. Still, she knew she had to be careful. She probably shouldn't have mentioned the hit man but then she hadn't planned to blurt all that out just to make Catarina feel better.

"Eli helped Elijah with that," Catarina said, making her feel better without even realizing it. "He didn't mention you to Eli."

"I guess if I'd kept my mouth shut no one else would know the most embarrassing moment of my life," Siena said.

"Jake provided a few embarrassing moments for me," Emma said. "It's that insane male leopard in them. Things get hot and passionate and they get all crazy on their women. The only thing you can do is learn to handle the fire. You'll come to love it, Siena. Elijah's so gone on you. Anyone can see that. I'd never seen him smile until you came into his life."

"How did Eli get you to give him another chance?" Siena asked.

"Sex. Hot, hot sex," Catarina admitted, a blush stealing up her neck and creeping slowly into her face. "That, and the way he loves me. He gives me the world. Just like Jake does with Emma, he shows me how important I am to him. He's very excited about the baby. He's already talking to it. Every night he puts his mouth on my belly and starts in. I *love* when he does that."

Siena splayed her fingers over her soft, growing belly. She was definitely far bigger than Catarina, but now, knowing she was carrying twins, she didn't feel so bad. The three of them were in different stages of pregnancy. She couldn't help but think how alike their lives were in many ways. The differences were just as great. Emma's husband, Jake, was a billionaire. He owned legitimate businesses and had no reason to dabble in crime. Catarina's husband, Eli, had been in law enforcement. He worked with Jake, doing what, Siena wasn't certain, but he also worked with Drake. And then there was Elijah. She didn't fully understand what Elijah was doing. What he was. He worked with Drake. Was surrounded by decent men, but she knew his life had never been decent.

"Siena." Emma's voice was gentle. So gentle, Siena winced. She knew she didn't have a poker face. She'd never been able to hide her feelings. "What is it?"

She shook her head. "Nothing. I just think it's rather wonderful to be sitting here with two other women discussing our very alpha men."

"Elijah's a good man," Emma said. "I know he's head of the Lospostos family. Everyone knows that. But he's a good man. I don't know how, Jake doesn't tell me anything about any of the men on Drake's security team, but they're all good men or they wouldn't do the things they do. They risk their lives to bring back kidnap victims from very remote areas. They do all sorts of things and all of it is good."

Siena nodded, but she didn't reply. What could she say? She knew Elijah was a good man, but he was hunting. Right at that moment he was hunting. And he wasn't hunting an animal, he was hunting a man. Eli and Drake were with him. She rubbed her tummy, wishing she'd insisted on Elijah talking to her, telling her straight up what was going on.

She'd allowed him to avoid the discussion because she was so in love with him. She'd always been in love with him. She felt as if she loved him from the day she sat across her grandfather's table and looked at his handsome face. She didn't want to lose that. As much as she didn't want to live—or have her children live—under a cloud of suspicion, she didn't want to lose Elijah. She knew she didn't have all the facts about his life. He was the head of a crime family—but then again, maybe he wasn't. Something else was going on. She just had to get him to tell her, or figure it out for herself. The sad truth was, she knew she didn't have the strength to leave him if he was what all the rumors said he was.

"He is a good man," she agreed. "And he's good to me. He'll be a good father. He hasn't gotten to the stage where he talks to them yet, but he rubs my belly every night and goes to sleep with his hand over them."

"Them?" Catarina hitched forward in her chair. "You're having twins?"

"Unconfirmed," Siena said. "My leopard said more than one, but I haven't gone to Doc yet to have him corroborate."

Emma cleared her throat. "Um, honey? That's how she put it to you? More than one? She didn't indicate two or give you that image?"

Siena eyed her warily. "What does that mean?"

"Just that Doc should check you, Siena. Carrying more than one baby can be hard on you," Emma said. "Jake would have had a fit if I'd had more than one baby inside me. As it is . . ." She glanced at her watch. "He's due to check on me any minute. It's been fifteen minutes and he pretty much is like clockwork."

Catarina and Siena giggled like a couple of schoolgirls. Right on cue, Jake slid the door open. All three women burst into full-blown laughter.

Jake scowled at them. "What's so funny in here? Emma's supposed to be taking it easy." He pinned his wife with a steely gaze. "I don't think that's actually resting, Emma, you're sitting up. Doc says to lie down."

"Doc is overprotective because he's afraid you'll kill him if he doesn't do everything you say. *You* were the one who said I had to lie down. I don't like that woman in my kitchen and I don't like someone else taking care of our children. I'm not in danger of losing the baby."

Jake was undeterred. He stepped close to the lounge where Emma was tucked with a soft thin blanket around her. He loomed over the chaise, his expression like thunder. Glaring. Eyes all cat. Definitely the dominant. Emma didn't even blink. She glared right back.

"The danger isn't losing the baby, woman. The danger is losing *you*. It. Isn't. Happening. So keep your sweet ass in that lounge until I come to carry you to our bed. And stop giving me grief."

"Next time, I'm not listening to either one of you," Emma declared.

His eyebrow shot up. "If you think I'm going to go through another nine months of hell, Emma, you can damn well forget that," he snapped. His hands framed her face, his gaze roaming over her features. "You're going to give me this."

Her eyes softened. "I'm lying down, honey. But you have to stop making me crazy."

His grin was slow. Heart-stopping. "Why? You've been making me crazy since I first laid eyes on you." He brushed a kiss across her mouth. "Cat, thanks for bringing dinner. It smells delicious."

Siena wished she knew how to cook. She would have brought them a dinner. "That reminds me. I'm trying out a recipe I found for Elijah tonight. I'd better get going. I don't know the first thing about cooking so I'm sure it will take me some time." She stood up. "It was really nice to be able to visit you both. I enjoyed it." Well, except the part where she didn't know what Emma meant about her leopard not being clear about twins. Was she carrying twins or not? Now she'd have to go to Doc and find out.

"Call me if you need help. I can maybe talk you through the recipe," Catarina offered. "And if you want lessons, I'm a fairly good cook. And Emma's a really good one."

"Catarina's being humble," Emma said. "She's awesome."

"I'll take you both up on it," Siena said. "I want to learn. Elijah promised he'd help me too." She said her good-byes, finding herself happy. Actually happy. She'd never had that before, just going to another woman's home and sitting down and talking. Laughing. Discussing men and babies. Being normal. She'd lived in her world of boarding schools, isolated from everyone. Elijah had given her that.

Her bodyguards surrounded her on the way to their car and again when they walked her up to the front door. Trey and Tomas went inside with her, disarming the alarm and doing a walk-through before Tomas led her to the kitchen.

"Is that always going to be necessary?" she asked.

Tomas looked startled, as if he hadn't expected her to actually speak to him. "What?" He was soft-spoken, but had the same intimidating build most of the leopards had, with the roped, defined muscles. His tee was stretched tight across his chest, and his shaggy hair looked as if it needed cutting weeks ago.

Siena shook her head. "Nothing. We're good. Thanks for walking me in."

He lifted his chin and left her there in the kitchen. A foreign, alien place. That didn't matter. She was actually excited. She wanted to find ways to take care of her man. To do more than have sex with him—not that she didn't love having sex with him—that was utterly glorious—but she wanted Elijah to feel loved in every single aspect of his life. She wanted him happy and, more than anything, to know she thought he was the most beautiful, wonderful man in the world.

She'd always wanted to learn to cook. She'd contemplated taking classes, but she'd been so busy getting first a business degree and then studying oenology and viticulture, learning everything there was to know about grapes and wine making, that she kept putting off the cooking classes. Washing her hands, she tied a makeshift apron around her clothes, using a towel.

The first recipe she'd decided to try was starred. The page was worn and smudged so she knew it was one of Elijah's favorites. The recipe was titled *Camarones a la Diabla: shrimp and spicy sauce*. She liked shrimp, and spice was good.

The recipe itself didn't look that difficult. Once she got it going she was going to make avocado dip to go with the meal. She had tortilla chips from the store. She would learn to make them another day.

The recipe seemed fairly straightforward as she studied it. She was to put all the ingredients in a pot along with a cup of water and cook it for twenty minutes. Once it came to a boil, she would put it in the blender and blend it. Not difficult. She could do that. The raw and peeled shrimp was then sautéed in olive oil in a frying pan with garlic salt and pepper. The salsa was added and the shrimp was cooked in that for twenty to twenty-five minutes on low heat. Elated, she laid out all the ingredients. She could do this. It was totally easy.

She cut up the two tomatoes and the small bunch of cilantro, added three pinches of oregano, two cloves of garlic and then studied the five small *chili de arbol* and the five serrano chilies. She wasn't certain how she was supposed to chop them up. The recipe didn't give specific instructions, only that they needed to be in the salsa that went over the shrimp. Taking a deep breath, she began, determined that Elijah would come home to one of his favorite meals.

ELIJAH frowned at Trey. "What do you mean, you haven't seen or heard from her? You didn't check on her?" The moment he'd come home, he expected her to be there. Right *fucking* there. Waiting for him. Glad to see him. Greeting him. Siena was nowhere around and that pissed him off. He'd been thinking about her the entire plane ride home.

"She went into the kitchen with Tomas and that was the last I saw of her," Trey defended. "No one's been in the house. My guess, she's still in there, waiting for you."

"When I leave her alone here, I want her checked on every twenty minutes or so," Elijah snapped. He'd cleaned up on the plane, wanting to come to her fresh, without the smell of gunpowder, feral cat or blood. Drake had sewn up the two places he'd needed stitches. He was good to go. *And she wasn't there.* Greeting him. Kissing him with that sweet mouth of hers. He fucking *needed* her. Right. That. Minute.

The moment he'd entered the house he had a bad feeling. He had no idea why, only that it was too quiet. He just didn't like the way it felt. He didn't like the fact that Siena wasn't right there. Or that anyone hadn't had eyes on her since she'd come home from Jake and Emma's. He didn't have time to waste snapping at security, he'd call a meeting later and lay down the law.

Turning on his heel, he prowled down the hall and took the shortcut through the atrium to the kitchen. The door to the kitchen was closed and he jerked it open. Instantly he smelled the potent aroma of *Camarones a la Diabla*. "What the fuck?" he snapped. His leopard was riding him hard. He still had the battle pumping through his bloodstream, the aggression. The need to conquer. The need to dominate. More, his cock was raging. *Raging* at him. None of that would disappear until he was buried inside his woman.

Siena didn't turn away from the counter where she was running the blender. And coughing. Choking. She obviously hadn't heard him come in over the blender, nor did she hear his angry question.

She was clearly affected by the potency of the peppers. Sometimes, when his grandmother had made the salsa to go over the shrimp, they'd had to clear out the kitchen and even a part of the house because it felt as if their throats were closing.

"Fucking chilies. What are you doing?" he demanded, stalking across the room toward her—not an easy thing to do when he was as hard as a rock. She half turned, and his heart nearly stopped. Even his raging cock settled. Tears streamed down her face. *Dios. Dios.* "What were you thinking? You didn't handle those chilies, did you?"

She turned all the way toward him, choking on the fumes. Tears spilled down her face, but she looked determined, still blending the salsa in the blender in spite of the fact that the fumes were closing off her airway.

He crossed to her, swept her up in his arms and turned off the blender. "*Dios*, Siena, what the hell are you doing?" Fury curled in his belly. Hard, tight knots that told him he hadn't taken care of her. He hadn't cautioned her not to use any of the starred recipes. The hotter-than-Hades recipes that a novice couldn't handle.

She buried her face against his shoulder, but she made no attempt to hang on. In fact she kept her open palms away from him. He could see they were bright red. He erupted into Spanish, cursing angrily. "*Fucking* hell." It was worse than he thought. "*Dios, mi amorcito*, you burned your hands."

Elijah stalked to the outside patio, carrying her away from the house and the fumes to set her down in the nearest chair. He took hold of her wrists, his hands gentle when the leopard was leaping close to the surface, raking and tearing at him for allowing her to be injured in any way. He turned her palms to face him. They weren't just bright red, they were actually swollen and inflamed. She'd still been trying to cook for him—with her hands like that.

Deep inside his heart stuttered. What the hell did a man do with a woman who loved him like that? Who would try to cook for him in spite of burns to her hands? In spite of her throat closing from the fumes? What did a man do with a woman who lapped at his cock to clean him after mind-blowing sex? A woman who *enjoyed* blowing him? Who swallowed for him? Who did what she could to *show* him she loved him, not just say the words?

His eyes burned, from the chilies he was certain, although that had never happened to him before. Along with burning eyes his throat felt raw. He knew anyone looking at him would see the stark fear on his face. Because Siena Arnotto could tear him apart easily. Rip him to shreds. She could do what no member of his family, no enemy, no one who had tried to hurt him had done. She could annihilate him. Destroy him.

"Damn it, Siena," he snapped. "Don't you fucking move. And don't touch your face. Keep your hands away from your body."

He rushed back into the kitchen, turned off the blender, yanked open the refrigerator, dumped a sizable amount of milk and ice into a large bowl and hurried back to her. He slammed the bowl onto the table hard enough that the milk splashed over the edges. Gripping her wrists, he yanked her hands over the bowl.

"Put your hands in that," he ordered. "You didn't run your hands under cold water, did you?"

She nodded, biting hard on her lip in an effort to control the tears streaming down her face.

He cursed more, tipping her face up toward him, inspecting her for any places she might have touched with her hands. "Is your face burning?"

She shook her head. "Just my hands. I was careful, once I realized they were burning, not to touch my skin anywhere else."

Dios, it could have been *so* much worse. The need for physical action was so great that he paced away, slammed his fist into the side of the house hard, three times.

She jumped, her hands coming out of the milk.

Instantly he was back at her side, forcing her palms into the ice-cold milk. "*Fucking* keep them there."

"Stop saying the f-word at me," she protested.

He ignored that. She had to stop crying. She *had* to. "Baby, what the hell were you thinking? Peppers contain capsicum. That's used in pepper spray. You can't get that shit on your skin, especially someone as sensitive as you. And sometimes when you blend those chilies the fumes can make you feel like you're choking. Seriously, Siena, what the hell?"

His hands actually itched to shake her. "I left for a few hours, baby. That's it. I come home to this. You could have really hurt yourself." He hit the tabletop with his fist, making the milk splash around her wrists. "*Fuck*. Don't you ever do something so stupid again."

"Elijah." She said his name. Low.

His gaze jumped to her face. He didn't want to look at her. He didn't want to see her tears, that just tore him up inside and the part of him that felt helpless because *he fucking wasn't there when she needed him* just pissed him off.

"Go away."

He scowled at her. "What did you just say to me?"

"I said, *go away*." She repeated it.

No remorse. Her chin wasn't even up defiantly. She just looked at him with soft green eyes. Eyes drowning in tears. Made his damn belly turn into hard knots.

"You did not just say that to me," he said. His male pushed closer to the surface. Raking at him. Clawing at his belly. Furious. Almost as furious as Elijah was at himself. They hadn't protected her. She was in pain, and it was such a simple thing to have avoided.

"I said it. I meant it. Now, go away."

"Siena," he warned. "You burned the crap out of your hands. You had no business cutting up those chilies without knowing how to properly handle them. What were you thinking?"

She lifted her chin. He'd been waiting for that little gesture of defiance. He liked it. It was perverse of him, but he did. She had attitude, and she could stand up to his foul temper. Still, everything dominant rose up to challenge her. To force compliance. To make her realize she was his, and he wasn't putting up with her hurting herself.

"I was thinking I would surprise you by fixing something that was a favorite dish of yours. A criminal offense, no doubt. Then I burned my hands and I was thinking my man was going to come home and comfort me—maybe tell me what to do to stop the burning and how to prevent it from happening again. But instead, my *idiot* man is a total *bastardo*."

Everything in him settled. The tight knots in his belly loosened just a little. He took a deep breath and studied her face. Most women looked like hell when they cried. Red, blotchy faces. Not Siena. No, she had to look even more beautiful. Her eyes looked greener than ever, brilliant, like gleaming polished emeralds. Tears sparkled on her lashes like tiny diamonds. Yeah. That was his Siena.

"My baby can say *bastard* but not *fuck*. Who knew?"

"Don't you dare laugh at me," she snapped. "I mean it, Elijah, I'll dump this bowl of milk over your head, although it is helping to take the burn away."

"Don't dump the milk over my head, *mi vida*. You can have *words* with me, though. I won't mind that. Although I don't have a clue what that might be since you can't say *fuck* or any other foul words beside *bastardo*."

"Apparently," she said in a very haughty tone, "your memory is going. I believe when I was very angry with you, I used extremely foul language and said the f-word several times, along with a few other choice words I was quoting from your *extraordinary* vocabulary."

"The f-word?" he repeated. "Extremely foul language?"

She glared at him. Gave a little sniff. The coughing and choking had stopped now that he had her out in the cool night air and away from the blender. The tears were drying up as well, because he'd gotten her angry.

"Go away, Elijah."

"It's not going to happen. I'll give you the world, baby, but not that. Besides, I have to cover your hands in aloe vera."

"I don't want your help. You're a total jerk. I don't know what I ever saw in you."

"That's not nice, Siena. And you're always sweet."

"I was nice, now I'm not because you're rubbing off on me."

He leaned down to kiss her. She turned her head away. Something in him tightened. Coiled. Something not nice. Not sweet. Something scary and dangerous and feral. "Baby, fucking kiss me." All over again, his cock hardened. He had the urge to put his fist in her hair and yank her head down right over it.

"I don't like you. I'm not going to kiss you when I don't like you. You were mean when I needed you to be sweet and understanding."

"You hurt yourself," he accused. His fingers delved deep into her hair, but he resisted the need to put her mouth on him. "You had no business cutting up those chilies, Siena. None."

"You knew I was going to cook tonight."

"Sure, but not that dish. Something easy. Something that didn't burn the shit out of your hands."

"How was I supposed to know which would burn and which wouldn't?"

"*Chilies.*" He snapped the word knowing this wasn't her fault. It was his. "I'm going to cut some fresh aloe vera stalks, but before I do, you are going to kiss me."

"I am *not.*" She glared at him.

He smiled. A predator's smile. She blinked rapidly and tried to turn her face away. One hand kept her jaw in place. "Don't take your hands out of that milk," he warned, his lips against hers. She tried to turn her head again but he didn't allow it. Her lips remained stubbornly closed.

He smiled against her mouth, enjoying her defiance, enjoying the effect it had on his body. He was harder than ever. Throbbing. Her defiance wasn't real. Siena didn't have it in her to hold a grudge. He'd learned that about her immediately. He'd hurt her feelings, but it wouldn't take much for her to forgive him. He coaxed her gently, kissing her with tenderness, his teeth tugging at her lower lip. When she still refused, he bit down harder, nipping her until she gasped. His tongue slid in.

She tasted sweet. She tasted hot. Sexy. His. And she kissed him back. No hesitation. Drowning in him. Giving him everything. Giving him—*her.* His woman didn't hold grudges and she could kiss like fucking sin. He felt her kiss go straight to his heart. Straight to his soul. Straight to his aching cock.

He lifted his head slowly, trailed kisses over her cheeks and up to her eyes, brushing the wet lashes. "Can't take it when you're hurt, baby. Breaks something inside of me, but this is my fault. I should have taken the time to go over those recipes with you. If you *ever* get hurt when I'm not close by, promise me you'll call one of the boys to help you."

She shook her head without actually thinking about it. Clearly she didn't want to call one of the men to help her. She didn't know it, but that was huge for him. He didn't like the idea of any of the men holding her hand or wiping her tears. Still. She should have had treatment immediately.

"Why didn't you call them?"

She shrugged. "It didn't occur to me. I was waiting for you. If I'm being honest, I'm not that comfortable with any other man but you."

He closed his eyes briefly. She definitely was killing him. He liked that more than a fuck of a lot. *Way* too much.

"And I wanted to finish the dinner. I might have burned my hands, but I think I did it right."

She looked up at him with her tear-drenched eyes. Her long, feathery lashes. Her bone structure. His heart started hammering in his chest.

"Do you think you could try to salvage the dinner? Maybe finish it? I want to see if I did the salsa right for you. It's important to me, Elijah."

Something inside him broke. Shattered. Maybe it was his heart, because his chest actually hurt. Her eyes moved over his face. Her eyes. Green. Piercing. Exotic. So beautiful. But she could see inside him to the small, vulnerable spot he kept hidden. It wasn't so hidden now. She'd exposed it to the world—at least anyone watching him would see it.

"You can kiss me again," she said softly.

"I can kiss you?" he echoed, not really following her.

She nodded solemnly. "Right there is the reason I can overlook all your f-bombs and ridiculous temper. That look you have on your face, right now. It's for me. It's mine. I love you like that, Elijah, so much it's terrifying."

He stared down at her upturned face. That face. He wanted to wake up to that face the rest of his life and still, it wouldn't be long enough. He was glad he was leopard, a shifter, living more than one life so he could find her again and again.

"Kiss me, honey," she ordered softly.

He crouched low, wedging himself between her legs. It was a place he liked to be. She lifted her face to his. His heart nearly stopped when, whisper-fine, her lips trailed fire from his jaw to the corner of his mouth. Her teeth tugged on his lower lip, bit down, pulled and then her tongue came out to soothe, just as he'd done to her.

He curled his fingers around the nape of her neck, his thumb sliding along her high cheekbone, making that sweep of her soft skin. His mouth found hers. Gentle. Rubbing his lips along hers. Sliding his tongue just to taste her. Taste the sweetness that always undid him. There was heat. Silk. The velvet rasp of her tongue along his. Need was there instantly. Hunger. But it was love he tasted, and it tasted fucking good.

Elijah deepened the kiss, feeding the burn between them. Her hands slid up his chest, leaving a trail of milk. She gasped. Whimpered. He lifted his head alertly and caught her wrists.

"Baby," he whispered softly. He brought her hands up to his mouth. "Let me get the aloe vera. We grow it fresh in the atrium. I'll coat your palms with it and this is going to feel a whole lot better."

She nodded. "Thanks, Elijah. I knew you'd know what to do. But really, finish the dinner."

"I'll make you something you can eat as well," he said, and stood up reluctantly. "Stay out here where the fumes won't get to you. I'll be right back."

He hurried back into the kitchen, saw that she'd blended the salsa properly and also had gotten the shrimp ready, peeling them. He caught up a frying pan, poured in a little olive oil and sautéed the twenty raw and peeled shrimp quickly with a little garlic salt and ground pepper. He added the salsa, and then turned the heat down to low to allow it to cook for the required twenty to twenty-five minutes.

Siena had already made the avocado dip and she'd used jalapeños. It was going to be way too hot for her to eat. He'd have to whip up something else for her. That wouldn't be hard. He strode into the atrium, cut some aloe vera stalks and made his way back to her. Truthfully, the aroma in the kitchen was making him hungry.

"Forgot to tell you, baby," he said, as he gently smeared the fresh aloe vera over her palms. "A notary is coming with the license for us to sign."

She went still. Her gaze jumped to his face. "License? What kind of license?"

"Told you, *mi vida*, we have to get the license before we can get married. Seventy-two hours or something stupid like that. So we need to get this done. Jake's lawyer knew someone who agreed to come out to the house."

"A marriage license?" she echoed.

"Baby, keep up," he said, a little impatiently. "We discussed this."

Her gaze remained steady on his. "You told me we were getting married and you weren't nice about it. I didn't think you meant it."

"You love me?"

She nodded.

"You carrying my babies in your belly?"

She nodded again.

"I love you too. So we're getting married before we have kids. I want my ring on your finger and your name to be the same as mine. Means we have to fill out bullshit papers, then we do it."

She stared up into his eyes for so long he was fairly certain she was going to have a few *words* with him. The idea made him hard all over again. Or maybe he'd remained hard even while he cooked. His reaction could have been from just looking at her. That could do it as well. That face. Those eyes. Her hair. Mostly that expression. The one that told him she loved him even when he was bossing her around.

"Honey, you came home to me. You came home you."

His heart clenched. "Yeah, baby. I did that."

"It was bad."

He didn't want her to see that. "Yeah, it was bad," he acknowledged, his tone warning her to leave it right there.

She nodded. "Thank you for coming home. I wouldn't do very well without you."

The knots in his belly unraveled just a little more. "Need to go whip up food for my woman, and I don't want the shrimp to overcook. It looked perfect." He gave her that because it had. He loved that she cared enough to cook for him. He didn't want her to ever do it again, but still, his woman wanted to do that for him. "The kitchen should be aired out enough for you to come back inside."

A slow smiled curved her mouth. Soft. Sexy. His. She stood up, and he wrapped his arm around her waist.

"You're not going to give me shit because the notary is coming tonight?"

"I don't give you the s-word, Elijah," she said primly. "I give you *words*. Do you want our children to talk like that?"

He pretended to think about it. *Dios*, but he loved his woman. Especially when she gave him that sassy voice. Standing up to him when few men dared.

"I like it when you give me words, *mi amorcito*. Makes me hard."

She rolled her eyes, just like he knew she would. He burst out laughing. Her green eyes jumped to his face, watching him. She liked watching him and he liked her doing it.

He pulled out a chair and she slipped into it while he made his way around the center island to pull out a pan.

"What's the difference between my leopard showing me

twins, or basically acknowledging two babies, and her indicating more than one?" she asked casually.

He was chopping vegetables and the knife stopped in midair. "Say again?"

Siena had been watching him intently but at his question she pulled back, looking a little alarmed. "Why are you saying it like that? In that tone? Emma and Catarina freaked me out already. Don't you start."

"Your female didn't specify twins or show you an image of two? She said more than one?" He felt his heart pounding. Hard. Without answering, he reached for his male. The lazy bastard was sleeping, ignoring the conversation. He'd done his work for the day, wasn't going to be able to be with his mate and was tired.

My mate is pregnant.

The cat acknowledged that with a lazy yawn.

How many?

His male had been around a long time. He knew what that meant. He immediately sent the impression of three.

Elijah drew in a deep breath. He felt Siena's eyes on him. Hell yeah, he'd gotten her pregnant. They'd been crazy wild on the floor together. But three? Triplets? Who had triplets? How hard was it to carry them? He needed to call Doc, like *now.*

He dumped the vegetables in the pan with a little bit of olive oil, chopped up a chicken breast and added that in as well, all the while avoiding her green eyes.

"I'm going to grab you some gloves while this is cooking."

"You didn't answer my question."

"I will in a couple of minutes, when we're sitting over dinner. Two minutes, baby, I promise I'll be quick." He was already on the move. "You can't eat without gloves."

He punched in Doc's private number as he hurried down the hall. "She's carrying triplets," he blurted out the moment the man answered. "Siena. My leopard told me she's carrying triplets."

"Don't panic."

He was *completely* panicked. "Listen to me, Doc. I mean every fucking word I'm saying to you. I want children with her, but not if she's in danger. If this is going to be too hard on her body, if there's a chance she won't survive, she's not doing this." He couldn't actually say the words to get rid of them. That would *kill* him, but he wouldn't survive losing Siena, not even if the children survived.

"Women carry triplets. She'll have to most likely go on bed rest at some point because we won't want them born too early. Stop panicking, go back and tell her. She's healthy. She's happy. She's got an overprotective bastard looking out for her. She's going to be fine. I'll want to do an ultrasound, just to confirm and get ahead of any potential problems. Is she having a difficult time with morning sickness?"

"It isn't just in the morning. She's sick a *lot*, any time of the day."

"That's not unusual with triplets. Bring her in tomorrow. We'll have a look."

Elijah snapped his phone off and shoved it in his pocket. Keeping Siena safe was a full-time job. He found some soft driving gloves that were going to be too big, but it was all he had.

She was up, mixing the stir-fry, holding the spoon between her thumb and index finger cautiously. She glanced at him over her shoulder. "You talk to Doc?"

"Yeah, I talked to Doc." *He* was the one who needed to sit down. What if they were all girls? Fuck him. He was dead in the water if she was carrying three girls.

"I'm having three, right? Please don't say four."

He nodded his head. There was just a tiny bit of panic in her voice. "Baby, we'll do fine." He took the frying pan from her before she dropped it. "Go sit down, *mi vida*. I've got this. And put the gloves on." He looked at her over his shoulder as she sat back in her chair at the table. "You scared, Siena?"

"Not as much as I thought I'd be. I've got you. I figure that means we can get through having triplets." She was silent while he put the food on the table and seated himself across from her. "You know I don't know anything about children, right? I've never even held a baby. Or changed one."

He put his hand over her wrist. "We'll do fine. We've got quite a few months, and there have to be experts that we can bring here to give us a few lessons. Doc will know someone and so will Jake. We've got this, baby. Emma's got two kids already and another on the way."

Her eyes lit up. With that look. The one that said she loved him and he could move mountains and raise three babies when they didn't have a clue what they were doing. He'd find a way because she believed he would.

20

ELIJAH lay in bed, one hand tucked behind his head, watching Siena as she emerged from the bathroom. Steam followed her. Perfumed steam. She always smelled good. Her hair was in a messy knot, spilling down her back even though the knot was high. He knew he was going to pull out that elastic the moment he could get his fingers in her hair.

"Appreciate the sexy camisole and panties, baby," he said, "but lose them. And do it slow for me. I like when you unwrap yourself before you give me you."

Her green eyes jumped to his face. Burned there. She never denied him. He could wake her up a dozen times in the middle of the night and she would turn to him, her body soft and warm and always, always welcoming.

"I'd do anything for you, Siena," he said softly.

"Would you give up being head of the Lospostos crime family for me if I asked you to do it?" she asked softly. Not moving. Not coming to him.

Everything in him went still. Tension knotted his belly so tight he thought maybe she could see the knots. "If I said no, will you still get into this bed with me?" he countered, keeping his voice soft. Neutral.

Her eyes moved over his face. She was an open book. The woman could never hide anything from him. Yeah. She'd get in his bed. She'd come to him and give herself to him and she'd do it completely.

"You're mine, Elijah," she said, still not moving. "You were born to be mine. I know it every single time I look at you."

She slowly undid the laces of her camisole so that her breasts spilled free. Already he could see the changes in her body. Her full breasts were even lusher. Her tucked-in waist was still there, but there was a definite baby pooch. A beautiful one. Soft and inviting like the rest of her. Still looking at his face, she hooked her thumbs in her panties and pulled them down until they fell free. She still wore the gloves and somehow, that was sexy, seeing her in soft skin and a pair of his driving gloves. He felt like he'd been aching for her for hours. And he had.

"Then come here, baby."

"You didn't answer me."

"I'm going to answer you, but I want you close." He patted his chest. "Very close. Right here, *mi vida*. I want your eyes on mine while I talk to you about this."

Because he wanted to see her reaction. The real one. The one in her heart and soul. He'd see that in her eyes. His belly was back to knots. She'd said she'd stay with him even if he didn't give her what she asked for. He watched her intently as she crossed the room and slid into the bed on the opposite side.

Instantly he turned, caught her to him and pulled her close, rolled until she was on top of him, sprawled across his chest. He roughly pulled the tie from her hair, allowing all that thick silk to cascade down. He loved the feel of it sweeping his skin.

"Honey," she whispered.

"Straddle me," he said softly, his hands at her hips, guiding her lower, until she was positioned over his hard, straining cock. "I need to be inside of you when I give this to you, baby."

She moistened her lips, but she lifted her hips and let him guide her over his cock—just like he knew she would because she always gave him what he asked for. *Always*. She slid down, watching his face as she took him. Like every single time he entered her, it felt like the first time. Tight. Scorching hot. Her muscles reluctantly gave way for his invasion.

He watched her face, and just like always, she looked as if he were her miracle. As if, when his cock pushed into those tight, hot folds, so slick with her welcome for him, she believed he was the greatest thing on earth. He didn't want to ever lose that look on her face. When she was seated on him and he was buried as deep as possible, he reached up to cup her breasts.

"You're the most beautiful woman I've ever seen," he admitted. "And you have the most beautiful heart. All this time, since we've been together, you thought you dragged me into your grandfather's shit, but the truth is, *mi amorcito*, I've brought you into a very dangerous world and I can't let you go. I told myself a million times it was the right thing to do and if I was any kind of a man, I'd get you away from me, but I can't do it. I need you. Just for survival. Just to breathe."

He watched her face the entire time he spoke. Her green eyes stayed glued to his. Just like he asked. Always like he asked. She killed him with the way she loved him. Her expression didn't change in the least. She didn't look apprehensive. She looked as if she believed totally in her man. Her body moved. Slowly. Oh, so slowly, lifting slightly, small circles, muscles clenching and clasping. She felt like paradise. She gave him that even when she knew he was taking her into hell with him.

"I want a clean life for you. For our children. Hell, baby, I want a clean life for me, although I have no idea how to live that way."

She leaned down and licked at his flat nipple. Sucked. Kissed her way up to his throat. "Honey, I love you. I didn't ask you to give up your life, I only asked you if you would."

"I wanted to do that, I even tried to do it. But this life, the one handed to me. It isn't easy to get out of no matter how hard you try. And then there's my leopard. Used to that shit. Hard to control. But still, I tried. Then when I realized it wasn't going to happen, not like I could live free and clean, before I met you, I made a decision. I didn't know it would ever be possible to find a woman like you, a woman who deserved so much better than I could give her, who would accept me as I am."

She pressed kisses to his jaw, slid her tongue up to his ear. "What decision?"

All the while her body rode his. Slow. Infinitely slow. Burning. Scorching hot. Gripping. Her sheath was so tight he felt like she was strangling his cock in the tightest fist possible. Milking him. The friction was exquisite. With the slow glide she was doing, his brain was beginning to fray around the edges. Still, that glide told him something important. She loved him. She belonged to him. She claimed all that was Elijah Lospostos, even his reputation.

"I made the decision, knowing I couldn't take all of them that route, to try to legitimize as much of my businesses as I could. I was doing that when I met Drake Donovan. Drake was running a crew of leopards in Borneo. They went after kidnapped victims and returned them. I went to Borneo to check on my sister, Rachel. I was at war with my uncle's soldiers to take over the family business and I was worried Rachel might be caught in the middle. There were rumors I put out a hit on her. I was really worried that there was a hit out on her and I wanted her protected."

Keeping her eyes on his, Siena arched her back, reaching behind her with her hands to run them over his thighs. The muscles there jumped in response. The angle allowed even greater friction. His breath caught in his throat. He especially loved the way her position allowed her breasts to jut out invitingly, swaying with every movement she made.

His fingers bit deep into her hips and then slid up her belly, over the soft resting place of his children. "Drake explained to me that there were more leopard families in organized crime than mine. Quite a few more. He came up with a good idea. At least I thought it was good, because I didn't have a family and was never going to have one."

His hands moved up her rib cage, the side of her breasts, and then he cupped the soft weight in his palms. "Stay like that baby," he whispered when she gasped as he tugged at her nipple. "Just like that." He loved that she was so sensitive and every roll of his fingers put that look on her face. The one that said she was close.

She slid down his shaft a little harder. A little faster. Trying to find it. He took his hands away from her breasts and caught her hips.

"Slow, baby. I like that slow burn."

"I need . . ." she panted.

"I'll give it to you," he assured. "But not yet. I like watching your face. So beautiful, Siena. So mine." His hands guided her pace back to slow.

The tip of her tongue swept out and moistened her lower lip. He was tempted to capture it, but instead, he rewarded her with his hands on her breasts again. Watching her face. Loving that look. So close. He wasn't going to let her take herself there. Not yet.

"Drake's idea was simple but dangerous, baby. I'm head of one of the larger territories. I already had the reputation and the soldiers. I had my finger in just about everything. If we legitimized some of it, but kept our hand in and our reputation, we'd know the violent players. The leopards. We aren't law enforcement, but we could take them down. Replace them with bosses of our choosing. No one can stop crime completely, but we can shut down a lot of it. Control the flow and how it goes. Keep civilians from getting hurt.

When violence occurs, we could essentially keep it to the crime families, not let it leak outside."

She stopped moving. Stared at him. Her exotic green eyes went emerald. Nearly glowed. Her cat was close.

"Elijah."

She breathed his name, and for the first time he couldn't tell how she was taking his news. His hands closed over her breasts, hanging on to her. Needing to feel her moving again. Needing the sweep of her hair against his skin.

"We just set up Joshua Tregre as the boss to take over Rafe Cordeau's territory. The council will accept him. He's one of Drake's main men, but his family has a violent past. He's believable, and his family is from the New Orleans area, although he was raised in Borneo. He'll be a huge asset to us and a valuable member of the team. Catarina has been feeding us information about Cordeau's business and his partners. We know where the money is and every trail to other leopard crime families. Jake is going at it from a different angle, following the businesses. His specialty is to attack them with hostile takeovers."

His hands slid down to her hips, urging her to move. Her face was utterly still. Her body was as well. She hadn't suspected that he was doing anything so dangerous. As if it wasn't dangerous enough to be the head of a crime family, but to deal in both sides of the fence, he was making himself a major target if anyone found out.

"Baby, you have to move." He lifted her, let her body slide down. The feeling was unbelievable and he thrust up to meet her.

She complied, more, he thought, because she was used to giving him whatever he wanted than because her body needed to move. She was stunned by his news. He didn't know if that was a bad thing or a good thing.

"I plan to set up Alonzo as head of the Arnotto family," Elijah went on. "He'll be another ally and one we can trust. I can help him learn the ropes. We'll try to legitimize what we can of the businesses. I figure you will run the winery and show the world that you and I and Alonzo are friends and business partners."

"Elijah." She whispered his name again and the sound went straight through his body. To his heart. Reached his soul. And vibrated right through his cock.

"I'm not going to lie to you and say we're not doing anything illegal, because we are. We have to in order to be able to stay in the game and make it work. I'm not clean, Siena," he confessed, hating the truth but knowing he had to give her that. "I'll never be clean. We can never get out."

"I love you," she whispered softly. "So much."

The burn went from slow and smoldering to pure fire. He rolled, sliding her body beneath his, pulling her legs up, forcing her to bend them at the knee. He slid one leg around his thigh and the other around his back as he drove deep. He forgot about talking. He couldn't think, his brain melting until he could only feel. She surrounded his cock with scorching silk, living, breathing silk, wrapping him tight and strangling him in paradise.

Her panting increased and then became a musical sob that vibrated right through his shaft. Then she was chanting his name. He used his thumb, sliding his hand between them, finding that magic little button and feeling her body instantly fragment around his. The quakes rocked him, took him closer, but he didn't want the ride to end. Liquid fire bathed his cock and flames danced over him, from crown to balls.

"Harder, baby."

He *loved* when she did that, panted in his ear, pleading. Sounded desperate for him. Wild for him. She loved his cock. She loved the way he gave her rough. Or gentle. She was uninhibited with him now, giving him everything. Showing him everything. And that only pushed up his own desire. His own lust. His own hunger and enjoyment.

He gave her harder. Rougher. Taking her wild while he could. He knew Doc would eventually curtail their brutal sexual escapades, but he had her now and he thoroughly enjoyed every second in her body. Her breath told him she was close a second time. He lifted her hips higher. She wrapped herself around him, giving him tight. Meeting him stroke for stroke. Just as rough. Just as hard. Just as needy and hungry as he was. He went over the edge, taking her with him, jetting hot and long, filling her, triggering another explosive quake in her. She whispered his name and his balls seemed to boil all over again at the sound. His cock jerked more, spasming, sending more of his seed spilling into her body. His name sounded like music. He found himself free-falling, floating in fire and a kind of happiness he never expected to ever have.

He buried his face in her shoulder, feeling every shudder and ripple of her body around his. "You with me, Siena? You going to stay with me through all this shit? Because I can't get us out. We'd have to hide, go on the run. We'd both be a target for the rest of our lives. No one would ever believe we're just looking to live free. We stay, it's dangerous, baby, but I have a better chance of protecting us. With Alonzo and Joshua in place, even more so."

Dios, she had to say she'd stay with him because he wasn't going to let her go. He'd keep her right there in his bedroom and talk until she listened, until he convinced her. Because there was no living without Siena Arnotto, not for him.

"Honey, I'm always with you," she replied softly, her gloved hands smoothing over his back. Her fingers went up his neck to find his hair. Stroking.

He rolled to take his weight off of her. Feeling her heart beat. Looking into her green eyes. She looked back at him. Soft. Gentle. His woman. She stayed there for a long time, holding him, gliding gently, giving him that sweetness until he finally slipped out of her. The loss hurt.

"It won't be easy, *mi amorcito*. The Feds will always be breathing down our necks."

"Why can't you just tell them what you're doing?" she

asked, kissing his throat. Sliding down his body slow. Making his heart beat harder in anticipation.

"Feds can be on the payroll too. We can't take chances. In any case, we're mainly after the leopards, because most of them are the ones who are the most violent, and no human can know about shifters."

She spread kisses over his chest, traced his roped muscles with her tongue and pressed more kisses along his rib cage.

"I didn't think about that," she murmured against his belly button.

The muscles in his abdomen contracted. His cock jerked. Even with her hands covered by his gloves, her hair swept over his body like silk and her mouth and tongue left caresses everywhere.

"It's much more dangerous, Siena, but we're trapped in this life. I want out for you. For the children. But even Drake admitted he couldn't protect us forever. They'd come looking, and they'd find us. I have too much information about the other bosses, what they do, their businesses, and no one will ever believe I'd keep my mouth shut."

She slipped farther down his body, fitting between his thighs, still spreading kisses and nipping occasionally with her teeth. Keeping him on edge. Making him wait. The anticipation kept his heart pounding. Kept blood roaring like thunder in his ears. Her tongue rasped along his hip bone. Slid over to the base of his cock. Blood rushed to center in his groin.

"Honey, can we keep the children safe?"

He closed his eyes. His hands found her hair. Sifted through it. He let the silken strands thread through his fingers over and over. She'd said *we*. That all important we.

"We'll keep them safe."

Her tongue slid along his inner thigh. Her hair brushed over his cock. The sensation was beautiful. Then she was doing something with her tongue that made his balls feel as if they were in heaven. Pure heaven. He didn't open his eyes.

He would when she moved up a little, but he savored the way she treated him, as if she worshiped his body.

"Will Alonzo be safe?"

That was a question he hadn't anticipated and he didn't have a good answer for her. Her tongue slid up the shaft of his cock. She lapped at him. So gentle. Almost reverent. Every fucking time she did it, his eyes burned. The woman could unman him so easily.

"I don't know, baby. He's smart and he's a really fast learner. He's a good man to have in a fight. We'll work with him, teach him everything he needs to know. If he's as intelligent as I think he is, he'll come to me or to Drake if he doesn't know how to handle something."

His eyes flew open as her mouth engulfed him. Took him deep, her tongue curling, stroking. Licking. Her mouth was hot and moist and felt even better than he remembered. It always did. Her eyes were on his, just the way he liked it. He hadn't told her this time, she'd just given him that. On her own. Just like she gave him everything.

"You're going to make me hard all over again, *mi vida*," he said, his fingers tangling in her hair. "We could be at this all night."

She smiled at him. Around his cock. "This is a problem?"

"I love you more than life, Siena. More than a man should love a woman. Terrifies me how much I love you."

Her tongue stroked and caressed. Laved and loved. Licked and lapped. Her mouth moved him. She ended with kisses. Lots of featherlight kisses, brushing them liberally over him. Then she crawled back up his body, and it was just plain sexy.

"I'm going to marry you in seventy-two hours, Siena. You're going to take my name. A lot of women in my culture don't do that, but you're going to."

She sprawled over him, one leg on either side of his body, her arms around his chest, head on his shoulder. "Mm-k."

"And you're going to Doc first thing tomorrow."

Something in his tone warned her and she lifted her head to eye him warily. "Don't go getting too bossy, Elijah. I love you and want to give you whatever makes you happy, but I can tell you've got this underlying reason for having me see Doc. If you think, even for one moment, that I would terminate this pregnancy, you have another think coming. You might be a crime boss, head of a family and your tentacles seem to be spreading out, but you are *not* going to dictate to me about our *children*."

"Not about our children," he said quietly. "Don't go all wild and crazy on me, baby. I would only put my foot down if there was a health danger."

"I don't go wild and crazy," she denied. "That's you. You have that hot head that makes you a little whacked sometimes. Me, I happen to be the voice of reason, which is good because one of us has to be. Women carry triplets, Elijah. Sometimes it gets tricky, but that's what women do."

"Not my woman. If Doc says you could be in danger, no fucking way am I taking that chance."

"Then prepare to live the next seven months without me. I'll go somewhere and get it done without you."

His hand tightened in her hair, yanking her head up so she could see the blaze in his eyes. "Don't even fuck around with that kind of threat, Siena. Not ever. You have no idea what I'd fucking do to keep you."

"Then don't you f-ing threaten to make me terminate my babies. That isn't your choice. They're real to me. Already alive. Already inside me. Growing."

She rolled off of him and tried to slide from the bed, but he shackled her wrist, rolled on top of her and pinned both wrists above her head with one of his hands. "Baby, you need to get this. Get me. Right fucking now. You're my world. You make me a decent man. You make me into someone worthwhile. You're gone, that man's gone and I'm a fucking killer. I'm what they made me."

She shook her head, not even struggling. "No, you're not,

Elijah. I didn't make you a better man. You always were that man. *Always*. You just didn't let anyone see him until me, but he was always there. I get that you're afraid for me, but honey, we make decisions together. That's how it has to work."

He shook his head. "It can't work that way, baby. And you know why."

"When it comes to your business, that's different and I understand that's your field of expertise. If you come to me to talk about things, and I hope you will, I'll listen, but I don't presume to know that life any more than you'd know how to run the winery or the vineyards. But between you and me, Elijah. Our personal life. Our home life. Our family. That's the two of us together. Not just you dictating to me. I would never be happy like that and you know it. We have to have a partnership."

He kissed the side of her mouth. Slid his tongue along her lower lip. "I'm all for a partnership, Siena, but not when you're at risk."

"Honey, everyone is at risk. You can't live your life being afraid of everything. I know. I've done that. I didn't even take a risk enough to have friends until you showed me what living is."

Her body remained relaxed against his, all tension gone. She was soft. Accepting. His.

"I'm taking a risk tying my life to yours. You may not be undercover, but you live your life that way and I'll have to do the same. I'm willing to do that, Elijah, because, for me, you're worth it. Our children are worth the risk to me as well. Just like Emma's child is worth it to her. And Catarina escaped Rafe Cordeau, and Eli claimed her knowing Cordeau was going to come after her. When something is worth it, you take that risk."

"Baby." It came out a groan. She didn't understand. How could she? The emotion tearing him up inside, ripping him to shreds, was too intense to describe with a single word like *love*. People loved all sorts of things. Elijah loved the way she took such care of him. But loved her? The feeling was far too powerful, too deep, such a force inside of him he knew if something happened to her, he would be gone.

"I need to clean up, honey. We'll talk to Doc in the morning and see what we're facing." Her voice was gentle. Loving. Turning his heart over.

Elijah buried his face in the sweet spot where her neck and shoulder met. Where he could bite down just a little bit and use his tongue to soothe that little ache. Where he could drag her skin into his mouth, suckling for just a moment, leaving his brand on her. She didn't move. Giving him that. He was like a fucking teenager who was hard every time he looked at a woman. One that was juvenile enough to give her love bites just to show off.

He let her up, rolling over, away from her abruptly. She wasn't going to carry three babies if the danger was too great. She could yell and scream all she wanted to, but it wasn't happening. And she wasn't leaving him to go off by herself to carry them if she didn't agree with him either. What the hell was wrong with her, saying something like that to him? She knew who he was. What he was. Didn't she think he'd be just as ruthless with her as he was in his business when he needed to be? Hell, more so?

He punched the pillow several times, listening to the sounds coming from the master bath. Brushing her teeth, the water running. He pushed himself up, snagged his jeans, hit the bar, caught up a bottle of Scotch and walked out, using the double doors that led outside to the covered, private patio. His leopard, sensing his mood, pushed at him, tried to comfort him. He felt restless. Edgy.

He paced back and forth, feeling the need to hit something. Wrapping his fist around the neck of the bottle, he took a long pull on the Scotch. It felt good going down. Maybe he could drink enough to lose the need to go back into his bedroom and shake some sense into Siena.

He tossed his jeans into one of the chairs and took another

drink as he stared moodily into the night. It was the kind of night a man like him could get lost in. Dark. No moon. Perfect. He could shift and run off the anger coursing through his veins, feeding the tension in his gut, or he could stay right there and drink himself into oblivion. It wasn't something he chose to do often, but his leopard wasn't going to want to run without his mate.

"Elijah?"

He closed his eyes and inhaled her, drew her deep into his lungs. The unique scent that was only Siena's. He could drown in that scent. As it was, he was surrounded by it. It floated to him on the night breeze and carried with it a million fantasies.

"Not a good time, baby," he warned. "The devil's riding me hard tonight."

"Tell me what you need."

He swung around to face her. She was there in the doorway, leaning one hip against it, dressed in her little camisole and nearly nonexistent lace panties. He liked that she had breasts and an ass he could get lost in. Soft. All woman.

"You need to fucking do what you're told and stop arguing with everything I say," he snapped, because the soft vulnerable spot inside of him continued to grow no matter how hard he worked at trying to shut it down. *She* did that to him. She exposed him like that. Keeping his eyes on hers, he took another long pull of Scotch.

She was silent a long moment, her green eyes searching his face. "Do you really want a yes-woman, Elijah, because you have to know, that's not me."

He swore, nearly threw the bottle, wanting to punch something. His temper was escalating. The cat was aroused now, raking and clawing, wanting domination.

"You've got to learn, Siena, there are just some things you have to yield on. There isn't going to be a question about it. You can't threaten me. You can't defy me. That isn't going to work. You just have to yield."

Her face closed down. Green eyes shifted away from him and he saw her fingers curl into two tight fists, so tight her knuckles went white. She slipped into the chair where he'd thrown his jeans. He took another swig of Scotch, using the neck of the bottle to lift it to his mouth.

"I can see you're not liking that, baby. But you have to know who I am. Who your man is. My woman stays safe. She has bodyguards. She lives free of the shit we're mired in, as free as I can make her and . . ." He crouched down in front of her. "Fucking look at me, *mi vida*, you need to see what I am." He kept his face close to hers, determined that she understand him.

The need for violence rode him hard. The leopard inside of him demanded she obey. The man that he'd been since his own family had shaped him was even more insistent. She stared back at him and there was that little chin lift. The flash of defiance in her eyes.

He threw the bottle. It smashed against the side of the house and shattered. He caught her face, framing it with hard hands. He slammed his mouth down on hers, taking hers. Not asking. Not coaxing. *Telling* her. He kissed her. Hard. Angry. Letting her know she belonged to him and she fucking well was going to do what he told her.

Her mouth was soft beneath his. Soft and warm. His tongue was aggressive. He dragged her into his arms. Right there on the patio, his hands moving over her body. Claiming her. Letting her know he would have her whenever and wherever he wanted her.

Siena melted into him. Kissing him back. Giving him everything without hesitation. Her hands slid up his back, and she'd removed the gloves. It was her touch, skin to skin, that shifted something inside of him, because the moment he kissed her, even angry, she turned wild.

He lifted his head, looking down at her. Her green eyes moved over his face. Slow. Studying him. Possessive. Hungry.

"What I see, Elijah, when I look at you, is my man. He

can be gentle and sweet and he can be angry and more leopard than human. But he's mine. The thing you need to get, honey, is that I love you. I'd do anything for you. I'd give up my life for you. But you have to see me. You have to know who I am. I can't be a yes-woman. If that's what you need, I'm not that woman as much as I'd like, for you, to be that. I love you with every single breath I take. Every single one."

She took his anger from him, wiped it away until he felt stripped bare. He pressed his forehead tight against hers. "I can't lose you. We talk to Doc about this, *mi vida*. If he says it's too dangerous, we go from there. Give me your word on that."

She hesitated. His grip on her tightened in warning. "Baby, I'm hanging on by a fucking thread here. I'm asking you to give me that."

"You're asking me to threaten the lives of our children."

He shook his head. "No. I'm asking you to follow Doc's advice. To listen to what he has to say. We'll do what we have to do, even if that decision is a difficult one."

She pulled back from him, her hand sliding to the nape of his neck, fingers curling even as tears welled up in her eyes. "Elijah."

His name came out a painful whisper, and his gut clenched. "I want the babies, Siena. Swear to God, baby, I want them. I'll do anything to help us keep them. I just have to know you're safe while you're doing it."

He touched one of the tears that spilled over and trailed down her cheek. Brought it to his mouth. Tasted it. Took it inside him as penance. He waited. Still inside. Waited for her slow nod.

He didn't know if she agreed with him, or if she was planning to leave him and make a run for it, but either way, he wasn't leaving her side until he knew what Doc recommended.

"You feel like letting your female run tonight?" he asked. His male was giving him hell now. He'd been settled until Elijah's temper had flared so hot.

She took a breath and then nodded.

He pulled her up and stepped close. Very close. Right into her, his thigh between her legs. "How can I want you again when I just had you?"

His voice was rough. Almost a growl, because his leopard was so close. His cock was as hard as a rock, the thick length standing straight against his stomach, jerking against her soft body, pulsing with need.

"I don't know," she whispered, hooking her thumbs in the lace of her panties and pushing them from her hips. When the lace dropped to the patio floor, she kicked them aside. Her hands slid between her breasts to open her camisole. "But whatever the reason, I'm burning up for you." She let the camisole follow the panties and then she cupped her breasts in her hands, lifting them toward him. "I want you right now, Elijah."

He didn't hesitate. He bent his head and took her right breast deep, suckling, using the flat of his tongue to press her nipple tight against the roof of his mouth.

"Honey," she whispered, her voice as hungry as he felt.

He lifted his head. "Put your arms around my neck, baby, and hop up."

He caught her ass and lifted her into his arms, already feeling her body, so scorching hot. He tipped her back against the wall and drove her down onto him. Her sheath convulsed around his cock, strangling him with fire.

He swore, gritting his teeth, driving into her as she rode him hard. Rode him rough. Matching his out-of-control hunger. Matching his savage. His wild cat. He drove her up twice. Fast. Brutal. Listening to her music, the panting sobs, the pleas, the chanting of his name. He felt every sound vibrating right through his cock. Each time he took her over the edge, she gave that to him, biting down hard with her small teeth, sinking them into his shoulder, saying his name. Her hot, silken muscles so tight, clamping down to seize him so tight he thought he'd died and gone to heaven.

She never stopped moving. Lifting her hips, riding him harder with each orgasm. Her face was a study in pure pleasure. Her eyes dazed. Lips parted. He fucking loved that about her. When she gave herself to him, she gave him everything. He tipped her farther, needing deeper. Needing to bury himself so deep she could never get him out. He pounded into her, his thick shaft driving through those tight, scorching-hot folds, jackhammering through her tight muscles, while the flames burned him clean.

He took her up a third time and knew he couldn't hold out this time. "Again, baby, give me that again," he said. It was his. Her orgasms. Her body. All of her. Heart and soul. She'd given that to him, and nothing was going to take it away from him.

Her breath was coming in ragged gasps. Little mews escaped and still he took her higher. Pushing her limits. He felt the score of her nails along his back, heard her sob, but she kept riding. Kept slamming her body down to meet his. Because he'd asked for it. Because he'd *asked*.

Then her body was rippling around his. Ecstasy. He felt the tidal wave start somewhere in his toes and sweep up his thighs to boil in his balls. He slammed home three more times and then planted himself there, feeling the eruption, the hot jet of his seed, the release that swept him away with her. Her tight sheath gripped him hard, clamping around him like a vise, holding him to her, in her.

He took his time, letting his lungs have air. Just holding her. Staying where he wanted to be. All the while, her fingers sifted through his hair, caressing. Stroking. Her body stayed soft, melted into his. Boneless. Pliant.

"I love you, Siena." What else could he say? He'd said it all. She'd seen him at his worst so many times, and she still held on tight to him. Still gave him everything.

"Let's let our leopards run, Elijah. I think they need it," she said softly. Still not moving. Still holding him tight, her legs wrapped around him, her heels digging into his hips.

She was laid out before him. Her back arched, partially

against the wall. Hair flowing down toward the patio floor. Breasts thrust toward him. Her body impaled on his. He'd never seen a more beautiful sight.

"I need the words tonight, *mi amorcito*. I need to hear them again."

She smiled at him. Her soft mouth. Her beautiful eyes. "I love you more than life, Elijah."

He let her back rest against the wall to hold her up just for a moment while he ran his hands from her shoulders, down over the curves of her breast, along her abdomen, his fingers splayed wide. Taking in his children. Holding them inside of her. He knew she saw the sorrow in his eyes when her body tightened around his. She pulled herself up, dropping her legs, trapping his hands there.

"Just wait to find out what Doc says," she whispered. "Let's go run, Elijah."

He knew it would help to lose himself in the freedom of his leopard. He nodded, took her hand and led her off to the edge of the patio. He liked their combined scents. He liked knowing it was his seed trickling down her thigh. He forced his mind away from the thought of losing their children to the joy of running free. And then he shifted.

21

THE male leopard took the lead, running free away from the sometimes suffocating house that belonged to humans. He kept his female close, mostly because he liked her that way. She was in a playful mood. He wasn't. He needed to run, to allow some of the aggression to ebb away.

The little female followed him for a long while as he led her deep into the center of the property, far from the house. The land was beautiful, rolling slightly rather than flat, and the vegetation wasn't manicured, it was wild and dense. His mate seemed happy enough to follow him once she got the idea that he wasn't playing, but then she began to lag behind him, stopping every few minutes to examine the ground, follow the trail of a fox, dig around a rotting log. Generally *not* complying with his wish to keep moving.

When he rushed her, glaring at her with his snarling mouth and focused stare, she simply rolled over and rubbed her fur along the ground and then came to her feet to rub along his body enticingly. Just like that his mood swung from temper to amorous. He gave her whatever she wanted, running beside her, playing, rolling with her in the deep grass, sliding his fur-covered side along hers, springing away when she swiped at him and moving into position when she crouched invitingly in front of him.

He lost his bad mood fast and remembered fun. Remembered freedom and what having a mate felt like. She tired easily, but she met his every advance willingly, letting him take his fill of her, just as loving back, rubbing her muzzle along his and winding her neck along his.

He kept them moving deeper into the property when he wasn't loving on her. Slower this time, with less purpose and more fun, but still moving. Even after taking her multiple times, the male needed the spacious land, the freedom of the night. Twice she lay down and he had to go back for her, standing over her protectively while she rested. Then he got her moving again.

He took her toward his favorite spot. A small rise with a grove of trees. The trees were old, a stand of oak with thick trunks and long sweeping branches that bent low to the ground. The rise was just high enough that when you leapt up into the trees and climbed, you could see most of the land—even the house.

More than once, when he wanted to be alone, Elijah had come here. Only Joaquin and occasionally his brother Tomas had followed him. They kept to the form of a leopard, their big males pacing a distance behind him, his shadows. They'd been doing it for so long, sometimes he could forget they were there—and why.

As he approached the grove of trees, he picked up the pace, eager to climb his favorite tree, rest with Siena and watch the sunrise before they had to go back and face the day. Face Doc. Elijah stayed buried deep in his leopard, trying not to think of what the morning might bring to the two of them. He wanted to just let go and think of nothing but living wild. Living free with Siena and his children.

The night was extremely dark with no moon. The air had stilled, not even a slight breeze blowing. Black clouds lay heavy above their heads, threatening rain, but there wasn't even a hint of a mist. He moved toward the grove, picking up his pace, and then became aware that Siena had stopped. She didn't follow him. Not only did she not follow him, but she lifted her lip in a snarl and first backed away, then turned to run.

The male leopard wasn't having any more of her defiance. He'd played her games, loved her, given her time to rest repeatedly, and his goal was just a short distance away. He went at her hard, mindful of her fragile state, but he used a hard, very muscular shoulder to turn her back toward the grove.

She resisted, stubbornly digging her claws into the dirt and then, when he continued to push at her with his larger body, she dropped to the ground, refusing to move. Elijah felt the burst of temper exploding in his moody cat and instantly shifted to keep the little female from the male's retaliation. He dropped his hand on the female's neck, digging his fingers into the beautiful thick fur.

"Baby, you'll love the grove," he whispered softly in the cat's ear, leaning his head against her. When in leopard form, he didn't have the human tactile feel of the leopard's fur against his skin. It was amazing, incredible, and he couldn't resist stroking caresses along her back.

Siena shifted out from under his hand, wrapping her arms around herself. Neither had brought a pack with clothes. Nudity didn't bother Elijah at all. He was comfortable in that form, and like all shifters, he stashed several caches with clothes and money around the property. He'd had his leopard almost as long as he could remember, and before that, he was aware of the creature. Siena, however, was clearly uncomfortable out in the open without her clothes. He locked his arm around her waist, pulling her front to his side, so he could shelter her a little with his larger body.

"I don't like the smell," she whispered, her hand sliding up his chest. It was trembling. "I can't quite catch what it is, but it makes me uneasy."

She was pregnant. Her cat would share her heightened sense of smell. Already, the leopard's ability was acute, but with the pregnancy, it would be even more so.

"Shift, Siena," he ordered softly. "Stay right here, in the taller grass and wait for me. I'll look around." He believed her. Siena wasn't given to unfounded fears.

The moment he recognized that she was afraid, the night went from beautiful to sinister. The overhead clouds became ominous. The entire atmosphere of the night changed, so that he felt that same uneasiness that her female had conveyed to her.

Siena wrapped her arms around his neck. "Let's just go, Elijah. We can go home and . . ." She obviously didn't know what, but her body trembled and her voice shook. She kept her tone very low, just a thread of sound, and she spoke against his ear as if she feared someone—or something—would overhear.

"You won't feel safe until I figure out what has you spooked, *mi vida*," he whispered into her ear, following her lead in order to show her he took her seriously. "Shift for me now, baby. Stay low, and I'll just scout around a little."

For a moment he didn't think she'd do what he'd asked. Her arms tightened around him and she pressed close for comfort, or to keep him with her, he didn't know which. He remained silent. Waiting. Because in the end, Siena believed in him. He got that now. She believed he would keep her safe. She was certain he would keep their children safe. If she didn't, she would never have agreed to stay with him. Threats wouldn't stop her leaving, only her belief in him. He got that now and it was huge, because it meant she wasn't going anywhere, no matter how tough things got.

He slipped his hand over her tummy, where his children were growing. He understood what she meant about risks as well. She was risking everything to stay and believe in him. He had to find the same courage when Doc gave them the statistics on a woman carrying triplets. He was intelligent enough to know that any pregnancy carried risks, and multiples had to come with their own set of problems.

"We'll handle it, baby," he murmured.

She turned her face up to his and smiled. *Smiled.* Her soft mouth curved, and even there in the darkness, with danger somewhere close, that smile lit her beautiful features and her gorgeous green eyes. She couldn't read his mind. She couldn't know he was referring to their babies, but somehow she did and she understood.

"Siena"—he wrapped his fingers in warning around her neck—"*shift.* Right. Fucking. *Now.* And you stay put. No matter what." Because his heart was in danger and that soft spot inside him was showing. He knew it. He knew she saw it. He had to be sharp because, although there was no breeze and he didn't smell whatever her leopard had, he *felt* the danger. And it seemed to be getting closer, as if something was stalking them.

She didn't argue. Right there, with his fingers curled around her neck, she shifted. She was still a little hesitant, a little awkward, but she was getting the hang of it. Her little female dropped her belly to the ground and curled into the high grass for protection.

Elijah shifted, already on the prowl, stalking back toward the grove of trees, lifting his muzzle, trying to catch the elusive scent that had warned Siena. He circled around the grove without entering, keeping to cover, using the slower, freeze-frame movements of the stalking leopard to cross any open areas so he wouldn't draw the eye.

He was a distance from Siena, something his leopard didn't like and he liked even less, when he caught the first scent. Instantly his leopard lifted his lip in a silent snarl. Paolo's leopard. There was no mistaking that odor. The leopard's scent had clung to Siena's body after it had mauled her so badly. Even after she'd showered repeatedly, it had taken awhile before Elijah didn't smell him on her anymore.

He'd never said a word to her, but more than once he'd gone into his workout room and pounded the heavy bag because the need for violence in him was too strong to ignore. He moved into the grove, keeping to the higher grass, and the scent of Paolo's leopard was even heavier. With it was another one. Paolo hadn't come alone. They were scouting the house, using the trees to do it.

Elijah knew this breech was his fault. Drake had pulled security in closer to the house, patrolling the surrounding grounds, but not the acreage itself. There was a lot of territory to cover and they just didn't have the manpower. But Elijah knew about that grove of trees and how a leopard could climb up there and see the house and any activity. They should have put someone on it.

He knew the tree one of them would be in and he guessed at that other. He couldn't get up the tree without being seen, not any of those, but he knew the tree on the far side of the grove had branches that looped and shaped long-reaching limbs toward the ground. Not only could he get up easily to the leopard highway in the trees, but he would be coming in from behind them. He made his way there.

Using pure stealth, his male ascended to the overlaying branches that formed a labyrinth in the canopy. His male knew every branch of every tree and exactly what branch could hold when it came to weight. He began his stalk through the trees, toward the leopard Paolo had brought with him. The trees reeked of their scents. They were male and they clearly wanted to claim territory, especially with a female in the area. Both had marked the tree trunks. The scent of Paolo enraged his male.

The large cat moved above his prey, the shifter Paolo had brought with him, looking down at the tawny cat, grateful for the stillness so the male hadn't scented him yet. His attention was fixed in the direction where Siena's little female was nestled in the deep grass. Elijah spared a moment to look that way. He couldn't spot her and his whiskers, eyes and nose picked up no movement or scent, so the male must have heard her.

He kept his gaze trained on the site where he knew he'd left her, worried now. If this strange male had spotted her, it was possible Paolo had as well. A few moments later, the sound came to him. He didn't see her, but he heard the slide of a body moving in the grass, moving *away* from the grove, back toward the house. Siena hadn't even given him a full half hour before she was on the move.

He knew if he heard that slide of fur in the grass, the other two males, already on alert, would hear as well. His large male launched himself, going for the kill, landing on the lighter-colored cat, teeth sinking deep, claws digging into the sides to ride him down as the branch broke.

They hit the ground hard, Elijah's leopard driving the other one so deep into the ground one leg snapped and the shifter's back broke. Elijah leapt off him, not taking the time to deliver the killing bite, which would have been merciful. Elijah didn't have mercy in him. He had fury. Absolute fury. Paolo Riso was about to pay for his multiple crimes against Elijah's woman. The beating. The mauling. Every broken rib. Every laceration and scratch. Every scar on her body. Every moment of her terror. Elijah planned to retaliate tenfold.

He dropped the screaming cat just as Paolo's large male, with a dark, almost charcoal coat and even darker rosettes, leapt from the tree he'd been in and landed a few feet away. Instantly he attacked, rushing Elijah's leopard. Elijah turned to meet him, running at him, gaining momentum. He'd learned speed in the rain forest. He'd learned how to utilize his flexible spine and how best to protect his body while tearing apart his opponent. He didn't plan to simply kill Paolo. He didn't want a clean kill. He wanted him to feel everything Siena had felt, including helpless terror.

At the last second before the two male leopards came together, he swerved, sliding past the other cat, raking a deep wound with his claw from shoulder, across the length of the heaving side to his opponent's tail. He made certain the claws went deep, well beyond the loose skin, almost to the bone. He dug out four furrows of flesh, fur and sinew. Two steps and he spun, raking the face of the cat, from the top of his head, down across his eyes to his nose. That fast his male sprang away a second time.

He leapt over Paolo's cat, striking with his back claws to rip open the back. In the course of less than a minute, he had already marked and injured Paolo's male in three places. Elijah was relentless, not giving the other male any time to gather himself. He struck over and over, fast attacks, rip-and-tear tactics, never going in for the kill, but shredding fur to get to the muscle. Tearing chunks of muscle to get to the bone.

There was nothing so painful as a claw digging into a bone and ripping at it. Or teeth settling around it and crunching down with powerful jaws. Elijah kept at the other cat, delivering a brutal, savage punishment until the eyes of the other male went from dominant, aggressive and confident to scared and then to sheer terror. The bloody leopard tried to run, whirling away from the heavy cat that was slowly ripping his body to pieces. Elijah was faster, hitting him hard from behind, using his entire weight and momentum to knock Paolo off his feet. He heard the crack as the back leg shattered and Paolo screamed.

Instantly Elijah hit him again on the side with his heavier weight. Breaking ribs. He leapt over the cat as the leopard tried to drag himself into a protective ball. He paced away from Paolo, snarling, fury riding him. A killing fury that took over. He saw her body, ripped and bloody as the cat mauled her, and Elijah rushed his fallen opponent again, crashing into his other side, breaking those ribs.

It took some time to come down from the killing madness. By that time he'd delivered the suffocating bite to both cats there was little left of Paolo's body that wasn't torn apart. His male still refused to back away from the dead leopard, despising his enemy, an enemy that would torture, beat and maul a woman.

His leopard heard the approach of two more males and whirled to face them, snarling, bloody from the minor lacerations Paolo's cat had managed to inflict during the mostly one-sided fight. Although he recognized both Drake and Tomas, he avoided them, unable to get near either one in his present state. They could deal with the bodies. He had something more to do.

His leopard took off running, his fury rebuilding with every step. He knew why Drake and Tomas were there. *Siena had gotten them.* She'd disobeyed him as usual, and she'd run for aid. He was going to kill her. Beat her. Spank her. Well. Not spanking. That hadn't worked out in his favor. But *something*.

Did the woman not know the meaning of *stay put*? How *fucking* hard was it to do that? He knew exactly what she was going to say, the excuse she would use. Drake and Tomas showing up to help him. He didn't need help. He didn't want help. He wanted to rip that fucking bastard Paolo from one end to the other. Shred him. Make him feel what Siena had felt. He didn't need help with that. At. All.

She was on the bedroom patio, pacing. His male both caught sight of her as well as scented her. In the dark, she looked ethereal, beautiful, her long hair up in that messy knot thing she did on her head to try to keep all that silk contained. She had pulled on one of her camisoles and the little shorts that went with it. They hugged her hips and accentuated her tucked-in waist. He could see the thickness forming and the cute little pooch at her stomach.

She drew in her breath sharply when the leopard vaulted over the low wall to land, already shifting right in front of her. Before she could say a word, he tagged her hand and dragged her back into the house. He didn't care that he was naked, bloody and sweaty. Neither did she. She didn't try to pull away, instead, the moment they were in the bedroom, she flung herself in front of him, her arms going around his neck, jerked his head down to hers, her mouth on his, tongue sliding in to kiss him. Wild. Wet. Hot.

He was angry. Furious. Leopard furious. But it didn't matter. It never did when the heat flared and the burn started. His kiss was angry. Ferocious. He took her mouth. Hard. Wet. Hot. More than wild. He bit her lower lip. She gasped. He took her mouth again. Her taste drove him crazy with need. Her sweetness was tinged with fear. With love. With hunger. With that wild he loved so much.

He was already naked, and he stripped her, lifting her, dragging first one leg and then the other around his hips while he kissed her, walking them right into the bathroom where the large shower waited. She didn't seem to notice they were moving. With the roped muscles of his kind, it was nothing to carry her, and he turned on the water, testing it with one hand, all the while kissing her. Feeding her hunger. Feeling her desperation. Feeding his own fierce temper with that building burn.

Water poured down over them, soothing some of the deeper scratches on him, so that blood and sweat ran in rivulets down his back and chest. All the while he kept his mouth on hers, kissing her. Biting at her lips, her chin, that sensitive soft spot he loved so much between her neck and shoulder.

She squirmed, her hips bucking against him, trying to impale herself on his hard-as-hell cock, but he held her just out of reach, allowing the flared head to penetrate, but using his strength to keep her from sliding over him with her slick, hot heat.

"Elijah," she protested. Panting. Needing.

"You disobey me, baby?" he demanded, his mouth at her shoulder. Teeth biting down in warning. She went still. He caught her messy knot and yanked her head back, forcing her eyes to meet his. "You disobey me? I gave you *orders*." His teeth bit down again, this time a little harder. More leopard. He kept his eyes on hers. Letting her see his leopard's fury. The man's temper. "Orders that would keep you *safe*."

She swallowed and stayed very still, pressed up against him, her heart beating fast and loud enough that he heard it.

"Fucking answer me, Siena."

She bit her lip, nodding. "I was scared for you," she whispered. "Elijah, I smelled the other male and I knew there were two of them."

"I told you no matter what to stay put. What part of that did you not understand?"

His fingers left her hair and went to her hips, both hands there now, and he slammed her down hard, right over him. Deep. Hot. Burning hot. *Scorching* hot, to match the fury of his temper.

She gasped. Her muscles were incredibly tight around him, that silken fist clasping him hard, reluctantly giving way to his violent invasion. She tried to move, but he held her there. His prisoner. His captive. His woman who didn't know how to do anything she was told.

"What *fucking* part of that did you not understand?"

"I was afraid for you," she reiterated, when she could get her breath. "Elijah, I knew I couldn't help you. I thought if I got Drake . . ."

"No, baby, you didn't think. I left you there safe. The moment you moved they heard you. They knew you were there. If things hadn't have gone right, if I hadn't incapacitated the first one before Paolo even knew I was there, he would have been on you. I had to worry about you instead of concentrating on killing that fucker."

He lifted her, feeling that tight burn all along his shaft,

that squeeze of her muscles, the intensity of the friction. Beautiful. Beautiful even in his fury. His eyes blazed into hers and he saw that change. The shift. She had known he would be angry. She *knew*. She still had gone for help, risking his wrath because she'd been afraid for him. Taking care of him. It was the absolute wrong thing to do, but she'd done it for him.

Her eyes filled with tears, accenting the brilliant green emerald. Her lashes looked like the feathery ends were dripping diamonds. He leaned forward and lapped at the wet there, taking her tears into his mouth. Tasting them. Tasting her.

"I love you, baby," he said, kissing his way down to her mouth. "But I swear, if you don't listen when I tell you something that important, I'm going to have to find a way to make you listen." He was dead serious. He didn't want to hurt her, and he'd always make certain she knew he loved her, but he wasn't living through that nightmare again. "I swear to you, Siena, and you'd better fucking believe me. I will find a way to punish you that you aren't going to like if you ever put me in that position again. Am I clear enough? Do you get me?"

She nodded, put her head on his shoulder and tightened her arms around his neck.

"Give me your word, not that nod. This is important, Siena. I have to know when it comes to your safety, you'll do what I tell you."

"I will," she murmured. Her voice hitched. "I swear, Elijah, I'll do better."

"Fucking don't cry. *Mi amorcito*, you can't cry anymore."

"I'm pregnant, Elijah," she whispered against his skin. The feel of her lips was exquisite. "That means I'm emotional. I'm going to cry."

He began to move, as desperate as she was for the contact, maybe more so. Needing the burn, feeding her hunger as well as his own. But really, it was that connection he needed.

To be inside her. Surrounded by her fire. To feel her body, real, alive, soft and all his, right at that moment.

"You scared me, *mi vida*," he admitted. "It isn't a good idea to scare me."

"I'm getting that," she whispered, and threw her head back. Turned her face up to the rain shower so the water fell soft over her. Over both of them. She rose up and came down hard, while he surged up to meet her.

He lost himself in her. Taking her over and over while she rode him. Wild. Driving her up twice. He wanted more from her. "Slide your hand down, baby. Use your finger. I want you to give it to me again, this time with me."

He felt the movement. Her palm slid down his chest. Lower. Between them. He loved that. He felt her fingers as he slammed home and then her breathing changed yet again. Giving him what he wanted like she always did. Her body convulsed around his, gripping him hard, milking him. Taking him over the edge. He held her a long while with the water washing him clean and then he set her feet on the tiles.

She kissed her way down his chest to his belly. He knotted her wet hair in his fist, used his hand to urge her down to her knees. Right there in the shower she loved on him. With her hands. With her mouth. With the water falling like rain all around her. Everything in him settled, and love rose strong. Intense. Far more intense than his leopard's temper. He knew she would always do this to him. Settle him down when he wanted to wring her neck. The funny thing was— he didn't mind in the least.

"MOST triplets are formed when three separate eggs are fertilized. Meaning they're fraternal. It isn't uncommon for one egg to split giving identical twins and a second egg to give a third baby," Doc explained.

Elijah waited. Doc hadn't gotten to the point. Not at all.

Siena, tummy still exposed, lying on the exam table, the machine next to them, didn't move at all. She was tense. More upset than he'd realized. Scared. He moved a little closer to her protectively.

"It is extremely rare, even in shifters, for a monozygotic event. A single egg splits three ways, or two ways and then one of those splits again."

"You're giving me nothing, Doc," Elijah said impatiently.

Siena squeezed his hand, and he looked at her. Her face was very still, and he could swear she was holding her breath.

"Siena." Doc looked straight at her. "There is one placenta and three babies. The babies will be identical and they'll all be the same sex."

Elijah's breath left his lungs in a rush. Not girls. Three girls looking like their mother would send him over the edge. He'd have to hire a fucking army to keep every male away from them.

"And the risks to Siena?" Elijah said.

Doc again looked at Siena. "Any time you have a multiple-birth pregnancy, the risks go up. With a monozygotic pregnancy, because you have a shared placenta, the risk is greater to the babies as well as to you. You can develop preeclampsia, which is a pregnancy-induced hypertension. Before Elijah panics, and I will admit that a good third of mothers carrying multiples develop this, they now have discovered that two proteins in the placenta may be the cause. We'll be able to test you and know right away if you're at risk for this and we'll be able to treat you if you are."

Elijah wrapped his hand around Siena's wrist, shackling it with his fingers while he stared down at her tummy where Doc's assistant had smeared some goo before doing the ultrasound. To keep his children, he could live with that. If Doc said he could deal with it, Elijah would believe him.

He bent his head and skimmed his mouth over hers. "We've got this, baby," he said softly. "Yeah?"

She smiled up at him. "Yeah." But it was forced. She was definitely afraid.

"Any multiple birth is at risk for preterm labor," Doc went on. "I'm sure both of you are aware of that fact, so we'll take every precaution that you hang in there as long as possible to give them the best start. You have to maintain a very healthy pregnancy and follow orders. I'll want to see you frequently."

Elijah was the one who nodded. Siena looked even more worried, and he didn't want her worried. He tightened his hold around her wrist. *"Mi vida,"* he said softly, and waited for her to look at him.

"No risky behavior, Siena, like scuba diving. Run it by me before you decide to do anything like that. You can swim, but you take it easy. Eat. Don't try to maintain your girlish figure by skipping meals. You're eating for all four of you, and you take your prenatals. Choose your food wisely because you also don't want to overindulge. Fruits and vegetables. I'll get you a list, Elijah."

Siena scowled at him, but Doc just winked.

"Drink water and stay hydrated. All the time. Of course no alcohol." Again he turned to Elijah. "When I say she needs to stay hydrated, I mean she should have water with her all the time."

"Got it," Elijah said, happy he was going to be able to oversee the pregnancy. He'd make certain she ate what she was supposed to, drank her water and took her vitamins. He could definitely do that.

Siena groaned. "Do *not* put him in charge, Doc. You have no idea what he's going to be like."

Doc grinned at her. "Sure I do. I'm leopard, Siena. That man is going to get you through this pregnancy, and you'll be healthy and deliver three healthy babies."

She rolled her eyes but smiled up at Elijah, shaking her head a little to let him know it wasn't going to be all his way.

Elijah knew better. It was going to be *all* his way. She was going to follow Doc's advice to the letter because, in spite of her smiles and eye rolling, he could see she was scared. Not for herself, but for her babies.

"Don't get overtired. She needs to rest, Elijah. A lot. And no hot tub. If she takes a bath, the water shouldn't be really hot. Also, calm the leopard sex down. You can have sex, but not too rough. Also, Elijah, no more shifting for her. Your male is going to have to be understanding and just stay close to her."

"He won't like it," Elijah said, and then wished he hadn't. Siena's gazed jumped to his face and then she looked away from him.

"He doesn't have a choice. You make that clear. Take him out and run him until he's exhausted, but Siena can't shift anymore. Not with three babies in her. It's too strenuous, not to mention, your male's going to want rough sex and then you two will."

"No problem, Doc," Elijah said.

"Why are you talking to him when you started out talking to me?" Siena demanded. "I need a towel to wipe this gunk off my belly." She was blushing, clearly uncomfortable with discussing rough sex of any kind, leopard, shifter or human—her gaze had stopped meeting Elijah's completely.

Doc handed her a small towel. He didn't look in the least remorseful. "Because I know Elijah will keep his eye on you and won't let you skip meals, eat the wrong foods, forget to drink water or rest. You'll have a tendency to want to overdo it, and he's not going to allow that. Also, he's going to know all the signs of preterm labor and you aren't to ignore any of them."

Siena made a face, pulled down her shirt, and Elijah helped her into a sitting position. His arm slid around her shoulders. "Just don't give me three girls, baby," he teased.

"You promise that and I'll let you have ice cream once in a while."

"I'm having ice cream," Siena declared. "Especially since it's the *male* who determines the sex of the child, and so you're responsible if we have daughters."

She teased him back, but he noted her gaze didn't go to his. Not once. Still, he kept trying to show her he was all right with everything. He gave a deliberate groan. "Don't put that on me."

"One last thing we need to discuss," Doc interrupted. "Transfusion syndrome will occur in about ten percent of monozygotic pregnancies. It's a condition when abnormal blood vessels may develop when a single placenta is shared. Basically one baby can become a donor for the others, endangering all of them. You aren't showing any signs of this, but I'll monitor you closely. There are a couple of advanced treatments now that have saved a good sixty percent or more of babies affected. I don't think that will happen, but that's because I've never seen it in a shifter."

Siena looked even more frightened and placed both hands protectively over her tummy as if she could shield the children. Elijah held her closer, moving into her so he could keep her beneath his shoulder.

"Elijah has my private number. Call day or night for anything," Doc said. "You're very healthy, Siena, and so far the babies are developing perfectly."

"We're getting married in two days, Doc, at Jake's. You're welcome to come," Elijah said, helping Siena down from the exam table.

He kept Siena close to him, his arm locked around her waist, as he talked to Doc for a few more minutes. Eli and Drake stood as they entered the waiting room. Drake went directly to the door and opened it, exiting first. Tomas, lounging against the car, came alert, opening the backseat passenger door, his eyes scanning rooftops while Drake was looking carefully up and down the streets for any sign of trouble.

Siena had made the announcement that she was taking over the Arnotto winery—the papers making a big deal of it. The winery was famous all over the world, and reporters had come the moment the word got out, along with the fact that she was engaged and soon to be married to Elijah Lospostos. She had also named her business manager, Alonzo Massi, who had been with her grandfather for years and was a man she trusted implicitly to oversee all the various businesses under the Arnotto umbrella.

Since the announcement had gone public, Elijah and Drake had tightened security. Locked it down, in fact. Siena didn't go anywhere, not even to step outside the house onto the patio without a bodyguard. She didn't like it, but so far she hadn't said anything. Paolo was no longer a threat and neither was Robert Gaton, but Elijah and Drake were taking no chances that any of the other bosses would object to Elijah and Siena forming an empire.

He helped her into the back of the car and slid in beside her, reaching to take her hand as she looked out the opposite window. She looked close to tears. Tomas started the car and they were away, the vehicle behind following close.

"Baby, for every bad thing he said, there was a solution. Our babies are going to be strong, and we'll do this right. They'll have every chance, and if you give a Lospostos a chance, he thrives."

When she kept her head turned away from him, he tugged on her hand. "*Mi vida*, I need you to look at me." He had to see her eyes.

When she turned her head he saw he was right and tears swam in her eyes. His heart reacted, just as it always did, clenching a little in pain.

"It was awful. The things he said were awful. I thought maybe there would be a little danger to me, but everything he said was about them."

Not everything. He'd heard more than she had when it came to some of the things Doc said, but he wasn't going to point them out. He brought her hand to his mouth, opening her fingers so he could press kisses over her palm to her inner wrist. "We are going to have three beautiful children. We're going to enjoy every second of the pregnancy and we'll follow the doc's advice to the letter. Everything will be fine."

He saw the shift in her tear-drenched eyes. Hope. Belief. In *him*. It nearly stopped his heart. That kind of thing was always an unexpected, beautiful gift. It shook him every single time.

"You think?" She wanted reassurance, and she was prepared to take it if he gave it to her.

"Yes, baby, I think we'll be fine. Now tell me what happened in there."

Her lashes fluttered. She looked at their joined hands. He had pushed her palm flat against his chest, over his heart and pinned it there with his.

"Siena," he said softly, insistently. And waited. It took a long time before she finally looked him in the eye. "We talked about the possibility of not being able to have sex. He didn't say that. He said no leopard sex. Not rough. Not wild."

"Not us," she whispered. "Elijah, that's not you. It's not us."

He smiled, because she was the most beautiful woman in the world and she was his. "That's me and that's us too. If I have you and that's what you need, that's what I need. Baby, we're going to do fine, I have no worries. You let me take care of you."

She shook her head. "I want to take care of *you*."

She was killing him. Each time he thought he loved her as much as possible, she did or said something that overwhelmed him. Filled him. He couldn't wait to make her his wife.

He leaned down, tipping up her chin. "You are *mi vida*. My life, Siena, and you always will be. I love the care you take with me. We'll make a deal. I get to take care of you while you're pregnant, and you take care of me when you're not."

She smiled up at him, her eyes going bright, the shadows moving out of them. "That sounds good, Elijah. I can do that."

He knew it wouldn't be that simple. She'd still find ways, but at least he got her brightness back. He leaned closer and took her mouth, because he'd found she was all he really needed.

Keep reading for an excerpt from
the next GhostWalker novel
by Christine Feehan

SPIDER GAME

Available February 2016 from Jove Books

TRAP Dawkins sighed as he tilted his chair back on two legs, automatically calculating the precise angle and vector he could tip himself to before he fell over. He was bored out of his fucking mind. This was the fifth night in a row he'd come to the Huracan Club, a Cajun bar out in the middle of the fucking swamp, for God's sake. Peanut husks covered the bar and round, handmade wooden tables with a crude variety of chairs covered the floor. The bar was constructed of simple planks of wood set on sawhorses surrounded by high stools, also hand carved.

To the left of the bar was a shiny, beautifully kept baby grand piano. In a bar that was mostly a shack out in the middle of nowhere, the piano looked totally out of place. The lid was open and there wasn't a dust spot or a scratch on the instrument. It was also completely in tune. The piano sat on a raised dais with two long steps made of hardwood leading up to it. There were no peanut husks on the platform or on the stairs.

Everyone who frequented the bar knew not to touch the piano unless they really knew how to play. No one would dare. The piano had gone unscathed through hundreds of bar fights that included knives and broken bottles.

Trap glanced at the piano. He supposed he could play. Sometimes that helped his mind stay calm when it needed action. He couldn't take sitting for hours doing nothing. How did these people do it? That question had occupied his brain for all of two minutes. He didn't really care why they did it, or how; it was just a plain waste of time. He wasn't certain he could take much more of this, but on the other hand, what alternative was there?

He'd come looking for *her*. Cayenne. In spite of the fact that—or maybe because—no one could accurately describe her, Trap knew she frequented the bar. This was where she chose her victims. The robberies in the swamp were only rumors, whispers, the men too embarrassed to say much. They were always drunk. Always on their way home. They were men with bad reputations, men others steered clear of. She would choose those men and they wouldn't be able to resist her. Not her looks. Not her voice. Not the lure she used.

He sighed again and glanced toward the bar, wishing he had another beer, but seriously, it was nearly one in the morning. She wasn't coming. He would have to endure this nightmare again.

"Fuck," he whispered crudely under his breath. He had discipline and control in abundance. But he couldn't stop himself from the destructive path he was set on. He *had* to find her, and that meant coming to this hellhole every night until he did.

"How you doin', Trap?" Wyatt Fontenot asked as he put a fresh bottle of beer on the very rickety table in front of his fellow GhostWalker and toed a chair out so he could straddle it. "You ready to leave? You're lookin' like you might be startin' a fight any minute."

Trap would never, under any circumstances, *start* a fight.

But he'd finish it, and he'd do that in a very permanent way. That was why half their team came to the bar with him.

"Can't leave," Trap said. Low. Decisive.

Not that he didn't want to leave, Wyatt noted. Trap said *can't*. There was a big difference. He'd told Wyatt he was looking for Cayenne, the woman he'd rescued from certain death, but knowing Trap, that was so far out of his reality that Wyatt hadn't really believed him. But now . . .

"Trap." Wyatt kept his voice low. Steady. His gaze on one of his closest friends.

Trap was a very dangerous man. He didn't look it, sitting there, legs sprawled out in front of him, his chair tipped back and his eyes half-closed, but there was ice water running in his veins. More, he had a brain that worked overtime, calculating everything even as he observed the most minute detail of his surroundings.

He had a steady hand and the eyes of an eagle. He was silent and deadly when he stalked an enemy, and he was known to go into an enemy camp alone, death drifting in and the reaper drifting back out. He killed without a sound and thoroughly, taking out the enemy without raising an alarm. When he returned, he was the same exact man—cool and remote, his brain already moving on to solve another problem.

Trap raised those piercing, glacier-cold eyes to his. An icy shiver crept down Wyatt's spine.

"I've known you for years," Wyatt continued. "You get caught up in problems, Trap. Problems that need solvin'. Your brain just won' let it go. This woman is a problem. That's what this is."

Trap sighed. "You know better. You, of all people, know better."

"You don' become obsessed with women. Hell, Trap, you hook up for an hour or two and then you walk. Not a night. An hour or two at the most."

Trap didn't deny it. "I fuck 'em and then walk away because

I don't need the entanglement but I need the release." He stated the fact mildly. Unashamed. Uncaring.

"This woman is a *problem* to solve to you. That's all she is. This has nothin' to do with the woman herself, just the mystery of her. You have to know that." Wyatt's Cajun accent was becoming more noticeable, the only thing that betrayed his wariness.

Trap's expression didn't change. His icy gaze didn't leave Wyatt's face as he took a long pull on the beer and set it down. "You grew up in that family of yours, Wyatt. You got your grandmother. Sweet and kind. You had all this." He gestured toward the swamp where Wyatt had grown up. "Running wild. Living a life. Having a *family*. You know what that's like."

Wyatt remained silent. Trap never talked about his past. Not ever. They'd met in college when they were both still teens and worked together on numerous projects that made both of them very wealthy. Wyatt had joined the service, and ultimately, the GhostWalker psychically enhanced Special Forces unit. Trap had followed.

In the years they'd known each other, Trap had never once alluded to his past. He sounded like he was gearing up to do just that, and Wyatt wasn't about to blow the opportunity to learn more about what had made his friend as cold as ice. He simply nodded, keeping his gaze just as steady on Trap's, mesmerized by the blue flame that burned ice cold under the glacier.

"I had two sisters and a brother. Did I ever tell you that?" Trap's fist tightened around the neck of the beer bottle, but he didn't lift it to his mouth. "My name wasn't Dawkins back then when I had them. It was Johansson." He said the name like there was a bad taste in his mouth. "Changed it legally in order to keep that shit out of the spotlight. To keep my enemies from finding me. Didn't work with the enemies, but it did with the press."

Had two sisters and a brother. Wyatt's heart clenched hard in his chest. He regarded Trap as a brother. He had for years. He shook his head slowly. What kid had enemies they had to hide from? Enemies so dangerous they needed a name change? Wyatt remained silent. Waiting. Letting Trap take his time.

"My brother, Brad, and my sister Linnie were younger than me by a couple of years. Drusilla was older by a couple of years. Dru took care of us while our mother worked. She worked because our father didn't." He raised the bottle to his mouth and took a long pull. Through it, his eyes didn't leave Wyatt's.

Dread built. This was going to bad. Really bad. Many of the GhostWalkers had difficult lives, which was probably why they made the military their home, but Wyatt knew the hell that was there under all that ice. Those blue flames that burned white hot and glacier cold meant whatever had happened to Trap was going to be bad.

He felt movement behind him and knew Mordichai, another GhostWalker and member of their team, was coming up behind him. He dropped his hand low, down by the side of the chair and waved him off, counting on Mordichai to understand—to know not to come near the table or allow anyone else to as well.

"My father despised me. I was different, even then, even as a child. He wasn't in the least bit logical and half the time he didn't make sense. He hated the very sight of me and Dru took to stepping in front of me when he was around, because the moment he laid eyes on me, he had to beat the holy hell out of me."

Trap shrugged, the movement casual. "I didn't understand what I did wrong and poor Dru tried her best to shield me. I was so young, but already too old in my mind."

Wyatt understood that. Trap's IQ rivaled some of the greatest IQs in history. Wyatt was intelligent, but like many others he was especially gifted in certain areas. Trap was just plain gifted at everything. Along with the brains, he had the fast reflexes and superb body of a warrior.

"My father wasn't proud of me for being gifted. If anything he took it as an affront. Dru always said he felt threatened by me, but I was a little kid and I didn't see how I was a threat to him."

Wyatt didn't make the mistake of letting compassion or anger show in his expression. Trap would shut down immediately. Trap kept his emotions under tight control and Wyatt realized why. There was rage coiled deep. So deep that it was never—ever—going to be purged.

"We never told Mom about the beatings, but one day she saw the bruises and the swelling. He'd broken my arm and a couple of ribs. She took me to the hospital and he was arrested. While he was in jail, she packed us up and moved us out of the city. I was eight. Dru, ten. We went clear across the country. His family bailed him out. He had two brothers, both as worthless and as vicious as he was."

The chair never moved, remaining balanced on two legs as Trap took another long pull of his beer. He put the bottle down on the table with deceptive gentleness. The movement was precise and deliberate. Just like Trap. Just like everything Trap did.

"They found us when I was nine. My father came into the house late at night while his two brothers poured gasoline up and down the walls inside and outside the little house we rented. He dragged my mother out of bed, down to the room where my little brother and sister slept. He shot them both and then shot Mom in the head."

Trap's expression didn't change. His tone didn't change. He might have been reciting a story he'd read in the papers. Wyatt's fist clenched beneath the rickety table but didn't allow his expression to change either.

"Dru and I were talking together in our secret hideaway. When we first moved in, we found a closet that was really shallow, and after Mom went to bed, we'd sometimes get up and read or discuss something interesting we'd learned that day. We heard the shots and we went to find Mom, to see what was going on. Dru threw herself in front of me when he came at us. He shot her twice and her body landed over the top of me. I could see her eyes, Wyatt. Wide open. Blank. She had beautiful eyes, but all of sudden, there was no light. No brilliance. My beautiful sister, so smart, so funny, the only one who could relate to me, who really saw me, saw into me, was dead. Gone. Just like that."

"Fuck, Trap," Wyatt said softly. What else was there to say? This was far worse than anything he had imagined.

"He should have just shot me," Trap said softly, almost as if he were talking to himself. "If he had any intelligence at all, he would have just shot me like he did Dru. She was so smart, Wyatt. A gift to the world. She could have done things, but he took her life for no reason other than because he was a fucked-up asshole."

Still, even with the language, there was no change in Trap's voice. None. That rage was buried so deep, so much a part of him, Wyatt doubted he actually knew it was there anymore. He held up two fingers, knowing Mordichai was watching them closely. Most likely the other members of his team were doing the same, not knowing what was going on, but willing to help in any way they could.

The GhostWalkers who had come with them were spread throughout the bar, one sitting on a barstool, one lounging by the famous piano the owner of the Huracan Club, Delmar Thibodeaux, guarded with a baseball bat, and a couple of others sitting at a table across the room. All would be watching Trap and Wyatt's backs, and at the same time appearing as if they had no cares in the world.

Neither man spoke until Mordichai plopped two icy cold bottles of beer on the table and sauntered away, pretending, like all the team members were, that he had no clue Trap and Wyatt were in a nightmarish discussion.

"How'd you stay alive?"

"He dragged me out from under Dru. I think he wanted to beat me before he shot me, but as I came up I rammed my head into his groin and twisted the gun from his hand as he went down. I'd already calculated the odds of success and knew I had a good chance. I shot him twice before he was on me. He had a knife in his boot."

Wyatt had seen the wicked scar that seemed to take up half of Trap's belly. He'd been what? Nine, he'd said. His own father had wiped out his family, killing his mother and brother and sisters. Wyatt pushed down the rage swirling deep in his gut. He drew in a deep breath to keep from annihilating the room. The peanut husks on the floor jumped several times like popcorn in a popper and the walls of the bar shimmered and breathed in and out. He took several breaths to get himself under control.

"He stabbed me twice. Once in my belly and again in my thigh. I hung on to that gun, but I went down in all the blood. That's when my uncles came in. They came at me, but I lifted the gun and both backed off fast. I guess they were either cowards or they knew my father was done for, because they left him there bleeding out, threw gasoline all over the floor, lit a match and told me to burn in hell. They got out. I crawled out. Still got the scars on my legs and feet from the burns."

Wyatt clenched his teeth and then carefully brought the bottle to his mouth. He needed action. Something. He almost wished a fight would break out as they habitually did in the bar. When he was younger, he often came there to drink, fight and find a woman, just like most of the other men in the swamp and bayou did. Now he came to drink and fight. He had a woman waiting for him at home.

"I had one living relative, my mother's sister. She was fifteen years younger than Mom, barely twenty-three, and single, but she came and got me and I lived with her. We changed our names, moved and thought we were going to be all right. At twelve I founded my first company after selling two of my patents. We lived good for a while."

For the first time something moved in his cold, piercing

eyes. Trap raked his hand through his blond hair, hair that definitely identified him as an outsider there in Cajun country. Had he not been with Wyatt, he would have been the first target chosen for anyone looking for a fight. The fight wouldn't have ended well. Trap wasn't a man who enjoyed a good friendly brawl. You didn't put your hands on him. You didn't threaten him. Even there in the Huracan Club with his team around him, he kept to himself. Wyatt could see the name Johansson suited Trap far better than Dawkins, with his build and blond hair. Trap definitely had some Swede in him.

Wyatt didn't want to hear what happened to Trap's aunt, but he had to know. There were too many flames burning icy-hot behind the blue glacier of Trap's eyes.

"For a while?" he prompted.

"Yeah. For a while. I made a lot of money, even through my early teenage years. Went to school, could have taught most of the professors. Did a lot of research in pharmaceuticals, and we both know you can make a fortune there. I just kept making money." He made small circles on the table with the edge of the beer bottle. His gaze once again held Wyatt's. "You know that money didn't mean a fucking thing to me, Wyatt. Not one damned thing. I can't help the way my mind works. The money made it easy to get the lab I wanted and the equipment, but that was all. I live simply. I don't use it."

Wyatt frowned at him. "Trap, I've known you for years. We went to school together. We were both younger than everyone else and, yeah, smarter, so we naturally gravitated toward each other. We went into business together. You don' have to convince me you aren' into money."

"She was kidnapped. They took her right out of the house when I was working in the laboratory. She would always come and get me for dinner. I could skip other meals, but not dinner. She didn't come. When I went into the house, the place was a wreck. She fought them and I hadn't heard a fucking thing."

Wyatt listened to Trap's voice, but he couldn't hear any expression at all. Just the soft monotone Trap often used.

"I paid the ransom, of course. Millions, enough to set them up for life in another country where they could change identities and live life large. I paid it immediately. They returned her body to me on my front porch. She was dead. They'd used her." Trap's blue eyes went so cold it felt like the temperature in the room dropped. "Hard. They made certain there was plenty of evidence so I would see that. They hurt her in every way possible before they killed her. They left me a note. Quoted 'an eye for an eye.' They made it very plain that any woman I was with would suffer the same fate."

Trap took another long swig of beer. "I knew it was my uncles. I pointed the cops to them. I hired detectives. They disappeared. Their tracks were so well-covered that I knew they had changed identities. Even bribing the best in the business, I didn't find out who they'd become. All that money I'd made wasn't worth shit, Wyatt. It didn't buy her back for me and it didn't find her killers."

Wyatt sank back in the chair and regarded his friend. He understood Trap's antisocial behavior much better now. He had buried himself in work, cut himself off from everyone, making certain he had few ties. He hadn't blindly followed Wyatt into the GhostWalker unit; he wanted the skills. He hadn't given up on finding the men who murdered his aunt. He would never give up. He didn't tie himself to a woman or let himself feel affection for one. He used his work to keep him apart, to keep his mind occupied so there would be no chance that he would ever put another woman in jeopardy.

"Trap," he cautioned softly.

"She isn't a problem," Trap said just as softly. "Cayenne. She isn't a problem. Fucking Whitney paired us together. I don't ever think about a woman, not even after I've fucked her. Not ever. I go to my lab and I work until there isn't a trace of her left. This woman I let out of a cage, not knowing if she was going to try to kill me. I only seen her a couple of times and I can't get her out of my head. I can't, Wyatt. She's no problem to solve. He fucking paired us together."

Both men fell silent. Dr. Peter Whitney had been the brains behind the GhostWalker program. He'd sold his experimental ideas to the military. They'd tested psychic ability. Those accepted into the program had to test off the charts for various abilities as well as have the personality and physical abilities to withstand Special Forces training. Once accepted into the program, they were enhanced and then trained in every type of combat situation conceivable.

There were four teams, and each had been enhanced not only psychically—as they'd agreed to—but physically as well—which they hadn't agreed to. The first team had many problems and a couple of their men had died, succumbing to brain bleeds. Whitney got better after that, improving with each new team, but it became obvious he had used animal DNA to make his superior soldiers.

It came to light that long before he had worked on adult men, he had first begun his experiments on female children he had taken from orphanages from around the world—disposable children. He believed they could be sacrificed for the greater good. If his experiments worked on them, only then did he try to duplicate them in the soldiers.

He kept the female prisoners in various facilities scattered around the U.S. as well as in some foreign countries. He went underground once his experiments had come under scrutiny, but he had friends in high places and they not only shielded him, but believed in what he was doing, so they aided him.

One of his experiments was to pair a male soldier with one of his female experiments, using pheromones to entice them to each other. No one knew how he did it, nor was there a way to undo what he'd done, so when the male soldier came across the female, and she him, they were so attracted, it was impossible for one to walk away from the other. What Whitney hadn't counted on was the emotional attachment the pair formed. Or the camaraderie of all GhostWalkers.

They were not only elite, but they were also different from every other human on earth. Some couldn't be in society without an anchor—another GhostWalker who could draw psychic energy away from them. The four teams had formed into a single unit looking out for one another. They trusted no one else and depended on one another. When one soldier found the woman he was paired with, she was protected by all of them—after all, Whitney had performed the same experiments on the women.

Each of the women was combat-trained and enhanced both psychically and physically. Some of them had been used for cancer research. Others had been forced into his "breeding" program. Wyatt had three daughters, little triplets, all of whom had snake DNA and were venomous. Trap had come to the bayou to help him find a way to keep them from hurting anyone if they accidentally bit while they were frightened or teething.

"How long have you known?" Wyatt asked. He wasn't going to argue. Trap wasn't a man given to fantasies, and the last thing he would welcome into his life was a woman—especially one he was paired with. One he couldn't ignore and set aside after he'd had her body.

"She bothered me on a level she shouldn't have from the moment I laid eyes on her. I thought—I hoped—it was because she was an experiment gone wrong and they issued a termination order on her. Maybe I could figure out what went wrong and I could fix her. My brain was already trying to assess her the moment I saw her and heard her voice, analyzing what her psychic abilities were and what DNA she might have been enhanced with."

"That makes sense." Wyatt wanted to pounce on that. Trap was holding himself together, but the rage deep inside was close—too close. He didn't dare set Trap off with so many innocents around. He felt the other members of their team moving into positions closer to them. Just in case. That meant they noticed the tension mounting as well. No one really knew Trap's full abilities, but it was generally considered that along with Ezekiel and Gino, he was the most lethal man on the team when it came to psychic enhancements.

Wyatt didn't want the building to shake apart and come down on half the men with families living there around the swamp and bayou.

"I tried to make it that, Wyatt," Trap said. "But she didn't let go. I think about her when I'm in the lab working on how to come up with a vaccine that will stay in the system for snakebite. Not once in my entire life have I ever been distracted from my work. I dream of her at night and I have always commanded my own dreams. Not just any dreams, erotic fantasies, and I'm not prone to those, not even when I've gone a while without a woman. When I consider finding another woman to get relief, the idea is not only repugnant but absolutely abhorrent."

"Fuck." Wyatt almost spat the word. "I see why you're putting yourself in this position now. It didn't make sense. You're the last person in the world to go to a bar every night. We've come here now for the last five nights. I thought maybe you wanted to get in better with the locals."

A faint gleam of humor moved through the ice in Trap's startling blue eyes. "Hardly. I did take your advice and hire a few of them to help with the renovations once escrow closed and the land and building became mine, but hanging out with them in a bar is going beyond the call of duty."

"How are the renovations coming?"

The humor deepened. "We're about finished. I know she's living there. No one has seen her, but things go missing and all of sudden the men are leery of working there, especially after dark. The workers think the place is haunted. Word leaked out that Wilson Plastics might have been a front for government experiments. I didn't let anyone go down into the lower region where the cells and the crematoria were until we'd gotten rid of all the evidence. Now it's a beautiful apartment I designed for her. Still, word got out and the men who really need or want the work show up, but they work in pairs and they won't stay late at all. I think she started the rumors and is sitting back laughing her pretty little ass off. Seriously, I only have a few odds and ends left anyway."

"Did you try to find her there? You hate coming here. That might be a better alternative."

"It's not going to happen. She's got her webs everywhere. The moment I come near there, she's gone. I don't want to risk driving her away."

Wyatt wished he'd had more than a glimpse of the woman Trap had rescued from those cells. Wilson Plastics had been a cover for a dangerous experimental laboratory and termination center for the experiments deemed to have gone wrong. His three little girls and the woman Trap was certain he had been paired with had been down in those cells, waiting to be killed and then cremated, their ashes taken out to sea so no one could ever know of their existence.

Prior to being Wilson Plastics, the land had been owned by Dr. Whitney. The huge building had been a sanitarium. Whitney had conducted his experiments on the orphans he "rescued" from around the world. The sanitarium had burned to the ground. Whitney's company had sold it and Wilson Plastics bought the land. Wyatt's GhostWalker team had exposed the company for what it really was, and when the land came up for sale, Trap bought it.

Their pararescue team had decided to make a fortress together right there in the swamp. Wyatt's little girls and his wife couldn't possibly leave the swamp, not until Wyatt and Trap came up with a vaccine that would stay in the system without daily injections. They also had to either remove the venom sacs or find a way to keep the girls from accidentally biting while they grew up. In any case, Whitney was trying to reacquire them, and that meant they needed protection at all times.

"So you think your girl is a squatter, living on your property."

Trap nodded slowly, the humor still in his eyes. "Yeah. She's there. And she's the reason we hear rumors about drunk men being robbed on their way home."

"Those men aren't the best of the bayou, Trap," Wyatt pointed out. "If she's the one doin' the robbin', she's pickin' the men who are particularly nasty to rob."

Trap shrugged. "Doesn't matter. That's not okay and she knows it."

"She's got to eat."

The humor faded from Trap's eyes. "Seriously, Wyatt, if I'm feeling this way, can you tell me she isn't? She could come to me. If not me, then you. She knows we're GhostWalkers, the same as she is. She could come to us. She doesn't need to rob anyone and put herself in danger like that."

There was an edge to Trap's voice, and a faint shimmer moved through the room. The opaque disturbance made Wyatt uneasy. He glanced across the room and Mordichai had a frown on his face. He felt it too. Trap had an energy about him now, one that was distinctly lethal.

"She doesn' think she's the same as we are, Trap. She was listed for termination. She considers herself flawed, just as Pepper always did. Not one of us, but a throwaway. She isn't goin' to come to us. She figures we'll look down on her. That we'll judge her in the way they did. It's possible she doesn't trust herself to be around us."

"She doesn't trust us," Trap corrected. "I can't say as I blame her, but she feels it, the same as me, that pull between us, or she'd be long gone. You know it's true. She had no reason to stick around here. She has no place to stay, no money, nothing. No clothes. She's staying for me."

"She's a GhostWalker, Trap. By now she has all those

things," Wyatt persisted. "She can slip in and out of any store or home without ever being seen. If she's the one robbing the drunks, then she's got money. You said yourself you're certain she's setting up her home there in the buildin' you just bought."

"I'm positive," Trap said. "So much so that I'll be moving there soon. I've nearly got the laboratory all set up. Most of my equipment is in. We've got a big workspace and I can protect it easier than the one we set up in your garage."

"I don' know if I like you livin' there alone right now, Trap, especially if she's there. We don' know how dangerous she is. I know you're close to finishing the renovations, but Whitney could hit us at any time. The boys haven't had enough time to set up all your security."

"She's there," Trap insisted. "If I'm there alone, she won't be able to resist coming to me. I'd never be able to resist going to her if I wasn't afraid of scaring her off. She won't hurt me."

Wyatt sighed. There was no arguing with Trap when he made up his mind. "If you're determined to do that, why are we here?"

"I need to see her in action. All of you have asked around. You know she's been here. She's gorgeous. Alluring. Almost as sexy as Pepper. You think these boys are going to forget her? Not be able to describe her? She does something to mute that either while she's here or when she's leaving. I believe it's when she's leaving. She'd want them attracted. She's looking for a type. Someone she believes deserves being robbed. A criminal. That tells me she's got a moral code of some kind."

Wyatt flashed a grin. "They couldn't have decided to terminate her because she's a straight-up killer."

"A black widow? She's that. She carries venom for certain. She can throw webs out. And there's her voice. She can lure with her tone and that damn French accent that's sexy as hell." Trap shuddered at the memory of her voice seeping into his body through his pores. The feel of silk on his skin.

Her long, thick hair that was so unusual. Black with red highlights right down the center. She had an hourglass figure—high firm breasts, a small waist and flared hips. Even with her curvy figure she was small, slight, so she could fit into places few others could get in and out of.

He was a big man. Solid. All muscle without an ounce of fat. He'd been with his fair share of women. He knew he was attractive physically and he was highly intelligent. But most of all he was rich. Not just rich. He was in *Forbes* magazine as one of the richest men in the world, yet he was in the military. He was a prize catch and women pursued him. He didn't do the pursuing. He never had wanted to take the chance that his uncles would rape, torture and kill another person he loved.

His brain needed to work. He had no choice, not if he was going to remain sane. He couldn't work as long as he was obsessed with Cayenne—and he was obsessed. His body needed relief, and soon. Right now his brain was occupied with fantasies of her and her body. Of the way she felt when she rubbed up against him. Of the way she smelled, that faintly elusive and mysterious mixture of storms and fresh rain. Sometimes he woke up with her scent in his lungs and he wondered if she'd been in his room. He was fairly certain it wasn't possible—he was staying with Wyatt and the rest of the team at Wyatt's grandmother's house and security was ultra-tight. Still, he wondered.

When he woke in the middle of the night, his heart beat too fast and his body was hard and tight and her scent was everywhere. Once he swore it was on the pillow next to him. He didn't sleep much. Sometimes he went days without sleep when he was on the trail of something he was developing for his pharmaceutical company. When he did regularly go to bed, he slept no more than four or five hours, and not all at once.

Often Trap got up to read or work out elusive problems. His scribbled formulas were on just about every scrap of paper in the room and a few had been written on the wall.

Sometimes he was certain those papers weren't in the same exact spot. He considered that he might be losing his mind. The last few weeks he'd been acting totally out of character, and that's what convinced him he needed to find her. To put a stop to whatever was happening.

If Whitney manufactured their attraction to each other, he should be able to find a way to undo it. Come up with an antidote. Cayenne would stay safe that way. It was the only way he could ensure no one would ever set hands on her again. He would have to give her up before the attraction grew to the point where neither would be able to resist.

Wyatt sighed. "You're going to move into that building before we have it ready, aren't you, Trap?"

Trap nodded slowly. "I can take care of myself."

"Yeah, under most circumstances, but if you're wrong about her, this woman could kill you, Trap. I couldn't harm Pepper. I doubt you could hurt Cayenne."

Trap's gaze turned glacier-cold. "You've always been sensitive, Wyatt. You don't like anyone pointing that out because you think that makes you feminine." He spoke entirely dispassionately, no judgment or expression in his voice. "That's what makes you such a good man. You care about people. You always have. I stopped caring when my own flesh and blood murdered my family. I couldn't allow myself to feel. If I did, I wouldn't survive. If this woman who is supposed to be *my* woman decides to kill me, she's an enemy. She isn't mine."

"She's scared, Trap."

He nodded. "I know that. I know she'll fight the attraction—and me. That isn't the same as wanting to kill me."

"When a wild animal is threatened—cornered—they often strike out. She's never known freedom or kindness. She has no idea how to live in the world. She's been locked up, experimented on, which means needles and God knows what else. She's never had anyone give her compliments or romance her. She knows nothing but enemies."

"I have a brain, Wyatt," Trap said. For the first time impatience crept into his voice. "I've had a lot of time to think this through."

"I don' want you to do something you'll regret, or worse, do somethin' that will get you killed."

The ice-blue flame in Trap's eyes deepened. Nearly glowed. "She's *mine*," he said softly. This time there was a wealth of expression in his voice. Possession. An underlying anger. That strange shimmer slid into the room again, filling the space where air had been, completely at odds with his intention to reverse whatever Whitney had done to tie Cayenne to him.

"Doesn' seem to me that you're so willin' to sacrifice your own happiness, or hers, to keep those uncles of yours in the shadows. Maybe you ought to consider courting her publicly. Get yourself in the tabloids, let the paparazzi take a gazillion photos of the two of you. That would bring them straight here. Right into a team of GhostWalkers waitin' for them." Wyatt flashed a cocky grin, knowing Trap was the most camera-shy man he'd ever encountered. "Whitney already knows where she is. It isn't like he'd suddenly find her."

Trap looked thoughtful as he took another pull on his beer. "That's not a bad idea. She isn't so easily compromised either. They try to tangle with her and she'd kill them in a heartbeat. I've been trying to find them for years."

"Maybe they're dead."

Trap shook his head. "Not a chance. They're out there, living the good life. Once I find them, I'm going to kill them."

Again his voice lacked expression. Still, that shimmer hung in the air. Trap took another drink and glanced toward the piano. If he played, it would get him through the last couple of hours before Thibodeaux shut the place down.

The door opened and the night breeze drifted in. Along with it came the scent of rain. Of storms. Of her. Of Cayenne. She was there. At last. He lifted his gaze, and for one moment, indulged his need to drink her in.

From #1 *New York Times* Bestselling Author
CHRISTINE FEEHAN

THE
LEOPARD
SERIES

"The Awakening"
(An e-novella)

Wild Rain

Burning Wild

Wild Fire

Savage Nature

Leopard's Prey

Cat's Lair

Wild Cat

PRAISE FOR THE LEOPARD NOVELS

"Dark, gritty and sexy." —Joyfully Reviewed

"Loaded with plenty of surprises, heat, thrills and suspense!" —Fresh Fiction

"Sultry…vivid…tantalizing [and] unforgettable." —Fallen Angel Reviews

christinefeehan.com
facebook.com/christinefeehanauthor
facebook.com/ProjectParanormalBooks
penguin.com

FROM THE #1 *NEW YORK TIMES* BESTSELLING AUTHOR

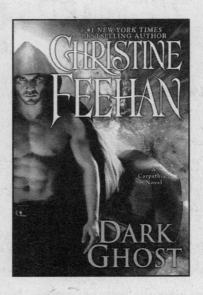

"The Queen of paranormal romance."
—J. R. Ward

"Intense, sensual, mesmerizing."
—*Library Journal*

christinefeehan.com
facebook.com/christinefeehanauthor
penguin.com